W9-AQK-863

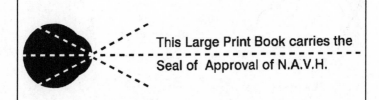

This Large Print Book carries the
Seal of Approval of N.A.V.H.

THE JACKALS

THE JACKALS

WILLIAM W. JOHNSTONE
WITH J. A. JOHNSTONE

THORNDIKE PRESS
A part of Gale, a Cengage Company

Farmington Hills, Mich • San Francisco • New York • Waterville, Maine
Meriden, Conn • Mason, Ohio • Chicago

Thorndike Press® Large Print Western.
The text of this Large Print edition is unabridged.
Other aspects of the book may vary from the original edition.
Set in 16 pt. Plantin.

LIBRARY OF CONGRESS CIP DATA ON FILE.
CATALOGUING IN PUBLICATION FOR THIS BOOK
IS AVAILABLE FROM THE LIBRARY OF CONGRESS

ISBN-13: 978-1-4328-6334-0 (hardcover)

Published in 2019 by arrangement with Pinnacle Books, an imprint of Kensington Publishing Corp.

Printed in Mexico
1 2 3 4 5 6 7 23 22 21 20 19

THE JACKALS

PROLOGUE

Front-page editorial from the Purgatory City, Texas, *Herald Leader*, Alvin J. Griffin IV, editor and publisher:

THE TIME HAS COME FOR OUR CITIZENS TO STAND UP TO THE JACKALS OF WEST TEXAS AND MAKE A STATEMENT FOR LAW AND . . . ESPECIALLY . . . ORDER!

The War Between the States is well behind us, the Mexicans have been behaving themselves of late, and the only thing that must be eradicated in the state of Texas — and our neighbors in the Southwest — are the menacing Apache marauders.

Yes, cowboys will be cowboys when they get paid, and most soldiers who risk their lives for our safety against these Apache butchers who torment our neighbors on the homesteads and ranches and small mines, or those lone travelers who make an "easy kill," yes, those soldiers get carried away much like cowboys when they have money to spend. Sure, we have gamblers who cheat and floozies who seek to soil our young men, and there is graft and dishonesty, even an occasional fistfight between friends.

All of this is part of progress, of sowing one's oats, of growing up. West Texas is seeing progress, and our towns and cities and communities are growing up. We have the telegraph. We have the railroad. We have stagecoaches. Our cities and towns have fine places to eat, comfortable beds that aren't ticky and are free of bedbugs. Our bankers are willing to make loans to reputable citizens at fine rates to build and build and build.

We must commend our fine city marshal, Rafe McMillian, and our county sheriff, Juan Garcia, for all they do. Likewise, we know MOST of the Texas Rangers under the command of Captain J.J.K. Hollister try to keep peace in our communities. Colonel John Caxton expertly commands the soldiers at Fort Spalding. Our district marshal for the federal courts, Kenneth Cook, and his valiant deputies are busy tracking down other offenders and law-breakers.

The only thing we should have to worry about, other than the Apache menace, is the weather.

But, of course, the weather must be left to the Almighty's hand.

We should be free of worry.

We should be free of most crime.

We should, and we must, be free of jack-als.

Yet, West Texas and the territories of New Mexico and Arizona, and even our neighbors below the Rio Grande, are not free of such beasts.

And as much as it sickens your editor of your best and leading newspaper, I feel it is time to single out the worst offenders, the jackals who could prevent corporations from investing in our communities. Those who tarnish our good standing, who smear our good name, and who, if we are not diligent, may destroy all of our hard work.

Certainly, Jake Hawkin and his band of desperate bandits have been rampaging our towns, stagecoaches, banks, and our decent citizens for far too long, and have started to rival the James-Younger gang and other bushwhacking border trash up in Missouri and elsewhere. Where there is

9

progress, where there is success, where you find money and people and beer and whiskey and wine and gambling halls, there will be a few rotten eggs. Jake Hawkin is a rotten egg. He and his cut-throats must be killed or captured and hanged by the neck until they are dead, dead, dead.

Marshal Cook assures your trusted editor this will happen, as his deputies are following leads and trails and believe that they have the outlaw butchers on the run.

But this paper — this editor — does not consider Jake Hawkin or his rogues to be *Jackals.*

A jackal, according to the dictionary on my desk, is "a wild animal of India and Persia, allied to the wolf."

Jake Hawkin is a coward. He wore neither blue nor gray during the late unpleasantness. He is too lazy to make the proverbial honest dollar. He is not wild. He has no allies, not even the men who ride with him, for all they want is that easy dollar. The men who ride with Hawkin, and Hawkin himself, have no calluses on their hands. Colt revolvers, Winchester repeating rifles, poker chips, and pastecards rarely cause calluses, and that's all these swine know.

10

In Thessalonians, it is written that we should reject every kind of evil.

We reject the Hawkin Gang, and they will be brought to justice. But we have not rejected all of our terrible jackals.

Alas, for the jackals in our midst, we must look closer to our homes.

At Fort Spalding, for instance.

Last week, Sergeant Sean Keegan all but destroyed The Killers & Thieves Saloon & Gambling Parlor on Acme Street. Oh, how we have asked saloon owner Ryan O'Doul to change the name of his establishment, but the fun-loving Irishman (meaning O'Doul, not Keegan, who speaks with not even the slightest brogue) says he wants people to have fun when they come into his place. According to O'Doul, "A man will remember The Killers and Thieves, no matter how much Who Hit John he drinks, and he will come back. Because, ladies and lasses, that name sticks out more than the Acme, the Place, and even The Alamo — saloons that line our streets on the other side of the railroad tracks." He went on by saying, "Folks, I try not to serve killers and thieves."

Yet he served Keegan and probably regrets it. The sergeant decided, after much too much Who Hit John, that he was being cheated at the roulette table. So he broke a bottle of rye whiskey over the operator's head, turned over the table, busted the wheel, drew his Remington revolver and began shooting out the lights that had been imported all the way from Saint Louis and were just installed a month ago to brighten the favored saloon in our great city.

Patrons ran out screaming in the street, as Keegan was the only man armed in the saloon, for bartender Saul Ferguson wisely left the sawed-off shotgun under the bar and helped Louie Roebuck, our lovable town drunk, out through the back entrance. Seeing he was alone, Sergeant Keegan walked to the bar and helped himself to more shots of whiskey. He then broke the mirror on the back bar with the whiskey bottle . . . that must have been empty. He kicked over the spittoons and as he walked out of the saloon, overturned tables and chairs — even busted three chairs — and tossed an entire table through the fine plate-glass window. He kicked open the batwing doors, ripping one off its hinges, and then holstered his still-smoking revolver, rolled a cigarette, and leaned against the hitching rail — which by this time was empty of all horses as the owners had wisely mounted up and moved at a fast lope for safer climes.

City Marshal McMillian and three deputies approached the drunken trooper, who finished his cigarette, offered his empty revolver, and was escorted to our new jail. Our fine constable said that the sergeant surrendered peaceably and has agreed to pay Mr. O'Doul for damages, by taking out a third of his monthly pay. Colonel Caxton insists that his officer in charge of payroll will make sure that this is, indeed, done. However, if you consider that a sergeant in our United States Army makes, perhaps, eighteen dollars a month, O'Doul might see those damages finally paid for in four and one-half years.

Sergeant Keegan, Colonel Caxton reminds us, was a decorated veteran for the Union Army during the war, riding for the Second Michigan Volunteer Cavalry Regiment, rising from private to brevetted major from his initial enlistment at Detroit in October of 1861 until he and his fellow soldiers were mustered out in August of 1865. He was decorated for valor at the Battle of Island Number Ten, the Battle of Perryville, the Battle of Resaca, the slaughter and carnage at Franklin, Tennessee, and again at the Battle of Nashville. He has, likewise, Colonel Caxton said, shown his bravery time and again since enlisting in the regular army in 1867. We do not argue with Sergeant Keegan's past bravery. But his actions last week were not the first time he has spent the rest of his leave in our jail.

Judge Preston Barnes says that, to the best of his memory, Keegan has been fined and jailed at least ten times over the past two years. Colonel Caxton said that the sergeant has spent several weeks in the guardhouse at Fort Spalding and has been demoted to private at least three times. Yet the sergeant's stripes keep being sewn again onto the sleeves of his blouse because, "Good sergeants," Caxton says, "are hard to come by, and the Apaches haven't all been turned into 'good injuns,' as we like to say."

The Army, we must say, needs to make a stand and weed out such jackals as Sergeant Sean Keegan.

"From their callous hearts comes iniquity; their evil imaginations have no limits."
— Psalms 73:7

But Sergeant Keegan is not the only

14

mad wolf and demon that Texas needs to weed out.

Two months ago, Jed Breen brought in another outlaw — dead. Breen does not live in one of our cities or towns. In fact, we doubt if Jed Breen has a home . . . or a mother or a father, for that matter, for he is, indeed, a jackal, a man kin to the wolf, and not any humans. Yes, Breen has rid our great state of vermin. It is said that he fights for justice, but, oh, what a sham that is. Justice?

Jed Breen wears no badge. He is neither sheriff, marshal, constable, Texas Ranger, nor Pinkerton agent. He has never been hired as a deputy. In fact, there are rumors that he is wanted for crimes in Kansas, Missouri, Louisiana, Alabama, Montana, and California. We have searched and made inquiries but have found no proof that Jed Breen is wanted for any crimes in any of those states, nor in our own glorious Texas. But who is to say Jed Breen is this vagabond's real name?

Breen, of course, is easy to recognize. He is lean, he is leathery, and although probably no older than his thirties, his hair is stark white, close-cropped. His eyes are a piercing blue. He has a unique countenance, and, indeed, many ladies have a tendency to swoon when he tips his hat in their direction.

Tipping his hat is about the only polite thing Jed Breen does, and I do not think that the man is recognized merely for his white hair.

You smell him before you see him. And the smell is that which reeks of death.

He brings in outlaws to various lawmen in towns from here to there. He collects the rewards posted for those men, but these wanted felons have not gotten their day in court. For they are dead upon arrival. Once, Jed Breen merely brought in the head of the criminal Fat Charles Wingo.

Dime novels are not noted for their veracity, but this quote from the author, Major Kiowa J. Smith (likely a pseudonym), rings true. It is from *The Last Days of Fat Charlie Wingo, Savage Outlaw and Comanchero; or Bloody Revenge on the Staked Plains of Texas.* "Why just the head? Well, Judge," the leathery killer said with a grin, "Fat Charlie runned his hoss to death in the middle of Comanch country, and the injuns weren't in no hospitable mood. Fat Charlie had to weigh nigh two hundred and fifty pounds, and that was before I put about a pound of lead into his

16

body. My hoss was fairly winded his ownself, and iffen it come to a runnin' fight with dem red devils, well, my mustang wasn't likely to come out the victor in such a race. That'd mean I was either dead or wishin' I was dead after the Comanch took their pleasures on me. My Bowie knife was sharp, and Fat Charlie's grain sack was empty. It just seemed like the thing to do, Judge. 'Sides, the head's all you need to identify that scoundrel. Ever'body this side of the Pecos River knowed Charlie had a mouthful of gold teeth, and if you peel up that eyelid you'll see his marled eye, which he's also knowed fer. The rest of his body I left for the coyot's, Judge, on account that coyot's gots to eat, too."

The body of Jimmy Martin was intact, head and all, and, yes, Jimmy Martin was wanted dead or alive for the robbery of the Lordsburg stage. But Jimmy Martin was all of seventeen years old, just a misguided youth who was hurting after the Apaches killed his father and older brother on the malpais. Jimmy Martin was wrong, yes, indeed, he was wrong, and deserved to be punished. But he was no jackal. He could have been reformed.

And no kid deserves to be shot in the back.

17

"I called for the boy to surrender," Jed Breen told Judge Barnes (this comes from the fine jurist himself, and not from Breen, whose quotes to this newspaperman could not be printed in even the most gratuitous and salacious and scandalous publication). "He popped a cap at me, and I returned fire. He just happened to be turning around to make a run for his horse, when I touched that trigger."

Young Jimmy Martin is not the first corpse this awful bounty hunter has brought to our courts, our towns, and our dedicated peace officers. He has claimed to have brought in men alive, but we find no record that has ever happened. Your intrepid editor did question Jed Breen, and the response was one that, as it lacked vile and profane language, was something we could actually print.

Editor of the *Herald Leader:* "Why must you always bring in outlaws for their reward, and not for a sense of duty and justice?"

Jed Breen: "Ink slinger, I shoot a Sharps rifle. You ever tried pricing a box of .50-caliber Sharps cartridges in this country? A man's gotta eat, and an officer of the court has got to buy lead."

For the record, upon checking past issues of your *Herald Leader* and other newspapers in Texas and the Southwest, we have learned that Jed Breen does not use just a big and powerful Sharps rifle (although that long brass telescopic sight affixed to his murderous weapon likely gives him an advantage when it comes to facing his "deadly" adversaries). Breen has also brought in bodies riddled with buckshot from his Parker double-barreled twelve-gauge shotgun, which is even more brutal since the Damascus barrels have been sawed off. And at least twice, he has killed men with his 1877 double-action Colt Lightning revolver.

And, no, your honest and busy editor did not walk across town to Dillon's Gun Shop to find out the price of a box of double-ought buckshot for a twelve-gauge nor a box of .38-caliber cartridges for a Colt revolver.

In short, Jed Breen hunts outlaws for the prices on their heads. But who hunts this jackal?

> "For it is from within, out of a person's
> heart, that evil thoughts come —
> sexual immorality, theft, murder,
> adultery, greed, malice, deceit,

lewdness, envy, slander, arrogance
and folly."
— Mark 7:21–22

Finally and most disappointing, there is another jackal in our midst — and perhaps he is the worst of the entire lot.

Matt McCulloch is a man of middle age, tall, lean, with a fine head of hair (yes, your balding editor is jealous of his black and gray mane). Once, he lived in our town, was respected, was honest, and the only time longtime residents recall him ever wearing a gun came when he went hunting for a deer or some rabbits to feed his family; or to rid West Texas of an unnecessary rattlesnake that had its fangs set to sink into the leg of one of the fine horses McCulloch and his sons raised and sold.

And then, some years back, Matt McCulloch returned home after driving six fine horses to sell to Texas Rangers Captain John Courtright — Courtright was killed in the line of duty four years ago, and ably replaced, but never forgotten, by our current Rangers leader, J.J.K. Hollister. McCulloch's home and barn were in ashes, his family butchered, and his horses stolen. The one daughter in the family was missing, kidnapped by those red-heathen butchers.

So McCulloch, after burying his beloved wife and sons, spent more than a year futilely searching for his daughter. Eventually, reluctantly giving the child up for dead like the rest of his family, he rode back to the Rangers headquarters and enlisted with Captain Courtright. He pinned on the *cinco pesos* star. He bought a long-barreled Colt revolver, and his Winchester carbine was replaced with a new, more current model, as his previous rifle had been consumed by the flames the murderous fiends had set to his home. The Texas Rangers in his battalion pitched in for the new carbine, I have been informed.

Of course, none of us at the *Herald Leader* can know how it must feel to lose one's entire family and home to such butchery. We do, on the other hand, feel Matt McCulloch's pain. And for a few years, Matt McCulloch wore his badge with honor and lived by the code of the Texas Rangers and by the law of the state of Texas.

Yet if you look at the stock of his Winchester rifle or the walnut butt of his revolver of .44-40 caliber, you will see the carvings that represent the men he has killed — as well as three Apache women, and one Mexican bandit woman — all reportedly as rough and wild as the brutes they rode with and all deservedly and justifiably killed. The brown stocks are now, literally, carved so much that the walnut is but a mass of ditches and scratches covered with grime, filth, and, yes, stained by blood.

"Sometimes," a former friend of the weary-eyed Ranger told me, "I get the feeling that Matt has to kill. He just doesn't know anything else after these years. He thinks every man he goes after, or every outlaw that comes after him, is responsible for the murders of his wife and children. And the truth of the matter is, it pains me to say, but we'll never know — not while we're living on this earth, I mean — who all committed that horrible crime. Those Apache vermin might be alive. Most likely, they're dead. And some think that maybe it was white renegades who made it look like the work of those red devils. And it just doesn't matter. McCulloch kills. He kills because he has to kill. He kills, I sometimes think, hoping that somebody will kill him."

It pains me to say this, too, but our state and our towns and our people and citizens and visitors and friends would be much better off if Matt McCulloch, the jackal with the Devil in his soul, would be killed.

"No one calls for justice; no one pleads a case with integrity. They rely on empty arguments, they utter lies; they conceive trouble and give birth to evil."
— Isaiah 59:4.

To these three jackals — Sergeant Keegan, the despicable Breen, and Ranger McCulloch — we quote from the Book of Kings: *"You have done more evil than all who lived before you."*

Yes, yes, yes, there are likely other jackals in our midst. And more will come. But for this town, this community, this county, this glorious state and the entire Southwest to grow, we need to get rid of — one way or another — this trio of jackals.

CHAPTER ONE

"Begging the lieutenant's pardon, sir, but, if you were to ask me, sir, that's not a trail I'd be inclined to follow."

Sergeant Sean Keegan, Eighth United States Cavalry, stood beside his dun gelding, tightening the cinch of the McClellan saddle, and sprayed a pebble with tobacco juice. He knew the lieutenant, proud little peacock that he was, kept watching and waiting for Keegan to look up before he began ridiculing the sergeant in front of the men.

Keegan let him wait.

Eventually, though, Sean Keegan did look up, and even pushed up the brim of his slouch hat so Second Lieutenant Erastus Gibbons of Hartford, Connecticut, fresh out of West Point, could see exactly what Keegan thought of the fool.

"Did Captain Percival put you in charge of this patrol, Sergeant?"

"No," Keegan said, and wiped his mouth when he added, "Sir." He thought, *But he should have.*

"And Sergeant" — Lieutenant Gibbons seemed to like this — "in what year were you graduated from the United States Military Academy?" It made him feel important. Made the kid with acne covering his face think that he was a real man. A soldier, even.

"Never went. Never even got to New York state." Keegan tugged on the butt of the Springfield rifle in the scabbard, just to make sure he would be able to pull it out cleanly and quickly. They'd have need of it in a few minutes if he couldn't talk some sense into the green pup.

"That's what I thought," the lieutenant said.

Keegan gathered the reins to his dun. "And when was it, sir, that you got your sheepskin from West Point?"

The eight troopers, all about as young and as inexperienced as the lieutenant, laughed, which made the lieutenant's face turn as bright as the scarlet neckerchief he wore around his fancy blue blouse.

"Quiet in the ranks!"

As Gibbons, who had been at Fort Spalding all of four months, took time to bark commands and insults at his enlisted men, Sergeant Keegan climbed into his saddle and lowered the brim of his hat.

The hat, he guessed, was likely older than Erastus Gibbons.

When he had talked himself into even a deeper red face, the kid sucked in a deep breath, and turned his wrath again on the sergeant. "Do you remember our orders, Sergeant?"

"Yes, sir."

"So do I, Sergeant. Captain Percival said if we were to come across tracks that we suspected belonged to hostile Apaches, we were to pursue — and engage — unless the tracks led to the international border. Is that your understanding of my, no *our,* orders, Sergeant?"

"Yes, sir."

"Have we crossed the Rio Grande, Sergeant?"

"No, sir."

"And what do you make of those tracks?" Gibbons pointed at the ground.

"Unshod ponies. Four. Heading into that canyon."

"Unshod. What does that lead you to believe, Sergeant?"

"Likely Apaches, Lieutenant."

"So why should not we, numbering *ten*

27

men, pursue, as we have been *ordered,* four, *four* stinking, uncivilized, fool Apache bucks?"

If the Good Lord showed any mercy, Keegan thought, *He would let Erastus Gibbons drop dead of a stroke or heart failure right now.*

The way the kid's face beamed, there had to be a fair to middling chance that would happen, but the lieutenant caught his breath, uncorked his canteen, and drank greedily. His face began to lose its color, and Keegan began to think that nobody lives forever, and that he had lived a hell of a life, but getting eight kids killed alongside him wouldn't make him proud when he had to face St. Peter, or more than likely, Old Beelzebub or Satan himself. He didn't care one way or the other about Erastus Gibbons's fate. The punk had become tiresome, a boil Sean Keegan couldn't lance.

"Orders say *pursue,* Lieutenant," Keegan pointed out. "I'm all for pursuing. Just not following . . . into there." He nodded at the canyon's entrance.

"Sergeant, you disgust me."

Still, Keegan tried again. "Four Apaches can do a world of hurt, sir. Especially in that canyon."

The kid shook his head. "All right, Ser-

28

geant. What would you have in mind?"

Keegan pointed at the tracks. "Those Apaches didn't hide their trail. Tracks lead right into that canyon, and this canyon twists and turns about a mile and a quarter till it opens up. They could be hiding anywhere in those rocks, waiting to pick us off."

"Or they could be riding hard to Mexico."

Keegan shook his head. "If they wanted to be in Mexico in a hurry, they wouldn't ride through this death trap."

"You haven't told me what you have in mind, Sergeant."

Keegan pointed. "Leave Trooper Ulfsson here with the horses in the shade. He don't speak enough English, I don't speak no Swede, and his face is blistered already. Leaving him here might keep him from dying of sunstroke. The rest of us climb up to the top. I work my way ahead, and when I spot where those bucks are laying in wait, I fetch you boys. We ambush the ambushers."

The lieutenant shielded his eyes as he examined the mesa then swallowed while still looking at the top. "How long would it take us to climb up there, Sergeant?"

Fifteen minutes if I was alone, Keegan thought, but answered, "Us? Forty minutes."

"The other side isn't as high, Sergeant," Gibbons said. "Why not try that side?"

"Because the Apaches will be on this side. And they'll see us up yonder."

The young whippersnapper shook his head. "How do you know which side the Apaches are on, Sergeant? *If* they're even up there."

"Because you're shielding your eyes from the sun, Lieutenant. And once we start throwing lead at those bucks, they'll be shielding their eyes to try to spot us."

The kid looked away, wet his lips, and stared hard at the tracks and the entrance to the canyon. "And what if we find no Apaches?"

Keegan shrugged. "Then we've rested our horses, gotten a good stretch of our legs, Ulfsson ain't dead, and you get to write me up in your report to Captain Percival that I'm a fool."

"And the Apaches?"

Keegan shrugged again. "We'll fight them another day." *If I prayed, would that change the punk's mind?*

No, no, that wouldn't do. If Sean Keegan prayed, God himself would drop dead of a heart attack — and that would be another black mark in the book on Sean Keegan.

The kid pulled down the chinstrap on his

30

kepi, and Sean Keegan knew the boy had made up his mind.

"Sergeant, there's no glory to be found ambushing four Apache renegades. More important, I don't think those savages are waiting for us. We're going through that canyon, Sergeant. Follow those tracks, and catch the Apaches wherever they might be."

"You're in command, Lieutenant." Keegan pulled the trapdoor Springfield from the scabbard and braced the carbine's stock against his thigh.

"I gave no order to draw your long gun, Sergeant." The boy's face was brightening again. "Return that weapon, soldier!"

Keenan sprayed the ground with tobacco juice, then hawked up the quid, and spit it out, too. "I don't reckon I'll do that, bub." He was done showing respect to this know-it-all who was about to get killed some young boys who might've made decent soldiers.

The punk stuck his finger, hidden underneath that fine deerskin gauntlet, at Keegan. "You better put that Springfield away, Sergeant. Or when we reach Fort Spalding, I'll have you up on charges of disobeying a direct order."

"*If* we reach Fort Spalding, boy." Keegan looked behind him. "And I suggest you

31

gents follow my advice and get your carbines at the ready. You'll have need of them soon enough."

A few Adam's apples bobbed, and some of the green pups even glanced down at their Army-issued .45-70 weapons. But none dared disobey the lieutenant. Not that Sean Keegan could blame them. He slightly recalled what it was like to be a young soldier after he had joined the Second Michigan in '61. Thinking that you had to do everything a fool officer told you to do. Not knowing any better. But Keegan had learned. Maybe some of these boys would live long enough to learn, too.

"You'll wind up a buck private, Keegan, and in the guardhouse for a month."

"I hope you're right, Gibbons. Means I won't be dead."

The kid turned around, angry, and raised his right hand. "Follow me! Follow me!" He rode, ramrod straight — Keegan would give the kid that much — into the canyon.

He let the other soldiers pass him, felt their stares, but he did not look them in the eye. Didn't want to remember what they looked like, for one reason. And he waited till the blond-headed, sunburned pup of a Swede, Trooper Ulfsson, passed by at the rear. Only then did Keegan nudge his dun.

"Hey," Keegan called out, dropping his reins over the horse's neck, and holding out his right hand. "I'll take the lead rope to the pack mule, sonny."

The Swede stared at him blankly.

"The rope, boy. The rope." He gestured again, and finally, just grabbed hold of the lead rope and waited till the raw recruit understood. "You'll need both hands soon enough, Ulfsson," Keegan said.

The boy likely only understood his name.

The Swede rode ahead, pulled up even with another soldier whose name Keegan could not remember.

Column of twos. Riding to their deaths.

Keegan sighed and rode behind them, pulling the mule along. Yeah, Ulfsson would have need of two hands in a short while, but that's not why Keegan wanted to pull the mule. The mule carried the kegs of water. It also carried ammunition.

They'd have need of both shortly.

Most of the troopers looked up as soon as they entered Dead Man's Canyon, but had to duck their heads, pull down their hat brims, or raise a gauntlet-covered hand to see. Keegan did not bother looking for Apaches. He knew he would never be able to see the butchers. He studied the terrain on the ground. Always looking for a place where he and anyone who lived through the first volley could take cover.

Two hundred yards into Dead Man's Canyon, Keegan figured, *They'll hit us now.*

Only they didn't, and Keegan gave a begrudging nod of respect. *Smart Apaches. Don't hit us where we figure you will. Make us sweat a little more.*

The first shot knocked Ulfsson out of the saddle. The second punched another hole in Keegan's hat, which did not fall off. A long time ago, he had learned to wear a hat that fit tight and snug.

He quickly lost track of the other shots, too busy shoving the carbine back into the scabbard, gathering the reins he had draped and cramming those into his mouth. He reached out as he passed the body of the Swede, somehow managing to snag the reins to that horse before it bolted away.

He saw Ulfsson and frowned. At least the boy wasn't suffering from sunstroke any-more.

Keegan pulled hard on the lead rope, spurred the dun harder, and grabbed the reins with his left hand. "To those rocks!" he yelled. "To those rocks!"

The Apaches had picked a good spot. No place for the soldiers to hide on the western edge. Just some rocks and a clump of juniper on the east.

One of the troopers didn't make it. Keegan saw the dust fly from the back of his blue blouse, saw the kid's arms fly out, and watched him topple onto the ground. Keegan cursed. There was no way anybody was going to catch up to his spooked gelding. The little gray kept galloping down the canyon.

Somehow, the other six troopers made it to what would have to serve as cover. Keegan credited that to the Apaches. They might have been younger than the kids wearing the blue of the United States Army. Of course, shooting downhill took a bit of knowledge. Mainly, Keegan figured, the Indians didn't want to kill the horses.

He saw Lieutenant Erastus Gibbons, trying to unpin his left leg from underneath his dead brown gelding. The boy was screaming as the rest of his command thundered past him. Keegan didn't stop, either, until he was behind the rocks. There, he quickly but deftly wrapped the reins to his dun around a juniper branch, and securely tied the lead rope around the tree's trunk, pulling the mule up short.

Next, Keegan started yelling at the frightened troopers. "Baker!" At least, he thought that was the boy's name. "Holster that six-shooter, kid. You need both hands. You're holding the horses. All but mine and the mule. They're not going anywhere. You kids, you can't shoot a carbine and hold your horse. One at a time, take your horses to Baker over yonder.

"You, you blasted fool, holster that pistol, son. Those Apaches aren't in range for a short gun. Do it.

"You. Get your horse over there to Baker. Pronto.

"Baker, don't you fret. These horses were sold to the Army four years back. These are Matt McCulloch horses. As good as the Army ever got, back in the day."

A bullet clipped a branch.

"But they will skedaddle if you don't keep a good hold on the reins. Whatever you do, don't let go of those reins, bub."

The boy held two horses, and Keegan was running ahead, keeping low, making himself as small of a target as he could, nodding at the next soldier to take his horse to Baker.

After sliding to a stop, Keegan peered over the boulder. Lieutenant Gibbons had managed to get his leg from underneath the dead horse, but was huddling close to the horse. Bullets slammed into the animal. Each shot made the kid cringe and cry out in terror.

"They'll find the range soon enough," Keegan said, more to himself. He looked at the redheaded kid with a face covered with freckles next to him. "Boy, where in blazes is your carbine?"

Tears welled in the boy's eyes. He made a vague gesture to Baker and the horses. "In the . . . holder . . . on my . . . stallion," he managed to choke out.

"It ain't a *holder,* kid. It's a *scabbard.* And it ain't a stallion, either, but a gelding."

"What's a gelding, sir?" the teenager asked.

Keegan shook his head, but somehow he smiled. "An unfortunate stallion, boy. And I ain't no sir. Here." He shoved his own Springfield into the redhead's trembling hands. "Don't blow your fool head off by accident. And don't blow mine off, either."

He fumbled with the flap on his holster and drew the Remington. "All right. I'm going out yonder to fetch the lieutenant. Soon as I light out, you start shooting up . . . that . . . ridge. Not at me. You won't hit a cursed thing, but you might keep those Apaches' heads down till I'm back."

He checked the loads of his Remington, drew in a deep breath, and let it out. "You got your cartridge boxes handy?" Not waiting for an answer, he rose. "Here." He handed the Remington to the kid. "This won't do me no good. All right. I'll see you when I see you."

He started running, moving this way, then that, hearing the weapons opening up, ricochets whining off rocks. Keegan couldn't tell who all was shooting, but he felt no bullets coming near him. For the first twenty yards.

Then one clipped his empty holster.

He dived the last few feet, slamming into the dead horse's bloody neck. Keegan rolled over, noticed his sleeve. and brushed off the blood from the bullet-riddled animal. Erastus Gibbons stared at him with sand covering his face and his trousers darkened by urine.

"Th-they," the kid stammered. "They . . . they . . . k-k-killed my horse."

"You killed your horse, sonny," Keegan said. "Shot him in the head when you pulled your short gun."

"But —"

A bullet zipped past Keegan's ear.

"Boy, we stay here, we'll be deader than your horse, and those bucks will start filling our carcasses with lead. Get up, Gibbons. We're rejoining what's left of your command."

Rolling over, Keegan grabbed the lieutenant's left arm in a vise-like grip. Then he was standing, jerking Gibbons to his feet as another bullet slammed into the dirt a few feet away. "Run."

Keegan did not release his hold, nor did he run in that zigzag fashion, fearing that would just trip Gibbons and bring them both to the ground. He ran, hoping that the fool West Pointer would somehow keep his feet. The soldiers in the rocks fired, reloaded, fired. Keegan's ears rang from the relentless explosions.

They reached the rocky fortress, and he flung the lieutenant into the dirt, toward the horses, before he slid to a stop, rolled over, and came up alongside the redhead.

"All right, boys," Keegan said as another Springfield roared. "Hold your fire! Stop wasting lead! All right. Reload your carbines, but don't cock them till I tell you to. There's no sense in blowing your pard's head off or blowing your own head off." He didn't know how much longer he could keep talking. His throat was parched.

Still, he laughed, wiped the grime and dirt off his head, and felt the reassurance of his hat — still on his head. "This ain't nothing, boys. I've been in tighter fixes in Purgatory City. Sonny" — he smiled at the redhead —

"you run back yonder and relieve Baker. You hold the horses for now. Have Baker come here and have him bring the canteens." He turned away. "One sip from your canteens. That's all."

He looked back at the redhead. "Sonny, why are you still here?"

The boy bolted away, keeping Keegan's Remington in his shaking hand, and Keegan picked up the Springfield, his Springfield, that the kid had left. He worked the breech, felt the heat, smelled the smoke, and reloaded the weapon. Baker was soon beside him, straps of the canteens over his shoulder.

"All right, Baker," Keegan said. "Pass the canteens out. Remember. One swallow for now."

"Here's your canteen, Sergeant," the kid said.

"You keep it," Keegan said. "For now."

That's when he heard the braying of the mule, and the sound of metal-shod hooves on hard Texas rock. Second Lieutenant Erastus Gibbons had untied the animal, swung in front of the packsaddle, and was spurring the frightened beast out of the fort of rocks and juniper.

"Gibbons!" Keegan shouted as the coward raced past him. "Get back here, you yellow-

40

livered piece of the foulest, runniest, smelliest dung ever squirted out of a jackass's behind!"

The lieutenant made no attempt to turn back as the heavily laden mule lumbered along.

"Gibbons!" Keegan yelled. He spit, then swung the rifle around, brought the stock to his shoulder, and put a .45-70 slug through the lieutenant's body. Shoving the smoking rifle into the hands of a pale soldier with his eyes and mouth wide in shock and terror from what he had just seen, Keegan ran. More shots thundered past him, but the mule stopped about ten yards from the dead body of Erastus Gibbons. The animal, loaded down with water and lead, was likely played out.

Keegan leaped over the corpse, slowed, and noticed that the bullets had stopped firing from the Apaches. The soldiers in the rocks, however, kept up volley after volley. Keegan found the lead rope, wrapped it around his right hand, and turned back to the rocks. He hoped the mule wouldn't turn stubborn, that it might actually follow him, and he breathed easier, when the animal did.

He hurried as fast as he could, sweating, feeling his heart hammering inside his chest.

The soldiers stopped firing, and Keegan heard another noise. He looked behind him to see an Apache on a brown and white pinto pony riding straight at him. Keegan reached for his revolver, only to remember he had given it to the redhead.

The Apache bore down on him and the mule. Keegan could run, but he refused to be killed by a bullet in his back. He stepped out away from the mule and watched the Apache work the lever of a Winchester.

"Hey!" Keegan shouted. He was addressing his fellow soldiers, but he kept his eyes on the charging warrior. "Will one of you boys kill this buck before he puts me under?"

Most likely, Keegan figured, any bullet fired from those wet-behind-the-ears recruits would hit him by mistake.

He didn't hear the gunshot, but he saw the Apache somersault off the back of the pinto, which turned in the other direction, and bolted. The Winchester reflected the sunlight as the shot went skyward, then plummeted to the earth. The Apache hit the ground first.

Keegan stepped back to the mule and pulled hard. The Indians in the rocks kept shooting, but the soldiers returned fire, and in a minute that felt like an hour, he was back in the rocks, holding the mule by the rope. He handed it to another soldier. "Take him back with the others."

"Yes, Sergeant," the kid whispered.

"Hey, boy." The kid turned. "Give the mule to the redhead. Then bring all of our horses. Mine, too. Bring them back here and turn them loose."

"What?" said one of the troopers behind Keegan. "We'll be afoot."

"We'll also be alive," Keegan said. "Those boys want our horses. And now that they know we have water and ammunition, they won't likely try to put us under. Fair exchange, if you ask me. They get horses. We get to live." He turned to stare across the canyon floor and stopped when he came to the body of Lieutenant Erastus Gibbons.

"How do we get back to Fort Spalding?" asked another.

"We walk," Keegan said.

"You shot the lieutenant dead," another soldier whispered.

"Yeah," Keegan said as he looked up and noticed Baker holding a smoking Springfield carbine. "I'm much obliged, Baker, for shooting that Apache brave."

The kid reloaded the Springfield and sank back against the rock. He stared at Keegan grimly while the redhead and the other trooper led the horses to the opening and reluctantly turned them loose.

"Sergeant," the boy said. "My name's not Baker."

Keegan reached inside his blouse for his plug of tobacco, and bit off a good-sized chaw. "It is now," he said and began softening the quid with his teeth.

CHAPTER TWO

Sitting alone at a table in the Enfilade Saloon in the dusty town of Crossfire, Texas, Jed Breen felt pretty good. Last night, the hotel clerk had sent out Breen's clothes for a good scrubbing, and Breen liked feeling clean. He had paid two bits for a hot bath, the barber had shaved him close and without any nicks, the tonic slapped on his bronzed face smelled good, too, and his white hair had been trimmed short — just the way Breen liked.

A poor excuse for a town, Crossfire lay in the middle of nowhere on the El Paso Road about halfway between misery and oblivion. But the owner of the Hotel Turret, who erroneously believed that the town had a bright future, had hired a French chef, so Breen had enjoyed a leisurely supper last night and a fabulous breakfast this morning. He couldn't pronounce anything he had eaten, but it certainly had tasted better than anything he had swallowed the past three weeks — jerky, hardtack, rattlesnake, rabbit, but mostly dust and sand.

No one would consider the Enfilade Saloon in the same class as the Hotel Turret, but the whiskey had been watered down enough so that it was almost palatable, and the bottle in front of Breen, with a label that said Glenlivet, actually tasted like Scotch. The barkeep certainly charged enough for it to be real Scotch whiskey.

Of course, the better saloon, Diamond Jill's, stood just across the street, but Breen liked it just where he was. He had a tumbler of Scotch whiskey in his left hand, his newly polished boots were propped up in the chair across from him, his horse waited in the alley that ran between the Enfilade and a general store, and the window before him was clean. Jed Breen had a clear view of Diamond Jill's batwing doors and the gelding of dapple gray tethered to the hitching rail.

Breen swirled the whiskey around, brought the glass to his nose, and breathed in the fine aroma. He took another taste, enjoying the Scotch on his lips and tongue, and set the glass on the rough table between his shotgun and a poster that had the likeness of a man's face drawn under the word

WANTED and above the words *DEAD OR ALIVE.*
He tested the double-action Colt Lightning
.38 in his holster, scratching the heel of his
right hand with the hammer, and glanced
again at the poster to be sure of Walker's
description.

CATWALKER

5-foot-9, 150 pounds.
Black hair, gray eyes, crooked nose;
left earlobe missing.

LAST SEEN riding Gelding, gray with dark
rings (predominantly on neck and rear),
branded "4/-W";
stolen from Eugene Wilson's ranch in
Presidio County.
Walker escaped the Owensburg town jail
after being convicted of robbing
Wyatt Mulholland of $300 and his life.
☞ HE WAS SENTENCED TO HANG.

INQUIRIES: Marshal Q.G. Livermore,
Owensburg, Texas.

Of course, it was the figure below the
particulars that interested Breen most.
$1,250.00.
That horse was across the street. In the

47

hotel earlier, Breen had checked the brand, using the telescope on his Sharps rifle from his room's second-story window. The big .50-caliber long gun was in the scabbard of his horse. A shotgun or .38 would likely be more convenient for that particular job. The only thing Breen didn't really like was that, if the map he had was right, Owensburg was two hundred miles northeast, and that was a long ride to carry a man like Cat Walker. Cat Walker would give a man a lot of trouble for two hundred miles. Anybody in his right mind would. To escape a hangman's noose.

Alive, anyway.

And dead. Two hundred miles was a long way to haul a carcass — especially in the Texas heat.

Breen reached for the glass and tasted more of the Scotch.

On the other hand, the horse tethered across the street was not necessarily ridden by Cat Walker. A man on the run had a tendency to swap a tired horse for a fresh one, and the man had to have covered at least two hundred miles. Maybe more.

Breen checked the dates on the poster. The murder had been done last year. The trial had been in March. There was no mention of when Walker had escaped, but the poster did not look too old. Breen had plucked it off the wall in front of the town marshal's office after his five-course French supper. It hadn't been up long. Cat Walker did not seem to be, from the description, the brightest of bad men, so he might have kept the dapple gray gelding.

Anyway, Cat Walker would be feeling confident along about now. He was only a two-day ride from Mexico.

"Hey."

Breen was swirling the whiskey around his glass again. He frowned and turned his head away from the window. A cowhand by the looks of him had wandered down the stairs with a buxomly if ugly crone wearing slippers, her undergarments, and a robe that did little to hide her undergarments or her large, if well used, gifts from God. Her hair was wet, and sweat had cut arroyos through the heavy rouge that tried its best to hide her face. The cowboy hadn't been too careful in his dressing, either. His boots were on the wrong feet, his trousers were unbuttoned, and his shirt wasn't tucked in.

"Hey," the cowboy repeated as he lifted his left arm — the one not wrapped around the big girl's waist — and pointed at Breen. "Yuh ain't supposed to have no gun in dis 'ere town. That lawdog, he don't likes it. He taken mine from me jus' after I rode in yes-tidy evenin'."

Breen looked back out the window and sipped his Scotch. He wondered what Cat Walker was doing inside Diamond Jill's. Probably the chirpies over there were better looking than the one here.

"Hey, mistah, I'm talkin' at yuh."

"The marshal and I talked yesterday afternoon. We came to an understanding." Sometimes, Breen reminded himself, it cost a few bucks for a lawman to reach this understanding, but the Crossfire constable turned very cooperative once Jed Breen told him who he was.

"Don't yuh look aways from me when I's talkin' at yuh, ol' man." The cowboy snorted. "Look at 'im, Sissy, he's dressed fer a fun'ral in 'em black duds of hissen. And dat hair! He's shore ol' enough to be headin' to the hereafter."

Breen finished his Scotch. Maybe he should've just stayed in his hotel room, and shot Cat Walker off the horse with the Sharps rifle. But, at that time of day, he had not expected to find many customers in the Enfilade Saloon.

"C'mon, honey," the chirpie pleaded with him. "You said you'd buy me a drink. And I'm thirsty something awful. C'mon. Let's get our morning bracer. You and me. Then maybe we can go back upstairs again. You got anymore money?"

"Shut up." The cowboy pulled away from her and staggered toward Breen's table. "What yuh use that little gun of yers fer, mistah?" He laughed. "A walkin' cane? A crutch."

"It's a Parker twelve-gauge," Breen said, without looking away from the dapple horse and Diamond Jill's. "The last time I used it was to shut up a loud-mouthed punk."

"Eddie," the barkeep called. "Leave him alone. Come over here. Have one on the house."

"And buy one for me," the chirpie requested, pulling on the kid's arm.

"Leave me alone." He staggered away, and had to use the chair at Breen's left to keep from crashing into the table, which would have sent the Parker to the floor, along with the wanted poster and the bottle of Glenlivet.

Breen pulled his feet to the floor. His right hand found the butt of the double-action .38 in the holster, but he tried not to look at the drunken kid.

"Eddie!" the barkeep shouted. "Get your arse over here now."

"C'mon, sugar," the chirpie pleaded.

"Shut up!" the drunk said.

"Eddie, for the love of God, boy," cried the bartender. "That's Jed Breen!"

"I don't know no Jed Breen," the punk said. "But I do know how that law dog tol' me I couldn't have my guns in Crossfire. An' it don't matter how fancy this feller 'ere dresses, he ain't no better 'n me, an' I ain't a-lettin' 'im keep no runt of a scattergun on 'im whilst mine Navy Colt's at the town jail."

"Honey, now c'mon." The chirpie put her arm on his. "You said you was thirsty, darlin', and so am —"

The drunk spun around from the chair at Jed Breen's table and buried his fist into the girl's stomach. She doubled over, gasping and then throwing up. While the bartender screamed out Eddie's name, Eddie then kicked the woman to the floor.

"You tramp!" the drunk said savagely. "You two-bit —"

Jed Breen stood up, pulling the Lightning from his holster and slamming the barrel down hard on the boy's shoulder. He wanted the boy to see what was coming. More important, he wanted the drunk to know *why*.

The collarbone cracked. The kid turned and yelled out in pain.

The revolver barrel next slammed into the

jaw, sending blood and broken teeth into the puddle of blood the chirpie was spitting up.

Eddie started to fall backward, but Breen's left hand grabbed the collar of the filthy shirt and pulled the kid close.

"You never, ever hit a woman, boy," Breen said in a deadly voice. "I don't care if she's a whore or a nun, my mother or your wife, you never lay a hand on any woman." He brought his knee into the kid's groin, and as he doubled over, Breen let him drop to his knees on the floor.

"Nooo," moaned the chirpie, but then she lost interest and fell into a ball, pulling herself into a fetal position, sobbing and moaning.

Frozen behind the bar, the bartender was smart enough to keep his hands in sight, palms down and atop the bar.

Breen's free hand grabbed the kid's mane of sticky hair, jerked the kid's head up, and pushed it back, managing to stop the boy from falling to make sure he could see what was happening, what else was coming.

"I ever hear of you mistreating this lady or any girl, even a hen, whether she lays or not, and I'll finish this fight, buster. If you so much as pass a woman on the street and don't tip your hat, I'll know of it. And I'll be back. You understand me, kid? If you do, blink once."

The kid squeezed his eyelids shut. When they opened, Breen jerked the boy's head up and down, up and down, and up and down.

"Good. Good. Because there's one thing you don't want to see, boy, and that's Jed Breen when he's mad." His left hand released his hold on the greasy hair. His right swung the Colt Lightning, and the grips slammed into the boy's head.

His eyes rolled back into his head as he sank to the floor.

Breen spit the bitterness out of his mouth and onto the kid's chest. He glanced at the woman, still moaning, and looked at the bartender. "You best fetch a doctor, mister."

As he moved back to the table, he reached into the pocket of his Prince Albert coat and withdrew the leather purse. Most of the double eagles from Sam Manning's reward had been spent, but the robber was only worth two hundred dollars. Breen pulled out a twenty-dollar piece and set it on the table near the glass and the bottle.

"For the doctor." Breen nodded at the girl. "Her only. Eddie pays his own way. I don't think there are any damages, do you?"

Most of the blood could be mopped up,

54

Breen figured. The barkeep's head bobbed slightly. That was the only thing about him that moved.

"What are you waiting for?" Breen called out, and the bartender nodded, muttered something underneath his breath, and hurried out from behind the bar and through the small door that likely led to a storeroom and a back door.

Breen returned the purse to his pocket and found the bottle. He hated feeling like that. Getting upset could ruin his day, but a man had his principles, and there were some things he could not abide. He poured two fingers of Scotch into his glass.

Glenlivet might settle his temper.

He brought the glass to his mouth, breathed in the wonderful smell, and started to drink as he looked through the window and saw the hitching rail in front of Diamond Jill's.

Swearing, he killed the whiskey, dropped the glass, grabbed his sawed-off twelve-gauge, and moved quickly. He stepped over the unconscious body of Eddie and stopped at the batwing doors. His cold eyes studied the street — to the north, down toward the south, and across from him. Nothing. Crossfire's Main Street was empty.

Over at the southern edge of town, the

marshal was coming out of his office. Someone must have passed by the Crossfire Saloon while Eddie was abusing the chirpie or while Breen was making the cowhand realize the errors of his misguided existence. The man in front of the marshal's office kept pointing toward the Crossfire. The marshal looked that way briefly before he turned around and stepped inside his office — probably for his own scattergun.

But that's not what really mattered to Jed Breen. He pushed through the batwing doors and headed for his horse in the alley.

What mattered to him was that the dapple gray horse that had been in front of Diamond Jill's was gone.

CHAPTER THREE

Cuervo Villanueva didn't have enough time to cross the border into Mexico, so he ran into the mission just north of the Rio Grande. He was trying to pull his horse through the wide door inside the adobe church when Texas Ranger Matt McCulloch put a bullet through the pinto's head. That dropped the horse.

"Damn you, McCulloch," Ranger Sergeant Ed Powell said. "There's at least a nun and a priest inside there."

McCulloch jacked the lever of his 1873 Winchester carbine, sending the empty brass cartridge flying over his head and beyond the stone-piled fence that bordered the graveyard in front and to the east of the mission. He moved closer to the crumbling adobe wall, ruins of the first mission the Spanish and put up a century or more ago, and ignored Sergeant Powell.

McCulloch turned to the youngest

Ranger, Timmy Burns, and pointed. "Get our horses. Take them to the side of the church. And keep a tight grip on the reins."

"Damn you, McCulloch!" Powell thundered. "I'm in command here."

"Then command!" McCulloch barked and gave the teenaged Burns a sharp nod.

The kid collected the reins to the four horses and hurried to the side of the mission.

"Keep your head down!" McCulloch shouted. He knew the other two Rangers, Sergeant Powell and Paul Means, were staring at him, trying to read him, and maybe understand him.

People couldn't guess Matt McCulloch's age. Older than thirty, most would guess, younger than sixty. His hair remained thick, with a wide cowlick that had been, and still was, the envy of many men, even though the deep brown was showing several streaks of gray. His face was deeply tanned, which made his cold blue eyes stand out. His lips were thin, his nose straight, his jaw stern, and his neck long. He stood tall, thin, and harder than the country through which he rode.

He let the two Rangers stare at him and focused on the church.

The river, flowing mighty wide for that

time of year, ran about thirty yards behind the church before cutting sharply to the south. Mountains, mostly tan but dotted here and there with green clumps of mesquite and cactus, rose beyond the Rio Grande. The church jutted out with its façade that resembled that of the Alamo over in San Antonio. The front door was wide, but blocked by Cuervo Villanueva's dead horse. Two tabled windows flanked the door, the windows shuttered with cutouts of crosses carved into the thick wood. So far, no weapon was sticking out of the crosses. Above the door was the opening to the bell tower, with a rugged wooded cross rising from its apex.

Another window on the side of the thick adobe faced McCulloch and the Rangers. The rectory was attached to the church, flat-roofed, and stretching about twenty-five feet to the east. Timmy Burns held the big Texas horses on the eastern wall of the rectory. The door, wide open, and the window with curtains hanging out of the opening faced McCulloch and the Rangers hiding behind the adobe walls.

McCulloch wet his lips, removed his hat, and looked at the Ranger who gripped a Remington Rolling Block rifle and peered over the side of the wall at the church's main entrance.

"Hombres!" shouted Cuervo Villanueva from inside the church.

"Paul," McCulloch said. "Get behind the building." He waited for Sergeant Powell to object, but the gray-headed hardcase just glared. Powell was a good man, and in time, he would become a very good Ranger, McCulloch figured. "There's got to be a back door. Get down by the river so you have a good shot if he tries to make a break."

The sharpshooting Paul Means looked at Powell, who confirmed the order with a nod and a sigh.

"Hombres!" the bandit shouted again.

"Best answer him," McCulloch said.

"Give yourself up, Villanueva!" the sergeant ordered.

"No *sabe*," came the outlaw's reply.

Powell looked at McCulloch, who shook his head. "He speaks English better than half the population of Purgatory City. When he wants to."

Feeding fresh cartridges into his own Winchester, Ed Powell cursed and shook his head. "Why didn't he keep riding? Fifty yards and he'd be in Mexico."

"River's wide," McCulloch said. "Means would've shot him out of the saddle before he was halfway across the Rio."

60

Powell thumbed back the hammer on his carbine, and pushed himself up for a better look. Inside the whitewashed adobe building came muffled shouts and bits of conversation.

"I don't like this," he said. "You reckon there might be some parishioners inside?"

McCulloch shrugged and looked at the entrance to the bell tower.

He was dressed in trail duds, which was about all he owned anymore, except for a frayed black coat and black string tie that he could wear to funerals. His boots had been made by a Mexican saddlemaker over in Presidio and could stand about four dollars' worth of repairs. His striped britches were faded, covered with old leather chaps. His shirt was a blue pullover, the bandanna a red calico, the vest brown with one pocket ripped off. His hat a battered gray, covered with dust. He thought about removing the linen duster the color of oatmeal, but didn't bother with it.

McCulloch wore no spurs. He had never worn spurs. He wasn't one to misuse an animal, he had told his sons. If you knew what you were doing, if you could communicate with a horse, a man had no reason to wear spurs. Spurs could hurt a horse, in fact *did* hurt horses.

61

Although he had never been one to mistreat any animal, he had just shot a horse dead. In front of a church. And he felt absolutely nothing about what he had just done.

A few minutes later, Cuervo Villanueva shouted, *"¿Que entre vosotros habla el lenguaje de mis padres?"*

"What's he saying?" the sergeant asked.

"He wants to know who speaks Spanish." McCulloch said.

Powell spit between his teeth. "I reckon you'd best answer him, Matt."

McCulloch called out, *"¡Dime ya! ¿Qué quieres?"*

Cuervo Villanueva responded with a long-winded speech that started with political statements, about how this land did not truly belong to the *Tejanos* but to the fathers and grandfathers of Cuervo Villanueva, and that he, a poor, peaceful farmer, had been driven out of his home, brutalized by the *Tejanos* and the lawmakers of the *norteamericanos* and other gringos, and that he did not want to do everything that he had been forced to do, but he had been given no choice. The wearers of the *cinco pesos* stars, meaning the Texas Rangers, should track down the truly bad men and leave Cuervo Villanueva to tend his garden and attend Mass and live his life in peace, as he had before all the troubles the *Tejanos* brought to this part of Mexico.

"What's he saying?" Powell asked McCulloch when the outlaw paused for breath.

"The usual wagonload of dung."

The lesson continued. Cuervo Villanueva had not killed that man in that store in that village south of Cienega. And he had asked the padre with him to pray that the Texas Ranger he had been forced to shoot on his way out of the village would be able to dance with a pretty girl in a few months. He said killing his horse was a terrible and mean thing to do and the padre and the two sisters were extremely annoyed with the Rangers who had done that terrible thing.

The more Cuervo Villanueva spoke, the more McCulloch studied the mission and the rectory. He also checked the position of the sun.

"What's he saying now?" Sergeant Powell asked.

"He wants us to send in some tequila," McCulloch said. "Communion wine only cuts so much dust. Enchiladas would be nice. Maybe a beefsteak." McCulloch pulled on his left earlobe and knotted his forehead. "I couldn't quite understand that last part."

Villanueva said something else. McCulloch's head bobbed. "And we owe him for his horse. He will take two of ours, but only one needs to be saddled and we can keep the saddle on the horse that we — I — shot dead."

Powell muttered a curse and reminded McCulloch, as though he needed any reminding, that Cuervo Villanueva had stolen that horse from outside the saloon in Cienega.

Eventually, after maybe fifteen minutes, Cuervo Villanueva fell silent.

"What do you reckon he's doing in there?" Powell asked.

McCulloch shrugged. "Probably dragging some pews in front of the front door. Maybe checking around, seeing how he can get out."

"He don't need to build no barricade," Powell said. "You did a fair job of that killing that horse."

"Means he can't get out in a hurry that way," McCulloch said. "And he has no horse to ride if he gets out."

"And that thing's gonna start ripening real quick," Powell said.

"Exactly."

McCulloch leaned the rifle against the crumbling wall and drew the long-barreled Colt from his holster. He opened the load-

ing gate, rotated the cylinder, and pushed a
.44-40 shell from the loops on his shell belt.
After sliding the cartridge into the empty
hole, he pulled the heavy pistol to full cock
and gently lowered the hammer, then
shoved the Colt into the holster. Glancing
at the sergeant, McCulloch found him staring hard in his direction.

"You shot a horse in front of a church
door," Powell said. "Don't that bother you,
McCulloch? Didn't you use to raise horses?"

McCulloch found his hat. "That was
another lifetime, Ed. Another man." Again,
he raised his eyes and considered the church
roof.

"Tell him to come out or we'll come in,"
Sergeant Powell ordered after a lengthy silence.

After McCulloch relayed the message, the
outlaw promptly responded.

"Well?" Powell asked.

It was the answer McCulloch expected,
but repeating it was far from palatable. "He
says if we come inside the church, he will
kill the priest, the two nuns, and the young
woman and her baby."

"He ain't got no baby," Powell said.

But the wailing of a child told the Rangers that Cuervo Villanueva was not lying at
all.

65

Powell swore.

"Sarge!" young Burns called out from the side of the rectory. "That's a little baby."

"I hear it, boy! Shut up." The sergeant swore, spit again, and scrutinized the front entrance to the church. "Well," he said finally. "Mexican standoff. We just wait him out. He ain't going nowheres. We can outlast him."

McCulloch shook his head. "Come dark, he can walk out of here with a priest or a nun or that young mother or her baby. It'd be too dark for Means to chance a shot with that long gun of his. Too dark for any of us to shoot."

"You said the river's running high," Powell said.

"I said it's wide for this time of year," Mc-Culloch corrected. "It's never deep. At least, not here."

"Well" — Powell was trying to think — "maybe he won't try that. Maybe —"

"Then he'll send one of the nuns out," McCulloch interrupted. "Over the horse and toward us. Before he puts a bullet in the back of her head."

"He wouldn't do that." Again, Ed Powell tried to convince himself of something he could not imagine and wiped the sweat off his brow with a dirty shirtsleeve. He saw

66

McCulloch's hard stare.

"What do you want us to do? Go charging in there like the Mexicans on the last day of the Alamo?" He pointed at the door. "That horse you killed not only will make it hard for that Mexican to come out, it'll mean he can pick us off as we try to climb over its stinking carcass to get inside."

McCulloch said nothing.

"We could let him go," Powell said. "Give him our word we won't shoot."

"He wouldn't believe you."

"We could ride off. Tell him he's free to go. We'll catch him and hang him next time."

McCulloch's head shook. "He'll remember Means's Rolling Block."

"We can leave that gun behind. And our long guns."

McCulloch stared hard. "You going to leave Cuervo Villanueva with three women?"

"By G-God, man," Powell stammered. "He wouldn't . . ."

"Have you forgotten what he did at Embarrado?"

Inside the church, the baby began yelling louder.

"Well, damn it, man, do you have any better ideas?" Sergeant Powell shouted.

That's all Matt McCulloch needed to

hear. He moved the Winchester, drew his Colt, came to his knees, looked once at the church door and windows, and bolted across the ground toward Ranger Burns and the horses.

An adobe column protruded from the rectory's eastern walls, all the way from the ground to about a foot from the flat roof. It was curved, more for design than function, but it was wide enough and heavy enough to support McCulloch as he climbed up it, laid his Colt on the rooftop, and then pulled himself up. He found the Colt and trod quickly but lightly across the rooftop toward the mission. When he reached the edge, McCulloch wet his lips and surveyed the roof of the church. It was flat, too, covered with gravel, sand, and the droppings of rats and birds from too many summers to count.

He was not a heavy man, but the church was at least a century old. If dust started drifting from the ceiling onto the church floor, Cuervo Villanueva would be ready. And angry enough to maybe pop a cap on a nun, a priest, or a young mother. Probably not the baby, though. Villanueva would be smart enough to save the baby as his bona fides, his passport into Mexico.

McCulloch frowned at the bell tower. He had hoped to find a door, but now that he thought about it, there was no need for a door. He did not look at the ground or anywhere near Sergeant Powell. McCulloch rose, moved his left leg up and over the adobe, and then pulled his right behind him. He was standing on the church's roof.

Listening intently, he took a tentative step toward the façade, and another. He felt nothing giving beneath his boots, so he moved faster, but still with precision and a dove's touch, and came to the tower. Grabbing the adobe with his left hand, he leaned over the front of the church and looked inside. It smelled of dust. Piles of guano covered the flooring beneath the bell, and he saw the rope that led through a hole. He also saw the trapdoor.

"No," McCulloch whispered, and moved away from the tower.

Cuervo Villanueva would be somewhere in the front of the mission, closer to the door. McCulloch had thought about opening the trapdoor, dropping himself into the church, and letting the chips fall where they may.

But that was no good. To kill or capture the Mexican outlaw, McCulloch needed to come in behind the killer. He sniffed, rubbed his left hand over the graying stubble on his face, blinked away the sweat, and looked down the roof. From there, he could see the river, the mountains of Mexico, and purple-necked sheartails darting around the flowering cactus between the church and the river. He didn't see Paul Means or his long rifle, but he saw another trapdoor.

McCulloch moved down the long rectangular roof.

When he reached the door, he knelt. Would it be locked from beneath? McCulloch took the handle and lifted, letting out a light breath when it opened. Seeing the rays of light shining from the roof to the floor, he stopped. He could hear the baby crying, the nuns praying, and the priest talking in hushed Spanish to the killer holding them all hostages. Villanueva yelled something that silenced the priest. McCulloch deftly eared back the hammer on his Colt.

Cuervo Villanueva began yelling again, screaming out his demands at Sergeant Powell. It was the final threat. If the Rangers did not lay down all their arms and ride away, he would be sending the oldest and ugliest nun out to the Rangers, and the Rangers would soon see what kind of man they were dealing with. Cuervo Villanueva was not a man to make idle threats.

This will be as good as it gets, McCulloch told himself.

He flung open the door and leaped through the narrow opening. Hitting the hard-tiled floor, he felt his right knee buckle — horse wranglers and horse breakers never healed completely — and slammed hard against a dark, unmoving pew.

It was darker inside the mission. Mc-Culloch's eyes had become accustomed to the bright sunshine of late afternoon. The baby cried louder, and the mother tried to hush her infant. They were behind Mc-Culloch. He sure hoped they were on the floor, protected by the heavy pews.

"*¡Maldita sea!*" Cuervo Villanueva shouted, and spun around.

McCulloch found him in the darkened front entryway. The outlaw was silhouetted by the sun shining through the partially opened door and cutouts of the crosses, and maybe three dozen candles lighted for Mass or prayer intentions. McCulloch's right knee hurt like blazes, and his shoulder had been jarred by the impact of the pew, but he still held the .44-40-caliber Colt, and it was coming up in his hand.

Although the priest had been kneeling in the aisle, he sprang to his feet, turned, and yelled something that McCulloch could not grasp. McCulloch had to shift his aim, but Villanueva was grabbing a tall, young, slender nun and pulling her in front of his own body.

McCulloch did not hesitate an instant longer. He pulled the trigger. The nun shrieked, the priest fell to the floor and covered his ears, and Cuervo Villanueva stepped backward, releasing the nun, who covered her face with her hands and dropped to the floor. The outlaw's revolver went off, disintegrating a candle. McCulloch fired again and drove the outlaw against the candles.

The gunshots reverberated throughout the church's thick adobe walls. McCulloch cocked and fired again, turning the Mexican bad man around as he knocked over more candles. McCulloch's next two shots caught Cuervo Villanueva in the back and pushed him against the door.

McCulloch considered pulling the trigger once more, but the older nun rose into McCulloch's line of fire. The revolver was slipping from Cuervo Villanueva's hand as he started sliding down the heavy door, and the mother of the child somewhere behind McCulloch kept screaming louder than her baby.

CHAPTER FOUR

Harry Henderson couldn't stop sweating. Of course, it was a hot day, and he was dressed in a suit of black wool, and he had just opened the bank that Monday morning in Sierra Vista, Texas. It had been closed Sunday, and Saturday, too, on account that Saturday was a holiday, Founders Day, so the bank was very stuffy. And, well, everyone in Sierra Vista knew that Harry Henderson, chief teller at the Bank of Sierra Vista, was a very nervous man, prone to sweating. But if the president of the bank, Mr. Jason R. Cox — or for that matter, anyone who knew Harry Henderson — had seen Henderson that morning they would have wondered if he was suffering from a relapse of his malaria. For even by Harry Henderson's standards, his sweating was extreme.

Someone pounded on the rear door to the bank.

Henderson almost jumped out of his tight-fitting shoes. He pulled the wet handkerchief from his vest pocket, mopped his brow for about roughly the hundredth time, and stumbled from where he was standing, peering through the closed curtains at Railroad Avenue. He heard the pounding on the rear door again.

There was no railroad in Sierra Vista. There were no mountains, either, and most people would recognize the fact that there wasn't much of a view. But the town's founding fathers had high hopes for getting a railroad and adding to the booming population. Sierra Vista had some major investors, two powerful ranchers, and one of the most successful whorehouses between San Antonio and Tucson — and they all banked at the Bank of Sierra Vista.

He whispered, "Oh, my," and wiped his face again, tried to return the white cotton handkerchief into the vest pocket — it took him three times — and hurried across the wooden floor. The echoes of his footsteps almost made him "jump out of his skin," as his mother might have said — God rest her soul. He pushed through the low wooden gate that separated the lobby from his desk, passed the door to Mr. Cox's office, and went past the bookcases and the filing cabinets. Turning around the corner, he came to the back door.

Four loud knocks sounded again.

Harry Henderson pulled back the three bolts — one at the top, one at the bottom, and a really big one at the side — twisted the lock on the knob, and opened the door.

Three men practically bowled him over as they rushed inside.

"What the hell kept you, you idiot?" said the biggest of the three, the one wearing the mustache and the hat that would've been blacker than Harry Henderson's suit had it not been covered with alkali dust.

Harry Henderson opened his mouth to answer, but he had no answer. He just tasted salt from his sweat.

"Well," said the man in black. "Shut the door, you idiot."

Harry Henderson made himself speak. "I thought there were four of you."

"Galloway's holding the horses."

"Oh." Henderson closed the door, but he just twisted the lock on the knob. He didn't bother with the bolts. He wanted to wipe the sweat from his face, but he couldn't get his hands to cooperate.

"Henderson," the man in black said, "do you want to wait for the bank to open to make our withdrawal?"

Harry Henderson blinked. He did not understand until the two men standing beside the man in black chuckled.

"Oh," Henderson said, realizing that Jake Hawkin had just made a joke. "Oh." He tried to smile, but could not.

Jake Hawkin glared. The man's eyes were blue, pale, and cold. Even as hot and as stuffy as it was inside the bank, Harry Henderson felt chilled. Jake Hawkin, he knew, was a very dangerous man. He was tall, solid, and wore two holsters carrying two guns, the one on his right hip with the revolver's butt facing the back and the one on his left hip with the butt facing forward. Harry Henderson had read enough dime novels to understand that such an arrangement likely meant that Jake Hawkin was right-handed.

The man in the tan clothes and Mexican sombrero — though he was not Mexican, but a white man — turned his head and spit tobacco juice onto the floor. He missed the spittoon. Maybe he hadn't seen it. Probably, he just didn't care. That man carried a Winchester repeating rifle, and he wore two holsters, too, one on his right hip, butt to the rear, and one on his belly, the butt toward his right hand.

Harry Henderson did not know that

man's name. He probably didn't want to know.

He did know the third man. That was Jake Hawkin's kid brother, Billy. Billy looked a lot like his big brother, only thinner, with no mustache, and eyes that were the same color but did not have that look of death about them. It was Billy Hawkin whom Harry Henderson had met while on a business trip to El Paso about four weeks back.

They had been gambling, not really speaking to each other, but then had seen each other at a café on Front Street, where Harry had met up with Catherine Cooper for supper. He loved Catherine Cooper. Especially now that she told him she was expecting a baby in six months, he was the daddy, and he damned sure was going to marry her pretty quickly. He wanted to marry her, but, well, the thing about it was that he already had a wife, Prudence, and two kids — neither of whom liked him one whit — from her dearly departed first husband. He also had a wife in Dallas, but he hadn't seen her in six or seven years after she had found out about the wife he had in Fort Worth, and as far as he knew, neither of those wives had divorced him, although the one in Dallas had threatened him with a shotgun.

He didn't want Prudence or Catherine to

know about any of his wives, so he told Catherine he would marry her as soon as he returned from Sierra Vista — he needed to settle up his affairs — and then they would be married, travel to San Francisco, and start all over. Catherine always said she really wanted to live in San Francisco. Henderson had said he did, too, although all he knew about San Francisco was that it was in California. He never really knew if it was in the southern part of the state or if that was the city called Los Angeles and that San Francisco was up north, or maybe in the mountains where they had found gold. Or was that some other place?

Billy Hawkin had been eavesdropping and had to have really good hearing because Henderson and Catherine had been whispering. He turned around in the booth behind Henderson and said, "So . . . you work at the bank in Sierra Vista . . . ?"

Now, inside that very bank, Billy Hawkin put his hand on Harry Henderson's shoulder and said, "Show me the vault, Harry. And stop shaking. We'll be done in a jiffy. Just relax." He slapped Henderson's shoulder. "Everything's gonna be fine, pard."

Henderson let Billy Hawkin guide him through the low gate and behind the counter to the vault. Billy would take care of him.

With his share of the money they were about to steal, Henderson could get to El Paso, marry Catherine, and head down to San Francisco. Or . . . well . . . maybe he wouldn't have to marry Catherine. With his share of the money they were about to steal, he could find him a pretty señorita in Vera Cruz or wherever he decided to disappear.

He stopped at the vault.

"Why didn't you have that thing opened before we got here?" Jake Hawkin demanded.

Spinning around, Henderson held up his hands, thinking he had heard the gunman drawing his pistol, but realized that the white man with the Mexican hat was pulling wheat sacks from the back of his waistband. He thought they'd put the sacks over their faces, but the man just shook the sacks.

"I asked you a question, bub," Jake Hawkin growled.

Oh, Henderson thought, *the sacks are for the money.* He smiled, then frowned, and looked at the outlaw leader. "I-i-it's a . . . t-t-time . . . ummmm . . ."

"Lock." Billy finished the sentence.

"You might have let us know that before," Jake Hawkin said.

Henderson looked at the Regulator clock on the wall. "Five minutes." *Man, it's ticking really loud this morning.*

Jake Hawkin cut loose with a string of curses.

They watched the clock, counted the seconds, and Henderson thought he had sweated enough water to fill the cistern in the center of town.

The clock chimed, and he almost jumped out of his skin. Shoved from behind by Jake Hawkin, he went to the vault and began working the dial. He prayed that he wouldn't suffer amnesia and forget the combination. He heard a click, stepped back, and pulled the lever. The heavy iron door barely budged.

"Here." Jake shoved Henderson aside and pulled open the door. Only then did he smile.

"Wait here." Billy patted Henderson's back and followed his brother inside the vault.

The other man with the sacks and the rifle followed.

Henderson listened to the clock. For a moment, he even thought of something completely insane. He could shut the vault. They couldn't open it from inside. He could picture his name in all the newspapers. He'd collect the reward on not only Jake and Billy Hawkin, but the other outlaw as well. Of course, there was the man outside holding the horses. He might come in and kill Henderson. Or worse, all those woodcut engravings of Harry Henderson's likenesses would appear in newspapers in Fort Worth and Dallas. And maybe even in Cincinnati. He hadn't married that girl, but he had left her in the family way.

Henderson decided he would just have to live with his share of fifty thousand dollars. Ten thousand. He could buy a lot with that much money, even in San Francisco. He could buy even more, he realized, in Mexico.

That's when he heard the clicking. He looked at the watch, and then at the vault door, and finally understood exactly what he was hearing.

The front door opened, and Mr. Jason R. Cox, president of the Bank of Sierra Vista, stepped over the threshold and stopped, his left hand still on the doorknob.

Henderson turned and looked at the Regulator clock on the wall.

"Harry," Mr. Cox said. "You're early this . . ."

Henderson looked back at his boss. Jason R. Cox never arrived until five minutes before the bank opened. The bank didn't open until 8:30.

"Harry?" Mr. James R. Cox was looking

at the open vault.

The man with the wheat sacks, the Mexican sombrero, and the Winchester repeating rifle stepped through the door way of the vault and brought the Winchester to his shoulder. "Inside. And be damned quick about it. Then close the door."

James R. Cox swallowed. His left hand left the doorknob, and he spun around and stepped out onto the boardwalk. He yelled, "Robbery!"

That's when the Winchester roared. Henderson felt the muzzle blast and his ears began ringing. He saw the burst of crimson appear in the center of Mr. Cox's tan jacket, and he saw Mr. Cox stagger out but stop himself from falling into the dusty street by using both hands to catch himself on the hitching rail.

The man with the Winchester worked the lever.

"Robbery!" Mr. Cox managed to cough as he lifted his head. "Murder."

The rifle roared again, and Harry Henderson saw the back of Mr. Cox's head just disappear. Then Mr. Cox was draped over the hitching rail.

People outside were taking up the cry.

"Robbery!"

"By thunder, the bank's being robbed!"

"Cox! Mister Cox! Get your guns, boys, they've shot Mr. Cox dead!"

Billy Hawkin came out of the vault first, holding the wheat sacks filled with money. The man with the Winchester and the two revolvers still holstered ran to the open front door. The curtains to the bank windows were closed, but not-small holes began appearing. Even though his ears kept ringing, Harry Henderson managed to hear glass shattering and bullets thudding against the wall of the bank. A moment later, the man with the Winchester began returning fire.

Jake Hawkin stepped out of the vault holding wheat sacks, too. "What the hell happened?"

Henderson blinked. He pointed. "He wasn't . . . he never. . . ."

"How many are out there?" Jake Hawkin yelled at the man firing the Winchester.

The big man worked the lever, ducked against the wall, and spit more tobacco juice onto the floor. "Looks like half the whole damned county."

"Keep us covered," Billy said. "We'll pick you up out front."

Jake was already making for the back door. "Galloway!" he yelled. "We're coming out!"

"Come on, pard," Billy Hawkin gave Harry Henderson a gentle nudge. "Come on. 'Less you want to hang."

Henderson had stopped sweating. He just couldn't stop blinking.

"Keep your head down." Billy shoved Henderson forward.

He swallowed and blinked, blinked and swallowed, and began moving past the tellers' counters, past the late Mr. Cox's office, and toward the bookcases and filing cabinets.

"Billy!" the big man with the Winchester called out, and his voice did not sound like it had earlier.

Billy Hawkin and Harry Henderson turned to see the man stagger away from the door, drop the Winchester, and put both hands on his belly.

"I'm kilt, Billy," he said, and blood began to seep out of the corners of his mouth. "Damn it all to hell, I'm kilt dead for sure."

Harry Henderson did not hear the gunfire, but more slugs must have slammed into the man's back, because he fell to his knees, grimacing with the impact. One bullet tore off the robber's left ear.

No, Henderson corrected himself. That was the *right ear,* because the killer was facing him and Billy Hawkin.

Another bullet grazed the man's right arm, and a moment later, he shuddered. A waterfall of blood erupted from his mouth as he pitched onto his face and shuddered.

"Move!" Billy shoved Henderson to the door, then pushed him out of the doorway and into the alley.

"Where's MacMurray?" Jake Hawkin was mounted on a big black stud horse. Another man was at the edge of the alley, his horse stepping this way and that as he fired a rifle while sitting in the saddle.

"Dead!" Billy Hawkin told his brother.

Jake swore. "What the hell is he doing here?"

"He's my pard, Jake. We're taking him with us."

"Are you daft?"

"MacMurray's got no need for his horse!"

The elder, meaner Hawkin swore again, reached out and took the sacks from his brother, and spurred his horse out of the alley. The man named Galloway followed.

Billy Hawkin helped Henderson into the saddle. The stirrups were too long. Henderson blinked. He started sweating again. Then Billy Hawkin pulled off his hat, slapped the pinto's rear, and Harry Henderson felt himself being carried away, out of the alley and into the street. The street where half the county was filling the bank with lead.

"Which way . . . ?" Harry Henderson managed to call out.

"There's only one place we're going," Billy Hawkin said. Amazingly, he was on his gray dun right behind Henderson. "Hell."

Harry Henderson sat in the private parlor of Miss Matilda's House of the Divine, the most successful brothel, people said, between San Antonio and Tucson. He still had trouble believing it. After all, Miss Matilda's House of the Divine was in Sierra Vista — on the edge of town, of course, and on the wrong side of the street — which meant he was still in the town he had galloped out of that morning. He could still hear the bullets whizzing past his head. One had even cut a hole through his black suit coat.

He sipped the brandy one of Miss Matilda's girls had given him. He tried to put together everything that had happened. Maybe he was dreaming. He took another taste of brandy. Maybe he was dead. In Hell.

The girl sat on Henderson's lap and pulled his face tight against her ample bosoms. "You poor, poor thing," she whispered.

No, Henderson figured, he was not dead. At least he was not in Hell.

He tried to remember.

■ ■ ■ ■

They rode west out of town, into the little arroyo where the two Hawkin brothers, the man named Galloway, and Henderson met up with maybe ten or twelve other men.

"Where's MacMurray?" one of the cutthroats demanded.

"Shaking hands with the devil," Jake said as he dismounted, handed the reins to one of the men, then noticed Henderson was still on his horse. "Get down."

"What?" Henderson mouthed, before looking down to see that Jake had stepped out of his saddle and the man named Galloway was walking into the mesquite thicket.

"Damn it, Harry, get off that horse now." Billy Hawkin did not wait any longer but reached up and jerked Henderson's sweaty body off the horse and shoved him into the thicket.

The men with the horses spurred their own mounts and galloped down the arroyo. Henderson tried to register what was going on. They had just robbed the Bank of Sierra Vista. They had just left Mr. James R. Cox, president of that very bank, dead with the back of his head blown off. And now, not even a quarter of a mile out of town, they had dismounted and moved into a thicket of mesquite trees that would tear a body to pieces if he wasn't careful.

"Don't move," Billy whispered. "Don't open your mouth. Don't even breathe." He pushed Henderson's head down.

The former bank teller did not move too much, nor did he open his mouth, but he breathed. His eyes saw Jake Hawkin, big revolver in his right hand, kneeling behind one of the trees. The wheat sacks filled with loot stolen from the Bank of Sierra Vista were at his feet. The man named Galloway had a couple of carpetbags in front of his feet while he gripped a long-barreled revolver.

Henderson heard the thundering of horses. He almost gasped, but felt Billy squeezing his shoulder and saying, "Shhhhhhhh."

His eyes widening in terror, Henderson saw the horses — a dozen, maybe more — tear through the arroyo and disappear. Four minutes later, several more horses galloped past. For the next few minutes, a few stragglers came along.

Then, for an hour, Hawkin and his men waited.

Finally, Jake laughed and holstered his revolver.

The man named Galloway shook his head, picked up one of the carpetbags, and tossed it to his boss. "I gotta hand it to you, Jake.

This one sure takes the cake."

"Give some of the credit to Billy." Jake opened the gaudy bag of pink and yellow and white and blue designs, and dumped the money from one wheat sack into the bag.

"We wouldn't have gotten this done without my pard here."

Henderson felt Billy's rough hand slam against his back. "Ol' Harry here, he done all right."

Jake snorted and poured the greenbacks and gold from the second wheat sack into the carpetbag.

Another carpetbag was tossed to the outlaw leader, who filled it, too.

"I don't —" That's all Harry Henderson could get out.

"The posse will chase Alfredo and our boys till they get tired of chasing," Billy Hawkin said. "They'll send telegraphs, of course, to the Rangers. To El Paso. Crossfire. Fort Davis. Van Horn. Presidio. Pecos. Fort Stockton. Purgatory City. Half of West Texas will be looking for a bunch of men traveling fast on horseback."

"We'll be enjoying some refreshments of the liquid and lady-of-the-tenderloin varieties," Galloway said with a laugh. He even slapped his own thigh.

"Right under the noses of the law and all

the fine folks in Sierra Vista," Billy said.

Henderson thought about his wife in town. Likely, the town marshal and the other clerks, cashiers, and tellers at the Bank of Sierra Vista had already informed her that her husband had been part of the robbery. They'd seen him riding out with the outlaws, and well, the vault had been opened, and only two people knew the combination, and one was James R. Cox, who had died defending the savings of the good citizens trusting him with their hard-earned money.

"We spend a day or two at Matilda's," Billy said. "Then we take a stagecoach ride to Purgatory City and on to El Paso."

"No one'll expect us riding a stagecoach," Galloway said. "You already got the tickets, didn't you, boss?" he called out to Jake.

The outlaw leader reached inside his vest and pulled out the tickets. "Too bad MacMurray won't be with us."

"Yeah," Billy said. "Too bad." And he laughed.

Jake dropped the tickets inside the carpetbag, the one with the green and yellow floral designs, not the pink, yellow, white, and blue.

"When we get to the House of the Divine," Billy said. "We'll get you a special room. Don't want any of the locals seeing you there. Your wife wouldn't understand."

Sitting in that special room, Harry Henderson managed to laugh. The girl asked if he wanted to buy her another drink, so he opened the carpetbag, found a double eagle, and handed it to her. Just as she stepped out, Billy Hawkin came in.

"How's it goin', pard?"

No longer sweating, Henderson grinned and raised his glass of brandy in salute.

"Good." Hawkin knelt by the open carpetbag and pulled out a handful of greenbacks. "Jake's got two girls with him. Galloway's snoring like my old man. And I'm gambling with Matilda herself in her own room." He shoved money into one of the front pockets of his trousers. "And I'm winning. Don't go anywhere with all our loot, pard." He laughed and walked out.

Harry Henderson couldn't believe his luck. He finished the brandy and moved to the third-floor window, slowly drawing back the curtain and staring down at Sierra Vista at night.

The westbound stagecoach had pulled in. He looked at the clock on the table in the private parlor suite. He looked at the carpetbags.

And an idea struck him. Galloway and the Hawkin brothers were, well, preoccupied. Most of the townsmen were off chasing the gang members who had led the posse away from the bank's money. The stage would be leaving in fifteen minutes. And Harry Henderson had a ticket. He could take those carpetbags, walk out of Miss Matilda's House of the Divine, and hand the ticket to the driver and messenger, who wouldn't know Harry Henderson from his Uncle Walter on his mother's side.

By the time the Hawkin brothers realized that they had been double-crossed, Henderson would be in . . . Mexico. With fifty thousand dollars all to himself.

He had never been one to take risks, except when it came to marrying several women. But now he would have a price on his head and a hangman's noose waiting for him. Jake Hawkin wouldn't be one to trust Harry Henderson forever. Even Billy might grow tired of him.

Henderson found his courage, snapped the two carpetbags shut, picked them up in one hand, and carefully opened the door and peered down the hallway. He could see the back door that led to the staircase that led to the ground that led to the walkway that led to the stagecoach station at the edge of Sierra Vista.

He stepped out and did not look over his shoulder. He stayed in the shadows then waited until the passengers were loaded and the rawhide-looking driver and the young messenger climbed aboard. The station agent disappeared into his office, and Henderson took a deep breath, exhaled, and hurried to the Concord.

The driver looked down.

Henderson handed him his ticket.

"Ya cuttin' it close, ain't ya?" the driver said, studied the ticket, shrugged, and shoved it into the pocket of his tan jacket.

"Working late," Henderson told him, opened the door, and climbed into the coach. His heart pounded as he smiled at the two other people in the coach, and he found a seat. He kept the carpetbags in his lap, waiting for Billy and Jake Hawkin to jerk open the door and gun him down.

Only then . . . the stagecoach lurched and the driver's whip popped and he cut loose with a string of curses. The Concord rolled into the darkness, its lanterns glowing to light the road ahead, and Harry Henderson was leaving Sierra Vista with something like $50,000.

He said to himself, "This is so terribly easy." And he laughed.

CHAPTER FIVE

Sitting in the most uncomfortable chair west of the Pecos River, Sean Keegan estimated the distance from where he sat to the spittoon at the side of Colonel John Caxton's desk. It was a risky shot. But then so was shooting Lieutenant Erastus Gibbons off the back of that mule five days ago in Dead Man's Canyon. This time, Keegan opted to hold his fire.

Behind the desk, Colonel Caxton sat, rubbing both temples with his hands and shaking his bald head. Captain Conrad Percival rolled a cigarette. Major Hans Ziegler, post surgeon, sat cleaning his monocle. First Lieutenant Nelson Wilmot sharpened a pencil with a pocketknife. Sergeant Major Titus Bedwell leaned against the closed door to the colonel's office. No one looked happy.

"You heard what everyone in your patrol said." Captain Percival had finished rolling his smoke, but he did not light it, just kept playing with it in the fingers of his left hand. His right picked up the notepad in front of Lieutenant Wilmot, who glanced up briefly before returning his attention to the task of carving the point of his pencil to the best angle for maximum writing.

"They all said the same thing," Wilmot said and nodded with approval at his pencil point.

"No discrepancies," Hans Ziegler said and settled the piece of glass over his left eye.

"I've never heard such a story in twenty-eight years of service," Colonel Caxton said. After sliding the notebook back toward Wilmot, the stenographer, Caxton leaned back in his chair. "You shot a West Point graduate, the commander of your patrol, in the back."

"It was the right thing to do, Colonel," Keegan said.

"The right thing to do?" Caxton rose from his seat. "It was cold-blooded murder!"

The hell with it, Keegan thought, and spit across the room. The ping the brown juice made when it hit the cuspidor's lip made him smile. He wiped his mouth with the sleeve of his blouse and stared at the colonel's blazing eyes. "I don't see it that way, Colonel. Cold-blooded murder? That was leaving six young troopers and me with only the water in our canteens and only the lead in our weapons to face a bunch of horse-stealing Apaches with a mind to kill as many bluecoats as they could."

"How many Apaches?" Lieutenant Wilmot flipped through the pages of his notebook. "Four?"

"Three," Keegan corrected, "after Baker took care of one of the bucks."

"Baker?" Hans Ziegler said. "Who's Baker?"

"Whatever the kid's name was." Keegan shifted the tobacco to his opposite cheek.

"Three Apaches," Captain Percival said. "Against a sergeant of the Eighth United States Cavalry and six able-bodied troopers."

Keegan shook his head. "Like I told the lieutenant, four Apaches could do a world of hurt in that canyon. Three could've done just as much damage. And would have."

"I don't believe that for one minute," said the affronted stenographer, who knew nothing of lead except the kind he sharpened.

"I don't believe I've ever see you, Lieutenant, out in the field, sir."

"That's enough of that, Sean," the sergeant major said from the door.

Keegan drew in a breath, let it out, and

nodded. He had always respected Titus Bedwell, and always would.

"Then," Captain Percival said, "you turned loose all ten of your horses to the Apaches. Just gave them up. Without a fight."

"Eight horses," Keegan corrected. "The lieutenant shot his dead when the ruckus started. Accident. And another horse took off for parts unknown after the rider got killed. Maybe the Apaches got him. Maybe the wolves. I don't know. But we kept the mule."

"The mule." The colonel spat onto the floor in disgust.

"Sergeant," the German surgeon said, "you had taken cover against the canyon wall. You had water — two kegs — and you had ammunition. You could have withstood a siege of four — I mean *three* — bucks. Why turn your horses loose?"

Keegan shook his head. This was getting nowhere. But he had served in this man's army long enough to know that. "The Apaches had Winchesters, Major. One of them could have kept us pinned down in that rocky part. The other two would've climbed up atop the ridge and rolled boulders down on top of us. That is, if I recollect right, how Dead Man's Canyon got that name."

"Ah!" The German's eye grew bigger behind the monocle as he stood, again gripping the notes the stenographer had taken. "But you said the Apaches wanted the horses. If they showered you with boulders, they would have killed the horses, too."

"Baker, or whatever his name is, killed an Apache. That meant the three others would want revenge. Or something in return. I gave them the horses."

"Eight horses," Major Hans Ziegler said. "For a comrade's life? That does not seem like a fair trade."

Keegan shrugged. "Maybe. I've made better."

"Such as?" the lieutenant said.

"Such as," Keegan said, "a yellow-bellied lieutenant for water and ammunition that might keep some of us alive."

That led to much bantering, name-calling and finger-pointing as the officers gathered around the colonel's desk. Even Sergeant Major Bedwell left his post by the door and stood beside Caxton's desk, waited, then bent to pick up the brass cuspidor by the handles. He carried it to the chair in the center of the room, and set it on Keegan's left.

Keegan spit, wiped his mouth, and smiled. "Thanks, Sarge."

Titus Bedwell just shook his head before he walked back to the front door.

When the commotion had dwindled into just a few heavy sighs and under-the-breath curses, Lieutenant Wilmot, no longer holding his pencil, said, "Answer this for us, if you'd be so kind, Sergeant. Why would Lieutenant Gibbons ride off on a mule, and not one of our fine Army mounts? Surely he did not think he could get away on a pack mule, especially one laden with two kegs of water and pounds and pounds of cartridges for .45-70 carbines and .44-caliber pistols."

"I wouldn't know, sir," Keegan answered. "Maybe since none of the horses had canteens, he figured he needed water. But that's just a guess."

"A bad guess," Colonel Caxton said.

"Could be. Better guess would be that crazy people and cowards do crazy things."

Caxton started heaving and clenching and unclenching his fists, but Captain Percival cleared his throat before the colonel could start frothing at the mouth.

"How many times have you engaged the enemy, Sergeant?"

Keegan shrugged. "I quit counting back

during the War of the Rebellion, Captain."

"Sergeant," Percival said, "we've served together for a number of years. We've lost men in battle before. Haven't we?"

"Yes, Captain. Yes indeed. Too many to count, sir."

"That's very true, Sergeant. But this is what really bothers me about the reports everyone gave us, Sergeant. At Rattlesnake Pass six years ago. Five of our men, including Sergeant Wilson, were killed. Do you remember?"

Keegan nodded. "Yes. Yes, sir, I do. Too well."

"The ground was practically frozen," Percival said. "But we buried them, didn't we? Maybe not six feet under. Certainly not with coffins. We couldn't even leave tombstones or wooden crosses, couldn't leave anything to mark their graves. The Comanches would have dug up the bodies. Desecrated those valiant, honored dead. But we buried them."

Keegan did not answer verbally, but that no longer mattered, as the stenographer had stopped taking notes after Trooper Baker, or whatever his name was, had finished his testimony forty minutes ago. Keegan's head bobbed. He remembered. There were fights you recalled, and those you forgot. Rattlesnake Pass was one nobody forgot. He wondered if he would remember Dead Man's Canyon ten years from now.

"What about the dead at Dead Man's Canyon, Sergeant?" Percival asked. "What did you do with the slain?"

Keegan spit into the cuspidor. Nobody seemed to notice that it had miraculously migrated from the colonel's desk to Keegan's hard-rock chair.

"Apaches carried off the one we killed. We, meaning, Baker, or whatever his name was."

"Baxter," Lieutenant Wilmot said.

"A murdering savage carried a dead buck away on a U.S. Cavalry horse," Colonel Caxton said. "That sickens me."

"Go on, Sergeant Keegan," Captain Percival said. "What about the slain soldiers?"

"We dragged Ulfsson, the Swede, and the other boy — Brackenburg, Brackenbury, Bracken-something or other. . . ."

"Brackendorff," the stenographer said.

"I guess so. We dragged them to the side of the canyon. Managed to collapse some dirt atop their bodies. Piled some rocks over them. That was about all we could do. Figured if we met up with a patrol, they could send some boys back with spades — we didn't have any — and a wagon. Bring them back here for a proper burial in the post cemetery. Or let their folks know if they wanted to come plant them closer to home."

"You didn't try to hide the graves, though?" the major asked.

"No need, sir. Apaches ain't like Comanches. They don't like dead men. Spooks them. If you can figure that out." Keegan spit again.

"So . . ." Captain Percival started walking toward Keegan, who crossed his legs and waited. He knew what was coming. "So Trooper Klaus Brackendorff and Trooper Nils Ulfsson are buried as deeply and as honorably as possible under the dire circumstances." The captain smiled. "What about Lieutenant Gibbons, Sergeant? What did you do about young Erastus's body?"

"Nothing," Keegan said. "We left him for the coyotes."

The hemming and hawking, the shrieking and fist-slamming, resumed, but about the only words Keegan caught came from the stenographer, Lieutenant Nelson Wilmot. "Erastus's recommendation for appointment to the Academy came from Senator Jacoby. The same senator who got me my appointment!"

Keegan shifted the quid to the opposite cheek again.

When the commotion silenced, Colonel Caxton rose from behind his desk and waved a finger at Keegan. "During the Rebellion, Keegan, I would have had you up before a firing squad. To blazes with a court-martial. I'd have had you shot. You're a mad dog, Keegan, and mad dogs deserve to be shot."

"He's a jackal," said the surgeon. "Just like that newspaperman wrote."

"Lock him in the worst cell in Leavenworth and throw away the key," Percival said. "Hanging, shooting, that's too good for the likes of this . . . animal. Let him rot."

"First we must bring charges against him for a general court-martial," said the lieutenant.

"You can't rightly do that." The voice came from the front door where Sergeant Major Bedwell brought his left boot down to the floor, and put his right boot against the wall. "Begging my superior's pardon."

The colonel went rigid. "Sergeant Major," he said, barely keeping his voice under control, "I am well aware that you served under Robert E. Lee as a colonel, too, but you lost the war and are a sergeant now, and you will not tell me what I cannot rightly do."

"Yes, sir," the old sergeant said. "You can

prefer charges on this soldier. You can watch him hang. You, as commander of this post, can do anything you please. But you might want to consider this. First, there's young Lieutenant Gibbons's family and friends. They'll want to think that their boy, their pride and joy, died in battle. Died facing the enemy. You let them find out that he was killed — and it won't matter how you explain it, shot as a coward abandoning his men or shot in cold-blooded murder — and you'll just break their hearts.

"But that's not all. How do you think, sir, General Thomason, head of the Department of Texas, is going to think of you when he finds out what really happened at Dead Man's Canyon? You're responsible for all your men, sir. And then there's you, Captain Percival. Sergeant Keegan was under your command. They'll certain remember that when the next vacancy for a major pops up in this man's army. Lieutenant, you're in the same troop as the captain and Sean Keegan. And you're the next in command. The brass won't forget you, either. Major, maybe you'll come out of this unscathed. But I think, and, yeah, I ain't nothing but a sergeant major, but I think if word of what really happened at Dead Man's Canyon gets out, that little write-up in that Purgatory

City paper won't hold a candle to what'll come down on all of you, maybe even me, and Fort Spalding."

The sergeant major shrugged. "But that's just the opinion of an aide to some old soldier named Robert E. Lee. Likely don't amount to much."

Stripped of his chevrons and forced to muster himself out of the Army, Sean Keegan shoved the last of his clothes into the saddlebag and tossed it on the back of the sorrel gelding. His clothes were still Army, except the chevrons had been removed, and his pants were buckskin.

"Here's a bill of sale for the horse," the sergeant major said, and handed Keegan a slip of paper.

Keegan folded the slip and shoved it into his shirt pocket. "How you plan on explaining the Remington and the Springfield?"

The old noncom spit between his teeth. "That's the quartermaster's department. If he can't keep up with his guns, that sure ain't my problem." Turning around, he studied the parade ground, and the commanding officer's quarters.

At that time of evening, most of the soldiers were in their quarters. It would be a good time to leave Fort Spalding, before the colonel decided that he could drum up publicity for himself by something he thought would be for the good of the United States Army even if it turned out to be completely stupid.

"You best ride, Keegan. The colonel, he changes his mind as often as a baby gets a diaper changed. He might decide it'd be worth all the hell just to see you hang. Or shot."

Keegan swung into the saddle. He looked down on the former aide to Robert E. Lee. "I should have shot that old horse's arse when he first took over command here."

Titus Bedwell shook his head. "No, Sean, if you wanted to stay in the Army, you should've gunned down those young troopers you led out of that furnace. Then nobody would've known what happened. You could've blamed all the deaths on the Apaches. You could have gotten yourself one of those Medals of Honor the major thinks they ought to put Lieutenant Gibbons in for." The old man shook his head, and gave Keegan another hard look. "To be honest, Sean, I'm surprised you didn't."

Gathering the reins, Sean Keegan spit tobacco juice onto the fence post of the corral. "I considered it, Titus," he said, and spurred the gelding into a lope, riding out of Fort Spalding into the darkness.

spurred the gelding into a lope, riding out
of Fort Spaulding into the darkness.

CHAPTER SIX

The man responsible for keeping the peace
in Crossfire, Texas, stepped out of his office
just as Jed Breen pushed his way through
the doors to the Enfilade Saloon and moved
down the warped boardwalk. The marshal
was holding a shotgun, but he stopped and
just stood there. Breen paid him no mind.
The lawman was too far away to do any
damage with a shotgun, and likely the lawman remembered that Sharps rifle with the
fancy telescopic sight that Jed Breen carried.

Breen turned into the alley and slipped
his Parker twelve-gauge into the scabbard
underneath the scabbard that held the long
Sharps. A moment later, he was in the
saddle and riding the black Thoroughbred
into Crossfire's main street. He reined up,
and looked down the street. The marshal
remained frozen, likely swallowing, praying,
resigning, or wetting his britches — perhaps

all four — but Breen couldn't care less about that worthless star-packer. He studied the road that led out of town. No dust. No rider. No nothing. And he could see a long way.

That meant Cat Walker had ridden north.

Breen turned the black in that direction, and pressed the spurs against the Thoroughbred's side. He left Crossfire, Texas, behind him, with the marshal still holding his shotgun and standing like a fence post in the middle of the street a few yards from his office and the town jail.

Crossfire ended with the livery stable and a warehouse. Beyond that stretched Texas, as far as a body could see. Breen saw the dust and kicked the black into a trot.

The dapple gray gelding he trailed was a quarter horse. That animal, no matter if it had covered two hundred miles or two, could outrun Breen's Thoroughbred for a little while, but not over the long haul. Breen rode casually, forgetting about the saddle tramp he had senselessly beaten in the Enfilade Hotel, forgetting about the saloon girl, the bartender, even the marshal with the shotgun. Before long, he wouldn't even remember the French food he had eaten or Crossfire, Texas, itself. What settled into Jed Breen's mind was Cat Walker. He didn't even think about the heat.

He followed the dust. He thought only of Cat Walker.

By the middle of the day, Cat Walker knew he was being followed. He made feeble attempts to hide his trail. Jed Breen was no Apache, no Kit Carson, no Tonkawa Indian scout, but he knew how to read sign, how to follow a trail. And Cat Walker was no Tonk, no Kit Carson, and certainly no Apache when it came to hiding his trail. Even when the country turned rougher, the ground harder, the land less hospitable, Jed Breen kept Cat Walker close.

He made a cold camp that night, watered and grained the black Thoroughbred, had a few swallows of water and a piece of jerky for supper, and climbed atop a mesquite-studded ridge to look around. The sky was clear, the stars dancing, and Cat Walker's campfire was easy to see. Three miles away? Four? That was all right. He could cushion the black's hooves with rawhide, and set out this evening. Probably catch Walker asleep. But over the course of the day's travels, he had passed signs of Apaches. They usually didn't like to fight at night, but Indians, even Apaches, were unpredictable.

The reward in Owensburg — twelve hundred and fifty dollars — was a good chunk of money. But you couldn't spend green-backs in Hell.

Breen slept easily, but not deeply, that night — the Lightning in his right hand. He had a few more swallows of water for breakfast and rode off on the black toward Cat Walker's camp.

He was gone, of course, but the ashes in the fire pit still gave off some heat. No Apache sign, either, and that pleased Breen a great deal.

As he rode, the country started getting more rugged, mesas and hills scattered about. More trees. Not ponderosa pines or anything like that; nothing even taller than a mesquite or juniper — but good enough cover for someone to take a shot at him from a nice distance.

Breen eased his way carefully across the country, and never rode along the skyline when he could help it. Sometimes, he even abandoned the trail and swung a long loop through arroyos, just in case Cat Walker was smarter than he acted.

Breen didn't need to follow the trail any longer. Cat Walker thought he was playing things smart. A simpleminded fool like Cat Walker would think all the posses, all the lawmen, all the bounty hunters would be looking for him along the Rio Grande. After all, he had been only a two days' ride from the Mexican border back in Crossfire.

Most likely, a good many of those boys were down that way, which would make things easier for Jed Breen. He rested that night down in an arroyo. When the wind blew, he could smell the smoke from Cat Walker's fire.

Tomorrow, Breen told himself. *Tomorrow.* He nodded, checked the loads in his Colt, and slept about a mile from where he had first made camp. A smart man never slept where he ate, where he had his fire going, and Breen considered himself a smart man. He moved from that fire because people could see fire and smoke, and slept in the cold just in case the Apaches were watching. Or Cat Walker was getting touchy about being trailed.

The next morning, Breen had it all figured. Culpepper's Station. Cat Walker would ride the dapple to the stagecoach stop. He'd trade the horse, saddle, and bridle for a ticket to El Paso. He wouldn't dare take the eastbound stage. Although that might not have taken him through Owensburg, it would be close enough, and those wanted dodgers on Cat Walker would be more plentiful.

Breen could make it to the station by keeping along the arroyo for about half the day. That quarter horse Walker was riding would be practically worn out already. Breen would beat him to Culpepper's by at least three hours. He could have some coffee, sourdough biscuits, maybe even antelope stew, and be waiting for Cat Walker when the worn-out murderer walked through the door.

That's the way it would work out, Breen decided. He kicked the black into a lope.

Of course, the arroyo didn't lead all the way to Culpepper's. It turned south, and Breen had to climb out and start easing his way through the garden of rock formations. The black's hooves clopped loudly on the ground.

Breen reined up. He drew the shotgun from its scabbard and braced the stock against his thigh as he studied the little pass through a collection of boulders. It was cooler there, but Breen had started sweating. With his left hand, he removed his black hat and wiped his white hair and forehead.

He studied the ground, but the pass was too hard to leave any tracks. No horse dung. Nothing. Breen had this nervous feeling about him. It was probably nothing, he thought, then corrected himself.

113

It was never nothing.

Apaches? No, no Apaches weren't that patient. And with a horse like the one Breen was riding, they would have killed him by now. Killed the horse, too. And started roasting the animal. If Breen remained alive, those red devils might roast him, too, but not to eat.

He returned the hat and wiped his face. He needed another shave. He took a look behind him and down the trace that led through more rocks and toward the desert, toward, maybe Cat Walker. Breen eased the black to a walk. He looked up the ridge and took in every nook, every cranny, and every shadow. No birds sang. No insects hummed. The only sound came from the creaking of Breen's saddle and the metallic rings of the hooves on stone.

Breen reined up again. He listened. Still, he heard nothing. Culpepper's Station was still a long way off, and if Breen kept up at that rate, Cat Walker would catch up with him. The canyon ended about a hundred yards from there, then it widened out and became much more passable, much less tense, until he would come to Culpepper's, which butted up against some mediocre mountains.

"To hell with it," Breen whispered to

himself, and eased the black into a faster walk.

Cat Walker came out of the shadows about fifteen yards in front of Breen and the black, up on the right.

Breen saw the flash of gunmetal, and he realized his mistake. He had acted like a greenhorn, thinking that Cat Walker had been lazy and stupid, that he had been lollygagging his way to Culpepper's. The man had fooled him with the campfires. Oh, he had left the fire burning, good and long, but he had ridden out of camp long before daylight. And there he was, laying the ambush Breen had planned for him.

Breen turned the horse as the six-shooter roared in Cat Walker's hand.

Breen heard the sickening impact of the bullet as it slammed into the fine black. The horse was screaming, rearing, and falling over as Breen dived off. He hit the ground, rolled over, heard another shot and the ricochet, and then took off running. Another bullet tore off his hat before he dived into the rocks. He hit the ground, came up, and looked down the barrels of his Parker.

They were cavernous, not clogged with dirt and sand from his fall.

Bootsteps sounded and another bullet whined off the rocks behind him.

"You back-shootin' swine!" the man roared. "Why are you trailin' me?"

Breen drew his Lightning with his left hand, pulled the hammer back to full cock, and tossed it over the rocks far to his right. The gun went off. He wasn't sure it would, but luck was with him, and the bullet whined off something.

While that was happening, Breen headed the other way. He cleared the rocks, and braced the Parker against his thigh.

Cat Walker had stopped and turned toward the direction Breen's revolver had spoken. Realizing his mistake, he spun around, keeping his Remington level, and bringing back his left hand to fan the hammer.

He was too late, of course. Maybe he knew it. Maybe not. It didn't matter. Both barrels of the Parker exploded, and Breen ducked underneath the clouds of white smoke.

He waited a moment and drew in a deep breath.

Cat Walker lay spread-eagled between cactus and catclaw. His chest was a bloody mess.

Breen walked to the rocks, found his Lightning, checked the action, and shoved the .38 into the holster. Later, once he was at Culpepper's he would give it a thorough cleaning. He shot Cat Walker another glance and moved past the body and to the black. It was dead, damn it all to hell, but Breen had known that already.

He popped the breech of the shotgun, ejecting the two shells, and opened the saddlebag and reloaded the twelve-gauge. He found his hat, frowned as he stuck a finger through the bullet hole in the crown, but still shoved it down over his white hair.

Four miles? Breen looked down the passage. Six? No more than that to Culpepper's. He managed to get the saddle off the dead black and found a good spot to leave it in the shade. If he took the eastbound, he could pay the driver to stop and pick it up. If not, well, a man could buy a horse and a saddle and a whole lot more with twelve hundred and fifty bucks. He kept the saddlebags, and the canteen, and especially the Sharps rifle.

Again, he ignored the dead man and looked around the rocks from where Cat Walker had emerged, hoping to find a horse hobbled there. What he found, however, was a saddle and a canteen. So Cat Walker had likely ridden the gray to death. He was making his way to Culpepper's, too.

All that meant was that Jed Breen had a long walk. But he could stretch his legs. He had a good bit of money coming to him.

He went to the body and saw Cat Walker's eyes staring up at him. Breen couldn't take the body to Culpepper's. He could cut off Walker's head — he'd had to do that with other men before — but that was messy. The air there was dry, though, and bodies didn't rot so much. Often, they mummified. He just had to keep Walker's corpse away from coyotes and buzzards.

He glanced down at the body and frowned, then lowered himself for closer inspection. Breen lowered his weapons and fished the wanted poster from the inside pocket of his Prince Albert. He reread the description on the poster.

5-foot-9, 150 pounds, black hair, gray eyes, crooked nose, left earlobe missing.

"Hell," Breen breathed again when he looked from the poster to the man he had killed.

Oh, he might have been five-nine, and maybe he weighed a hundred and a half. But the hair was sandy brown, the eyes were dark brown, his nose was big, but not what you'd call crooked, and both ears, while too big, still had the lobes.

"You're not Cat Walker," Breen told the dead man.

"Maybe Walker traded that horse to you," Breen told the corpse after he had shoved it into a hole in the rocky wall, deep, and out of sight. Had there been any witnesses, Breen might not have had to hide the body. The dead man, whoever he was, had opened fire first — even killed Breen's horse — and Breen had shot the trigger-happy fool in self-defense. Only, there weren't any witnesses, Breen's friends in that part of Texas numbered zero, and he couldn't keep track of all the sheriffs, marshals, competition for bounties, judges, and hangmen who would jump at the chance to see him swing.

"Maybe you're even wanted for something," Breen said, concluding what amounted to a prayer or eulogy. "But this is where I leave you."

He went through the dead man's clothes and his saddlebags, but found only three dollars and seventeen cents, and chewing tobacco — Jed Breen couldn't stand chewing tobacco — no watch, no identification, and nothing carved into his saddle. He tossed the saddle into the arroyo, and collapsed the side of the wall to bury the cheap slick-fork saddle.

Finally, Jed Breen, three dollars and seventeen cents richer, picked up his canteen, his Sharps, and his Parker, and started walking toward Culpepper's Station.

It was shaping up to be a lousy day.

CHAPTER SEVEN

Jacob Jackson Kenneth Hollister appeared to be on the verge of dropping dead from an apoplexy. It took him several seconds before he could actually utter a complete sentence. "We are paid to keep peace in our communities!"

He must have been reading Purgatory City's *Herald Leader,* Matt McCulloch figured, and he waited for the captain of Company G, Texas Rangers, to finish his tirade.

"Not shoot a church to pieces. A church. By God, how could you have done it? Why did you do it? What were you thinking, Mc-Culloch?"

McCulloch answered in a flat, deliberate tone. "I was thinking that the only way to bring peace to that little community on our side of the border was to shoot Cuervo Villanueva to pieces."

"Inside a church?"

"Cuervo picked the spot. He could have stayed outside and faced us like a man. He could have made for the Rio Grande."

"How many times did you shoot him . . . inside that place of worship?"

"I don't rightly know."

"Enough to splatter a nun's face with his blood and brains. Enough to cause eighteen dollars' worth of damages to the church."

"I paid for those damages, Captain. Out of my own pocket. And I buried Villanueva myself."

"You splattered that nun's face with blood and brains," Hollister repeated.

"Would you have rather had Cuervo splatter *her brains* across the church?"

Captain Hollister sank into the big chair behind his big desk.

The newspaper editor wrote a few notes onto his pad and began to talk. "The only reason the good citizens in Purgatory City have not taken up arms against Ranger McCulloch is because this gunfight happened to have occurred in a Mexican church."

McCulloch saw that he had balled his hands into fists. One of these days, he knew, Alvin Griffin would get his nose broken, and his jaw, and, with luck, every finger on both hands. That might keep him from writing those hate-filled stories, at least for a while.

"But, as I will point out in next week's editorial, what happens when our Lutherans or our Episcopals or our Baptists and good Methodists see their sanctuaries riddled with bullets? But this is not just about religion."

"No, sir," the Ranger captain said. "It most certainly is not." He gathered several telegraph sheets in his right hand, balled them up, and held them high over his balding head. "Do you see these, McCulloch? Do you know what they are?" He tossed them aside, but again, somehow, did not collapse of stroke or heart failure.

McCulloch figured, if he kept it up, he would likely splatter his own blood and brains across the Texas Rangers in the captain's office, the editor of the muckraking newspaper in Purgatory City, and the circuit judge — once Hollister's head exploded like an over-pressurized steam engine.

"The governor. Two senators. A representative from my hometown. The state attorney general. The attorney general from Washington, our nation's capital. Six newspaper editors. The Archdiocese of San Antonio. The bishop in El Paso." Hollister shook his head, and next brought his fingers to his temples to begin a hard massage. "The only person I haven't heard from is the Pope. Every one of them wants my head on a platter."

McCulloch said, "I can think of some who don't want that, Captain."

The massage stopped, the hands fell atop the desk, and the captain looked up. He waited.

"The priest down there. Two nuns. A mother and her four-month-old daughter," McCulloch told him.

"That's a bunch of bull —"

"You think so? You think that priest would rather 've read the last rites over that girl? That baby? We had to get Cuervo out of that building before the sun went down, and that job fell to me."

The two other Rangers, Burns and Means, shifted uncomfortably in their chairs.

Sergeant Powell cleared his throat. "Well, now, Matt, I don't think I actually ordered you to —"

"Because you were thinking about negotiating," McCulloch barked back. "Having a little parley with a butcher. Begging him not to hurt those fine people inside that mission, letting him cross the border to rape and rampage over there till the *Rurales* chased him back across the Rio Grande and he became our problem again till we ran him back into Mexico." He paused just long enough to catch his breath, and when Sergeant Ed Powell's mouth opened, McCulloch closed it. "And, Sergeant, you asked me if I had any better ideas. I did. I took that as an order. I wasn't about to let Cuervo Villanueva start another Embarrado."

The Ranger sergeant sighed. "You're right, Matt." He looked at the Ranger captain and the newspaperman. "I didn't exactly give Matt McCulloch the order, but he did what had to be done. There are times when I think too much. Matt knows what has to be done, and he knows thinking can get folks killed. You might be getting a lot of criticism for having a gunfight in a church, but, well, we don't always get to pick where we have to make a stand. You folks seem to forget that the Alamo was a Spanish mission back in 1836. And Matt was right. We couldn't afford another Embarrado."

"Embarrado." The town's newspaper editor and owner, Alvin J. Griffin IV, spoke the village's name with a mix of contempt and skepticism. "You and Ranger McCulloch pull that name like you draw your guns. Embarrado. Massacre at Embarrado. Bloody

Embarrado. The Embarrado Bloodbath. It's like a dime novel, McCulloch. And I don't believe anything ever happened at —"

"If you say one more word, Mister Newspaperman," Matt McCulloch said, his voice steady, soft but cold. Very cold. "I'll rip out your guts just like Cuervo Villanueva did to that woman in Embarrado."

The newspaper editor's faced turned white.

"You don't believe it happened, fine. But I was there, Griffin. I had to bury those people. And they were chopped up so much, I wasn't sure I got the body pieces in the right graves. And if you say it didn't happen in front of me ever again, and I'll show you what I saw."

"Ranger McCulloch!" the captain snapped. "I will not allow —"

"Captain," Sergeant Powell said. "I was at Embarrado, too."

"Well." The editor had recovered. "Cuervo Villanueva was never convicted of what you allege happened at that dirty backwater —"

"And that's another reason I have half a mind to run your sorry hide through that press you operate. See if I can't squeeze all the black ink that flows through your black heart out of your body."

126

The newspaperman shook his head. "You're nothing but a jackal, McCulloch. Just as I pointed out in my newspaper. You don't belong behind a Texas Rangers badge. You belong on a wanted poster. And you're angry at me because I print the truth."

"Print whatever you want," McCulloch said. "Judge me all you want. You're not the judge I'll answer to. You're just a seedy little man who wants to make a name for himself."

"I think you're the one who wants to make a name for himself," Griffin said. "And you're making one, too. I find you more offensive, more vile than those other jackals I singled out. The Army sergeant. He's used to killing. He killed all through the war. And he's a drunkard. An Irishman. He can't help himself. The bounty hunter? Well, we all know what bounty hunters are. Scum of the earth. Low class. Killers. Their blood is as cold as a rattlesnake's. But you . . . you're a Texan. You were a family man. You were a man of peace. And now . . . you're pathetic."

"Gentlemen," the Ranger captain pleaded.

"No, no, you will hear me out, Captain," Griffin said. "I don't want to see Purgatory City slide into oblivion. We are on the verge of greatness. But if we are not careful, if we do not weed out the sinners in our community, those who put a blight on our good name, we will become just another dusty, forgotten place. Like those ungodly backwater communities in our county that —"

McCulloch swore and shook his head. "Every town that's not Purgatory City, especially every town with more Mexicans than white folks, is a dirty, backwater village. You might remember that the Mexicans were here long before we were, Griffin."

The newspaperman spit into a spittoon. "That's right. I keep forgetting, McCulloch. You actually married one of those greasers."

The Colt leaped into McCulloch's hand, and the report of the big .44-40 sounded like a howitzer in the close confines of the Ranger captain's office. White smoke filled the room. Alvin J. Griffin IV soiled his britches as he dived to the ground, clutching the top of his head where the lead slug had passed by perhaps half an inch.

The youngest Ranger had dived onto the floor, while Ranger Means dropped his right hand for the big Colt on his holster before deciding otherwise.

"McCulloch!" Captain Hollister had stood. He pointed. His mouth hung open, but he could not find the words as Matt McCulloch walked slowly toward the writhing journalist.

"Ed!" Hollister said when he could remember how to talk again. "Stop him. Don't let him."

Ed Powell sat where he was, cleaning a fingernail with the blade of his penknife. "He won't bother him, Captain," the sergeant said. "If he wanted to kill him, he would've killed him."

Yet at that moment, Matt McCulloch was aiming the long barrel of his smoking revolver at the wild-eyed face of Alvin Griffin. "You ever mention my dead wife again, there won't be another warning shot. You savvy?"

Griffin's head bobbed.

McCulloch lowered the hammer, holstered the Colt, and walked up to the captain's desk. Hollister sank deeper into the chair. His face revealed that he thought Matt McCulloch was going to part what was left of his hair with another .44-40 bullet.

Ranger Burns was finding his chair again, but stopped, too. Ranger Means looked toward Sergeant Powell to know what should be done, but the sergeant kept his focus on his fingernails.

When McCulloch reached the desk, his right hand left the butt of the Colt and came up to his vest. He unpinned the small badge made from a Mexican five-peso coin. He held it in his hand for a while, and then tossed it on the crumpled telegraphs that littered the captain's desk.

"You probably want this, Captain. And to be frank, I don't really care for wearing it anymore. I've grown tired of being bound to that oath I took." McCulloch turned, gave a quick look at the three Rangers he had ridden with, and moved toward the door.

He stopped beside the newspaperman, who remained on the floor, though he had risen enough to lean his back against the stone wall, and his hand kept rubbing the top of his head.

"If you feel like your honor has been affronted, I'll be gathering my traps from the quarters before I ride out. Otherwise, just remember what I said about my wife. And if you print something in that rag you call a newspaper, I'll consider my honor affronted. Duels have come out of fashion in Texas, but it would give your competition across this county something to write about." McCulloch tugged the hat down on his head and strode out the door.

Sergeant Ed Powell met McCulloch at the corral but did not speak as McCulloch secured the saddlebags behind the cantle, tied on his rain slicker — like it ever rained in that part of the world — and led the buckskin through the gate.

"Where you bound?" the sergeant asked as he closed the gate.

McCulloch shrugged then pointed to the gate. "Thanks."

Powell struck a match against the corral post and brought it to his smoke. When he had the cigarette going to his satisfaction, he shook out the match and tossed it onto the dirt.

"The captain give me the rank of sergeant, McCulloch," Powell said, "but it should've been you."

McCulloch's head shook. "No. And you know that, Ed."

"Well." Powell stared at his boots. "I ain't rightly figured out what I'm supposed to do. Probably would've gotten everybody killed four times over if not for you, Mc-Culloch."

"Maybe. Maybe you'll keep learning. If you live."

"If I live." Powell managed a slight smile. He swallowed, and tossed the cigarette, practically unsmoked, to the ground. "You going to look for her?"

McCulloch's head shook. He didn't like

131

to think of his daughter, but he never could stop thinking about her. Or his wife, or those sons. "Been too long, Ed. She's dead. Like me."

"Yeah."

McCulloch eased into the saddle like a much younger man, and he turned the horse around. "You think too much, Ed. Fighting Indians, bandits. It's just like breaking a horse. Don't think when you're in a ticklish situation. React."

"I'll try to remember that."

"You do that. Might keep you alive. Good luck."

He didn't offer his hand. Powell did not expect it.

Matt McCulloch just pulled his hat down low, kicked the buckskin, and rode out of Purgatory City.

Heading back to his own personal hell.

Weeds had taken over the graves, or as much as weeds could grow in that climate. McCulloch reined in and stared bitterly at the cemetery in front of what once had been his home. The corrals that the raiders had not taken down were gone. Wood was scarce in that part of the country, so most likely some homesteaders had taken the poles to use in their own homes . . . along with the stones for their chimneys. Yet, maybe out of decency, they had left the fence around the cemetery.

McCulloch frowned as he sank into the saddle, hearing the creak of leather. He remembered the cemetery next to the Catholic church and rectory down along the Rio Grande. It had a fence around it. Not much of one, but a fence, at the least. The post cemetery at Fort Spalding had a big stone fence, solid and thick and well-kept, enclosing it, too. Every cemetery McCulloch had ever seen, or at least all that he remembered, had been protected, or at the least, bordered by a fence.

So was this one that housed the graves of his wife and his sons and two of the Mexican hands who had worked for McCulloch. But he had never put up the fence. All he had done was bury them all, place crosses at the heads of the graves. Then he had ridden off to find his daughter Cynthia until he thought he could never find her — or decided he wouldn't want to after more than a year living among the Indians.

He could put up a marker for Cynthia, just a cross, and then some other people, neighbors or the priest or the Rangers or whomever, could come along and replace the shoddy markers he had put up for his family.

Easing the buckskin, McCulloch left the hardscrabble boneyard and rode to the house. Winds and rains had scattered the ashes and sent the adobe walls back to the earth from which they had been made.

He tried to recall when he had returned last, but soon he quit trying. The settlers, the predators, or whatever had taken bits of the limestone slabs used for flooring McCulloch had brought in on wagon beds. The barn was nothing but a memory, too. The outhouses had fallen into themselves and vanished. He couldn't exactly remember where the bunkhouse would have been.

The horse snorted, and McCulloch pulled the reins, turning the buckskin around. He tried to figure out why, after all those years, he had ridden back there. Had he expected the memories to come flooding through him? Did he think he would hear voices? Hear his wife's cousins, who rode with him and knew the country better than the Apaches, and horses better than he? Hear them playing music at sunset, Carlito strumming the guitar and Benito singing in that rich, haunting, soulful voice? See his kids when they were little? The time the oldest had stepped on that nail? Or see his wife standing on the porch, waiting for him to come up the steps and sweep her into his arms?

There was nothing, of course. Nothing there. Even the wind had blown all the visions and memories from his mind. The ranch was dead. Like Matt McCulloch. He did not look at the graveyard as he rode past it. He did not look behind him as he kicked the buckskin into a lope.

He rode away.

CHAPTER EIGHT

"Do you really need these?" Gwen Stanhope raised her arms, letting the sleeves of her blouse fall down and reveal the iron manacles that chafed the flesh and rubbed against the bones in her wrists.

The deputy sheriff met her gaze briefly, sniffed, and worked his jaw. "Yeah. I do."

"You could loosen them some," she said, still holding her arms up for his inspection. "Couldn't you?"

"No, I couldn't."

Gwen shook her head, looked at the benches in the station, and settled onto the closest one. She couldn't really blame the deputy. He had a job to do, and he had done it . . . so far. The county paid the deputy, whose name was Glenn Reed, and the sheriff of the county was Charles Van Patten. Charles Van Patten was the brother of Kirk Van Patten, and Kirk Van Patten owned half the county. Kirk Van Patten was the

136

man Gwen Stanhope had killed. She had been tried. She had been convicted. She had been sentenced to hang. Her lawyer had filed appeals. The appeals had been denied. Gwen Stanhope had managed to escape the jail at El Paso — but practically everyone who had ever been imprisoned at the El Paso jail had managed to escape. She had managed to escape into Mexico, but the deputy sheriff had broken the law, crossed the border, found her dealing faro in some cutthroat saloon, shoved a pistol against her spine, and brought her back into the United States. Into Texas. And was taking her back to El Paso.

To hang.

They had arrived at Purgatory City, where the deputy and Gwen waited for the stage-coach to pull into the city. *Nobody lives forever,* she thought. That had been one of Kirk Van Patten's favorite sayings, and he had lived to see it come true.

She settled onto the wooden bench and thought back to the circumstances that had resulted in her arrest.

He found Gwen dealing faro in Albuquerque, New Mexico Territory, and she let him woo her. He certainly was not an ugly man, physically, at least. He was tall, but not too tall. He

137

wasn't fat, nor was he skinny. He had a wonderful laugh, an engaging smile, and he could talk about politics, about business, about gambling, about faro, about Shakespeare and Milton and Nathaniel Hawthorne. Plus, he owned thousands of acres in the county and had business interests beyond his ranch and the gambling hall he operated. He could afford good wines, and his library held hundreds of books.

Gwen decided that she might even let Kirk Van Patten marry her. After all, she was thirty years old, and after too many years on her own, realized that she wasn't getting any younger and that, eventually, women gamblers would see their luck play out.

What happened to women gamblers when the cards turned cold usually was not a pretty sight to behold.

She grimaced, thinking *Nobody lives forever.*

Kirk Van Patten took Gwen out to supper at the Acme Saloon and had escorted her back to the Bolivar Hotel in El Paso. He invited himself into her room for a drink. Gwen said she was tired, and she was tired, after seventeen straight hours of dealing faro in a high-stakes game. She quickly learned that Kirk

Van Patten did not like being told no. He pushed the door open, and shoved her inside, then slammed the door shut, locked it, and wagged his finger in her face.

Gwen had learned to take a lot from some people, but she was not the kind of woman who would let herself be pushed to the floor and have a fat finger waved in her face. She came up and slapped Kirk Van Patten hard across the cheek.

The blow stunned the man.

She cursed him, told him to get out of her room and that when he was sober he could come and apologize and maybe — but no promises would be guaranteed — just maybe she would give him another chance.

Kirk Van Patten, gentleman that he was, slammed his fist into her stomach. She gasped, fell to her knees, bent over, and vomited on the floor. The next thing she knew, the drunken rancher and state representative was dragging her to the bed in her hotel room. He jerked her up by her hair, shoved her onto the bed, and pressed his body against hers. His breath stank of beef, whiskey, and cigarettes. He put his hand on her throat and pressed hard until she thought she would die.

"You won't be the first witch I killed," he told her. He spit in her face. He laughed. He slapped her until her nose and lips bled. And when he stood, still grinning, the fine, upstanding Kirk Van Patten began to unbutton his britches.

"No," he said after a moment's thought. "No." He laughed. "You deserve something special."

His right hand moved and he reached inside his coat. He pulled out a pocketknife, which he opened, and ran his thumb across the blade.

"Let's see how many customers you get at your faro layout after your nose has been cut off." He laughed again. "That's what Apache bucks do to their squaws when they find they've been unfaithful."

"Kirk," she whispered, pleading, begging, and hating herself for being such a coward, but she was in a great deal of pain, and the crazy eyes of Kirk Van Patten let her know that he really meant to disfigure her. Possibly even kill her.

Gwen's right hand fell toward her pillow. It disappeared briefly under the pillow, and when it came out, it held the .41-caliber Remington over-and-under derringer. "Get out, Kirk." She cocked the pistol. "Get out before I kill you."

He spit into her face. "You ain't got the guts, child. And now you're really going to get it. Nobody pulls a pistol on me. You're gonna hurt more than you thought you could ever hurt. And when I'm done with you, ain't nobody, not even a leper, would want to be caught in bed with a crone like you."

He changed his grip on the knife, took it by the handle, raised it over his head, and was about to bring it down into her chest.

She shot him in his privates.

When he spun around and screamed and gripped his crotch, she put the second .41-caliber slug into the back of his head.

She hadn't meant to. She had wanted to shoot him in the heart, let him see it coming, but he had twisted as he fell, and she was hurting, and not thinking properly, and she was terrified of what he might do.

Her lawyer pleaded self-defense. The way Gwen thought, it *was* self-defense. If she had not killed Kirk Van Patten, she would have been buried in what passed for a Boot Hill.

The twelve jurors, *all men,* all men who feared and/or idolized Kirk Van Patten, had not seen it as self-defense. They convicted Gwen of murder in the first degree and sentenced her to hang.

The judges in the appeals process brought up one indisputable fact. According to the undertaker, Kirk Van Patten had been killed by a single shot to the back of his head. Yeah, he might have died, eventually, from the bullet in his groin, but he was killed by a shot from behind. It was quite hard to find for an acquittal of a murder charge when the deceased was killed by a bullet fired at close range and into the back of a man's head.

The door to the station opened, and in walked another businessman. He saw the handcuffs on Gwen Stanhope, stared, and found the deputy. The man walked to Glenn Reed and handed him a business card. "Sheriff, I am Alvin J. Griffin the Fourth, editor and publisher of the *Herald Leader* here in Purgatory City."

Glenn Reed shook the hand of the journalist and told him his name, but added that he was not the sheriff, just a deputy.

"We do not see many women with handcuffs, Deputy Reed," Alvin Griffin said with a beaming, pleasant smile. "So perhaps you can tell me what crime she has been charged with?"

"She ain't just charged," Deputy Reed said. "She's been tried. She's been convicted. She busted out only to get caught again —"

"Illegally," she told the newspaperman.

"Well," Deputy Reed said, "that may be so, but you're here, and you're in my custody, and you're gonna swing in El Paso when we get there."

"Do you mean she's a murderess?"

"I mean to tell you," Reed told Griffin, "that you don't turn your back on a woman like this. She'll slit your throat."

Gwen rolled her eyes. "I didn't slit his throat," she told the journalist.

"No," Reed said. "She simply blew his head clean off."

"That's not true." She had shot the fiend with a derringer, a lady's hideaway gun. She had not used a double-barreled shotgun with buckshot or a rifle in a heavy caliber.

"All right. I guess you're right," the deputy said. "She just shot him in his testicles and then put a bullet through his brains. She's one hard customer, Mr. Griffin."

"Fascinating," the editor said. "And she's hanging in El Paso."

"That's the plan."

"Charles Van Patten might have something else in mind," Gwen told the newspaper editor.

"Like what?" the journalist asked.

"Like killing me before I ever get to El Paso," Gwen told him.

"I've heard that name before," Griffin said.

"Don't listen to nothing my prisoner has to say," Deputy Reed said. "She's a . . . a . . ."

"A jackal?" the newspaperman suggested.

"Well . . . it's . . . umm. Well, you see . . ." Reed sighed. "I don't exactly know what that there word means."

Griffin did not have a chance to define the word.

The door flung open and a Mexican youth, who could not have been older than twelve, yelled, "The stagecoach! It come! It now come!"

"Get up." Deputy Glenn Reed kicked Gwen's shoes.

She stood, refusing to give the lawman the pleasure of seeing how much his kick had hurt. The newspaper editor and publisher stood, too, and made his way to the door.

Glenn Reed put his right hand on the butt of his holstered revolver and said, "Don't you try getting away from me, woman."

Her head shook in disgust, and she followed the journalist out of the adobe hut and into the sun. The dust rose thick and furious as she saw the team of mules and heard the popping of the whip and the curses of the driver. She had to turn her head to keep from being blinded by the dust as the wagon skidded to a stop.

"Purgatory City!" she heard the driver call out. "All out for Purgatory City." He set the brake. "You can stretch your legs, folks, but don't run off, because we'll be leaving here as soon as they change the teams."

The door squeaked open, and two men leaped out and began dusting off their clothes. The newspaper editor walked over to the driver and the shotgun guard to ask about any news, the two men who had jumped off went into the station, probably for coffee.

The deputy shoved Gwen from behind. "Let's get aboard."

She moved to the stage, climbed into the wagon, and saw a timid-looking man in a black suit sitting in the front bench, his back pressing against the driver's side of the stagecoach. He was pale as a ghost, and was craning his head so he could look through the window facing the street. When Gwen cleared her throat, the little man practically jumped out of his skin.

"Didn't mean to give you a fright," she said, and moved to the rear bench.

Glenn Reed came in with his revolver halfway out of the holster. The man in black went rigid, except for his arms, which pulled the two obnoxiously colored carpetbags on his lap closer to his stomach and chest.

"Don't talk to the prisoner," the deputy warned the timid man.

145

"P-pris-n-ner?" he stammered.

Gwen Stanhope rattled her wrist bracelets. "That would be me."

"Oh," he said. "My."

When the two other men returned to the stagecoach, Glenn Reed gave them a similar speech. "No talking to the prisoner. She's a hard customer. I'll stop anyone who I think is trying to rob the hangman of his duty."

"Hangman?" the timid man said.

"I said no talking to the prisoner," Reed said.

"There won't be much conversing to anyone," said the red-bearded man in the plaid suit. "Once we start rolling west."

"Lessen you want a mouth filled with Texas dust," said the potbellied man in tan trousers and a blue brocade vest.

Glenn Reed sat beside Gwen Stanhope, but kept his right hand on the butt of his revolver, which was halfway out of the holster.

The door opened again, and the timid man and Deputy Reed almost wet their britches. The guard, a man with a drooping yellow mustache, buckskin jacket, and curly hair that touched his shoulders, butted the shotgun's stock on the floor of the coach and smiled.

"Folks, there was a telegraph waiting for

us." He stopped as a voice sounded behind him, and he stepped away to allow the newspaperman to climb into the coach. He moved to the front bench, and the man in black pulled his carpetbags even tighter.

The shotgun guard returned to his position. "Mr. Griffin, this might interest you."

The newspaper editor leaned forward.

"The commander at Fort Spalding sent a telegraph warning that the Apaches under Holy Shirt are acting up again. Another party of those red devils have come up from across the Mexican border. Maybe to join Holy Shirt, who's preaching big medicine. Maybe just to rob, rape, and butcher their own way. Anyway, some scouts and a couple of patrols have reported seeing plenty of sign. The company here will refund any tickets for anyone who don't want to risk their hide and hair. It's a far piece to El Paso, folks, and once we start rolling, we ain't stopping except to change the teams. So if you want to be safe, now's the time to step off this Concord." He nodded at Gwen Stanhope. "Ma'am."

"She don't got a say, Rourke," the deputy told the guard.

"But you do," the guard said.

"She's going to El Paso."

Gwen's head shook and she laughed. "A

hangman's noose or the Apaches? Not much difference, I reckon."

"You don't know Apaches," Rourke said.

"She's going," Reed told him.

The guard's head shook. "And the rest of you folks?"

The newspaper editor scribbled quickly on the back of an envelope. Taking notes, Gwen figured, on whatever paper he had handy.

The man with the carpetbags said, "I . . . well . . . my . . . business in . . . El Paso . . . it . . . just won't . . . wait."

"You folks certain?" Rourke asked.

"Dead certain," said the man with the red beard.

"Must you say *dead*?" whined the one with the big belly.

The guard turned his head and spit into the dust. He lifted his shotgun, shouldered the big weapon, and shook his head before he looked up at the driver's bench. "Petey, they're all bound and determined to ride with us."

"It's their funeral," the driver said. "We're burnin' daylight, Rourke. Haul your buttocks up here before I leave your sorry hide behind."

The door was closed, and the wagon leaned and squeaked and then righted itself

148

on its suspension as Rourke climbed into the driver's box and settled onto the bench to the driver's right. The brake was released, the whip popped, and Petey began cursing the mules as the Concord pulled out of Purgatory City.

"Are you covering the Indian uprising?" the man with the potbelly asked Griffin.

"My newspaper covers all the news," the editor said. "That's why our circulation is the largest between San Antonio and El Paso."

"I see," the potbellied man said.

"Are you covering the hanging, too?" asked the one with the red beard.

"The hanging of a woman will be news indeed." Griffin smiled at Gwen Stanhope. "It's just a pity that it must be on a bright, charming and beautiful woman such as you."

"No talking to the prisoner," the deputy said, "even for a member of the working press."

The stagecoach hit a hole or ran over a log or slapped across a boulder. Rourke cursed Petey outside, and the man in black bounced up and dropped one of the ugly carpetbags at his feet. The one with the red beard reached down to pick it up.

The man in black shrieked like a baby.

149

"Don't you touch that! It's mine!"

The man with the red beard straightened and glared at the timid man. "Then you pick it up yourself, bucko."

The pale man grabbed the handle to the grip with his left hand as the red-bearded man added, "After you apologize."

The timid man gripped the handle tighter and kept his right arm securely over the other hideous bag as he glanced at the man with the red beard. "I . . ." he started. "It . . . I . . . well . . . this . . ."

"Just say you're sorry for your hot temper," the one with the potbelly said. "So Nelse can forget that you slighted him and we can save all our fighting for when the Apaches hit our stagecoach and try to kill us all."

"I wish you'd shut up about the Apaches," Glenn Reed said.

The stagecoach rounded a corner. Outside, in the driver's box, Rourke was screaming at Petey to watch the road, and Petey was yelling at the guard to keep his eye out for Apaches and let Petey do the driving.

"How many miles do we have before we get El Paso?" asked the man with the two ugly carpetbags.

"Depends on the roads," answered the man with the red beard.

"And the Apaches," added the one with the fat belly.

"Let's just everyone shut the blazes up," Glenn Reed said.

"This is going to be one long ride," the newspaperman said.

Gwen Stanhope stopped listening to the useless conversation. She just looked at those two carpetbags that the man in the black woolen suit gripped like the cases held life itself. *What,* she wondered, *would possess a man to keep such a grip on such hideous luggage? A gun?* Glenn Reed had shackled her wrists in front of her. She'd be able to get a gun cocked, aimed, and have the trigger pulled before he knew he was dead.

But then she'd have to kill everyone else riding for El Paso, and that couldn't very well happen, which made her smile as she thought again.

Nobody lives forever.

CHAPTER NINE

Billy Hawkin kicked open the door to the private parlor and suite on the top floor of Miss Matilda's House of the Divine. The chirpy let out a scream as she sat upright in her bed.

Raising the lantern in his left hand, and leveling the Colt .45 in his right, he saw clearly by the dim, flickering yellow light from the lantern that the prostitute was in bed alone.

"Where the hell is he?" Billy demanded.

"Who?"

"The guy who paid you!" he snapped.

Behind him, Galloway stepped inside the room. Galloway carried a double-barreled shotgun, and he moved toward the bed. The chirpy pulled the covers up to cover her unmentionables.

"You mean that pale little feller?" she asked.

Galloway dropped to his knees and peered

152

under the bed. Then he stood, jerked open the door to the armoire, and trained the shotgun's barrels on the chirpy's shoes, purses, some black stockings, her pills and bottles of laudanum, and a small suitcase.

"Who else?" demanded Billy.

"He ain't here," the girl said, and watched as Galloway kicked over a chair and looked behind the changing curtain, moved to the window, drew the curtain, and looked onto the pitched roof.

"He was with you!" Billy said.

"Well, yeah."

Galloway turned, shook his head, and butted the stock of the shotgun on the bed. He sighed heavily, and turned his eyes to the chirpy.

"What happened to the thief?" Billy roared.

"I don't know," she said. "He said he was thirsty. Maybe." Her head shook. "I don't know exactly what he said. But I went downstairs to fetch him some more brandy, and when I got back upstairs, he was gone."

"Gone?" Billy Hawkin swore. "You didn't tell Matilda?"

"No." She lowered the covers and gave him a stare that could match he one he was trying to give her.

"Why not?"

"Because he left enough money for the rest of the night."

"Then you could have entertained more customers and made a killing tonight. You expect me to believe you'd —"

"You can believe anything you want to believe, Billy Hawkin. What I saw was enough money and a nice note that meant I could catch up on my sleep. And that's something girls in my line of work don't often get to do. You understand what I'm saying to you, Billy Hawkin? That's all that interested me. Getting some shut-eye. Which is what I was doing until you barged in here and scared six months off my life."

He swore, kicked at something on the floor, or maybe just his shadow, and carried the lantern to the window and stared outside.

"He ain't there, Billy," Galloway said.

"Why don't you let me find that out for myself?"

"Fine," Galloway said. "You do that. And why don't you let me find your brother?"

"No!" Billy sang out in a voice that was filled with terror. He inhaled quickly, held the breath the longest time, and finally let it out. "Not yet, Galloway," he said softly, and tried to paint a smile across his face, but that failed miserably and he looked again into the blackness at the roof. "What did he write in that note?" he shot out.

"It's none of your business."

"Let me see it," he bellowed, turning and shoving the .45's barrel in front of the chirpy's nose.

The prostitute swore, slid over toward the nightstand, and pulled a crumpled yellow slip of paper out of the ashtray. "Here!" She shoved the paper directly at him. "Read it your ownself."

That was exactly what Billy Hawkin did, before he shook his head, and offered the paper to Galloway.

Thanks for everything. Here's an eagle for your kindness. Come see me in Kansas City sometime.

No signature. No date. But Billy Hawkin had read enough of what Harry Henderson had written to know the writing belonged to that double-crossing cowardly bank teller . . . or cashier . . . or clerk . . . or whatever title he held at the Bank of Sierra Vista.

"Well?" Galloway asked.

Billy held the piece of paper out toward the gang member.

"You know I don't read," Galloway said.

"Yeah." Billy crumpled the paper again and pitched it toward the ashtray. It bounced out of the ashtray and rolled over the side of the table and landed on the edge of the rug on the floor. "It doesn't say a damned thing, doesn't tell us one thing. All it really says is that he's going to Kansas City."

"Maybe we should go to Kansas City" Galloway stated.

"No," the prostitute said.

"Why not?"

"Because that thief isn't going to Kansas City."

"Oh." Galloway nodded, comprehending the levels at which Harry Henderson, a coward no one had considered as a threat or a thief ever, could operate.

"So you just came upstairs and found him gone," Billy Hawkin stated, and waited for the chirpy to confirm.

"Yeah. And I read his sweet note and I pocketed the money he give me, and I drank a little brandy to take the taste of laudanum out of my mouth, and I was sleeping real good and having not one bad dream till you boys came barging through my door." She pointed at the door. "Matilda's gonna add that to all the money you'll owe her and me and all the girls you've bothered tonight."

"Yeah," Billy said. "Shut the hell up. Where do you think he went?"

The girl was silent.

"Answer me," he demanded.

Galloway shook his head. "Billy, you just told her to shut up."

The punk growled. "Don't you get me started, Galloway."

The man shook his head and asked the girl, "He didn't give you any clue about where he might be headed?"

"No," the chirpy snapped. "I done told you all. I went to fetch him some more brandy, and once I came back here, he was gone. He paid me plenty, and I am real tired."

Billy Hawkin jumped up and down and cursed and kicked at the air.

"Let's go find Jake, Billy," Galloway began.

"Absolutely not. We got to find Henderson."

"Well, we can find his home," Galloway said.

"He won't be there, Galloway!" Billy spit on the floor.

"Hey," the chirpy said. "That's disgusting."

"Shut up. We're trying to think here."

"Well, think someplace else. I'm going

back to sleep."

Billy swore and shook his head, and finally took time to lower the hammer on his Colt and slide the big weapon into the leather holster. "He could be anywhere."

Galloway was looking outside. He tapped on one of the panes of glass, then turned away from the window with a wide grin stretching across his face. "Billy. The stagecoach."

Billy stepped over to the glass, knelt a little bit, and stared through the panes of glass.

"The westbound," Galloway said. "That's where he's bound."

"Yeah."

"We gotta tell Jake."

Suddenly, Billy grinned. "I bet, since the stage will travel along that road, and have to stop at The Crossing, Meade's Place, and Purgatory City, I could cut across the country and beat it to Culpepper's."

"You might run into that posse," Galloway said.

"They won't be looking for one rider."

"You might run into Apaches."

Billy chuckled. "That's better than running into Jake."

Galloway let out a long breath. "You still gotta let Jake know what happened. You gotta tell him."

"You tell him," Billy said. "Just give me till daybreak to get out of here."

"That ain't smart."

"Maybe not. But Jake gets real touchy when you wake him up in the middle of the night." He slapped Galloway's shoulder. "Tell him I'll catch that turncoat and gut him like a fish. And I'll fetch him back the money."

"He won't like it."

"You've been riding with Jake long enough to know that he don't like nothing."

Galloway shook his head and sighed again.

Billy nodded. "It'll be fine. Once I get that fifty grand back."

Jake Hawkin kicked the prostitute out of his bed, tossed her a robe, and told her to fix herself a morning bracer.

"This is my room, Jake!" the girl yelled.

"Get out."

"Well, when I tell Matilda what you're. . . ." The threat died in her throat and fear enveloped her when she saw the deadly look in his eyes. She quickly looked away, grabbed a robe to throw over her unmentionables, and left him with the man called Galloway.

"That pipsqueak of a banker! Where did he find the backbone to take my fifty thousand bucks?" Jake pulled on his pants, grabbed the Colt he had underneath the pillow, and shoved it into the holster. He dressed in a hurry, peppering Galloway with questions all the while.

"Billy left all that money with . . . what the hell was that dude's name, anyway?"

"Henderson," Galloway answered. "Harry Henderson."

"What was Billy thinking?"

Galloway shrugged. "Like you said, Jake, we didn't think he'd have gumption to try to cross you."

"Gumption? He don't know the meaning of the word. He's just stupid."

"I guess so."

Jake stomped the boots onto his feet. "Where's Billy?"

"He took off after him."

"When?"

Galloway had to think. He had been testing various answers since Billy had ridden out. "I don't rightly know, Jake. Sometime during the night."

The killer froze. Only his eyes looked up as he buckled on his gun rig. "During the night?"

Somehow, Galloway managed to swallow. "Yeah. Billy rode off. He thought he could catch up to the stagecoach at Culpepper's

160

Station."

"How late in the night?" Jake shoved his shirttail into his pants.

"Two, I guess. Maybe three."

Jake swore. "And you let me sleep."

"Billy said not to trouble you till daybreak."

The gang leader cursed even more vilely. "How did Billy figure out that yellow-livered snake took the stagecoach?"

"He was downstairs, playing poker. Maybe faro. This dude just off the stage come in. He said as he looked back just before the stagecoach left, that this gent in a black suit came out of the shadows and hopped into the stage. The dude thought it peculiar. Billy stopped gambling and came upstairs. When he found Henderson gone, and the carpetbags gone, he woke me up. Then went back down and found the dude as he was sipping a beer and asked him about the fellow who got on the stagecoach. The dude said he couldn't tell what the gent looked like, it being dark and all, but the fellow was in black, or brown, or some sort of dark suit and was carrying a couple of god-awful-ugly carpetbags."

Another blue streak of curses filled the prostitute's room. By time that time, Jake Hawkin was jamming his hat atop his head and storming out the door.

They stopped downstairs at the bar. That early in the morning, no one was there, so Jake found a bottle of bourbon and poured stiff drinks for himself and Galloway. "How much money do you have?" Jake asked.

"I did all right," Galloway said. "Fifty dollars. Little more, a little less."

"That's all?"

Galloway shrugged. "Didn't want anybody to get suspicious, flashing around a whole lot of money."

After pulling out his pouch, Jake dumped a few double eagles onto the bar, pried out some cash money. "All right," he said, and slid most of it to Galloway. "All right. Get to the livery. Get us good horses that won't let us down. Saddles and tack, too."

"We gonna try to catch up with Billy?"

Jake refilled his glass. "First, we need to get to the hideout. That's where Alfredo's supposed to meet up with us. He damned well better lose that posse in a hurry."

"Alfredo's good," Galloway said.

"So was MacMurray. They'll be burying him."

"Then we ride for Culpepper's? To catch up with Henderson?"

"We ride after my fifty thousand dollars. And then we kill Henderson, if Billy hasn't already done it. And if Billy has done it, I might be inclined to kill my stupid brother. Because I wanted to kill Henderson before we left the damned bank. That stupid brother of mine has cost us a fortune. And shot my perfect plan all to hell."

The thought Billy Hawkin could not get out of his mind was that his brother was going to kill him. And it would not be a quick, merciful death.

Billy Hawkin had stolen a horse — one he'd thought was a good one — in Sierra Vista, but miles into the West Texas emptiness, the horse had gone lame. Billy was afoot, walking with his rifle and his canteen, stumbling through cactus and over stones, and a long, long way from Culpepper's Station.

An hour later, Billy Hawkin understood that he did not have to worry about being murdered by his big brother Jake.

Three Mexicans came out of the rocks before Billy knew what was happening. He had started for his revolver, but staring down the barrels of a scattergun and two revolvers stopped him from drawing the pistol. He merely smiled and raised his hands.

The burliest of the three motioned with

the shotgun, and Billy unbuckled his belt and let it drop.

"We shall take your *dinero,*" said the man with the shotgun.

Billy laughed. "There's not much money, amigos."

"It had better be enough," said the big man with the shotgun.

Billy withdrew the billfold from his pocket and tossed it into the dirt. It had become one *lousy* day. He had helped pull off one of the Hawkin's Gang's most successful robberies — a whopping $50,000 — and had eluded a vengeful posse. Then a stupid coward of a teller and cashier had made off with almost all the loot they had stolen. And big, arrogant brother Jake would blame Billy for all of it.

Billy had to agree, rightfully so. They should have shot Harry Henderson dead. But Billy had tried to do what he thought was the right thing. Well, *right* had nothing to do with it. He just wanted to contradict his know-it-all older brother. It turned out, Jake had probably been right, and Billy was in the middle of nowhere, about to be robbed and murdered by a bunch of no-account greasers.

Life was not fair. It was not fair at all.

The Mexican in white cotton shirt and

pants, black boots, and a black sugarloaf sombrero looked at Billy Hawkin's money. Frowning, he turned to the big dude with the shotgun and spoke in rapid Spanish.

"Is that all you have?" asked the shotgun-wielding leader.

Billy shrugged. "Yeah. It'll take some explaining, but it has been a bad day for me."

The Mexican in blue denim pants and jacket grinned. "Amigo, you do not know how bad your day is about to become. It has been very nice . . . until now."

"I can make it a whole lot better for you," Billy tried.

"And how is that?" asked the one with the shotgun.

"Would you like fifty thousand bucks?"

The burly one with the shotgun squinted.

"He is lying," said the one wearing denim.

"How could we get such a sum of money?" asked the one with the shotgun.

"I robbed a bank in Sierra Vista," Billy told them. "And then I got robbed by one of my associates."

"That is a lot of money," said the one in denim.

"It is."

"Too much for one man to spend," the one in black said with a glittering smile.

"But it would split well four ways."

The Mexicans laughed. "We came here to get us scalps from the Apaches we planned to kill," said the leader, still holding the shotgun. "But killing Apaches is dangerous work. How do we get this *mucho dinero*?"

"Take me to Culpepper's Station," Billy Hawkin said. "We have to get there before the stagecoach arrives from Purgatory City. Then we find the man who stole the money from me. We kill this man. Kill him dead. And kill anyone else who gets in our way. We split the money. And we're all rich."

Of course, he had no plans to split any money with a bunch of Mexicans. But he would have to figure out how to kill the three men before Jake rode onto the scene.

"I do not believe you," said the one in denim. "Kill him now."

Billy started to dive for his gun, even though he knew such an act would result in his death, but the youngest of the trio, the one carrying the pistol, barked out something in his native tongue, and the others turned to look at the dust.

"One rider," said the man with the shotgun, speaking in Spanish. "He must be a fool to travel this country alone."

"Good," Billy Hawkin said. "I will take

his horse after we kill him. Then we will go after all that money."

Chapter Ten

Jed Breen didn't like what he saw at Culpepper's Station one bit.

The corral was empty when it should have been filled with mules for the changing of teams. What's more, the poles had been knocked down. Now, it could have been that one stubborn mule had kicked the poles to the ground, and the mules had wandered off. That might explain why the door to the station remained open. The two men who worked there could have hurried off to bring back the wayward animals. But Breen did not think that had happened, and he would not think it — not in a thousand years.

There were tracks . . . a lot of tracks . . . with a mix of shod and unshod ponies. That told Breen that Indians had been through there, and though he saw no arrows sticking into the walls or doors of the station, he knew that Apaches would reuse the arrows that had not killed a human being. They would have plucked the arrows out of the wood and adobe and returned them to their quivers — much the same as he would pick up the empty casings of his brass cartridges to reload them. Bullets were expensive in that part of the country.

And Apaches were practical. Making arrows took a great deal of time.

He looked around. It could be that the Apaches had stolen the mules and killed the employees. It could be that the employees had abandoned the station because the Army had warned them that Indians were on the prod. It could be a lot of things Jed Breen could easily explain.

But there was just one peculiar thing.

Somebody was inside the station, and that somebody likely was owner of the wagon that was parked along the side of the station. The wagon was no coach, but more of an ambulance painted red, black, green and blue, with colorful lettering on the side.

Sir Theodore Cannon's
~ F A M E D ~
SHAKESPEAREAN TROUPE
and Acclaimed Improvisatory Company

"Hailed by Queen Victoria!"
London. New York. Paris. Rome.

169

San Francisco. Quebec.
And now HERE ! ! !

From inside, a man sang. Had Jed Breen heard that tenor anywhere else, he might have been moved. It had been years since he had heard anything by Gioachino Rossini, and *La Donna del Lago, The Lady of the Lake,* had always been one of Breen's favorite operas. It was based on a great poem by Sir Walter Scott. It had been a long time since Breen had read Scott, too.

The voice was spectacular. The man was singing the *canzoncina* "Aurora! ah, sorgerai," and Breen heard himself whispering the English translation, "Dawn! Ah, will you always arise inauspiciously for me?"

He stopped himself. Culpepper's Station was a long, long way from the French Opera House in New Orleans. He squinted and thought of something else. Would the French Opera House have staged an Italian opera based on a Scot's narrative poem?

Breen smiled at his private joke and then sprinted from his place in the rocks to the wagon. He braced his back against the wagon, expecting arrows or bullets to start raining in his direction. All he felt, though, was the wind. All he heard was the tenor voice.

170

He sidled against the side of the wagon and peered around the corner, still holding the rifle and shotgun. The station's door was open, and he could see the splintered wood in the wagon's side and in the cottonwood posts of the station. An arrowhead remained lodged just above his head. The Apache had managed to jerk out the arrow, but the point had broken off.

That confirmed what Breen had figured. Apaches had run off the livestock. Maybe the station tenders had been killed. Maybe they had survived. But the man singing the opera inside the station had been in the wagon. The arrow point seemed to confirm that. So why wasn't he dead or gone?

Breen wasn't going to stay there trying to figure out the answer to that question. Those Indians might still be in the area.

He sucked in a deep breath, let it revive him, and exhaled. Then he was running, leaping over the tongue, ducking underneath the hitching rail, and stepping onto the rough porch. His boots thudded on the planks and then he went through the door. With the stocks braced on his hips, he aimed the shotgun and Sharps toward the voice.

Hamlet stood before him wearing a blond wig and a fake goatee, with a cloak of scarlet trimmed with gold lace. His face was caked white with makeup paste, and he held a heavy staff in his right hand. *Hamlet. Singing in Italian.*

The man belted out the final notes and then took a bow, pulled off his fake beard, and laughed. "Good God, man. I thought you were another one of those bloody savages!" He filled a stoneware cup with black coffee, passed the cup to Breen, and began scrubbing the makeup off his face.

Breen walked to the open door, the Sharps rifle held in his left hand, and studied the hills that surrounded the station.

"I had to make the Apaches think I was crazy," Theodore Cannon said.

Breen had to smile. "You pretty much convinced me."

"I can be a very good actor."

"You have a good voice," Breen said, and sipped the coffee. "And you make good coffee."

"Well, the manager of the theater in El Paso told me that Apaches won't kill a crazy person."

"Unless they feel like it," Breen said.

Cannon tossed the towel onto the table, poured himself a cup of coffee, and walked to the doorway. "The Indians hit me while I was about a quarter of a mile from here. I

172

whipped my team into a frenzy, made it here, and saw the empty corral and more Apaches. So I reined up, stood in the driver's seat, set the brake, and began reciting Hamlet's soliloquy."

He turned and began again.

"To be, or not to be — that is the question:
Whether 'tis nobler in the mind to suffer
The slings and arrows of outrageous
    fortune,
Or to take arms against a Sea of troubles,
And by opposing end them: to die, to
    sleep —
No more; and by a sleep, to say we end
The heart-ache, and the thousand natural
    shocks
That Flesh is heir to? 'Tis a
    consummation —"

Breen stopped him with a stare. He smiled and shook his head. "Where's your troupe?"

"Alas, Rachel married a rancher in Tucson, August was arrested in Lordsburg, James abandoned me for another company in Las Cruces — he thought he should have been the head of the company, get all the lead roles, but he just never could command stage or crowds the way I can — and he had trouble remembering his lines. We'd be doing *Macbeth* and he'd suddenly think he was Falstaff in One Henry Four."

"What happened to the station tenders?"

Screams began from somewhere deep in the hills.

"That," Theodore Cannon said. He set the cup of coffee on an overturned bucket, and placed his hands over his ears. "There were two last night!" he shouted. "I guess one of the blokes is dead now."

"Lucky him," Breen said.

Ten minutes later, the screams stopped, and the actor lowered the hands from his ears.

"Listen," he said. "When the Apaches come again, you should join me. We can pretend that you are crazy as I am. Do you sing?"

"I wouldn't call it that."

"But you know opera. And you know theater. Perhaps you can dance?"

"I'm not going to meet my Maker acting like a fool," Breen said. "No offense. Because it might be nice to spend my last few moments of this earth listening to your fine voice singing a wonderful opera while arrows and knives are cutting me to pieces."

"I have a suit of armor in the back of the wagon," Theodore Cannon said.

Breen was bringing the cup of coffee up,

but he stopped, and studied the thespian a little closer.

"Sometimes I am asked to recite Malory," the actor explained. "*Le Morte d'Arthur*." Cannon cleared his throat, his left hand over his breast, and began. " 'Then Sir Arthur looked on the sword, and liked it passing well. Whether liketh you better, said Merlin, the sword or the scabbard? Me liketh better the sword, said Arthur. Ye are more unwise, said Merlin, for the scabbard is worth ten of the swords . . .' "

"I'm familiar with that one, too, sir."

"But the armor could protect you from arrows," Cannon said.

"Not bullets," Breen explained.

"Ah, but there's the rub, my good man. These Apaches, they are not using bullets. Hatchets. Arrows and bows. Lances."

Breen stared. "That's not like the Apaches I know. They'll use anything they can get their hands on."

The actor's head was shaking. "These savages are being led by a medicine man called Holy Shirt. Or something like that."

"You speak Apache, do you?" Breen said, having determined that Theodore Cannon wasn't acting like a crazy man. He was quite, quite mad.

Cannon grinned. "No, but I read the

newspapers. And I listened to the Army officer at Fort Stanton who was telling me
about the warriors who had come up from
Mexico to start a little uprising in New
Mexico Territory and West Texas. This Holy
Shirt, he got some young bucks to come
with him. He's preaching that the reason
the Apaches haven't been able to kick out
the white men was because they were using
the white man's weapons. He was saying
that to kill white men, to make the Apaches
more powerful than the white men, that the
Apaches had to go back to their own ways.
White man's weapons were poison. White
man's weapons were poisoning the Apaches.
The only way to win was to burn or bury
all the white man's things. No bullets. No
guns. Not even white man's clothes. You
won't find these warriors wearing cotton
shirts or anything they could have gotten
from the agent on the reservation. Nothing
they might have stolen from a raid in
Arizona or Texas or even down in Mexico.
The ones I saw — the ones I made think I
was insane — were dressed in deerskin.
They're not even wearing silk or cotton
headbands. Just rawhide or deerskin over
their heads. Or a headdress from some
varmint. So, yes, Mr. Breen, you are absolutely right that a suit of armor — actually,

I have two suits — would not stop many a bullet." He pointed his cup of coffee at Breen's Sharps. "But they most definitely will stop an arrow."

He sipped his coffee, pursed his lips, squinted a bit, and added, "Well, I think they'll stop an arrow." His head nodded. "Yes. Sure. That's how the conquistadores whipped the Indians all those years ago."

Breen finished his coffee and set the cup on the bucket. "Well, Mr. Cannon, that might be well and good, but there's one little problem. It's a long walk to El Paso, and it's a long walk to Purgatory City from here. You have a wagon, but we don't have any mules to pull that wagon. And I'm not sure we'd be able to get very far walking . . . in a suit of medieval armor."

The actor's head bobbed again. "I know, Mr. Breen — might I call you Jed? You can call me Theodore. Or even Teddy. There's no point in addressing me as Sir Theodore. That's just on my wagon. I'm not even from London. Or even England. Born and raised in Syracuse, New York, sir. Have you ever been to Syracuse?"

"Teddy," Breen tested. "Actually, I like Sir Theodore, but don't worry, I'll keep your Syracuse upbringing a secret. This is Texas, you know, and many haven't forgotten that late war. London is a little bit more palatable to former Johnny Rebs than New York. You may call me Jed, but we still don't have anything to pull that wagon. And it'll be hotter than hell walking across that furnace, especially wearing a tin suit."

Cannon slapped Breen's shoulder, tilted back his head, and cut loose with a deep laugh. "Jed, Jed, Jed, my boy. We won't walk. Obviously, we'll just shoot some Apaches off their horses and use those animals to pull my wagon."

Breen stared at the actor. "Obviously."

CHAPTER ELEVEN

The arrow sang past Sean Keegan's left ear and cracked against the limestone boulder behind him. Instantly, Keegan went into action, jerking the rein, turning the sorrel gelding around, and driving the spurs into the horse's side, He felt the explosion of power as he leaned low and heard the second arrow as it whistled past. An instant later, he was reining in the sorrel, immediately stepping out of the saddle and pulling the gelding into the rocks for cover. With the Springfield carbine in his arms, he peered into the canyon country and waited.

Slowly, he removed his battered old campaign hat and rested it crown up on the rock next to him. He listened, but only the quietness of West Texas reached him — a silence that Keegan had seen unnerve many brave soldiers like himself. No. He had to remember, he no longer was a soldier, just a civilian. A civilian alone in the middle of one empty expanse, with an Apache somewhere in the rocks.

The Indian wouldn't have been with the young bucks that had ambushed Keegan's patrol in Dead Man's Canyon. Those renegades had had rifles. This one was using his bow and his arrows, which could have meant that he was one of Holy Shirt's boys. Keegan had heard about what that medicine man was preaching, and he hoped more and more Apaches joined that cause. Bows and arrows? Against Springfield carbines, Colt revolvers, mountain howitzers and Gatling guns? That was a fight the Army would be sure to win — no matter how many Lieutenant Erastus Gibbonses the United States Military Academy kept sending to the West.

On the other hand, Keegan figured, it could be an Apache who didn't want to waste powder and shot or who wanted to kill in silence.

And it could be a white man who wanted to put the blame on the Indians.

Keegan immediately eliminated the theory about the white man. If it had been a white man, Keegan knew he would have heard him by now.

Silently, Keegan rose and inched his way to the sorrel gelding. He made his way to the saddlebags and removed the hobbles, which he then placed on the horse's front feet. While he was on his knees, he took time to loosen the cinch. He came up, found the canteen, and took a heavy pull. His first thoughts were to take the canteen with him, but he knew he would have to be quiet. Sloshing water inside an Army canteen could get him killed. Carefully, he picked his path away from the rocky corral.

He kept his back against the rough wall, and when he found himself in the shadows, he studied the country again, thinking of his options. With the sorrel standing silent and contented, Keegan stepped around a massive garden of prickly pear cactus and knelt behind the green. The boulders to the side were massive. Lying atop of one another had created a little cavern where he could hide. Hide and wait, but that wasn't Keegan's style. He also could find himself trapped inside the small little opening, and if that Apache decided to forgo Holy Shirt's preaching and start using firearms, he wouldn't even have to have a good aim. Ricochets bouncing off those rocks would eventually tear Keegan to pieces.

On the other hand, the top of the rocks might be exactly the place he needed to be. Again, after watching the land all around him, he rose and backed against the rocks, a mix of white, rust, brown, and grayish colors. He moved between the boulders and creosote bush, lifted his free hand, and found a natural hold. He pulled, bent his knee, and let his left heel find another hold. A moment later, Keegan was on the first level of the rocky path. He glanced behind him at the piles of rocks leaning one way or the other. Too heavy for even a man of Keegan's size to move. Turning around, he slid the Springfield carbine on the flat, rocky roof of the boulders. His hands stayed there, feeling for something, and eventually he gripped something firm. The rocks bit into his fingers, and he knew he wouldn't slip.

Keegan climbed onto the roof and lay there, his head feeling the warmth of the sun on the hard rock, and his nose taking in the scent of creosote.

Gripping the Springfield, raising it carefully, he rolled over onto his back and pointed the carbine's barrel at the highest point of the canyons — maybe a hundred yards away from where he lay. Mesquite and creosote lined most of the path between Keegan's rooftop and the slanted, dark peak of bare rocks topped by a mound of oblong boulders — the smallest of which would have crushed the stockade at Fort Spalding — that appeared to be leaning to the west.

The Apache would not have been up there, Keegan knew. At least not when he had sent those two arrows that just missed striking Keegan's flesh. The brave would have been off to the east, out of Keegan's view, probably closer to the trail.

The question was, would the buck be able to see Keegan if he sprinted up the slope?

It did not matter, Keegan decided. That Apache could hide in those rocks and see just about everything.

Old scouts had a saying that went along the lines that stillness was the key to survival. The first to move, usually became the dead. Keegan never bought into that theory. He was like a shark. As long as he kept moving, he kept living.

He rolled onto his belly and dragged himself about twenty yards, then stopped, kept the Springfield in his right hand, and sank his left into the water.

That was another reason Keegan had left his canteen behind. The country around there had been drawing Indians probably before the Apaches ever settled in that part of the world. Igneous rock — Keegan had had to ask the sergeant major to explain just what igneous rock was — had burst through the limestone, and the hollows in the rock held water after rainstorms. He brought his cupped hand to his lips and drank. It wasn't the briny water you'd find at most of the watering holes, nor water with so much iron it would weigh you down. It was rainwater, cold and sweet and satisfying.

The tanks had been bringing men for centuries. Off to Keegan's right he saw another small cavern created by how God had arranged the boulders, and inside the opening, he could see crude, ancient drawings between the saltbush and purple prickly pear.

Keegan knew not to drink too much water. He just wanted enough to wet his throat, to keep the dust down. Bringing the Springfield around, he rose to his knees and waited. He breathed. He listened. Finally, he came to his feet, although he kept in a crouch. After wetting his lips and listening to just the wind in the rocks, he began moving quickly but with little noise across the rooftop, leaping to the stony path that weaved between the mesquite and creosote, heading down before the slope began to rise again to the rocky watchtower above.

As soon as he cleared the shrubs, he stopped and turned.

The sorrel gelding whickered and danced on the hard ground.

Swearing vilely, Sean Keegan turned and

ran back through the thorny mesquite and gangly creosote. He did not care who heard him. He just ran.

The Indian who had attacked him was trying to steal Keegan's gelding.

He heard the horse's whinny and its iron hooves striking the hard rocks. Saddle leather creaked. A crash followed, accented by a human's groan.

Keegan reached the edge of the roof. He had a clear view of the rocky corral-like hiding place where he had left the Army horse. Lying on the ground, the Apache kicked free of the stirrup, and came to his feet and reached again for the gelding's reins.

That was why Keegan had loosened the cinch. A man in a hurry doesn't always take the time he should to check the little things, although the Apache had noticed the hobbles and had removed them. The saddle had slipped, spilling the Apache warrior, who now saw Keegan.

Keegan drew a bead on the warrior's buckskin shirt and touched the trigger.

The .45-70 gave a deafening roar and its echo bounced across the canyon walls and caverns. The Apache slammed against the rocks that were sprayed with blood from the hole the big chunk of lead tore as it passed completely through the brave's body. Keegan blinked, and cursed. The bullet had hit the warrior just below his ribs, and the bullet had exited most likely in the small of the lithe man's back. It should have dropped the Indian into a ball — if not killed him dead in moments — but the Indian staggered toward the rearing, snorting gelding.

With a savage curse, Keegan jumped off the ledge and landed in the road. His knees bent then straightened, propelling him to the ground. He dropped the Springfield and rolled over, jumping up to his feet while reaching for the Army-issued revolver that came holstered butt-forward, per military regulations.

"No," he yelled, and drew the Remington from the holster.

The Apache jabbed the sorrel's neck with a knife, twisted it, and was pulling out the bloody blade when Keegan's bullet from the .44 struck the warrior in his left breast.

That bullet sent the buck flying over the wall and landing on a mess of purple prickly pear. The sorrel shuddered, tried to scream, and fell onto its forefeet before collapsing onto its side.

"Damn it!" Keegan listened as the echoes of the gunfire faded. He shifted the Remington to his left hand, grabbed the Springfield off the ground with his right, and moved toward the Indian.

The Indian was an Apache. And he carried no white man's things. So he had to be one of Holy Shirt's boys. Or men. The Apache's face showed that he had lived a long life, and that he was not afraid to die. He might have been older than Sean Keegan.

As he started to sing his death song, Keegan stepped closer. He didn't let the brave finish. Keegan rammed the stock of the Springfield into the man's face, crushing the skull.

"That's for my horse, you dumb ass," he told the dead Indian, then looked over the rocks at the sorrel.

Keegan backed away and into the little cavern he had spotted earlier. There, he waited for an hour, listening, sweating, and wondering. But when no more Apaches came, and when the birds began singing in the hills, he want back out.

He stripped the dead sorrel of saddle and bridle and then scalped the dead warrior. The bloody trophy he flung into the cavern and wiped the blade from his knife and his hands on the Apache's leggings.

Inside the dead Indian's leather haversack, Keegan found carved, bloody steaks. He sniffed the meat. *Mule.* Probably two days old, greening up a mite. That would explain why the Apache was alone, and not with Holy Shirt. He had lost his horse, and was trying to steal Keegan's. Maybe that's why the Indian was dead. He hadn't followed Holy Shirt's vision. He had tried to take property from a white man.

Keegan thought about cooking the mule meat, for he had not eaten anything much for the past few days, but he heard rumblings from far across the tanks and the canyons. Gunfire. More to the east.

This country wasn't getting any safer for a man, a white man, and especially a white man with no horse. Keegan loaded the Springfield and shoved it into the scabbard. Lugging the saddle, tack, and his canteen over his left shoulder, and keeping the Remington revolver in his right hand, he began walking.

He could make it to Culpepper's Station in a couple of hours.

If he lived that long.

Chapter Twelve

There were three of them. Mexicans — one holding a shotgun, the other two armed with pistols. The one with the shotgun made the young, thin white man fall to his knees and turn around to face Matt McCulloch. The big man laid the top of the shotgun on the young man's head.

But the young man was grinning.

McCulloch was close enough to see that. He was also close enough to hear everything the men had said.

"Un jinete," the big one had said. *"Él debe ser un tonto para viajar solo a este país."*

"Good," the one forced to his knees had responded. "I will take his horse after we kill him. Then we will go after the gold."

McCulloch nudged his horse forward toward the trio. *Actually,* he corrected himself, *the quartet.*

Since the Mexicans kept their guns out, he eased the Winchester from the scabbard with his left hand and braced the stock against his left leg. He thumbed back the hammer, figuring that since the wind was blowing toward him, the sound might not be picked up by the four men waiting to waylay him.

He reined up about twenty yards in front of the four. He said nothing, but he saw the smile on the white kid's face vanish. The boy whispered in Spanish, border Spanish, and not even good border Spanish but enough for the Mexicans and Matt Mc-Culloch to understand.

The kid had said, basically, that the rider was a Texas Ranger, and hell with a gun.

"Half right," McCulloch said as he draped the reins over the horse's neck and shoved his right thumb into the belt of his chaps, casual-like. But he kept tilting the Winchester in his left hand to his left and right, just enough to keep the eyes of the outlaws on the carbine.

"Meaning?" the Mexican said in English.

"Meaning I'm not a Ranger anymore." He did not stop moving the Winchester.

"Bueno." The one with the shotgun grinned. "I do not like *Tejanos."* That smile widened, and the others copied the grin when the big man added, *"Me gustan los Rangers incluso menos."*

"Then we're even. I don't like Mexicans." McCulloch's rifle froze in its position.

His wife, McCulloch figured, would understand. You said things that you didn't mean, to rile those men you had to go after. Men with tempers don't fight as well as even-keeled folks. They rush their shots. They become blinded by rage. Usually. Sometimes, on the other hand, a hotheaded man can become tougher than leather and mean as hell in a fight. So angry, so furious, that you have no choice but to put the man down, dead.

In this situation, though, Matt McCulloch figured it didn't really matter. He would have to kill the three Mexicans one way or the other. And the gringo? Well, maybe he'd have to die, too.

No one was smiling.

McCulloch spoke. "I'd like to ride on. Like I said, I'm no longer a Texas Ranger. That means I got no authority to stop you from killing this punk." He smiled. "It'd be to your liking, boys. That's Billy Hawkin. There's a two-thousand-dollar price on his head."

The kid's face reddened, and he balled his hands into fists. "Kill that lawdog. He's lying."

Actually, McCulloch *was* lying. The last

poster he had seen on the kid had the reward at only five hundred dollars. His big brother, Jake, was the one worth two thousand.

One of the Mexicans with a pistol had turned away from McCulloch and studied Billy Hawkin, and that was the break McCulloch had been looking for.

The others were looking at the Winchester butted against McCulloch's left leg, so he drew the Colt revolver with his right hand, thumbed back the hammer, and put a bullet between the shotgunner's eyes.

The big Mexican was dead when he touched the twin triggers of the shotgun, but the bullet had driven him backward, and the barrels pointed toward the sky. Buckshot exploded into the air and rained down on the ground like sleet moments later, while Billy Hawkin rolled away from the dead man's body. The young outlaw kept cursing and pounding the ear that had been closest to the double-barreled scattergun.

Matt McCulloch barely saw that. He was leaping out of the saddle and slamming the Winchester's barrel against the horse's rump. As the animal thundered across the big empty, McCulloch was winging two shots at the men with the pistols. As those bandits tried to return fire, McCulloch dropped to the ground.

He had chosen the spot carefully, lying on the hard ground that was slightly downhill from where the others had positioned themselves. They kept spitting lead from their pistols, but didn't have a clear view of him as he lay on the ground. They were also shooting pistols, and one of them kept fanning the hammer like some dime-novel trick artist.

Having holstered the big Colt, McCulloch brought up the Winchester and squeezed the trigger, the gun catching the sunlight as the outlaw on his right spun high in the air and disappeared behind creosote. He dropped to his knees then tried to stand, but McCulloch had already worked the lever of the Winchester, and the second round from the carbine punched a hole in the man's back and drove him facedown into a soaptree yucca. With luck, the Mexican was dead before the sharp plant cut his face to shreds.

The last of the Mexicans tossed his empty pistol to the ground and unsheathed the machete at his side. Screaming in his native tongue, he charged, waving the long blade over his head.

"Stop!" McCulloch shouted. Then, in

Spanish, yelled, *"Alto."*

The man kept running, screaming, and McCulloch knew he had no choice. The carbine roared, and the Mexican spun around, fell to his knees, his right shoulder a bloody mess, and the big machete skidded across the hard rock. To McCulloch's surprise, the man rose, staggered, and snatched the handle of the machete as he staggered closer to the former Ranger.

"Damned fool," McCulloch whispered. Once more, he turned to Spanish, asking, "Do you want to die?"

The Mexican did not reply, but lifted the machete over his head.

Out of the corner of his eye, McCulloch saw Billy Hawkin staggering toward the corpse of the shotgunner and quickly put a bullet in the Mexican's brisket. He watched him slam to the rocks on his back, the machete still in his left hand, as the eyes lost their focus and the death rattle escaped from his throat.

Working the lever on the Winchester, McCulloch turned around quickly and lined up Billy Hawkin in his sights. But McCulloch decided to give the fool kid a chance. He adjusted his aim and put a bullet into the dead Mexican's waist, just inches from Billy's fingers as the outlaw tried to snatch the dead man's pistol from the sash across his stomach.

Hawkin's hand jerked back, and the killer turned around, saw the Winchester and Matt McCulloch.

"That's the only warning you get, Billy!" McCulloch said.

The kid straightened and grinned. "Well, Ranger, you know what Jake always told me."

"No, I don't."

"Die game!"

The boy leaped atop the dead Mexican and rolled across the body with the nickel-plated revolver catching the sunlight. Mc-Culloch rushed his shot, knew he missed, and jacked another cartridge into the carbine. By then Billy Hawkin had fired twice from the prone position, but those bullets did not even come close to the former Ranger.

McCulloch's next round kicked up sand in Hawkin's face, and that caused him to come up. On his knees, he gripped the revolver with both hands, thumbed back the hammer, and took careful aim.

"Don't make me kill you, kid!" McCulloch yelled, but did not wait for Billy Hawkin to touch the revolver's trigger. The Winchester roared, and Billy Hawkin was catapulted back.

He lay in the dirt, his right leg bent at the knee with his foot on the ground. The leg kept twisting left and right, much as Mc-Culloch's Winchester had done. The punk kept moaning between coughs.

After cocking the Winchester again, Mc-Culloch considered Billy Hawkin briefly, then moved toward the nearest Mexicans. Both were dead, eyes open, faces registering shock. He walked toward the other two men, but kept scanning the countryside for any sign of Apaches. McCulloch figured those Indian raiding parties would be more of a threat than what was left of the bunch of outlaws.

He stepped over the shotgunner's body with little more than a glance and finally squatted beside Billy Hawkin, who lowered that one leg, turned his head, and spit out blood onto an ant mound.

"You . . ." Billy Hawkin squeezed his eyelids tight and moaned.

"You called it, Billy," McCulloch said.

"I . . . ain't . . . ain't . . . dead . . . yet," the kid said and coughed.

"You're gut shot."

"You done it a-purpose." He rolled to his right, then his left, cursed McCulloch,

196

cursed the Mexicans, cursed his mother, cursed God, and cursed Jake Hawkin. When the profanity stopped, he spit up more blood. "Mercy, Ranger, can you give me . . . a . . . drink . . . of . . . of . . . w-w-water."

"That'd kill you, Billy, and put you in more pain than you're feeling now."

"You bas—" Bloody phlegm cut off his curse.

"Where's your horse?" McCulloch asked.

"Dead."

"And your comrades'?"

Billy Hawkin managed a laugh. "Comrades . . . my . . . a-a-arse. They was gonna . . . do me in . . . till they . . . spied . . . you." The eyes shut again, and he tried to hold the blood inside his body, but both hands were already stained crimson.

McCulloch stood. "I'll see if I can find their mounts."

He did, after catching up his own horse, and led them from the arroyo bed back to the dead men and the dying killer.

"What you lookin' at?" Billy Hawkin managed to say.

McCulloch dropped his gaze from the skyline to the boy. "Smoke."

"Smoke?" Billy laughed. "I bet the Apaches kill you before I'm dead."

"I'll take that bet."

The kid cursed again. "Jake'll kill you."

McCulloch did not answer. He shoved the Winchester into the scabbard, checked the cinch on his saddle, and took a pull from his canteen. "Billy, I can do you a favor and kill you now. It'll be cleaner and quicker. You'll be dead in an hour anyway. If the Apaches find you before you're dead" — he let out a sigh — "well, Apaches can keep a man alive a hell of a lot longer than he wants to be breathing."

The kid coughed up more blood. "You ain't puttin' me under, Ranger."

"Suit yourself." McCulloch lifted a foot to the stirrup, and grabbed the horn.

"Wait."

McCulloch looked at the dying man and waited.

"Put me on one of them Mezkin's horses," Billy managed to say.

After pushing back the brim of his hat, McCulloch asked, "What for?"

"So I can ride, find Jake, tell him who done this." The boy screamed in agony, writhed for a moment, and coughed up more blood. "So he'll know. So he . . . he . . . can . . . come . . . killing . . . you."

McCulloch was looking over the distant hills. More clouds of smoke were lifting into the blue sky. He didn't want to be caught in the open and tried to figure out where he might find the nearest shelter.

"Oh, Lord a'mighty," Billy wailed, "I'm hurtin' something awful. Please, God, end this misery." He grimaced and tried to spit, but only managed to cry out in pain.

"Billy," McCulloch said.

When the kid looked up at him, Mc-Culloch palmed the Colt and put a bullet through the boy's head. "That was for mercy, son." He knelt by the body. "And this is for your last request." He opened his saddlebags and found the book that the state issued to all Texas Rangers. *List of Fugitives from Justice* cited all the men wanted, their crimes, their descriptions, and other important details.

He found the page on which Billy Hawkin was described, fetched a pencil from his vest pocket, and wrote BILLY HAWKIN. SHOT DEAD BY MATT MCCULLOCH WHILE PROTECTING HIMSELF. He ripped the page out, folded it, and stuck it inside the kid's vest pocket.

Not that he expected Jake Hawkin to find it. In fact, McCulloch wasn't sure anyone would find the body of Billy Hawkin or the bodies of the three dead Mexican bandits. Except the buzzards. And maybe the Apaches.

If McCulloch didn't hurry, the Apaches might find him, too. So he swung into the saddle, and using a lead rope to pull the horses of the Mexicans with him, he kicked his horse into a lope.

And rode toward Culpepper's Station.

CHAPTER THIRTEEN

There had to be a better way to cross West Texas.

Gwen Stanhope sat, but far from still. The Concord stagecoach bounced this way and that, and swayed like a small boat in a strong gale. The potbellied man, who called himself Brant, had gotten sick — a common occurrence for passengers traveling on a stagecoach, as it tended to make many people feel seasick even a thousand or more miles from the ocean. He kept vomiting into his hat. The other passengers tried to give him room.

It was hotter than the Hades' hottest hinges inside the coach. The men she traveled with stank, and the timid little man who kept his two hideous carpetbags close to him like they were his infant kids had demanded that the curtains be drawn. That did keep most of the dust out. On the other hand, it kept most of the wind out, too, and trapped the stink and heat inside.

Mr. Brant looked up, his face whiter than alkali dust, his pupils dilated, and his lips red. For a moment, Gwen thought he was going to pass out, but then he sucked in a gasp, and dropped his head into the awful-smelling hat.

"I paid how much money for this journey?" the newspaper editor said, sneering as he brought a handkerchief to his nose.

The man with the carpetbags turned away.

The traveler with the red beard, who had introduced himself as Timmons of Toledo, Ohio, sniggered at the fat man's misery and dealt a jack up to Deputy Sheriff Glenn Reed.

Once Brant raised his head, he leaned back against the padded wall. "I feel awful," he said, and closed his eyes.

"Mister . . ." Gwen said, and she saw Reed's eyes narrow. He ignored the jack he had been dealt, and stared hard at his prisoner.

Gwen raised her manacled hands off her lap and pointed a slim finger at the sick man. "Your hat is leaking."

Reed looked at the hat, as did everyone else in the coach, before he turned back to his card and motioned for the red-bearded gent to hit him. They were playing blackjack without any betting, just to pass the time and take their minds and noses off the vomiting man.

"Oh, God," said the newspaper editor. "For the love of human decency sir, dump that reeking waste outside."

The sick man slid over toward the window.

"Don't be a fool, Brant," Timmons called out. "As fast as we're going, that slime will fly right back into the coach. Spray us all with your sickness."

"M-m-maybe," stuttered the timid fellow who had introduced himself as Harold and Harry and Homer with a last name of Harrison, or Harris, or Henderson. He wasn't the best liar Gwen had ever met. He might have been the worst, but only Gwen and the deputy seemed to notice. Or maybe everyone else just accepted the Western ways. If a man called himself Jim one minute and Joe the next, you never questioned him. You didn't even ask a person's name. If he told you, that was fine. And if he couldn't quite pick the name he wanted to use, well, that was fine, too.

"M-m-ay-be . . . the . . . they . . . will . . . s-s-stop the c-c-c-coach," the man said hopefully.

That caused the newspaperman to laugh. "They'll stop for nothing that's not on the schedule."

"Damn right," the deputy sheriff said, smiling as he flipped over his hole card after Timmons dealt him a nine. "We've got a hanging to make." He tapped the cards. "Nineteen."

Timmons grinned and showed his cards. "Push. I got one, too."

"Good thing we're not playing for money," Glenn Reed said. "Else I might have to arrest you."

Timmons gathered the cards and started shuffling. "Indeed." He set the deck at his side after one shuffle and pointed to the curtain. "Brant, pull up the curtain, lean out the window. The fresh air will do you some good. And lower your hat and let gravity and physics do their duty." He pointed at the timid man. "You. Latch hold to Brant's suspenders. In case he starts to fall out. He's sick, you know."

The timid man straightened and went rigid.

"Those bags you're toting won't be out of your sight, mister. You're closest. Just do it. Before we have to ride all the way to El Paso with vomit on our boots and clothes."

It was the newspaper editor who rose from his seat and drew up the curtain, securing it above the window. Sunlight bathed the coach, dust immediately drifted in, but the air rushing by felt cool. The editor fell back into his seat, the carpetbag-carrier left his grips on the floor, and slipped his right hand at the base of the Y-styled suspenders as Brant eased over, climbed onto his knees on the bench, and leaned out of the window.

Outside on the driver's bench, the jehu named Petey cursed the team of mules and slapped his whip, while the guard named Rourke remained quiet — probably to keep from choking on the dust.

Timmons leaned forward and slapped the deputy's leg, reached across the aisle and slapped the journalist's thigh, hooked a thumb at the little man who had his eyes closed as he held the suspenders to the fat man, who hung out of the coach from his fat gut and above.

After winking at Gwen, the man with the red beard settled back into his seat, and laughed. "Amazing what you can get a fool to do."

Alvin Griffin chortled, and the scared man's eyes shot open. He looked hard at Timmons, whose grin widened.

Suddenly the timid man was jerked toward the window as Brant's body seemed to go limp.

"Hell's bells!" shouted the newspaper editor.

"Don't drop him!" Gwen heard herself shout.

Glenn Reed stared, but did not move. It was the red-bearded man who stepped between the lawman and Gwen, and hurried the short distance. He grabbed the waistband of the fat drummer's pants and began pulling. The small man, who released his hold on the suspenders, jumped back and found his carpetbags.

From above, Rourke's shotgun roared.

"What the hell?" shouted the newspaper editor.

"Get this team movin', Petey!" Rourke thundered, triggering another blast of buckshot.

Reed whipped out his pistol, thumbed back the hammer, and shoved the barrel near Gwen's breasts. "If it's your friends, you might not hang, but you'll be dead sure enough."

"What friends do I — ?" She didn't finish because Timmons had managed to pull Brant inside.

The scream did not sound human. Gwen covered her mouth, her eyes widening in terror, and slowly she understood that she had not screamed. That had come from

Henry or Harold or Harry or whatever name he was using at the moment.

The body of the drummer bounced off the seat, hit the floor, and knocked the door open.

Once again, Rourke's shotgun thundered. Timmons stepped across the body and grabbed the door. "God have mercy on our souls." He slammed the door shut, dropped to his knees, and opened the satchel he had set by his feet.

Gwen couldn't take her eyes off the drummer. An arrow was jammed into his side, almost all the way to the feathered shaft, and another had gone right into his ear. A third was lower, in his side. His eyes remained wide open, unblinking, and as she looked at his face, she did not see the fat drummer but Kirk Van Patten, whom she had killed. Another shotgun blast by Rourke snapped that mirage.

"Apaches!" said Glenn Reed.

"You take that side," said Timmons, who opened his Schofield, snapped it shut, and moved to the far side, bracing his feet against the dead man's head, and extending his arm out the open window.

"I'm guarding my prisoner!" Reed said.

"The hell with your prisoner, Sheriff!" the newspaper editor shouted.

The shotgun roared. So did the Schofield in Timmons's hand.

Gwen stared at the deputy sheriff incredulously.

The lawman grinned. "It might be fun to let the Apaches have you, but then Charles wouldn't pay me . . ." One minute he was talking. The next second blood was pouring out of his mouth like water from an artesian well.

Gwen blinked, trying to comprehend, and at last saw the revolver he had dropped onto the floor, and the two hands clutching the shaft of the arrow that had somehow struck him in the center of his throat.

Deputy Sheriff Glenn Reed slowly tilted onto his side, clutching the bloody shaft of the arrow, sucking for air until he stopped breathing and just stared across the coach, looking completely shocked and completely dead.

On the other side of the stage, Timmons fired the Schofield. Gwen looked at the newspaper editor, who seemed even paler than Brant had when he was just sick and not dead. The coward with the carpetbags remained rigid. The deputy's pistol lay where it fell, and Gwen realized that neither Alvin J. Griffin IV, editor and publisher of the *Purgatory City Herald Leader,* nor Harvey Harrison or whatever his name was had any inclination or backbone to save their hides. She leaned off her seat, swept up the pistol in her manacled hands, and slid onto the seat that had previously been occupied by Timmons of Toledo, Ohio.

She set the revolver on her lap to raise the curtain, and once she had that secured, she felt the arrow whistle past her ear and thud into the padding on the wall behind her. That almost shattered her nerves, but she choked down the fear, snatched the revolver, and aimed.

All she saw, however, was dust. The coach hit a hole or a rock or something, and the Concord rocked, almost overturned, and slammed her against the wood. After choking back a curse and fighting off the pain, she looked again, searching for a target.

On the other side of the stagecoach, Timmons's Schofield boomed. Timmons, maybe, had a better view. The wind was blowing toward Gwen, so the dust might not be as thick on his side. Or perhaps he was just pulling the trigger to scare off those Indians, or let them know that customers inside the coach were armed and ready.

Wetting her lips, Gwen kept the pistol level and cocked, but no warriors rode into sight. She became aware that she no longer heard Rourke's shotgun above, and feared that he might be dead. Another thought jarred her. Both the jehu and the messenger could be dead and the team was carrying the coach pell-mell and out of control. Curses above did not make her relax, but at least she knew someone was up there driving the team.

The coach banged skyward again then landed on the two wheels nearest Gwen, and she saw the ground coming up to meet her. She also saw a figure slam onto the road as the coach righted itself. She looked before the dust flew inside and saw the figure rolling into the ditch. She blinked. That man wasn't dressed like the messenger. That had been the driver, Petey.

"Damn your sorry hides!" shouted the voice above. "Move, mules. Run. Run, damn your hides. Else we're all dead!"

That was Rourke. Petey, the driver, was dead, and his body was just off the road. That explained why the shotgun was no longer being fired upstairs.

Gwen saw a white figure emerge from the dust. She blinked, wondering if she might be hallucinating, for the figure looked like an angel. But that thought died quickly, too, because the figure was an Apache, dressed in light-colored buckskin, with long black hair dancing in the wind. And the horse was not white, but gray.

The revolver shook in her hand as the warrior drove his magnificent stallion closer to the stagecoach. The derringer had been impossible to hold steady when she had killed Kirk Van Patten, too. She never quite grasped how she had managed to hit him, let alone kill the brute. But that memory helped her find her nerve, and the dead deputy sheriff's gun stopped shaking. She no longer saw an Apache warrior with a lance in his right hand, preparing to throw it into Gwen's body. She saw that miserable swine of a man who was going to beat her to death. The gun bucked in her hand, the lance flew off to the side of the road, the warrior clutched his chest and toppled off the horse, and the gray went galloping into the dust.

She could breathe. No longer did fear grip her. Cocking the revolver, she waited.

The wagon sounded different, and the scenery vanished, replaced by rocky walls. They had made it to the canyon country, and if Gwen's mind were not playing tricks on her, that meant they would soon be at the stagecoach station. The dust grew thicker, funneled down the narrow entrance of the canyon.

Another rut or stone or hole bounced them around, but the stagecoach kept moving.

"Folks!" yelled the man driving the Concord. "If anyone back there's alive and can hear me, we'll be at Culpepper's in a few minutes, God willing! As soon as this bucket stops, pile out and don't be lazy! Don't be stupid. Leave everything that ain't breathing where it is. Go through the doors and take cover. And you best know what to do with that last bullet. In case things get —" He did not finish. "Here we come, folks! Remember. Into the station and make it snappy!"

Bracing herself, Gwen felt the stagecoach slide to a hard stop. Dust blinded her as it swept inside the coach. Just breathing hurt, and with her eyes clamped shut, she tried to find the latch to the door.

Suddenly, the door swung open with a bang. She heard a curse, felt someone move past her, and then she managed to open her eyes. It was the newspaperman. Alvin Griffin wasted no time departing the coach. Gwen tried to shake her head, but before she could stand, the little coward had leaped past her, out of the door, and into the dust. She would not have recognized him had she not caught a glimpse of the hideously colored and designed carpetbags he was carrying.

So much for leaving behind personal items that were not breathing.

She made it out of the coach and felt her legs on solid ground. She reached out to help Mr. Timmons, who, still gripping the Schofield in his right hand, was coming toward her.

She heard the unmistakable sounds of arrows cutting through the air, then the jarring, numbing sound of arrows striking flesh. The Schofield flew out of Timmons's hand and struck Gwen in her chest. She fell backward onto the dust, and her head struck the ground hard.

Arms reached under her, lifted her up. Gwen's eyes opened to see Mr. Timmons, his left hand sticking out through the window of the coach, his right slapping at his back. Another thump and the look on Timmons's face told her that another Apache arrow had found its mark. The messenger, Rourke, was at the side of the coach, reaching for Timmons's hand.

"Forget it," the red-bearded man said. "I'm done for."

Timmons, that brave man from Toledo, Ohio, closed his eyes and slowly slumped into the coach. She couldn't see his face or his body, just that hand, fingers curled, hanging out of the window.

We're all going to die.

That would be her last thought.

Her eyes closed, but opened as she heard herself say, "Nobody lives forever."

Her shoes dragged across the ground. That's the first thing she saw. Next, she spotted Rourke. With the shotgun in his left hand, he scooped up the Schofield with his right.

Only seconds had passed.

Gwen felt shade and saw the roof above her. She was inside a building. The door shut, and she saw Rourke and a . . . a . . . a . . . man from the Bible, no, the Middle Ages help slam the heavy cottonwood bar onto the holds on the sides of the door. It was like she was in the Leadville Opera House watching *King Lear.*

She was being laid down, fairly gently, and she looked into the face of the man who had dragged her from the stagecoach to the inside of Culpepper's Station.

"Ma'am." He tipped his hat and disappeared.

CHAPTER FOURTEEN

Picking up the Sharps, Jed Breen hurried across the practically barren quarters of the stagecoach station. He heard the hooves of horses, the yips of the warriors, and the thudding of arrows as they struck the door, the shutters, and the stone walls. Back during the days of the original Overland Mail, Culpepper had been no fool when he had erected the stagecoach stop. The solid walls, some adobe but mostly stone, were two feet thick, and the roof might have been made of wood, but it had been covered with three feet of dirt and more rocks. Nobody, not even the Apaches, would be burning them out. The doors looked to be wood. So did the shutters. But those heavy cottonwood boards covered an iron interior.

The place had been built better than any Army gunboat.

He rammed the rifle barrel through the gunport, bent, and tried to find a target.

Laughing, he pulled back the Sharps and stepped away from the closed bolted window. He shook his head. You had to respect those Apache bucks.

"What?" asked the man from the stage-coach.

"They've already pulled the mules out of their harnesses and vanished," Breen said.

"How about the coach?" the man said.

"It's still out there. For now."

"Well, the president of this company will hear from me and my paper," said one of the men from the coach, the one who wasn't hugging two ugly carpetbags as he huddled in the corner. "This is an outrage. I'll —"

"Shut up," Breen told him, and walked to the woman, picking up a cup off the table. He held it to the handsome woman as he knelt. "Ma'am, it's not hot. It's not even good. But it might perk you up."

She smiled, and the metal cuffs jingled as she lifted her hands. She hesitated, maybe embarrassed or maybe just annoyed at the handcuffs.

"Silver is becoming on most ladies," Breen said. "But I expect even brass would look wonderful on you, ma'am."

She tested the coffee and smiled.

"Keys?" he asked.

"I . . . um . . . stagecoach."

216

"Colonel, open the door."

"You're not going out there just so you can unchain this wench, sir!" the newspaperman bellowed.

Breen turned. "If you want to show your chivalry, I'll let you do your good turn for the day, mister."

"I will not have you risk my life — or the lives of these other good people — to free a concubine and a murderess bound for the gallows."

Breen glanced at the blonde, sizing her up.

"Leave her chained!" said the coward in the corner.

Sir Theodore Cannon climbed atop the table, put his right hand inside his cloak, closed his eyes, and began speaking.

"I begin to find an idle and fond bondage in the oppression of aged tyranny, who sways, not as it hath power, but as it is suffered. Come to me, that of this I may speak more. If our father would sleep till I waked him, you should half his revenue forever and live the beloved of your brother."

"What the hell?" said the newspaper journalist.

217

Breen grinned. "Well said, Earl of Gloucester. Get that bar off the door."

"I forbid you to risk our lives for a woman who is doomed to hang." The newspaperman had found his backbone and was standing, pointing a finger. "Do you know who I am, sir? I am Alvin J. Griffin the Fourth, mister, and I edit and also publish the renowned *Herald Leader* in Purgatory City, sir."

That stopped Breen, who turned around, and looked over the gent.

"You've heard of me, I presume," Alvin J. Griffin IV said.

"Indeed I have. I've even read some of your editorials. My name's Breen, Mr. Editor. Jed Breen. Or maybe you should just call me . . . a jackal."

Breen looked at the man drawn up into a ball in the corner, clutching the carpetbags, and then at the shotgun who had driven in the stagecoach. "I don't know how many bucks are out there, folks, but we stand a better chance if this lady has both of her hands freed to kill some Apaches before they kill us. Anybody else want to argue with me?"

The stagecoach employee and the actor lifted the bar, and Breen darted outside and stepped toward the coach.

It stank of death. After climbing over the body of the corpse that partially blocked the door closest to the station, Breen saw the body of another man lying faceup on the floor. He guessed that the lawman was the other dead man who lay on the seat in a pool of blood. Anyway, that's the one that looked like a lawman, and bounty hunters like Jed Breen could pretty much spot any lawman.

Sure enough, when Breen pushed back the dead man's coat, he saw the badge pinned above the top pocket on his vest. He stuck his fingers inside the coat pocket, pulled out a wallet, and looked through it quickly.

And he started to sweat.

The first vest pocket held a few matches. The second one held a cheap watch. The third had the keys, and one of those Breen knew from prior experience was a key that could lock and unlock manacles. He stopped searching, and with his free hand, gripped the butt of the Lightning on his hip.

An Apache in buckskins jumped in front of the door, and raised a knife over his head. With the .38 revolver already in Breen's hand, two quick bullets drove the warrior over the hitching rail. Instantly, the door opposite Breen jerked open. Breen dived over the body of the Indian who had died in the doorway. Turning back toward the opening, he saw the Apache raise his arm to thrust the lance. Suddenly, the Indian's face disappeared in an eruption of bone, blood, and brains, and he slammed atop the dead white man.

"In the station!" a voice yelled from the desert. "I'm white. I'm alone. And I'm coming in!"

Breen was crawling out. He dropped to the ground, turned around, and using the front wheel for cover, aimed the Colt at the corrals.

The door behind him opened, and the man from the stagecoach rushed outside, taking cover behind the rear wheel. "Who in hell is that?"

"I don't know, but when he shows, if he's not a white man, gun him down." Breen saw dust behind the barn. "Because I detest a liar."

The man came from the side of the cistern by the corrals. The first thing Breen noticed were the buckskin britches. That briefly made him think it might be an Indian because the rest of the man's outfit was that of a soldier. Apaches had been known to use white man's duds to sneak closer to their prey.

But not those Apaches, he remembered. They were Holy Shirt's boys, those that shunned all white man conveniences.

Crouched low, the man was running at angles from the cistern. He held a big revolver in one hand, a Springfield trapdoor in the other, and a few canteens were slung over his shoulder.

"Let him come," Breen told the stagecoach man when he lifted his shotgun.

An Apache dropped off the roof, swung a tomahawk, and dropped the shotgun guard into the dust. Breen shot the brave dead, as an arrow cut across his collar, drawing blood. Breen rolled to his side and saw another brave coming at him. A gun roared, and the warrior's chest exploded crimson. He staggered awkwardly and dropped to his side as about a dozen riders galloped into the yard.

From the doorway, Sir Theodore Cannon blasted two barrels from a shotgun that dropped a horse and sent an Apache toppling over. As the thespian reloaded the double barrels, he began screaming at the top of his voice.

"Blood and destruction shall be so in use
And dreadful objects so familiar

That mothers shall but smile when they
  behold
Their infants quarter'd with the hands of
  war;
All pity choked with custom of fell deeds:
And Caesar's spirit, ranging for revenge,
With Ate by his side come hot from hell,
Shall in these confines with a monarch's
  voice
Cry 'Havoc,' and let slip the dogs of war;
That this foul deed shall smell above the
  earth
With carrion men, groaning for burial."

The shotgun barked again.

The soldier, or ex-soldier, or whoever he was, swung the Springfield like a club. The actor stepped outside and fired the shotgun from his hip. Breen brained one young Apache with the barrel of his Lightning, sending the warrior through the doorway. A lance flew through the open doorway.

Breen thought *This is it. But Death comes for us all!*

Dust. Sand. Breen could see little, but pulled the trigger on the Lightning anyway. He felt his back pressing against the jagged walls of the station as Apaches sang out war songs. They yipped. They shouted. Their horses screamed. Arrows whistled overhead, bounced off the stone walls, and then a grinning warrior stepped out of the dust and prepared to gut Breen with his knife. Breen turned the Lightning at the warrior's black-painted face and squeezed the trigger again. Nothing. He pulled the trigger once more, saw the hammer drop, and heard nothing. The Lightning was empty. He wondered how long he had been dropping the hammer on empty shells.

The lance that had been thrown inside the station now drove the warrior through his gut. The knife slipped out of his fingers, and the point of the spear slammed into the coach. The warrior gagged on his own blood and died. Breen saw the woman, still in her handcuffs, gripping the shaft of the lance. She must have picked up the weapon, and charged out like a knight right out of *Ivanhoe.* She was saying something, but Breen couldn't hear. Holstering the .38, he reached over and grabbed the blonde's left shoulder. The man in the buckskin pants and Army duds took hold of her right shoulder. They stumbled, cartwheeled, and practically fell through the empty doorway, with the actor, Sir Theodore Cannon, right behind him.

As another warrior stepped into the opening, the soldier raised his Remington, and the pistol barked. The brave slapped his bloody ear and stumbled before the soldier could finish him with another .45 slug.

By that time, Breen and the stranger were standing. The door slammed, peppered with arrows. In the maelstrom from Hell, Sir Theodore Cannon lifted one end of the cottonwood bar. The blonde grunted and tried to raise the other side. Breen helped her, and the bar fell into place. Everyone dropped to the floor.

Eventually, a silence, eerie and foreboding, and a tenuous peace settled over Culpepper's Station.

Breen stared at the soldier. The sleeves of the Army boy's blouse showed that he had once held the rank of sergeant, but the chevrons had been stripped off. Breen then looked at the canteen.

The soldier was studying him and smiled. He pulled off one of the canteens and tossed it to Breen.

"You'd make my day if you told me it was brandy," Breen said, hardly recognizing his voice.

"If it were brandy," said the soldier, "I wouldn't have passed it to you."

Breen grinned, almost chuckled, and handed the canteen to the woman.

"Thank you," she said.

Then he fished out the keys to the handcuffs. But before he unlocked them, his
head jerked around. He saw the unconscious
Apache brave on the floor, and the coward
with the carpetbags and that ass of a newspaper owner far across the station. Breen
sighed, rose, and cursed. "The driver. Or
shotgun. Or whoever he was! He's outside."

"Oh, my God," said the woman.

"I thought he was dead," Sir Theodore
Cannon cried out.

Breen and the soldier were already at the
door. There was no time to reload the
Lightning. With luck, the Apaches had run
off. The bar came out, and the actor took it
and held it. The girl picked up the 1875
Remington that the soldier had placed on
the floor.

She cocked the pistol, brought it up, and
aimed at the door.

Breen nodded at the soldier, who returned
the nod, and Breen jerked open the door.
The soldier started, stopped, and leaped
back in.

Breen did the same. "Damn!" He and
Cannon returned the bar.

"Is he dead?" the woman asked.

"Worse," the soldier said. "He's gone."

"Maybe . . ." Theodore Cannon tried.
"Perhaps he escaped."

"They're all gone," Breen said. "Dead and wounded carried off. And . . ."

"Rourke," said the woman. "His name was Rourke. He was a brave, brave man."

Sir Theodore Cannon cleared his throat. He was still dressed in his Macbeth garb. " 'A coward dies a thousand times before his death, but the valiant taste of death but once.' "

"*Julius Caesar*," Breen said. "But Shakespeare didn't know about the Apaches. Because the Apaches will have the valiant tasting death a thousand times, and that valiant man will be a coward long before his life is mercifully ended."

The actor did not seem to hear. " 'It seems to me most strange that men should fear, seeing that death, a necessary end, will come when it will come.' "

"It's coming." The woman chuckled without any humor. "Nobody lives forever." She knelt by the Apache that Breen had brained with his revolver's barrel. "This one's still alive."

"Kill him!" shouted the newspaperman in the corner.

The man in the black suit nodded in agreement. "Kill him. Before he's awake and he kills us all."

Breen started reloading his pistol, but the

soldier had moved to the Apache. He looked at the bloody gash on the brave's head, checked his pulse, and ripped the headband off his head. "We'll keep him alive, for the time being." He rolled the buck onto his stomach, pulled his hands behind the warrior's back, and used the cord that was serving as a headband to tie the warrior's wrists. Next he opened one of the canteens and poured water over the Indian's wrists.

"By Godfrey, sir!" shouted Alvin Griffin. "How dare you waste water like that. We don't have much water. What on earth do you think you are doing, sir."

The man looked up but did not answer, did not even consider the Purgatory City journalist. He merely corked the canteen, picked up his Springfield, took the Remington from the woman, and moved to the door to keep an eye on things.

Breen knew exactly what the soldier was doing. Wet rawhide would shrink as it dried. Those bindings would be so tight in an hour or so that the Indian would never be able to free himself.

Breen went to the woman and showed her the keys to the handcuffs. "You did well."

"You, too," she said.

Breen's head shook. "If I'd done better, Rourke — isn't that what you said he went

227

by? — well, he'd still be with us."

"Nobody lives forever," she said again.

"Not in West Texas," Breen said, and fitted the key into the slot.

Moments later, the handcuffs were on the table, the woman was massaging her wrists, and Breen was collecting the brass cartridges from the floor.

"A place this remote is bound to have gunpowder, lead, and bullet molds," he said, thinking more to himself.

"This is no armory, sir," Griffin countered.

"I beg to differ," said the soldier.

"Where do you think?" Breen asked.

"Outside," the girl said. "So it wouldn't blow up the entire station."

Breen's head and the soldier's head shook in disagreement.

"They'd want it here," the soldier said. "Because *we're* here. And *we* need it. *Here.*"

"Right," Breen said.

"But protected," the soldier said. "Because of what the girl said."

"It's Gwen," she said. "Gwen Stanhope."

The soldier tipped his hat. Breen did the same.

"A safe?" She looked around.

"Ceiling," said the soldier as he lifted his head. "Attic?"

Finally, all of them started staring at the floor.

"Cellar," Breen said.

"Uh-huh," said the soldier.

The thespian cleared his throat, and pointed at two tables pushed against each other. "Under the rug, but you'll need every hand in here to move those tables to get to the rug. Damn things weigh a ton."

Breen grinned. He thanked Sir Cannon and looked at Griffin and the coward. "You two. Lend a hand."

Griffin came up instantly. The coward hesitated, but finally pushed himself to his feet.

"Leave the grips," the soldier told him. "You'll need both hands."

The man stopped, looked at the ugly luggage, and slowly placed them where he had been cowering.

Once the tables and rug were moved, Breen opened the trapdoor. Another idea came to his mind. "Maybe there's a tunnel. For escape."

"There's not," said Sir Theodore. "I asked."

"All right."

A half hour later, a keg of gunpowder was out, and the stove was fired. A heavy pot lay on the lid, and lead bars were beginning to melt. At the table sat the current residents of Culpepper's Station — except the Indian, who was awake on the floor, his legs also bound, and his back against the wall. He stared at the others with malevolent eyes, but did not speak, did not complain, just sat and stared.

"This," Breen said, "is a bullet mold. It's .45 caliber, but that'll work for a lot of our weapons. I'll trim the lead down with my knife for the forty-fours and my thirty-eight. And I'll show you how to load the cartridges with powder and primer."

"Maybe all this is unnecessary," said the newspaper editor. "Perhaps the Army has a patrol, an entire troop, galloping to us right now."

"No," said the soldier.

"But you're no longer in the Army," the editor said. "I can see where your stripes have been ripped off. Or perhaps you are just a deserter. How do you know the Army's not riding here?"

"Because I haven't been out of the Army that long, Mister Alvin Griffin the Fourth of Purgatory City's leading newspaper. The Army's down south toward Dead Man's Canyon trying to track down some other Apaches on the prod."

The editor leaned forward.

The soldier removed his hat. "Don't you remember me, Mister Newspaper Editor? I mean, you've wrote about me enough, sir. Keegan. Sean Keegan."

Breen laughed and held out his hand. "Well, Keegan. This is a pleasure. From one *jackal* to another. I'm Jed Breen."

CHAPTER FIFTEEN

He needed one extra hand.

Hiding in the rocks, Matt McCulloch put his hands over the muzzles of two of the Mexican bandit's horses, a roan and a black, to keep them from whinnying. He figured he could trust his buckskin not to call out to the approaching riders. It was the fourth horse, a pinto, that worried him. If that horse whickered or made any kind of noise, McCulloch knew one thing.

He was a dead man.

Holding his breath, feeling the sweat trickle down his cheeks, he listened as the ponies thundered past. The rocks blocked most of the dust, but he still had to lower his head to keep from being blinded. He tried to count the number of riders. More than ten, he figured, but no more than twenty. For Apaches, that was an entire cavalry regiment. He waited till the dust had settled and the sound of the horses faded.

Finally, he released his hold on the roan and the black, rubbed them gently on their necks, and grinned at the pinto, the last of the horses on the lead rope. "You're a good girl," he told the mare, and went to her to rub her neck, too.

His gelding grunted.

"I know, you're good, too," he said, and removed his hat and wiped the sweat off his face with his shirtsleeve.

Now, he pulled the Winchester from the scabbard and moved to the conglomeration of boulders. "Stay," he told the horses, and smiled at a memory.

"Stay," he said to the ponies.

His wife grinned and said in that wonderful Spanish accent, "My love, those are *caballos,* not *perros.*"

He ducked underneath the waving stems of ocotillo cactus, stepped onto the square boulder, and pulled himself onto the giant goose egg of a rock. Keeping the Winchester in front of him, McCulloch crawled to the edge and watched the fading dust of the Apaches. At such times he wished he owned a pair of binoculars, but those spyglasses could get a man into trouble. If the sun reflected off the lenses and the Apaches saw it — and everybody knew that Apaches had eyes in the backs of their heads — well, that could lead to trouble.

Apaches, however, weren't the only ones with that extra sense, those proverbial eyes in the backs of their heads. Slowly, Mc-Culloch rolled over and saw more dust down the trail.

"Hell," he whispered, and shot a quick look at the four horses.

The rider was coming along at a good lope, probably aiming to catch up with the war party after scouting along the back trail. With luck, McCulloch reasoned, the brave would keep riding to join his fellow marauders. With even more luck, none of the horses would whinny a greeting to the solitary rider. McCulloch couldn't risk trying to climb back down and keep those animals silent. For one reason, he didn't have time. For another, the Apache might see him. Hell, he might have already spotted Mc-Culloch.

Flattening himself on the warm rock's surface, McCulloch listened to the approaching Apache. Gradually, he slid his right foot up and stretched his right hand until he found the walnut handle of the knife he kept sheathed inside the boot. This he drew and brought up, but kept the blade close to his body. The sun was shining brightly, and though the chances were slim that the riding Indian could spot a reflection, McCulloch wasn't one to take those kinds of chances.

Keep riding, McCulloch thought. *Keep riding. It could be a white man, though. Or a Mexican.*

He grinned. That was nothing but wishful thinking. No sane man would go chasing after dust made by Apaches. The rider had to be an Indian. And when the horse slowed down, McCulloch knew from the sound of the hooves that this rider was Indian. The horse he rode was unshod.

The hiding place McCulloch had picked was the best he could find nearby, and it was a great spot. The ground was hard rock. No white man could see any sign that four horses had turned off the trail and into the forest of boulders. No white man . . . but the man below was an Apache.

McCulloch drew his left hand from the Winchester. A gunshot would carry far in that country, and the Apaches would send enough of their party back to investigate the shot. Likely, they would send some men back anyway, eventually, to check on the man guarding their back trail.

The horse stopped, snorted. The Indian below whispered something. McCulloch tensed, waiting for one of the four horses to whicker or snort or even begin to urinate. One noise, no matter how slight, would give him away.

The metallic click caused McCulloch to raise his head just a fraction. Few men in West Texas would fail to recognize that sound, and certainly every Texas Ranger understood what it meant. That was the triple-click of a single-action revolver being cocked.

So these Apaches weren't the same ones who had been riding with Holy Shirt. They had to be part of another bunch. It also made his situation a little bit more ticklish. The Apache had a cocked revolver, and if he squeezed off that shot, McCulloch would have to start dealing with more than one Indian. Maybe the string of horses he had could pull away from the fleetest of the warriors' mounts. Maybe not. He'd rather not have to run a few good horses to death.

Wetting his lips, controlling his breathing, but sweating like a leaking water bag, he listened. The hooves of the Apache's pony clopped. The warrior had found the entrance to McCulloch's hiding place and his makeshift corral for the four horses. You had to admire a man with that kind of talent, but it was like the Texas Rangers always said, *We can find a man if you give us enough time, but an Apache can find that man in no time.*

McCulloch waited, listening and trying to guess where the Apache rider was. To his amazement, the horses remained quiet, although he heard them moving, nervous, unsure of what the new horse would be bringing with it. McCulloch came up on his hands and knees, before he finally lifted himself just a fraction, rocking on his haunches in silence, waiting . . . listening . . . waiting . . . waiting . . . listening . . . waiting . . . until . . .

He leaped off the rock.

The Apache sensed the movement and was turning quickly in his Indian saddle, bringing the pistol — an old Navy Colt — up. McCulloch saw everything and knew exactly what he had to do.

His left hand slammed onto the old .36 in the Indian's right hand, the pinky finger just managing to slip between the brass frame and the casehardened hammer as the Indian squeezed the trigger.

The hammer bit and broke the finger, right between the middle knuckles, but Mc-Culloch felt no pain at that moment. Even better, he heard no shot. His finger had stopped the hammer from striking the percussion cap and detonating a round. All the while, his body was driving the Indian off the saddle. The Apache's head cracked against the limestone wall just a few feet from the horse, which whinnied, reared, and bolted toward the other animals. McCulloch slashed with his knife but everything was moving too fast, and he felt the blade sing off the hard rock wall.

He grimaced at the impact as he and the Apache bounced off the wall and into the dirt. Grabbing his knife, McCulloch rolled away, rose, and started for the brave, then stopped suddenly and leaped back to avoid the Apache's dun horse. It had turned around and was bolting down the small, narrow canyon and out to the main trail.

The other horses, except for McCulloch's buckskin, started to follow, but McCulloch and the Apache had come at each other in the middle of the canyon. The horses stopped, turned, danced, whinnied, snorted, and then hurried back to the far wall of their pen.

The Apache's knife slashed, but McCulloch leaped back, avoiding the blade, and saw the Indian spin halfway around. Dazed from his head slamming against the wall, he had swung too hard. He tried to dive to his left to correct his mistake, but McCulloch was driving his knife into the brave's back, slamming him against the wall. As McCulloch twisted the blade and drove it deeper, he used his right hand to grab the brave's long, shiny black hair and jerk the head back. Then he slammed the head against the rock wall again. That cut off the man's scream.

He groaned as McCulloch jerked the knife free. He slammed the Indian's face into the wall once more, then turned him around, and let go for just an instant. His right arm came up quickly and smashed the Indian's throat, crushing the larynx, preventing any sound. His left hand drove the blade into the center of the man's heart. Again, Mc-Culloch twisted, just to make sure, before he jerked the knife free, lifted his arm from the man's throat, and watched him drop hard onto the ground.

McCulloch had little time. The bleeding, broken pinky would have to wait. He looked above the rocks and saw the rising dust. The dead brave's pony was bolting toward the rest of the war party, and that meant, once the other warriors saw the riderless horse, too many Apaches would be back. Mc-Culloch picked the Navy Colt off the ground, shoved it into his waistband, and moved to the horses.

He could leave them, just take the buckskin, but he saw no need in abandoning the animals and giving them to hostile Indians. Besides, the Apaches would likely just eat the roan, but McCulloch saw some potential in that horse. He wiped his blade on the Indian's calico shirt, returned it to the sheath in his boot, and checked the lead rope. Whispering soothing praise to the dead bandits' horses, he swung into the saddle and rode to the dead Indian. The buckskin remained calm, but the other animals became skittish at the smell of blood and death.

"Easy," McCulloch said. He stood in the stirrups and stretched his left hand to the rocky top. His broken finger hurt like blazes. He couldn't bend it but the other fingers and thumb gripped the barrel of the Winchester, and he pulled it down. He did not bother to shove it into the scabbard. He might have need of it real soon, and those horses behind him were about to bolt — if he didn't get them away from the dead Indian quickly.

He kicked the gelding's side and maneuvered through the narrow path, came to the main trail, and loped away. He did not follow the trail, but dipped past a garden of ocotillo and into a winding arroyo to put as much distance between him and the dead Indian as possible.

Yet he did not keep the horses at a gallop for long. Running horses raised too much dust, and a drunken white man would be able to follow his trail once he entered the sandy arroyo. An Apache would find him a lot quicker.

The horses wanted to lope, but if those Indians caught up with him, McCulloch knew he would need all four of those horses, and they'd have to be fresh and ready to run. For the time being, he decided to take a leisurely journey across the emptiness. He climbed out of the arroyo, dodged between cactus plants, up and over rocks, and through narrow passes. The Apaches might follow him, but they wouldn't enjoy the torment he put them through.

By dusk, he was still alive. Surprising, perhaps, but McCulloch felt no reason to complain. He wasn't sure he'd still be walking around on this earth by morning.

He had heard the gunfire earlier, and figured it had to be coming from Culpepper's Station. Maybe that's why he had decided to make for the old Butterfield stagecoach line. If the Apaches had attacked there, knowing Apaches the way he did, they would have moved on. The place seemed as permanent as the mountains in the Big Bend country. Old Culpepper's place would still be standing all the way to Armageddon — and maybe even afterward. Maybe he would find white men still there, or maybe not, but he knew he'd find water — the Apaches would do a lot of things, but he had never heard of one poisoning a well — and a place to sleep. The horses needed the water. He needed water, too, and he wouldn't frown on a chance to catch a few winks.

Roughly a mile or so from Culpepper's, McCulloch reined in his horse in a small box canyon and swung to the ground. He had managed to wrap and splint the pinky on his left hand. It had stopped bleeding, but the throbbing remained persistent. He slaked his thirst and gave the last of the water from the canteens to the horses.

Wish I had some grain for you boys, he thought. He knew better than to talk.

He removed his boots and opened his saddlebags, withdrawing Apache-style moccasins. They made less noise than his boots, and even an Apache could not tell if moccasin prints were made from a white man or an Indian. He pulled them up over his ripe-smelling socks, over his britches, and laced them tight around his calves just below the knees. He took the horses to the deepest part of the canyon, where he hobbled his gelding, and then used the lead rope to manufacture hobbles to the other horses. He didn't like the idea. If he got killed, and the Apaches never found the horses, they would all die of starvation or thirst — or even worse, be ripped to death by hungry wolves or coyotes before they were dead.

But if the horses wandered off, McCulloch would be in a bigger pickle than the one he was trying to get out of.

I'll be back, boys, he thought as he rubbed the horses' necks. He wrapped the canteens in his bedroll and strapped that over his shoulders like he'd been taught to do in what passed for an army during the late War Between the States.

Infantry. He shook his head. Why in hell had he enlisted in the Texas infantry? He was a horseman. He probably would have been promoted to colonel in the Rebel cavalry.

He shook his head again. The bedroll, of course, would keep the canteens from rattling, and with Apaches all around him, Mc-

Culloch knew he had to make little noise if he wanted to stay alive.

He checked his Colt, the Winchester, and the Navy .36 he had taken off the Apache he had killed. Then, he started to make his way across the broken country toward the stagecoach station.

The drums started a quarter of a mile later, and he smelled smoke.

If the Apaches did not care who smelled their fires or heard their music, then they must be settling in for a siege. That meant people were still inside Culpepper's Station. McCulloch considered heading back to the horses. A man could cover a lot of ground in the night, even if the moon was new.

But there would be water at Culpepper's. And maybe even something stronger to drink.

He moved past cactus and into the rocks, picking his path quickly but practically, moving with little sound. When he could see the station, he sat down. The stagecoach was parked in front, doors open, tongue down, and no sign of any horses. Not hitched to the stage, nor to another, smaller wagon off to the side that, from the words on the side and back door, belonged to some theatrical troupe. No horses in the corral, either, and no smoke coming from the chimney. He looked at the barn, the lean-to, and the other corrals. His eyes locked on the well, and then the cistern.

Behind him, the drums continued to beat, and the voices of Indians carried in the gloaming. The Indians were arguing, but that figured. Comanches might be argumentative, he liked to joke, but Apaches made Comanches look like Quakers.

There was nothing else for McCulloch to do, so he stretched out, kept the Winchester in his arms, and waited and watched. Eventually — though it felt like an even hundred years — the sun disappeared. Darkness dropped the temperatures. There would be no moonrise, so he remained patient. When the blackness seemed complete, and the Indians continued to pound their drums and scream and shout, and McCulloch was as certain as he could be that no hostiles remained in the barn or near the station, he rose and picked a long, arduous, time-consuming path down the rocks to the edge of the barn.

With his eyes accustomed to the dark, he slid past the big barn, more wood than adobe, and moved one step at a time, almost not moving at all till he smelled the stench from the stagecoach.

It was a smell you never forgot. And McCulloch had smelled it too many times in the West Texas country.

The penetrating, lingering odor of death.

He moved around the tongue of the wagon, not even daring to step over it, then felt the nearness of the hitching rail before his thighs brushed against it. He slid past it, and moved like a snail until he was on the porch. With one ear pressed against the rock wall, he listened.

Someone was . . . snoring? McCulloch rolled his eyes. What kind of fool would be sleeping with Apache war drums beating? McCulloch looked behind him. He could even see the glow of the fires in the hills above Culpepper's Station.

The snoring stopped. Footsteps sounded inside, just faintly as the walls were thick. Whoever was snoring inside must have sounded like an approaching tornado.

Five minutes later, McCulloch knew he was at the door.

He brought the rifle out about half a foot, then slammed the butt against the heavy door. Once. Twice. Thrice.

CHAPTER SIXTEEN

Jed Breen trained the Colt Lightning on that big door maybe a fraction of a second before Sean Keegan was cocking the Remington. Or maybe Keegan had won that draw. Breen wasn't exactly sure.

The only light came from the faint glow from the fireplace off in the corner.

"Mother of God!" shouted the man who called himself Harry Henderson as he shot upright from where he had been sleeping and snoring like a platoon of drunken cowboys.

"Shut up!" Keegan barked.

Outside, three more thuds pounded the door.

"Apaches!" cried the coward.

A muffled voice called out from behind the door. "Matt McCulloch. I'm alone. Let me in."

At that moment, a match flared, and Breen and Keegan spun to find Gwen Stanhope starting to light a candle. "Douse that!" both men shouted simultaneously.

To her credit, the woman shook out the match, and both men moved toward the door.

"Wait!" cried out the newspaper editor. "It might be an Apache trick."

"Shut up." Breen holstered his Colt and reached for the bar on his side of the door.

Keegan gripped the other side and called out, "When I say come, get in here. We're not opening the door wide, and don't tarry, because it's shutting quicker than you can pop a cap." He nodded at Breen.

Once they lifted the bar, Keegan took three steps away from the door and yelled, "Now!"

The door opened and almost immediately, it was slamming shut, and the two men were dropping the bar into its holders.

A man dressed like some ordinary cowboy picked himself off the floor. He held a Winchester in his hands, but as soon as he stood, he leaned the carbine against the wall and began removing the bedroll strapped over his left shoulder. When that fell to the floor, he breathed in deeply, exhaled, and pushed back his hat.

"Much obliged." He nodded at Keegan and Breen. "Sergeant. It has been a while."

"Uh-huh," Keegan said. "You'd be a hero in my eyes if you told me a company of Texas Rangers was out there with you."

"You'd be a hero to me if you told me you were just holding down the fort till the Seventh Cavalry came riding down to save our hides."

Keegan's head shook. "Ain't part of Uncle Sam's Army no more. And it was the Eighth Cavalry. Not the Seventh. There ain't much left of the Seventh these days."

"I would have taken a brigade of invalids." McCulloch sighed. "And I'm afraid to inform you that I'm alone. No longer a Ranger."

Keegan spit.

Breen scratched his nose and studied the newcomer. "Did I hear you right, mister? McCulloch. Matt McCulloch. Texas Ranger. Is that what I heard?"

"Got the name right." McCulloch studied Breen with cold eyes. "But like I told Sergeant . . . I mean, Mister Keegan here, I'm no longer packing a *cinco pesos* star."

"Yeah." Breen hooked both thumbs into his gunbelt, the right thumb just inches from his holster. "That's what I thought. Two years ago. Del Rio. You caught up with Joe Morse. Blew his head off with a rifle in the Carolina Saloon."

McCulloch's head nodded as his right hand moved to the Colt holstered on his right hip. He scratched his palm with the heavy hammer.

"Yeah. Kin of yours?"

Breen's head shook. "No. I was looking for him. You beat me to him. Cheated me out of fifteen hundred bucks."

McCulloch laughed, and it was a gentle, true laugh. His right hand did not raise far from the holstered Colt, but his left hand came up and settled on his cheek, just below the left eye. It traced along an old scar for about two inches before it stopped. "I kind of wish you had caught him. He spoiled my handsome features."

Breen had to laugh. Shaking his head, he crossed the station and held out his right hand. "I hope you spent that reward money well, Ranger. Breen. Jed Breen."

They shook briefly, and Breen stepped away, noticing that everyone was awake.

"I guess that makes this a poker hand worth betting on," Sean Keegan said. "Ain't that right, Mister Newspaper Editor? You've drawn three of a kind. Not jacks. But jackals."

Slowly, McCulloch turned around. He saw a man in a black suit clutching two carpetbags as he cowered in the corner, a striking woman, and a man pulling a goatee off his face. McCulloch blinked at that sight, then realized that the beard was fake. The clothes the man wore were . . . well . . . more like the latest fashions being illustrated in Godey's magazine. And last, McCulloch saw the *Purgatory City Herald Leader*'s editor and publisher, Alvin J. Griffin IV, who did not appear any happier to see Matt McCulloch than McCulloch was to see him.

"Hello, McCulloch," the editor managed to say. "Haven't seen you since the meeting."

"Uh-huh." McCulloch turned back to Breen. "Any chance a man could find a shot of rye here? Or coffee?"

"No rye," Breen said. "And I'm not sure I'd call it coffee, but it's strong and it'll fortify you."

"What do you think, Griffin?" Keegan said. "The three men you singled out as blights on your community are all here. Like the Three Musketeers. You'll have a hell of a newspaper story, sir. If we live out tomorrow."

"I write the truth," the editor said, though his voice cracked. "You read it, too. You must. Or have it read to you, Keegan."

Keegan stiffened, and that made Griffin grin. "And you read it, as well, didn't you,

McCulloch?"

Holding the cup that Breen was filling with coffee, the former Ranger smirked. "I wouldn't say I read it, exactly." He turned around and took a sip of the awful brew. "But it does come in handy in the privy."

That made Breen and even Keegan laugh, and the tension that had been filling Culpepper's Station vanished.

Until the drumbeats up in the hills intensified.

"We killed a fair number," Keegan said as he followed McCulloch and Breen to the nearest shuttered window. "Wounded a few. Apaches don't ride in big numbers."

McCulloch sighed. "They've likely got between ten and twenty reinforcements."

Keegan and Breen swore.

"I barely missed their company on the trail here. Killed one."

"And you brought them here!" The little man with the carpetbags had been eavesdropping. "You brought more Apaches here. You let them follow you. My God. Now we'll all be butchered."

"Shut up."

Breen, McCulloch, and Keegan turned to see the woman, who spit, rather unladylike onto the floor, and eyed the man in the black suit with pure disgust.

"He didn't bring those Indians here. He didn't even know we were here. And he's an extra gun, mister, and obviously willing to use it. What have you done? Except hide behind those god-awful grips you've been toting?" She spit again.

The three men smiled.

"Well," Breen said. "Ten or twenty, they're still following old Holy Shirt. Shooting only arrows and the like. They can nock arrows faster than some people can shoot, but they're no match for Winchesters, Colts, and my Sharps."

"They might be." McCulloch set the coffee cup on the main table. He drew in a deep breath, exhaled, and nodded at the shuttered window. "The one I killed, he was bringing up the rear, probably watching their backs."

Drawing the Navy Colt from his waist, he laid it beside the coffee cup. "He had this on him. And he was ready to use it." McCulloch raised his left hand and painfully wiggled his pinky. "Would have gotten off a shot had I not stopped the hammer from falling."

"Damn." Keegan's head shook.

"We might have killed too many Apaches today," Breen said.

"What are you blokes talking about?" said

the man in fancy clothes.

"Oh." Breen shook his head. "I've forgotten my manners. Matt McCulloch, this here is Sir Theodore Cannon, actor extraordinaire. That's his traveling wagon outside, if you could see it in the dark, or if the Apaches haven't dragged it away. Sir Theodore, meet a former lawman and rancher in these parts, Matt McCulloch. You know our illustrious journalist. The woman is Gwen Stanhope."

McCulloch studied her, removed his hat, and said, "Ma'am. A pleasure." But his eyes told the woman that he knew all about her, and that maybe he read the newspapers more than he was willing to let editor Griffin know.

"And this" — Breen nodded at the coward — "is one Harry Henderson. He's quiet most of the time, except when he's snoring, and doesn't talk much unless he's screaming for mercy. We tend to think that he's a carpetbag drummer."

Harry Henderson moved the two grips behind his back.

McCulloch still nodded a greeting and turned toward Breen and Keegan, but his eyes turned to another figure.

"Oh," Keegan said. "That's one of Holy Shirt's boys. We took him prisoner. I'm still not certain why. Anyway, it's one less we have to worry about."

McCulloch frowned. "If he's alive, I'd worry about him."

"We are civilized, McCulloch," Alvin Griffin preached.

"Uh-huh." McCulloch changed the subject. "I didn't get a good look at the Apaches who were riding this way."

They could hear the drumbeats increasing and the faint echoes of singing.

"Could be," Keegan said, "that the leader of the ones who joined Holy Shirt's boys are preaching that the only way to win this here battle is to fight with white man's weapons."

Breen nodded. "And Holy Shirt's preaching that they must follow his vision. Bows and arrows. Nothing tainted by us white folks."

"That's probably the size of it," McCulloch said.

Gwen Stanhope was listening. "So the question is, Who wins the argument?"

McCulloch, Breen, and Keegan nodded.

"I'd say that's about the size of things, ma'am." McCulloch looked around, first at the people in the station, and then at the fireplace. "You've been busy," he said, and finished his cup of coffee.

255

"I like to be prepared." Keegan nodded toward the fireplace and motioned for Mc-Culloch to follow. "What caliber you shooting? .44-40?"

McCulloch nodded. "Both carbine and revolver."

"Makes things handy. I think we've got some casings that'll fit you, if you need to restock your shell belt."

McCulloch nodded. "I've spent some lead myself."

"And we'll be spending a lot more before this merry adventure's over," Keegan said.

Breen was watching the woman as she wandered back to her bedding on the floor. He drew in a breath, let it out, and followed her, calling out her name, and smiling when she stopped.

"Ma'am," he said when he caught up with her. "I didn't mean to snap at you when the Ranger started pounding on the door." He motioned at the shuttered window. "But you light that candle, and if Indians are outside, they might just poke their weapons through the gunports in those shutters and open fire. Arrows, of course. But that light would provide some fine targets."

Gwen nodded. "I figured. I just wasn't thinking."

"It's hard to think," he said.

They looked at each other. Breen found it hard to look away from such a good-looking woman. He ran his hands through his white hair while trying to think of something to say. She opened her mouth and said something, but by that time, something had caught his attention.

Without a word, he walked past her to the shutter. He bent and looked through the opening, a thin rail up and a thin rail across, either a lowercase *t* or a cross, depending on your view of such matters. He saw nothing but darkness, but that wasn't what was bothering him. It's what he heard.

"They've stopped singing," Gwen said from behind him.

"Yes, ma'am. And they're not pounding the drums, either."

"Do you think they're planning on attacking?"

His head shook. "That's not in the nature of Apaches."

"Then . . . what — ?"

They heard the answer before Gwen Stanhope could finish her question.

It was the most terrifying scream anyone at Culpepper's Station had ever heard.

CHAPTER SEVENTEEN

"Mother of Mary," Harry Henderson wailed. "Is that some wild animal?"

Jed Breen felt the bile rising in his throat. He started to answer, but then he remembered Gwen Stanhope right beside him.

"No," Sean Keegan said bluntly. "It's not."

The shriek sounded like complete agony and terror, but not human, more like the screams one would expect to find in the deepest pits of Hell. The newspaper editor walked toward the closest window, drawn by his ingrained curiosity as a journalist — or maybe by some unholy trance.

"Stay away from that window, Griffin," Keegan said.

Griffin stopped, and his face cringed tightly when the scream pierced the black night again.

"My God," Gwen Stanhope said.

Henderson clamped both hands over his ears and squeezed his eyes shut as though that could block out the terrifying, demoralizing yells.

Tied up and stretched out on the floor, the Apache grinned.

McCulloch and Breen walked to meet with Keegan.

"You know what that is?" Breen said. "Don't you?"

Keegan nodded a grim nod.

"*Who* is it?" McCulloch asked.

They spoke in whispers. Breen nodded at the woman: "She came in on the stagecoach with Griffin, Henderson, and some others that didn't make it."

"I smelled them when I snuck past the stage," McCulloch said.

"Yeah," Breen said. "The jehu was dead. He's somewhere along the side of the road, I reckon, or what the Apaches left of him, I imagine. The shotgun took over in the seat and got the coach here. Got brained with a tomahawk when that second band of savages swarmed us. Anyway —"

"Rourke?" McCulloch interrupted, but still kept his voice down. The three men were quite aware that Gwen Stanhope, Sir Theodore Cannon, and Alvin Griffin were staring at them, desperate to hear what they were saying. Henderson, on the other hand, kept his hands over his ears and his eyes clamped shut.

"Yeah," Breen answered. "You know him?"

"He served with the Rangers for two years. Got a better offer from the stagecoach company." McCulloch spit the foul taste out of his mouth. "Thought it was safer, too."

"And would be," Keegan commented, "if the Apaches weren't on the prod."

"Go on," McCulloch told Breen.

"That's about it. Apaches were chasing the stagecoach. They pulled up. I went out to help and we all made it inside. Barely. Rourke came out to cover me when I fetched the handcuff keys from the dead deputy. That's when he got beaned with the tomahawk. I swear, I thought he was dead."

"Nobody's blaming you," Keegan said. "I was out there, too, and I could've dragged him inside."

"If you had tried that," McCulloch said, "chances are the Apaches would have gotten inside. Then you'd all be dead, and I'd be alone. Don't blame yourself. I know Rourke. Rode on many a mission with him. He wouldn't want you to have risked your hides for him." Suddenly, McCulloch grinned and shook his head. "He always said if he lived past thirty it would be a miracle." He nodded. "By my recollection, he'd be thirty-four about now."

The scream echoed, sounding like ten other men being crucified.

Gwen Stanhope sucked in a deep breath and held it for the longest time. The cabin was fairly dark, but the three men could see that the woman was on the verge of tears. The actor, the newspaperman, and Henderson didn't look steady, either. And no one could blame them.

Clearing his throat, Keegan turned around and looked at the Stanhope, Griffin, and Cannon. He didn't care if Henderson could hear him or not. "All right. You've probably figured it out by now. This is the Apache way of fighting." He shrugged. "And, if you think about it, and not think like Christians or regular folks, it's not a bad way to fight. The Apaches, they think that by torturing a man, they take away his power, and that power comes to them. You can call it hogwash or pagan or anything you like, but that don't change the facts. And power or not, they also do it to get under our skin.

"Nah. That ain't exactly right. They do it to crack us up. Drive us crazy. You folks are doing good right now. I've been on patrols with soldiers who couldn't stand it. Seen it break down officers from West Point, even officers and enlisted men who fought in the late war, and those had seen and heard some of the most horrible things that nobody ought to go through. That's about the size of it. Maybe the carpetbagger over yonder's got the right idea. Try to block out that fellow's misery. And when the bucks come at us in the morning, you remember this night. That man out there suffering. And you remember that if they catch you alive, that's what you'll have to endure. It'll make you fight harder. I hope. For all of our sakes."

He stopped and stood, waiting, but he did not have to wait very long.

"What about that poor man out there?" Gwen Stanhope said.

"Ma'am —" Breen stopped. He couldn't think of anything to say.

"Surely, you can't let him suffer."

"That's what the Apaches want, sister," Keegan said. "Draw some of us outside. Then they'd have someone else to torture. One less gun to fight. One more agonizing torment to drive us mad."

"I'm mad," the woman said. "And if you aren't going to do the right thing, then by God I am."

She started for the door, but stopped when Matt McCulloch walked to the Apache and kicked the man's moccasins.

The Indian looked up.

Breen and Keegan walked to McCulloch, standing on either side of him.

"She has a point," McCulloch whispered.

"You know better 'n that," Keegan said. "And remember what Rourke said."

"I remember." He looked Keegan hard in the eye. "And I know something I won't want to remember. And that's that I let a pard, a onetime Ranger, die like that."

"Well, when you get caught, and it's you that they're ramming that heated barrel of your Winchester into holes in your body they've cut or even natural ones, you'll be remembering that it's us that'll pay the price for your bravery when they kill us all tomorrow morning."

"Keegan's right," Breen said. "The Apaches will be expecting one of us to try to put Rourke out of his misery."

"Uh-huh." McCulloch stared down at the glaring Apache. "So I'm thinking that we do something that'll occupy their minds. Drive them mad."

Breen and Keegan looked at the warrior.

"Fight Apaches," Keegan whispered, "like Apaches."

The thought made even a hard man like Jed Breen swallow down the bile crawling up his throat. "Risky," Breen said after a long pause.

"Could get us all killed," Keegan said.

"Nobody lives forever," Gwen Stanhope said.

The men turned. She had come up behind them. Her face, lighted only by the coals of the fire, showed no shame, no soul, perhaps. She seemed to be agreeing with the three men.

"Yeah," Keegan agreed. "And if we don't do something to change the odds, ain't a one of us going to be living after tomorrow."

"Especially," Breen said, "if old Holy Shirt loses his argument and the Apaches arm themselves with repeaters."

The newspaperman had found his courage and come to them, too. So had Sir Theodore Cannon, but he said nothing.

"You can't be serious," Griffin said. "You're white men. You can't fight . . ."

"Oh, but we can," Keegan said, warming to the thought.

"Listen," Griffin continued. "First, he's an Apache. He won't scream if you torture him. He's not human."

"He'll scream," Keegan said. "Because he can't stop himself. I've learned a lot during my time out West. I've learned a lot from Apaches like him."

"We can hold out here," Griffin argued, moving to another front of attack. "When the stage isn't at El Paso tomorrow morning, the manager will alert the authorities. A posse will come. Probably a patrol from Fort Bliss."

"By the time the Army gets here, we'll be dead," Breen said.

"But," Griffin continued, "this place is solid. Impregnable. The Apaches can't get in here. Unless we let them."

"They won't have to get in here," McCulloch said. "If they decide to fight with bullets and powder." He pointed to the shutters. "Those gunports. Good in some ways. We can shoot out. But all a man with a repeater would have to do is stick barrels through there and just cock and pull the trigger, cock and pull the trigger."

Keegan picked up the thought. "Lead will be bouncing around this place like a swarm of bees. Or hornets. We butchered about thirty Apaches once the same way. They were in a cave. We just fired into the cave. I can still hear the whines of those ricochets. And the screams of the Apaches. Women. Kids, too. And a few bucks. It was a bloody mess when we went down to bury them all."

"Four windows," Breen said. "Four rifles. It wouldn't take them long. Be a regular enfilade. Messy way to die."

The newspaperman paled.

"There's the trapdoor," said Breen, looking at the woman. "When it comes to that, you need to get down there. There's just room for you. That'll keep you alive."

Gwen Stanhope shook her head. "No," she said, and managed a smile. "But thanks. I won't meet my Maker and hear him saying I showed yellow."

"Well . . ." the newspaper editor began. "We must . . ."

"If you suggest that you hide in that little cellar, know that that trapdoor will never open to let you out, you lily-livered peckerwood," Keegan told him.

The journalist turned even paler.

Harry Henderson wet his lips but did not attempt to plead his case to hide in what was little more than a cubbyhole dug into the hard rock.

"I shall go," Sir Theodore Cannon said. "Not into that pit of despair. No. I couldn't fit in that thing. Trust me, before Mr. Breen arrived, I tried. Nay, I mean I shall go to do my duty, to put one poor, tortured soul out of his misery. Why, lady and gentlemen, in Baltimore, the *New Republican Enterprise* raved about my death scene in *Julius Caesar*. I shall —"

Keegan cut him off. "I'd like to see you play that part, Sir Theo. In El Paso. And I'm sure Mr. Griffin here will write up the fact that you were the first to volunteer. But we'll need you here, sir. In case this don't turn out the way we hope."

"Rourke's my responsibility," Breen said.

"No," McCulloch said. "I knew him. Rode with him. And he's my friend."

Breen held out his Sharps. "But I have this."

McCulloch held out his hand. "Thanks. You take my Winchester."

The bounty hunter sighed and slowly extended the big rifle to the former Ranger, who exchanged the long rifle with the telescopic sight for his Winchester carbine.

"Apache's mine, then." Keegan reached down and jerked the Indian to his feet, then shoved a balled-up bandanna into the warrior's mouth, and shoved him toward the door. The old Army sergeant moved to the fireplace and stoked the coals until they glowed red. He tossed some kindling onto the coals, and once they ignited, added two pieces of wood.

Motioning toward the windows, he turned and said, "Stay away from here. Apaches aren't ones to fight at night, but they damn well might be charging here directly. They see you through the ports, they'll try to send you to Hell." He grabbed a crowbar, and tossed one end into the fire. "I'll be back for this directly."

Breen removed his hat, and reached inside his jacket, withdrawing a woman's stocking of black lace. "Don't say a word," he warned as he slipped the stocking over his head. "White hair. Dead giveaway."

"Why don't you just dye your hair with bootblack?" Sir Theodore Cannon asked.

"Because ladies like my white hair." Breen rubbed the stocking over his hair. "This one in particular. Said it makes me look distinguished. And Apaches see like nighthawks." He picked up his shotgun in his free hand.

A moment later, they stood at the door. Gwen Stanhope lifted one end of the bar, and the actor did the other. Henderson still sat in the corner, his eyes still closed, and his hands still over his ears.

The newspaper editor blinked. "You can't do this. You simply cannot do this."

No one listened. The door opened just a crack, and McCulloch slipped outside. The door shut. They waited as Keegan silently counted to sixty.

"You can't —"

"Shut up," Gwen Stanhope told Griffin, and the editor obeyed.

The door opened again, and Breen went outside with his shotgun and McCulloch's carbine.

Keegan counted only to thirty.

The door cracked again, and he pushed the Indian through. He glanced at those who would remain inside, saying, "Stay here. Give me five minutes, maybe ten. I'll be back, but just for a jiffy."

And he was gone.

McCulloch made it to the cistern by the corral. Rourke, God bless him, helped him make it that far. Those excruciating screeches bouncing off the walls of the canyons and hills around Culpepper's Station covered any noise he made. The fact that there was no moon helped him, too, but the stars, millions of them, and bright, allowed him to find his way.

The fires in the hills told him where he would find Rourke. But there was an Apache he needed to deal with first. The Indian was on the other side of the cistern, dipping his hand in the water, bringing it up, letting it drip, slaking his thirst. Probably a boy in his teens. Laying the Sharps next to the wall, McCulloch unsheathed his knife. He heard another noise and turned his head, catching the light as the door to the station opened

269

ever so slightly. A shadow appeared, and McCulloch knew Keegan was slipping back inside.

The Apache knew it, too, and stopped drinking water. He moved to McCulloch's right.

Sean Keegan remained silent as he crossed the room, ducked into a crouch when the light from the fireplace reached him, and eased his way to the fire. Finding a heavy canvas pad, he used it as a mitt to grip the end of the crowbar. He examined the glowing end of the iron and nodded his approval.

Thirty seconds later, he was back at the door, nodding at Stanhope and the actor. "Bar the door this time. Two knocks, two seconds, four knocks. That'll be me. Three knocks, four seconds, one knock. That'll be McCulloch. Four knocks, six seconds, that'll be Breen. Any other sequence, keep the damned bar on the door." With his free hand, he tipped his cap at Stanhope and nodded at Sir Theodore Cannon. "If this don't work out, it's been a pleasure knowing you folks — except you, Griffin."

Once the door closed behind Keegan, Stanhope and the thespian slipped the cottonwood bar into its holders.

■ ■ ■ ■

Jed Breen never considered himself a patient man. This just wasn't his kind of fighting, and the black stocking over his head wasn't comfortable as after so many years he could no longer smell the scent of Alice Portis's body, or at least her legs, on that black silk and lace. He would have to get back to Denver sometime. Maybe see if Alice had some new stockings she could give him. This one was starting to run.

He had positioned himself in a clump of creosote bushes, not even four feet high, and Alice Portis's stockings did not diminish the tar-like stink of the creosote. Off to his left grew a spiny ocotillo, its arms waving in the wind like the tentacles of a squid.

Neither the creosote nor the cactus would provide him any cover if the Apaches started shooting. That's why Breen had picked this spot. Apaches wouldn't expect a man to hide there.

They had to know the three men were out there. The light from the fireplace would have revealed the moment Breen, Mc-Culloch, and Keegan had exited the station. Now that Keegan had gone back inside and come out again, Apaches had to be everywhere, searching, smelling, and getting ready for the kill.

Breen could see one over by the cistern, not even bothering to hide. He could also make out the figure of Matt McCulloch, lying on the ground on the other side of the Apache. Breen could kill the Apache easily with McCulloch's carbine. But that would give away his position.

"Will you hurry up?" Breen whispered.

A moment later, as if Sean Keegan had heard Breen, the yell cut through the starry night.

"Aiiiii-yeeeeeeee-iiiiiiiiiiiiiiii!!!!!"

It bounced around the barn and station, louder, more horrifying than the distant yells from Rourke. Breen lifted the Winchester, and when the Apache yelled again, he used the screams to cover the sound as he eared back the hammer. The Apache kept yelling, so Breen cocked both barrels of the shotgun at his side.

Breen had to smile. Sergeant Sean Keegan had learned a lot, after all, during his time on the Apache frontier. What would newspaper editor Alvin Griffin IV be thinking inside the station about now? And would that squirt with the grips still be covering his ears? Breen didn't have to wonder about the Apaches. He could hear them now that the buck's screams, even the echoes, had died.

The Apaches began talking. Breen tried to pinpoint the locations, but the voices came from all over the compound.

It was going to be interesting. If Jed Breen were a betting man, and he was, he'd bet that not a one of them got out of that mess alive.

CHAPTER EIGHTEEN

"Nooooo!!! Yiiiiii-eeeeeeee. *¡Dios mío!* Ohhhhh-yiiii-eeeeeeeee!"

"Got you speaking in tongues, eh?" Sean Keegan hissed into the Apache's ear as he drew the poker and raised it underneath the Indian's nose. "At least Spanish. Ever wondered how it felt? The ones you give this to? Yeah. Yeah. Don't worry, buck. I'll kill you soon. But let's try to see if you can yell in French or Russian or Greek this time?"

He stepped behind the Apache he had secured to the beams across the top of the lean-to and brought the poker, not as hot as it had been, and shoved it.

"Arrrrggggh, yiiiiiii-eeeeeeeeeeeeeeee, ohhhhhhhhh!"

Two of them came bounding out of the barn, raising their tomahawks over their heads, and yipping like mad dogs.

Breen made a quick decision, and laid McCulloch's Winchester on his lap. He picked up the sawed-off Parker twelve-gauge, and waited.

He touched one trigger, and looked away to save his eyes from being blinded by the muzzle flash. The shotgun roared, the stock slammed against his shoulder, and Breen was moving away from the ocotillo and creosote, and diving toward a boulder.

Only then did he look at the two Indians. Both were down, one not moving, the other writhing, and gagging, and trying to sing his death song. Arrows thudded into the clump of creosote where Breen had been moments earlier. One barrel. Two Indians.

The odds, Breen thought, *are improving.*

Once the two Indians dropped from Breen's shotgun blast, the young Apache let out a guttural cry and raced around the cistern. He never saw McCulloch, who jumped up as the young Indian raced by him. McCulloch's right hand grabbed the Apache's hair, and jerked him back. The brave dropped the war club he was holding and kicked at McCulloch's leg, but it only glanced off his shin.

The kid was tough. Brave. And seasoned as a fighter for one not out of his teens. He would have made a good warrior for his people. McCulloch hated to slice the throat, but such was war. He carved deep into the neck, cutting to the bone, preventing the Apache from crying out. Then he shoved the dead or dying brave forward, away from the cistern.

Two flashes leaped out of Keegan's pistol, and Breen's shotgun roared again. McCulloch ducked and found the Sharps. As more Apaches rushed toward the station, he disappeared into the rocks and headed toward the campfires. And toward the screaming of his friend named Rourke.

Inside the station, Gwen Stanhope grabbed an old Henry rifle, jacked the hammer, and moved to the nearest window.

"You heard what they said!" Alvin Griffin yelled at her. "Stay away from the windows. The Apaches will cut you down."

"Not if I kill them first." She slid against the wall, rammed the barrel through, and tried to see anyone moving in the coal-black night.

"You might kill the bounty hunter!" Griffin yelled. "You might shoot the ex-Ranger by mistake."

The rifle roared, and Stanhope worked the lever.

Off in the corner, Harry Henderson removed his hands from his ears, clasped them together, lifted them to the rafters. "Everlasting Father, for the sake of the love which Thou didst bear to St. Joseph, whom Thou didst choose above all to occupy Thy place on earth, Have mercy on us and on those who are dying . . ."

Gwen Stanhope said, "Our Father, Hail Mary, Glory be to the Father." She fired again.

Henderson continued. "Everlasting Son of God, for the sake of Thy love toward St. Joseph, who didst protect Thee so faithfully on earth, have mercy on us all and on those who are dying . . ."

Whispered the blonde, "Our Father, Hail Mary, Glory be to the Father . . ." And the Henry .44 spoke again.

While Henderson kept praying, Theodore Cannon moved to another window, sticking a Dragoon Colt, converted to take modern cartridges, through the cross-shaped slits, and pulled the trigger.

"You're all a bunch of damned fools!" Griffin yelled, barely able to hear his own voice as the guns roared inside and outside. "You'll all be killed." To his surprise, he saw that sniveling coward Harry Henderson rise, cross himself, and leave his carpetbags on the floor.

He found Keegan's carbine, the Springfield trapdoor, and rushed it over to the actor. "I can reload. I can't shoot. But I can reload."

"An actor is nothing without his stage manager!" Cannon cried, and handed the empty, smoking Dragoon to the little coward. He took the big cavalry long gun and pushed its barrel through the opening.

"Fools!" Griffin told them.

They answered with gunfire, then Sir Theodore started in.

"These famish'd beggars, weary of their
    lives;
Who, but for dreaming on this fond exploit,
For want of means, poor rats, had hanged
    themselves:
If we ben conquer'd, let men conquer us,
And not these Bretons; whom our fathers
Have in their own land beaten, bobb'd, and
    thump'd,
And in record, left them the heirs of shame.
Shall these enjoy our lands? Lie with our
    wives?
Ravish our daughters?"

He pulled out the smoking carbine and handed it to Henderson, who lifted the heavy .44 in a trembling hand.

Alvin Griffin could not believe what was happening. Madness. Everyone in the station had turned insane, except for himself. It was the screaming of the Apache that had caused it. He had to blame the jackals. And then he saw the two carpetbags on the floor, one lying on its side. That innate curiosity of a newspaperman grabbed hold of him. The woman and the two men kept up their barrage, so Griffin eased his way to the ugly grips. He wet his lips, knelt beside the nearest bag, and started to open it.

Keegan held the poker in his left hand and the Remington in his right. He thumbed back the hammer and waited. McCulloch was gone. He felt certain of that. He couldn't find Breen's location, not since he had emptied the shotgun a few moments earlier.

Apaches yipped across the yard, and guns roared from inside the station.

He nodded his approval. When he recognized the report of his Springfield carbine, and saw an Apache grab his leg and roll in the dirt, he figured he had underestimated the fight and spirit in some of those people. Another Apache grabbed the wounded one and dragged him out of sight. Keegan was aiming his pistol at the hero, but did not touch the trigger. That would have been a difficult shot. Even for a man like Sean Keegan.

He heard the noise behind him and dropped to a knee as he spun. He felt the lance sail over his head and saw the outlines of two warriors. The one on Keegan's left had thrown the spear and was jerking a long-bladed knife from a fringed sheath. The one to Keegan's right was about to cut loose with an arrow.

He couldn't kill them both, but he could send one to hell with him.

Keegan squeezed the trigger, and the arrow sliced between his legs as the Indian fell backward. Turning toward the Apache with the knife, Keegan cocked the Remington, but before he could touch the trigger again, the Indian was being catapulted into a yucca. Keegan had felt the blast of the bullet against his ear.

He spun back, and saw what had to be Jed Breen jacking another load into Mc-Culloch's Winchester.

Though he doubted if Breen had seen him, Keegan nodded his thanks then went back to the Apache, now unconscious with his head hanging down. Keegan sighed. Apaches had ways of keeping a man they were torturing awake. That's why Rourke remained alive, unfortunately, and was still screaming — although the explosion of bullets was drowning out that sound of agony. Keegan knew he had a lot to learn before he became that adept. And now that he had a taste of it, he figured he didn't want to learn any more.

He looked at the Apache. "I want you to know," he said, though the Apache probably heard nothing, and even if he did, it would be unlikely that he understood English. "That I hold you in the highest regard, warrior to warrior, man to man. I respect you. I respect your valor. I respect your people, though we are enemies. Maybe in the next world, we can smoke a pipe and learn from each other. Until that day comes, adios."

He shoved the barrel of the Remington under the Indian's chin and pulled the trigger.

McCulloch was pretty high in the hills now, and he could see the flames from the Apache camp. Figures moved in easy sight. If he had to guess, he was about four hundred yards from where Rourke was being tortured. That had to be where most of the warriors and a few squaws were gathered. Maybe Rourke was dead.

Anyway, McCulloch knew he couldn't get any closer. The top of the ridge was flat, hard, and devoid of any place where a man could take cover. He figured he was maybe a quarter of a mile from the station — but that was as the crow flies. It would take about a half-mile of traveling, and probably a little bit more, for a man to get back to the shelter of the station.

He heard just the wind and the muffled voices of the Apaches. He thought about finding the Indians' pony herd. He could drive off the horses, but that wouldn't work. It certainly would not help matters. The Sioux, the Cheyenne, the Comanch', and the Kiowa, those Indians depended on horses. Get rid of their ponies, and you had practically won the battle. But Apaches? They were foot soldiers. They used horses, but they sure didn't need them.

Movement caught his eye. He remained still as he studied the camp. Some bucks who had been down below had returned to camp, and were gesturing wildly, pointing, shouting in Apache — one even stamped his feet. McCulloch nodded. Keegan and Breen, and — from the gunfire he had heard — others inside the station had all done their job. Done it well.

They had helped get McCulloch that far.

Now he had to do his job.

He swallowed in disgust. The Apaches had grabbed a pole, and something dangled from that pole as they carried it to what appeared to be a mound of . . . something. It was too far, too dark, for him to see exactly what was up there.

The pole's bottom edge was rammed into the ground, then tilted upward, and secured.

"Damn," McCulloch whispered, because now he knew what the Apaches were planning. "They're going to burn Rourke alive."

The din of battle had stopped. An eerie silence fell over Culpepper's Station. Even Rourke's yells from the hills had been stilled — for the time being.

His back against the well, Breen reloaded the Winchester and his Parker. The night was cool, as nights tended to be in that country, and it chilled Breen because he had been sweating so much. He watched the figure take a roundabout way before Keegan sank to the ground on Breen's left. The old Army sergeant pushed the empty casings out of his revolver, picked up the brass, and thumbed those into his shirt pocket.

"He should be there by now," Breen said.

"If he's alive," Keegan agreed.

"I guess Holy Shirt's still in charge."

"Good thing." Keegan wiped his brow. Breen wasn't the only man who had been sweating. "But his power's gotta be slipping after the hurt we put on those boys tonight."

"The Apache?" Breen asked.

Keegan knew what he meant. "I shot him. Couldn't stomach what I was doing no more."

"You're not the demon Griffin pegged you as."

Keegan smiled. "Oh, I am. But even a jackal's got his limitations."

"Should we go inside?" Breen asked.

"Best wait. If we don't hear a shot in the next half hour, and that stagecoach guard starts yelling again, we'll have to finish the job McCulloch started out to do."

"That's what I figured you'd say," Breen said, "you righteous trash."

"Don't give me that, bounty hunter. You was thinking the same damned thing."

"Is it over?" Harry Henderson asked in a plaintive voice.

"I don't know," Gwen Stanhope said. "I think someone's over by the well."

"It's Breen," Sir Theodore Cannon said. "Actors," he added, "have to be able to see in the dark. Wait." He took the Springfield out of Henderson's hands and began to shove it through the slit in the wood and iron shutter. The hammer cocked ominously, but a moment later the thespian softly lowered the hammer, and pulled the cavalry carbine out of the gunport. "No, that's the old sergeant."

"They're not coming in," Gwen Stanhope said.

"Waiting on the Ranger," Cannon said.

"Well . . ." Henderson said, "what do we do?"

Alvin Griffin IV saw his chance. "You keep an eye out. I'll be at the door. I'll let them in. You just keep a sharp eye outside. There are plenty of Apaches still alive. You can warn the soldier and the bounty killer if you see them. I'll be here at the door. Ready to open it. Henderson!"

The drummer, or whatever he was, looked up. Griffin pointed at the middle window. "Take that one. Three pairs of eyes are better than two."

His bout with bravery must have taken root, for the man in the black suit rose and stumbled toward the other shutter. Griffin couldn't believe his luck. The coward had found his backbone, but so had Alvin J. Griffin IV. He picked up one of the carpetbags and moved in the shadows to the door. Newspapering could be prosperous, but a carpetbag full of currency seemed much more inviting. He would sneak out in the darkness, Apaches be damned. He would take some of the canteens. He knew a good place to hide and a Mexican family about five miles south. Apaches did not like to attack in the dark, and sure wouldn't be inclined after the beating they — Griffin decided that he had done his part — had given them this night. He doubted if the three vermin would go looking for him.

Money — especially that much money — was worth the risk. Besides, he was only taking one bag. Once the bounty hunter and those other scum realized how much money Griffin had left behind, they'd be fighting amongst themselves for it.

By that time, either the Apaches would have killed them all or they would have killed themselves. And if they happened to survive, Griffin would already be across the border in Mexico. Maybe he could start up a newspaper in San Blas.

A .50-caliber Sharps rifle took getting used to. By the time Matt McCulloch had joined the Texas Rangers, the company had forgone those single-shot rifles and opted for repeating rifles. The previous captains had seemed to prefer single shots, saying that a Sharps put a man down with one bullet, but likely figuring that Rangers would waste lead if they had repeaters. By now, the Texas government knew that Texas Rangers weren't ones to shoot recklessly. They shot to kill, and made every shot count.

The fire was going.

McCulloch raised the rifle and leaned closer toward the telescopic sight. He heard Rourke screaming again and begged his friend for forgiveness. "I had to wait for the flames, pard. I couldn't see you without that fire." In his friend's face he saw the pain, the wildness of the eyes, desperate and pleading for mercy.

And Matt McCulloch granted Rourke, that brave, brave soul, the mercy he so deserved.

CHAPTER NINETEEN

The Sharps sounded like a cannon, and Rourke's screams stopped instantly, replaced by the whoops and curses of the Apaches.

By that time, Matt McCulloch was already racing down the hillside. After all those years on horseback, riding to catch mustangs, riding wild mustangs till they were broken, riding, riding, and riding, McCulloch's legs had bowed something considerable. Running was not his strong suit. Apache moccasins might be better than high-heeled cowboy boots, yet they did not make running easier. The soles of boots were thicker and reinforced much more than the moccasins, which let him know every time he stepped on a sharp rock or cactus. But he ran. He had to run. Or he'd die.

An arrow sparked as the obsidian point glanced off a boulder. McCulloch bowled through creosote, hurdled a yucca, and almost tripped over a loose rock. Behind him, the Apaches ran, angry and ready to kill.

He ducked underneath a mesquite, but not low enough. The thorns tore through his vest and shirt and carved into his shoulder blades.

Out, he leaped over a narrow arroyo, rounded a rock, and saw a young Apache standing a few feet before him. The Apache seemed just as surprised as McCulloch, and, being only in his teens, was slow to react. McCulloch rammed the barrel of Jed Breen's Sharps into the brave's bare stomach. The boy groaned and staggered to his left, falling to his knees and gagging as he clutched his bruised belly. McCulloch almost dropped the rifle, but somehow secured it, and dodged in and out of a few ocotillo cacti.

His lungs burned. His right hand gripped the heavy rifle. His left hand clutched his side. His chest seared with pain, and his heart felt as though it might burst.

He reached the hill, gritted his teeth, and churned his legs as he climbed the hard rock, leaping to a stone, slowing down only when he had to climb. The rifle slipped from his grip, and McCulloch cursed, fighting for breath, and let himself slide down the slick but hard rock. He had gripped the rifle and started to pick it up when another Apache appeared. The brave growled, and McCulloch buried the heel of his left foot into the man's nose. The warrior cried out, let go of his hold, and fell backward, crashing into at least two of his comrades.

McCulloch scrambled to his hands and knees, somehow managed to push himself to his feet, and made himself climb again. He had not realized just how close his enemies were behind him.

When he reached the peak, he saw the light shining like a beacon through the slits in the shutters of the station.

He just might make it.

"I don't think he made it," Keegan said.

Breen spit in the dark. "Yeah. Hell."

"I'll go," both men said at the same time.

"I'm going," Breen said.

"Why you?" Keegan asked.

"Because I spent a hell of a lot of money on that Sharps. I ain't about to let some Apache take it."

They ran back to the cabin, stopping on the porch.

Keegan drew his revolver and started to pound on the door, but stopped. He let loose with a string of blasphemy.

"What's the matter?" Breen asked.

The old soldier chuckled. "You won't believe this. But I can't remember what sequence I told that ink-slinger I'd use to get inside."

"Are you kidding me?"

"No."

"Just bang on the damned door."

Then they heard the shot. It echoed in the darkness, and both men stared at the yellow glow of distant fires in the hills.

"That's my Sharps," Breen said.

"I'll be a suck-egg mule," Keegan said, and let loose with a regular belly laugh. "That sorry turd of a Texas Ranger. He made it."

"He got a shot off, at least," Breen said, and slapped Keegan's shoulder. "And my Sharps don't miss."

The door started to open. Both men turned. A figure slipped out of the shadow, and Keegan banged into him. The man cried out, something hit the floor, and then the man followed. Keegan glanced back at Breen.

He nodded and waved McCulloch's Winchester. "I'll cover McCulloch. And don't wait for any damned password or such tomfoolery. When we're banging on that door, let us in damn quick."

The bounty hunter scurried toward Sir Theodore Cannon's wagon while Keegan went inside and pulled the door shut.

"What the hell were you doing?" Sean Keegan looked at Alvin J. Griffin IV sitting on his hindquarters and rubbing his elbow.

The actor, the blond woman, and the little pipsqueak were standing by the front shutters, each one armed. Keegan had to blink and look closer. Yeah, that was Harry Henderson, lover of carpetbags, standing by the middle window.

The newspaperman came up, swallowed, and said, "I was letting you in. Where are the others?"

Keegan was about to answer, when a pistol shot popped outside. It came from the hills. Keegan swore. A rifle shot followed. Then another.

"They're shooting," Sir Theodore Cannon said.

"Hell." Keegan kicked one of the carpetbags and watched it slide past Alvin Griffin and hit the leg of the table.

The Apaches were using firearms. Holy Shirt had lost his hold on at least some of his people.

"Get those guns out," Keegan commanded. "Be ready. With a little luck, Mc-Culloch will be coming hell-bent for leather for us. And a whole lot of Apaches will be right behind him."

When Keegan turned back to the door, he saw the newspaperman at the door. "Don't bar the door, damn it."

Griffin whirled around.

"Stay there. No. Get to that other shutter. The corner one. If any buck shows his shiny hair, part it." Keegan drew the Remington and tossed it. "You've got six. Make them all count."

He moved to the table, realized that it was two tables shoved together, and that the tops were thick wood. He wet his lips, snatched the Navy Colt off the top, and went back to the door He opened it and yelled again, "Don't bar the door!"

As soon as he was on the porch, he dropped down and pulled the thick door shut behind him.

At first, Jed Breen thought the streak below the stars was a shooting star. And another. And another. But meteorites did not last that long, and as the light began to descend, he cursed.

Those were arrows. Flaming arrows. One thudded on the roof behind him. Another struck the ground.

He heard the popping of guns, and realized what that meant. Some of the Apaches were shooting bullets, ignoring Holy Shirt's message.

Another arrow bounced off the roof.

Then two hit the top of the lean-to. Another struck the barn. One whipped into the side of the Concord stagecoach.

The roof of the lean-to was already burning, and smoke smoldered inside the barn.

"They're lighting us up!" Keegan called from the porch of the station.

"So they'll be able to see McCulloch when he hits the yard!" Breen fired back.

Two more arrows glowed. Another went through the window of the stagecoach. The third bounded in the dirt.

About that time, McCulloch rounded the side of the barn and somehow managed to bound over the corral fence and cover its distance in a matter of seconds. Diving between the lowest and middle rails, he hit the ground, rolled over several times, and scrambled to his feet.

Three, no, four, Apaches appeared a moment later.

And Breen was standing, firing the Winchester from his hip, moving away from Cannon's touring wagon to the front of the stagecoach, feeling the intense heat from the fire raging inside the old vehicle.

He worked the lever and trigger practically at the same time.

"That damned door better be open, Keegan!" he yelled and watched the Apaches scatter.

A bullet blasted the door of the stagecoach, sending sparks into the air like fireworks on the Fourth of July.

Matt McCulloch ran past as Breen pulled the trigger and heard the loud snap of the hammer fall on the empty chamber. A bullet punched a hole through the crown of his hat, knocking it to the ground. He whipped off the stocking and tossed it to the ground.

He'd be good and damned if he met his Maker wearing a woman's stocking over his face and fine white hair. He ducked underneath the hitching rail, and saw the open door. McCulloch was already inside. Keegan was holding it open and firing some toy pistol. The muzzle flashes practically blinded Breen, but he moved toward the opening as a bullet plucked his collar. Keegan leaped inside, and Breen followed him, diving onto the floor, and sprang up to help Keegan bar the door.

He didn't have to.

Summoning the strength of Hercules, the veteran sergeant managed to do it himself.

CHAPTER TWENTY

"You said Apaches don't attack at night!" Alvin J. Griffin IV yelled.

"I said they don't like it!" Keegan yelled back, and pointed at the shutter the editor had turned away from. "Shoot, damn it. Show them why they don't like fighting at night!"

He was too late.

A rifle barrel rammed through the cross carved into the wooden shutter, and sixteen inches of smoke and flame shot out of the barrel. That bullet thudded into the wooden mantel over the fireplace. As Gwen Stanhope withdrew her weapon to reload, a rifle barrel slipped into that opening, and the gun roared. That bullet ricocheted off the stone wall — Keegan just glimpsed the spark — and heard the deadly pinging as it whined three times more before the chunk of lead either disintegrated into several slivers or landed in something wooden.

The woman reached up, grabbed the barrel, and shoved it forward as the Indian pulled the trigger again. Stanhope screamed as the heat of the rifle barrel burned her hands. Sir Theodore Cannon turned away from his shutter and rushed to help her as the rifle went up and down, with the Indian and the murderess fighting for control. Another barrel, this one from a pistol, came through the arms of the cross, and spoke.

Jed Breen rushed forward, stuck his Lightning between Stanhope and the pistol, grabbed the barrel of the Apache's gun, and pulled the trigger of the double-action .38 six times, emptying the revolver. The pistol fell out of sight. Stanhope dropped to the floor as the rifle barrel fell, too.

Then Sir Theodore Cannon screamed, clutching his head, and fell to the floor, where he rolled over, back and forth.

"McCulloch!" Keegan shouted. He wasn't sure the former Texas Ranger could hear over the din of gunshots echoing and the whining of ricochets off the walls, but the Ranger looked up. He was kneeling over the actor.

Keegan was already at the nearest table.

"Help me get these things turned onto their sides!" Keegan shouted, and McCulloch abandoned the actor and rushed to the tables butted together.

A ricocheting bullet punched off Keegan's hat and burned the top of his head. He gripped the table's thick, wooden side, saw McCulloch doing the same, and they managed to get the table onto its side, then moved to the next one, and pushed it over, as well.

"Take cover!" McCulloch and Keegan shouted together. "Get behind these tables."

McCulloch rushed back, helped the actor to his feet, and they lunged forward. Breen was guiding Stanhope forward. The newspaper editor and the man with the carpetbags stumbled in the darkness.

Seeing the small barrel on the floor beside the glowing fireplace, Keegan dived toward it. He picked it up, thinking it was the gunpowder they'd been using to reload their cartridges, and cursing the imbecile that had left the deadly powder that close to an open fire.

The bullets fired from the windows sparked on the walls, like fireflies on a summer night.

A bullet scratched his calf right above his boot, before Keegan managed to slide behind the heavy wooden tabletop.

The newspaperman dived over Henderson and rolled as close to the table as he could. Breen shoved the woman over the table, turned and grabbed the man in the black suit, and dragged him behind the cover.

Matt McCulloch was the last to take cover, bleeding from a scratch on his neck. He held a small barrel, too, and as he leaned next to one of the tables' legs, he nodded at Keegan.

"Nails?" McCulloch asked as the gunfire and pinging of ricochets ceased for a moment as the Apaches reloaded.

Keegan glanced at the small barrel he had risked his neck to get away from the fireplace — or a stray bullet. Nails. Eightpenny most likely. "What the hell?" he snapped.

"Oh," Harry Henderson said. "We thought we could melt them down. Use them for bullets."

"They didn't melt," said the actor as Breen moved to him and wrapped his head with a bandanna.

The gunfire and the ricochets resumed. The men and the women cringed, hearing the bullets whip over their heads and bounce off the floor and the walls, and jumped as a bullet or parts of a bullet struck the tops of the table.

Again, a silence returned.

The smell of gun smoke mingled with the

scent of the burning barn, lean-to, and stagecoach outside.

McCulloch drew in a deep breath, exhaled, and shook his head. "It's just a matter of time."

Keegan nodded. The tops of the heavy tables covered two sides. A potbellied stove gave a little protection on one of the openings, but they had no way to keep a ricochet from hitting them from the open side facing the main door or the opposite wall.

"When anyone's killed," McCulloch said, "whoever's closest, pull the dead body over you. That might keep you alive."

"Ladies first?" Breen asked.

"No," Keegan said. "Closest. There ain't no chivalry here. Besides, she's going to hang in a few days anyway."

"M-m-maybe," Harry Henderson stuttered, "th-th-they're out" — he swallowed — "of . . . of . . . of . . . b-b-b-bullets."

They weren't. The hellish gunfire continued.

The actor screamed in pain. "Those swine!" he said, gasping for breath. "They shot off my big toe."

Pings and sparks came from everywhere. A piece of the table leg lodged in Keegan's cheek.

When the noise died, the actor yelled

again, "Stop pulling on me, Griffin! Confound you, I'm not dead. And few would call a bullet to a toe a mortal wound!"

Breen slid away from the woman to the center of the makeshift fortress. "Give me that gunpowder."

"Are you reloading?" Harry Henderson cried out.

Breen did not answer, but took the small keg McCulloch slid across the floor.

"And those nails." The bounty hunter motioned at Keegan, who looked at the small keg he had set to his side and pushed it toward Breen.

The gunfire resumed. Everyone except the bounty hunter huddled closer to the floor. Breen lifted the small container of nails and dumped them into the five-pound gunpowder keg. He set the nail keg down at his waist, and a ricochet slammed into it, spinning the keg around. Breen did not even notice what had happened, or how close he had come to catching a ricochet in his hip, leg, or side. He focused on pounding the top onto the container of gunpowder.

"A bomb?" McCulloch asked.

Breen shrugged.

The gunfire stopped again.

"Wagon's out front," Keegan said.

"Let's hope it's still burning." Breen came

to his knees, knocking over the empty nail container, and rose to his feet.

Keegan and McCulloch stood up, too.

"Stay low, folks," McCulloch said, and the three ran to the barred door.

Keegan took one end of the bar and Mc-Culloch the other, while Breen braced himself against the rocky wall near the door.

Then, the muzzle flashes lit up the deadly station, the roar of gunfire turned deafening, and sparks explode once more to the accompaniment of pings and screams of those behind the table.

"Go!" Keegan barked as he staggered and held the bar across his body.

McCulloch left the Army man holding the heavy piece of wood, and took hold of the handle of the door. A bullet slammed into the wood inches from his face. The former Ranger did not even flinch.

"Ready?" he asked Breen, who held the barrel of powder and nails in both hands.

"Go!" Breen barked, and jumped slightly as a piece of a bullet carved the inside of his left leg.

The door opened, and the flames in the night almost blinded the bounty hunter as he stepped outside. McCulloch leveled his gun, ready to fire at any Apache guarding the door. To his surprise, all the Indians

303

were at the shutters. He stepped through the opening and saw an Apache ramming a ball down an old Enfield rifle. He fired. The Indian crumpled, and others turned. A muzzle flashed, but by then McCulloch was stepping back to the open door.

Breen got as close as he could to the old Concord completely engulfed in flames. He heaved the keg, saw it swallowed by the inferno, and heard it crash inside what had once been the coach. He also recognized the smell of the burning flesh of the corpses the Indians had left inside. It smelled like a beefsteak roasting on an open fire.

McCulloch got through the door first, Breen a second behind. Indians whooped as they rushed from all but the corner window where a repeating rifle sent bullets bouncing off the wall. One thudded into the heavy brace Keegan held, and it drove him against the door. That helped push the door shut. But the Indians were ramming it.

"Get it on!" McCulloch yelled as a bullet from the rifle in the far window cut across his side.

"Can't," Keegan yelled and dropped the heavy wood on the floor.

Turning toward the gunfire coming from the window, McCulloch fired one shot, knowing his chances of putting a bullet through the cross were nonexistent. As the Indians tried to push the door open, he joined Breen and Keegan and leaned against the door.

The rifle opened up again from the shutter.

A second later, the explosion rang in their ears. The concussion almost drove them away from the door.

Screams followed. The Indian stopped firing from the shutter. Resistance ceased and the door slammed shut. Keegan and McCulloch quickly picked up the heavy wood, got it in its holders, and dived to the floor, expecting the gunfire and the deadly whining of ricochets would resume.

But all they heard from the outside was the agonized shrieks of Apaches who had been riddled by eight-penny nails — an obscene form of grapeshot.

Keegan sat, legs stretched out, both hands clutching his stomach.

"You hit?" McCulloch asked, noticing the grim look on the old sergeant's face.

"Yeah." Keegan turned and grinned. His right hand came up, and he held a flattened bullet between his forefinger and thumb.

"Hell's fires!" Breen yelled.

Keegan let out a little chuckle. "Bullet went right through that bar, popped me right in my navel." He shook his head. "Hurts like a son of a gun."

"Would've hurt a lot worse had that chunk of wood not stopped it."

Keegan nodded.

Outside, the Apaches began yelling at one another, mixing with the moans and intense screams of the wounded and the dying.

"We ought to get behind those tables," McCulloch said, but he made no effort to move.

"Yeah," Breen said. "We should."

"You boys go ahead," Keegan said. "I'll be there directly."

No one moved.

Behind the tabletops, Sir Theodore Cannon moaned about his shot-off toe, the woman reloaded the weapons around her, and the newspaper editor prayed.

"We need to move," McCulloch said. "They'll open up on us directly."

Breen nodded. "Be madder than hell after what I just gave them."

"Yeah," Keegan said. "Good thing I fetched that keg of nails."

"Good thing," McCulloch said. "You coming?"

Keegan nodded. "In a jiffy. Don't wait for me."

"Me, either," Breen said. "Soon as I can

get my legs to work, I'll be over yonder." He nodded at the table.

"Yeah. I'll see y'all then." But Matt Mc-Culloch did not move, either. They sat there, backs against the door, legs stretched out before them, breathing in and out, and looking at the shutters.

They were still sitting there when rays of sunlight began peeking through the crosses on the shutters.

CHAPTER TWENTY-ONE

I've been brave, Harry Henderson thought. *That newspaper editor, Griffin, he'll write all about what I did here in the Purgatory City newspaper. I bet newspapers back east, and in California, maybe even in London and Dublin and Paris and Berlin, they'll write about me, too. I wasn't a coward. Not tonight.*

He frowned, then, thinking of those children of his. They wouldn't care, one way or the other. Prudence, his wife in Sierra Vista, she wouldn't care, either. She was such a hard woman. And that girl he had married in Dallas — *what was her name?* — well, that didn't matter. Nor did the woman in Fort Worth.

He wanted to reach over and find his carpetbags, pull them closer, but he could not take both hands from his belly.

For most of the night, he had prayed, but he no longer called to the Lord for help or for saving his life. It did not matter. What mattered . . . the only thing that mattered . . . was Catherine Cooper of El Paso, Texas. Catherine was his latest love. She was pregnant with his son . . . it had to be a son. That son would love him, even if the poor boy would never really know his father.

Harry Henderson smiled and felt blood run over his lips and onto the cold floor.

He needed to make things right with Catherine Cooper. That's all that mattered. God would see that, deep down, Harry Henderson was a good man. God would forget those little dalliances. Fort Worth and Dallas, those women weren't good women. Prudence over in Sierra Vista, she was more like the Devil's right-hand man. No, it was Catherine Cooper that Harry Henderson decided was his true love. Maybe because he had not married her yet. She was clean. Now, maybe if he had made it to Mexico and had met some pretty señorita, things might have changed, but that wasn't going to happen.

His stomach began burning. He spit out more blood.

Morning was breaking. *Morning. Sweet morning,* he thought. Maybe it was a Sunday morning. He had lost track of the days. It was good to die in the morning, especially around dawn. To die at night was kind of frightening. But now, he could see, a new day was coming, and God was welcoming him, brave man that he was, into his kingdom along with the rising of the wonderful, glorious West Texas sun.

He mouthed *Catherine* as he heard Gwen Stanhope behind him. She knew he was brave, too.

"Mister Henderson."

She sounded just like Catherine.

She touched his shoulder. "Are you all right, sir?"

She had the gentleness of an angel. Just like Catherine.

Henderson could not resist her pull as she tugged on his shoulder, and he rolled away from the tabletop and onto his back.

"Oh . . ."

He heard Catherine Cooper say it, then thought *No, no, this was the woman named Gwen Stanhope.*

She covered her mouth, lifted her head, and turned toward the door. "He's been shot!" she yelled, and tore off part of her sleeve, and pressed it to Harry Henderson's stomach.

But he turned toward her and said, "Don't bother, ma'am." *That was a brave thing to say.*

Behind her, he saw the actor — a good

actor, a fine man, but not as heroic as Harry Henderson — who was busy wrapping bandannas and napkins over his bloody foot. The newspaperman was standing, suddenly grinning, but that vanished and he made himself seem sad, or strong, or something.

Slowly, he backed away as the three jackals he had written about stood over Henderson.

The man who called himself Matt McCulloch was the first to kneel. McCulloch had been a Texas Ranger. Henderson had heard of him, and at first, had feared that the Ranger was coming to arrest him. Henderson might have hanged for the bank robbery in Sierra Vista, for the murder of Mr. Cox, the president, but now that Henderson knew McCulloch no longer worked for the Rangers, he no longer worried. Besides, Matt McCulloch knew that Harry Henderson was a brave man. And did not even know, most likely, that the bank in Sierra Vista had been robbed.

The Ranger, the *former* Ranger, pulled Henderson's hands from his belly. "Hell," he whispered.

He should not be cursing, Harry Henderson thought, but he decided to forgive Matt McCulloch for using profanity in front of a dying, heroic man. God would forgive Matt McCulloch, too.

The bounty hunter came to the other side of Harry Henderson. Jed Breen had frightened him, too, because bounty hunters sometimes did not like to see men hang. Bringing a man in alive could be burdensome, and a whole lot of trouble, but Henderson realized that it was much, much too early for the board of directors of the Bank of Sierra Vista to have put up a bounty on him. They might, somehow, not have even realized that he had helped the Hawkin Gang pull off that robbery. Maybe they thought the outlaws had taken him hostage.

That would make me even more heroic. Sort of.

The bounty hunter was poking a hole through the tabletop.

"Knothole. What are the odds?" Breen's head shook, and he turned around and stared down at Harry Henderson. Those eyes had been hard, but they softened.

Harry Henderson knew Jed Breen — a brave man even if his occupation verged on, well, criminal — respected Harry Henderson, who was dying a hero's death.

"Are you kidding me?" The old sergeant Sean Keegan dropped to a knee and looked over Henderson's body to the hole in the table. He shook his head and looked into the former bank teller's eyes.

Henderson managed to smile. He wanted to say to Sergeant Keegan that everything was all right. But blood kept rising in his throat, spilling over his lips, and he couldn't say anything at the moment.

"Should I get him some water?" the woman asked.

Gwen Stanhope, thought Henderson.

"Not gut-shot," Matt McCulloch said.

Henderson shivered and turned his head. He tried to see the knothole, but gave up and looked again at the men around him.

So, the bullet that hit him in the stomach had not punched through the top of the rough table. It had gone through a natural hole in the wood.

Yes, Mr. Breen, what were the odds? Henderson tried to shake his head.

"You did fine," the old Army man said, giving Henderson a nod of approval. "Last night, you were brave. Your family will be proud."

Harry Henderson shuddered. His legs were cold. He no longer felt his feet. He swallowed blood, coughed, and tried to talk.

"Easy . . ." Matt McCulloch rested his hand on Henderson's shoulder. "Don't talk."

"Got . . . to . . ." Harry Henderson managed.

The former Ranger looked at the bounty hunter, then at the woman and the Army veteran, and moved over, slowly lifting Harry Henderson's head.

That somehow eased the burning in Henderson's belly. He drew in a deep breath and let it out. The rattle of death frightened him, but then he remembered that he was a hero. And when he looked into the eyes of Gwen Stanhope, he saw Catherine Cooper in the house where she lived in El Paso and worked as a dressmaker, alone, unwed, pregnant with his child. He had to make things right for the only woman he ever loved — well the only woman he had loved since Prudence, before she turned into a wretched old hag . . . and before Candace — that was the name of that slender beauty in Dallas, before she turned into a fat sow . . . and, of course, Elizabeth of Fort Worth, but she was lucky that he had married her because how many whores actually ever became honest women. And once Elizabeth had stopped charging . . . well . . . none of that mattered anymore. All that mattered was Catherine Cooper. Maybe she'd name her son Harry. Yeah, that's what would happen.

"Water?" he managed.

McCulloch frowned.

"Give him some," the bounty hunter said. "It's not going to matter."

McCulloch nodded, and the woman rose and headed to the bucket.

"We might need that water," the newspaper editor said. "I would not waste it on a dead —"

"Shut the bloody hell up," Sir Theodore Cannon told Alvin Griffin.

The dying man heard it and thought, *A fine actor and wounded hero, too, though not as brave as Harry Henderson.*

"Who are you to call anyone a jackal, sir, when you deny this poor, brave man a drink of water before his untimely demise?"

Harry Henderson wanted to smile at the great thespian, but the woman was back with a ladle that dripped water.

The former Ranger lifted Harry Henderson's head, and the woman knelt beside him and poured sweet, wonderful water down his parched throat until he coughed, and shivered, and gagged, and almost died.

"My wife . . ." Harry Henderson never knew that speaking could hurt a body so much. His eyelids closed. His legs were numb all the way to his hips. He knew that he had to hurry.

315

"Ca-Catherine Cooper —" He groaned and felt more blood leak between his lips. "Owns The Dressmaker's Shop . . . four blocks . . . from . . . the . . . old . . . Cath . . . Cath—" He had to paused. Then, miraculously, his stomach stopped tormenting him, and Harry Henderson knew that God was relieving him of his pain so he could do the right thing. Yeah, Catherine Cooper wasn't really his wife . . . not yet . . . but that didn't matter. God knew that they would have married. It would have been a blissful existence. And, well, Juárez was just across the border and Harry Henderson could have gone down there — He shook his head at such awful, prurient thoughts. He had to finish. He could not feel anything beneath his ribs.

"Catherine Cooper. The Dressmaker's Shop. Across from Gomez's Café and just down from the . . . Catholic . . . church."

"Your wife?" McCulloch said, and when Henderson nodded and grinned, the one-time Ranger looked at the bounty hunter and the former soldier.

"Yes. Catherine Cooper. My name is Harry Cooper." God would forgive him the lie as he was protecting the reputation of a fine woman who put Sunday dresses on El Paso's best. "Tell her that Harry sends her his love." She would understand. She once told him that he was the first man named Harry she had ever known. Harry was a common name, too. Hard to figure.

His left arm was numb.

"Tell her I sold the business." His right arm, about the only part of his body that he could control, other than his mouth, went this way and that. He panicked, coughed violently, and looked around. "My carpetbags!" he cried.

The sergeant rose. "Griffin. Get this man's grips."

"But —"

"Now, damn your hide!"

Harry Henderson twisted this way and that. The bounty hunter and the woman tried to restrain him, but he knew that if those carpetbags were gone — *had the Apaches stolen them?* — that Catherine would never name her son Harry.

"Here." The newspaperman set one grip on Henderson's thighs.

Harry Henderson reached over, took the handle, and remembered. "Both . . . of . . . them . . ." he moaned.

"Damn you, Griffin. Get the other grip."

"I couldn't find it."

The sergeant pointed. "It's right there. Are you blind?"

"Oh."

A moment later, Harry Henderson was clutching the handle of the grip at his side. He couldn't feel it. He felt nothing except a contentedness. He saw the angels — all resembling Catherine Cooper — dancing in the rafters of Culpepper's Station.

"This . . . is the money. Fifty thousand dollars." He remembered that Billy Hawkin and his mean brother and that other fellow, Callahan or Calloway or Gallagher . . . no Galloway . . . had taken some of the money and spent it in that awful den of inequity in Sierra Vista. May God have mercy on their souls. "Or something slightly less than fifty thousand dollars."

The sergeant straightened his head. The woman looked down at the grip on his thighs. The sergeant reached over and pulled the grip to the floor. He opened it. He looked inside. Then he looked into Harry Henderson's eyes.

"You'll get it to my wife?" Harry Henderson asked. Somehow, he managed to turn his head and find the bounty hunter. "Won't you?"

Jed Breen wet his lips.

Harry Henderson looked up at the Ranger. "You'll see to it?"

These three brave men deserved a reward,

too, Harry Henderson decided, because jackals that they were, they would never see the streets of gold, feel the touch of the Lord, be lifted into the clouds and enjoy the wonders of Heaven.

"You can take five thousand dollars for yourselves."

They were looking at each other.

"Divided amongst yourselves. Not five thousand each." That wouldn't have left Catherine with hardly enough to raise a son bound for Harvard. "Promise me!" Henderson felt nothing from his neck down.

"Give me your word!" he shouted. At least, it sounded like a shout to him. It might have been a whisper.

"You've got it," said the bounty hunter.

"My word," said the Ranger.

"All right," Sergeant Keegan said.

"You're good men." Harry Henderson felt himself slipping. "Good men and true. Tell Catherine that Harry's dying thoughts were of . . . Elizabeth. . . ." No, he remembered. Not Elizabeth. That was the wench from Fort Worth. He had meant to say *Catherine.*

But before he could correct himself, an arrow slammed between his ribs, piercing his heart, and Harry Henderson's head was cracking against the hard floor as the Ranger was diving to his side, and everyone else

319

was scattering before the world turned black.

CHAPTER TWENTY-TWO

The .50-caliber Sharps lay at Jed Breen's feet. He picked it up, recognized the unmistakable sound of an arrow flying past his head, and the *thwack* as it struck the back of a chair, the force sending the chair crashing to the floor.

Breen saw the shadow through the cross cut in the shutter, drew back the hammer of the heavy rifle, and braced the stock against his shoulder. Another arrow slammed into the tabletop, but that one came from the side window. He ignored that and peered through the telescopic scope. He touched the set trigger, heard the click, and when the crosshairs lined up what looked like a bone breastplate, he let out his breath and squeezed the second trigger.

The Sharps jarred his shoulder. The white smoke slowly raised, and Breen started to reload the Big Fifty while Matt McCulloch sent two rounds from the Winchester carbine at the attacker in the corner.

"Give them hell, boys!" former sergeant Keegan commanded. "Let's remember Harry Cox . . . or Henderson. Whatever the hell his name was. Give them hell for Harry, boys. You, too, Stanhope!"

"Arrows," Jed Breen said after the Indians had withdrawn.

"Yeah." Keegan nodded. "Which means Holy Shirt won his argument, thanks to that bomb you made up. Must've hurt those red devils pretty good. Other buck, the one pushing for rifles and such, must be shamed."

"For now." Matt McCulloch fed cartridges into his Winchester carbine. "But Apaches can be like red-blooded stallions. Fickle. Gentle and obedient one minute. Bucking you to heaven the next."

"I never knew any Apache to be gentle and obedient," Keegan said.

McCulloch grinned and leaned his carbine against the wall. "Who wants coffee?"

Outside, the Apache drums began.

"What does that mean?" Gwen Stanhope asked.

"Probably asking the gods to show them the way to kill us," Keegan answered. "Bullets or arrows. Holy Shirt's way or gunfire."

■ ■ ■ ■

Outside, the drums beat on.

Inside Culpepper's Station, they'd turned one of the tables over, pulled up the chairs, benches, and kegs, and were sipping coffee.

"They're still beating those damned drums," Gwen Stanhope said.

"As long as they're beating drums, dancing and singing, and praying," Breen said, "they're not trying to kill us. You got to look at the bright side of things, Gwen."

Her head shook, but she grinned at the bounty hunter and lifted the cup of coffee to her lips.

Alvin J. Griffin IV sidled up beside Sean Keegan. "Fifty thousand dollars." The newspaper editor whistled.

"I don't recall asking you to sit next to me, jackass," Keegan said.

Griffin grinned. "Well, hear me out, Sergeant. Fifty thousand is a lot of money. And what's this crap about Henderson having a wife? A wife named Cooper. He's *Henderson*. Did you hear about a bank robbery in Sierra Vista?"

"Make your point," Keegan said.

Griffin rose. "Hear me out, folks. I don't think the late Harry Henderson owned anything to sell. I think that money came from the Hawkin Gang's bank robbery in Sierra Vista. The telegraph came to Purgatory City just before I got on this stagecoach. What I think, *what I know,* is that there are five of us, and fifty thousand dollars. Split five ways, that gives us ten grand each."

"There are six of us," Sir Theodore Cannon said.

"The woman's bound for the gallows," Griffin said.

"Chances are she won't hang, and none of us will be alive to spend that loot," Breen said.

"Ten thousand dollars ought to give us a reason to fight like hell," Griffin said, "and get out of this pickle. Maybe the Indians will give up. After that excellent and deadly bomb you gave us, Breen."

Keegan finished his coffee, rose, and walked away from Griffin.

"You've got gall," Matt McCulloch said as he pushed his cup away.

"If we all get out of here alive, I'd be willing to give Gwen Stanhope a cut, too. I'm not greedy."

"You're greedy," Keegan said. "And you're a real snake in the grass."

"Fifty thousand dollars," the editor said.

McCulloch busied himself wiping the barrel of his revolver with his bandanna. Without looking up from his chore, he said, "You tend to forget one thing, Griffin."

"Such as?"

"I gave my word to Mr. Henderson that I'd get his money to his widow in El Paso. Catherine Cooper."

The editor laughed. "But he has no wife."

"Maybe so. But I gave my word."

"You're —" Griffin stopped when McCulloch looked up over his Colt. The editor turned to Breen.

"Not many outlaws in Texas or anywhere bring that much reward. Isn't that right, Jed?"

The bounty hunter shook his head. "It's a right tidy sum. But you tend to forget, Mr. Honest Newspaper Editor, that I also told Henderson I'd see this job done. If I live."

"You told —"

"I told a dying man I'd do something. My ma and my pa brought me up that you never, ever, go back on a word."

"Your word —"

Breen looked up, and those eyes silenced the newspaper editor, who quickly turned back to Sean Keegan.

"Ten thousand dollars, Sergeant, and with the power of my newspaper, I could have your rank restored. Maybe even a promotion. First Sergeant. Sergeant Major. How would you like to be an officer, Keegan? The power of the press is stronger than —"

"Most everything, I imagine," Keegan finished. "But nothing's stronger than my word. I told Henderson I'd do my job. I aim to do it."

"Your word?" Griffin's fist pounded the table. "*Your word.* The word of —"

"Jackals?" Sir Theodore Cannon laughed.

"I think they're just greedy rats," Griffin said. "They get their five thousand dollars a dying man said they could have. We get —"

"To live," McCulloch said. "If we're lucky. If we manage to survive."

"Which," Keegan said, "most likely . . . we won't."

"And if Holy Shirt has his way" — Breen leaned back his head, and laughed — "they won't take the money, either, because it's been tainted by the white man."

"Poor Catherine Cooper," Gwen Stanhope added. "She'll die a widow. She'll die poor."

"And some lucky so-and-so will find fifty thousand dollars," Sir Theodore Cannon, "and maybe pay for a nice funeral for us."

Griffin fell silent and sulked away to the corner.

Outside, the drumbeats sounded.

They had grown accustomed to the sound of the drums. Suffering intense pain, Sir Theodore Cannon sat on an overturned keg and looked down at the bloody mess that was his foot. Kneeling by him, Gwen Stanhope began rewrapping a bandage over the wound.

"Perhaps I shall give Richard, Duke of York, a limp when next I play him," the actor said, and grimaced as the blond woman tied off the bandage.

After wiping her hands on the hems of her skirt, Stanhope looked in the direction of McCulloch and Keegan as Breen moved to the counter at the far side of the station. She asked, "If they're going back to bows and arrows, anything without the taint of the whites, that gives us a better chance, doesn't it?"

Neither the Ranger nor the soldier answered. Breen fingered the cartridges on the countertop and said, "We still have to find a way out of here." He did not turn around. "And that bomb I made means these are all the bullets we have left."

"How many?" Keegan asked.

Breen turned his head and shook his head. "Just make every shot count." His head turned another way, and he touched the double-action Colt's grip. "Griffin, get your hands off that carpetbag."

The newspaperman turned around, laughed, and raised his hands. "I was just putting them together in a safe place."

"Uh-huh."

"Listen." Griffin stepped back toward Keegan and McCulloch, stopping and bowing his head at the body of Harry Henderson, now covered. "All we have to do, as I've mentioned, is wait out the Apaches. Till help arrives."

"Help may never arrive," Keegan said.

"But —"

"We're low on lead, Griffin, and powder. The Apaches will come at us again, and once we've shot ourselves dry, by the time the Army does get here — if they ever get here — they'll find our bodies looking like porcupines."

"We're dead," Stanhope said, and sighed.

"Come now," the actor said, "let's show some fortitude here. 'Fortitude,' that grand Francis Bacon said, 'is the marshal of thought, the armor of the will, and the fort of reason.' "

The men and the woman stared briefly at Sir Theodore Cannon and let silence fill the room until Breen's boots sounded as he walked toward the door. He stopped, said, "the armor of the will," and began pushing up the heavy bar.

Keegan went to him and assisted. The former soldier drew his Remington, eared back the hammer, and opened the door.

By the time Breen stepped outside, Matt McCulloch was standing beside Keegan and holding the Winchester .44-40.

"What the hell is he doing?" McCulloch asked.

"Not a clue," Keegan answered, and he reached up and pulled out a nail that was driven about an inch into the wood. "But that was some bomb the old boy gave us."

McCulloch looked at the dried blood that stained the ground and the walls, the bent and twisted nails littering the ground, and bits of Apaches — a finger here, an ear there — and carnage everywhere. Little remained of the Concord stagecoach, which had been blown to charred pieces by the keg of gunpowder and nails. The barn remained a skeletal wreck of smoking mess, and yet there was no sign of any Apaches. The dead and wounded had been carried off. At least, the parts of the bodies the Indians could find.

After a minute that felt like thirty, Jed Breen walked back. He had not gone far, but he had felt the presence of Apaches watching him. When Holy Shirt decided to attack, they would attack. But at the moment, they were just watching, out of curiosity or making sure the men trapped like rats in Culpepper's Station were going nowhere.

Breen stopped at Sir Theodore's wagon, which had some nails drilled into the side from the bomb and was blackened by the smoke and explosion. Otherwise, it seemed in pretty good shape. He opened the back, stared at it briefly, and then heard the voices of Apaches.

He wasted no more time. Quickly, he shut the wagon's door and hurried back onto the porch and through the door. McCulloch slipped in next, and as Keegan pulled the door shut, an arrow cut through the air and lodged into the wooden beam next to the door.

"Did you see anything that struck your fancy, Breen?" McCulloch asked in an angry, sarcastic voice.

"Yeah," Breen answered. "You didn't tell me, Sir Theo, that you had armor for a horse with all your goodies."

The thespian looked up, squinted as though trying to remember, and finally shrugged. "It comes in handy for promo-

330

tion. When we first arrive in town, Sir Lancelot rides his trusty steed, Merlin."

"I don't think that was his horse's name," Breen said, shaking his head.

"What are you thinking?" Keegan asked.

The bounty hunter grinned. "That Apache arrows won't pierce a medieval suit of armor."

"Kind sir," Cannon said, "I have only armor for one horse."

"Yeah." Breen looked at the fireplace. "But I think I can rig something to protect at least one more horse."

"There's one thing you're forgetting, Breen," Alvin J. Griffin said. "We don't have one damned mule. We have nothing to pull that wagon. Unless you want to put armor on me and" — he looked around — "well, the sergeant's strong enough. Is that what you plan to use for livestock?"

Breen eyed the journalist. "I hadn't thought of it. But now that you mention it —" He laughed, shook his head, and looked at Matt McCulloch. "But I think I know where we can find some horses. Well, I've heard enough stories about a Texas Ranger and horse wrangler who's never far from a horse. Isn't that right, Matt?"

The drums fell silent. The chanting had

stopped. And no one spoke or even breathed hard inside Culpepper's Station.

CHAPTER TWENTY-THREE

"All right." Keegan broke the silence. "Let's get ready."

He and McCulloch walked to the body of Harry Henderson, pulled off the blanket covering his body, and carried him to the far window facing the front. They propped his corpse against the cross in the shutter, and McCulloch held up the dead man's right arm, while Keegan found the hammer and nails. Holding some nails in his mouth, he fitted one in the center of Henderson's forearm, brought back the hammer, and began pounding.

"Good God in Heaven." Alvin Griffin almost vomited.

"Makes sense," Sir Theodore Cannon said. "Plug up one hole. One less place from which those heathen savages can shoot at us."

They left Harry Henderson propped up on a desk they had moved to the window, his arms stretched out as though he had been nailed to a cross, which, in a morbid way, if you considered the cutout in the wooden shutter, he had been. His head slumped forward onto his chest. His bloody stomach had dried brown. No one looked at the dead man, the barricade, as McCulloch and Keegan walked back to what Sir Theodore Cannon had christened, "Fort Hopeless."

Having time to prepare, they had arranged the tables, which they now overturned, so that they formed a *V* pattern, with the potbellied stove offering some protection, though not complete, at the base.

McCulloch pulled open the trapdoor and nodded at the woman.

She frowned.

"We cut cards," he lied. "You lost. Get in."

When she hesitated, Keegan said, "Lady, there's not enough room for all of us to hide, unless you cram yourself into that hole. I promise you, we won't take it for a privy."

"Nobody lives forever," she said. "Put the newspaperman in there."

"Then," Breen said, "we probably would use it for a privy. Get in. Before the Apaches start filling this place with lead or arrows.

Get in."

"Before," McCulloch said, "I throw you in."

Reluctantly, she sat down, pushed her legs into the opening, and dropped, bending her knees, and finding something hard to sit on in the cramped, damp but cool miniature cellar.

"We've put all the ammunition down there," Keegan said. "We can't shut the door. So we'll hand you guns when we need reloading."

"Which," McCulloch said, "shouldn't be much."

"On account that Keegan and I will be the only ones throwing lead." Breen cocked the heavy hammer of the Sharps.

"And there isn't a whole lot of .45-70 government cartridges left," Keegan said.

"Nor Big Fifty shells for my Sharps." Breen brought the heavy rifle up, used a table leg to steady and balance the weapon, and aimed at the opening of one of the shutters.

Keegan aimed at the corner window.

Sir Theodore Cannon lay on his belly, but his wounded foot hung over the opening. "The coolness eases the pain in my toe, or where my toe once was, madam," he called out to Stanhope. "I hope I do not bleed on you."

Alvin Griffin hugged the far table, groaning at what he had just witnessed. "Jackals," he whispered, over and over again. "Jackals. Beasts. Fiends. Warriors for Lucifer."

An arrow cut through the cabin, fired from the corner window, and lodged in a barrel of trash. Another arrow whistled past Keegan's ear and thudded into the wall, shattering the shaft.

"Holy Shirt won," McCulloch said.

Breen sank down behind the table. He had not fired his Sharps. "So you want to talk to me about those horses?"

Keegan went down, too, his Springfield carbine still cocked, unfired.

"Four," McCulloch said. "In a slot canyon. A mile from here."

"Four?" Breen asked.

McCulloch shrugged. An arrow bit into the table over his head. "Long story."

"Were you planning on ever telling us?" Gwen Stanhope asked from the pit below.

McCulloch felt another arrow slice over his head and slid down as low as he could. "Maybe. Maybe not."

"You're one self-centered scum, McCulloch," Sergeant Keegan said.

"I could have run to those horses after I

put Rourke out of his misery. Four horses would have carried me a long way from here, folks. I ran back here. So you best mind your manners. Because I'm the only one who knows where I left those animals."

Keegan spit, but remembered to turn his head before he sent saliva into the pit and onto Gwen Stanhope. "I best return fire, so the bucks don't think we've all been called to Glory." He did not lift the Springfield, however, instead pulling the Navy .36 from his waistband, took careful aim, and did not even blink when an arrow came inches from his ear. The gun popped, and he swore, thumbed back the hammer, and adjusted his aim. The second lead ball went through the arms of the cross. Outside, an Indian yelped.

Keegan ducked again behind the table.

"Can any of those horses pull a wagon?" Breen asked.

McCulloch shrugged. "Well, I know mine hasn't, and I doubt if the others are trained for the harness. But horses aren't stupid, and it wouldn't surprise me if they'd do just about anything. They know that Apaches like to eat horse meat."

An arrow splintered against the chimney of the stove then clanged off it. Keegan swore, cocked the Navy, and rose again, firing at the nearest window, then dropped again behind the safety, so to speak, of Fort Hopeless.

"Four horses," Breen said. "You couldn't get them to us. Alone."

McCulloch's head shook. "Not with Apaches around. I wouldn't even bet on me making it with two horses. Not alone. But it's our last chance."

"If we send him, he'd just ride off," Alvin Griffin said. "Leave us to die. Then come back and take all that fifty thousand dollars for himself."

"That's a possibility," McCulloch said, "except I wouldn't keep it for myself. I'd deliver it to Catherine Cooper in El Paso. And take my five thousand."

Breen spit on the floor next to the editor. "He's already told us, Griffin, that he can't bring back four horses. This job will take two men."

"Indeed," Sir Theodore Cannon said. "Two men. Two horses."

"But there are four horses," Griffin said.

An arrow came down from the ceiling, it seemed, and dropped into the hole.

"Gwen!" Breen yelled. "Are you all right?"

"Yes. But where the hell did that arrow come from?"

"Indians have wised up." Keegan cocked

the Navy again and sent a .36-caliber ball through the main post of the cross cutout in the nearest window. "Angling their shots now. Smart devils." He lowered himself again and looked at the smoking revolver in his right hand. "Two shots."

"Want me to let them taste my Sharps?" Breen asked.

"Best save your lead," McCulloch said.

"You need to send four men," Griffin demanded. "Four men for four horses."

"Sir Theodore's wagon can hitch up only a team of two," Breen said.

"Then two others amongst us will ride hard and fast alone. In separate directions. To give us a better chance."

Keegan shook his head and spit again. "I suppose you'd be one of the riders, Griffin, going hell-bent-for-leather toward the Mexican border."

Rising on one knee, Breen aimed the Sharps and touched the trigger. The explosion left most of the ears inside Culpepper's Station ringing. He sank back down, removed the spent cartridge from the breech, and lowered his left hand into the pit. "Sharps," he called out.

Gwen Stanhope, just a few seconds later, put the cold brass cartridge with the massive bullet into Breen's hand.

The .50-caliber bullet had silenced the Indians for a minute. Maybe Breen had managed to kill one, though he had barely aimed.

"What do you think?" Keegan asked McCulloch.

"Our friend in the newspaper business has a point," McCulloch said.

"Damned right I do," Griffin said.

"But I think we send two men, each to bring back two horses. Better chance of one of us getting through."

"I was thinking the same thing myself," Breen said.

"And if both of us manage to make it," McCulloch said, "we tie up two horses behind the wagon. If things don't work out, two of us ride out, try to make it. The rest of us make our stand."

"Our Last Stand," Keegan said.

"Yeah."

The room had turned silent, except for some sickening slicing noise.

"What, by thunder, is that?" Sir Theodore Cannon asked.

Keegan spit again. "They're spearing Henderson's back. Trying to push his body from plugging up that hole."

"My God!" Griffin said.

"And I'm no hand when it comes to

carpentry. They'll knock him loose before long."

"You men are pathetic!" Griffin said, gagging again.

"Well, old Harry bought us some time," McCulloch said.

Five minutes later, the body of Harry Henderson rolled off the desktop and slammed with a sickening thud onto the floor. An arrow stuck through the opening, but Sergeant Sean Keegan was ready. The Springfield sounded like a cannon, and the Apaches began yelling again.

Keegan sank down, ejected the shell, and called for a new bullet. He handed the carbine to the actor, and popped up again with the Navy Colt in his right hand. He sent one bullet through the arms of the cross on the corner window, and the last .36-caliber ball through the top of the cross carved into the nearest window. Then he threw the Colt like a tomahawk, and it thudded against the shutter.

"All right," Keegan said. "McCulloch goes out tonight for the horses. Who volunteers to go with him? And you ain't volunteering, Griffin."

"Best wait," Stanhope said from the pit, "till we see who's alive come sundown."

"If anyone's alive," Matt McCulloch said.

CHAPTER TWENTY-FOUR

"Here," Gwen Stanhope said. "Let me help you, Sergeant."

Sean Keegan had slammed the desecrated, mangled body of the late Harry Henderson against the shutter of the middle window. He held the hammer in his left hand, and could not speak because of the nails he kept in his mouth, but he tried to, anyway.

"Ma'am, I don't —" Giving up, he shoved the handle of the hammer into his waistband and pulled the nails from his lips. "Ma'am —"

"Sergeant" — she put her hands on her hips — "nobody has called me ma'am since I was fourteen. That was Bobby Turner, and he said it as a joke. Call me Gwen." She drew in a deep breath and brushed against Keegan's arm as she reached up, put both hands against the dead man's black coat, and threw her weight into him as she tried to keep the corpse from sliding. "Hurry,

Sergeant," she said, straining.

With muffled curses, Keegan turned around. McCulloch and Breen were guarding two of the other windows, and he knew he'd never be able to persuade the actor or the editor to do the sordid job. Slowly, he fetched a nail, drew the hammer, and went to work.

"Oh, my." Stanhope put a hand to her forehead. "That —"

One knee buckled, and Keegan caught her arm. She smiled, but her face was turning paler with each second, and he guided the gambler to one of the chairs still standing. "Let me help you, ma'am." He turned his head. "Griffin! Get your arse, you yellow-spined coward, to that window. Touch my carbine, and I'll rip off your head and feed it to javelinas. Just keep an eye on anything that moves outside."

He helped Stanhope into a chair. "Let me get you some water."

The woman's head bobbed ever so slightly, and Keegan hurried, found a canteen, filled a cup, and returned to the condemned murderess, easing the tin container into her trembling hands.

"Thank . . . you. . . ." She took a sip, brought the cup down, and smiled. Then she made the mistake of looking at the window they had just barricaded with a dead man.

"I suppose . . ." Her head shook, she lowered it, and finally looked Keegan in the eyes. "Will you do that to my body when I'm dead?"

"No, ma'am. Won't have to. My plan is to kill the actor and the newspaper piece of filth and use them."

She stared at him, her mouth fell open, and then she grinned, shaking her head. "I . . . well . . . there's still one window left."

He nodded.

"Breen?"

Keegan shook his head. "McCulloch's bigger."

Galgenhumor," she said.

He blinked, uncomprehending.

"A German I played poker with in Waco," Gwen Stanhope explained. "He used it. He said it meant 'gallows humor.' "

"I don't know what —"

"You're not German. It's making a joke, in bad taste, or at least rather morbid. Say someone's on the gallows about to be executed. You make a crass joke. *Galgenhumor.* Gallows humor."

"We're not getting hanged."

"Yes. I know. It's just a saying, Sergeant. You said that about McCulloch. Gallows humor. A bad joke. Morbid. Crass."

Keegan suddenly grinned. "Oh." The light in his eyes died and he said, "I didn't think it was bad, though."

"It was funny as hell, Sergeant. I needed a laugh. Thanks for the joke."

"What made you think I was joking, ma'am?"

Her face turned blank. She stared at him and could not look away. Finally, Keegan smiled, and she laughed.

"Galgenhumor," she said again, and her head hung down. "Gallows. I wonder if I can find any humor when I'm standing on that scaffold in El Paso."

"Drink your water, ma'am. Don't worry about El Paso."

She tried to sip, but looked again at Keegan. "You don't have to ma'am me, Sergeant."

"Yes, ma'am, I do. Way I was brought up. Even if you was my wife, or my sister, or a whore, I'd ma'am you."

"Well." She finished the water. "You have manners, Sergeant. That's a rare commodity in this harsh land."

"You don't have to call me Sergeant, ma'am. That's past."

"I know." She tilted her head and smiled. "I was dealing in El Paso once when you came into the saloon."

"I remember."

"Do you?"

"You're not the kind of lady a man forgets."

Her head straightened, and she reached out and touched his leg. "No one has called me a lady in a long time." She patted the thigh, and quickly pulled her hand away.

"What will you do, Sergea— . . . well . . . ummm . . . ?"

"Name's Keegan, ma'am. No Mister. Just Keegan."

"I like *Sean,*" she told him.

"Well, ma'am, I like the way it sounds when you say it."

"Sean?"

He waited.

"Why don't you try *Gwen*? At least once."

He stared at her, frowned, stared some more, and at length said, "All right . . . Gwen."

Her eyes brightened. "I like the way you say that, Sean."

"I'm just glad your name ain't Desmondonia," he told her.

And she laughed.

"You busted our saloon up pretty good," Gwen said, and leaned back as if remembering that time, maybe a year, perhaps as long as two years ago.

"I had help," he said.

"Yes, you did. Van Hickson was our bouncer, and he was really big and really mean."

"And swung a bung starter like no man's business." Keegan rubbed the back of his head and grinned.

"Well, he was eating soup for about a month after that ruckus, Sean. Everton, our boss on the floor, he couldn't spin a roulette wheel until they took off both casts six weeks later. One arm was shorter than the other after you broke both of them."

"I tried to tear them both off."

"I wish you had, Sergeant . . . I mean, Sean . . . because he was lousy."

"He cheated."

She nodded. "That's what I mean. He was lousy. He was a sorry cheater. We all cheated, Sean. At least, we all cheated when we were working for Jules Hazelwood. The problem is that Paul Everton *got caught* cheating." She let out a sigh, shook her head, and looked deeply into Sean Keegan's eyes. After a moment, she made herself take in the rest of the station. "How much did that cost you, Sean?"

"Two months in what you call a jail in El Paso. Two months' salary from the United States Army. I think it was ninety-eight dollars that I had to pay —"

"For the roulette wheel."

Keegan nodded. "And the mirror behind the back bar. And the chair I busted over Van Hickson's head."

She shook her head in amazement. "Sean, do you know how many hellholes across the West I've worked?"

He waited for her answer.

"Fort Worth. Houston. Dallas. San Antone. Baton Rouge. New Orleans. Jacksboro. Caldwell. Baxter City. Sedalia. Springfield. Kansas City. Abilene. Ellsworth. Great Bend. Newton. Dodge City. Cimarron. Santa Fe. Mesilla. Tucson. Yuma. Trinidad. Denver. Cheyenne. Deadwood." She grinned. "All those towns and cities. All those railroaders and cowboys and miners and soldiers. All those tinhorns and outlaws and gunfighters. I've seen my share of fights, Sean. Veritable brawls that pretty much wrecked the joints. But until that evening I had never seen one man inflict so much damage in such a short time."

"Wasn't even my best, ma'am . . . I mean . . . Gwen."

"It was glorious, Sean. Simply glorious."

He rose. "Glad I could entertain you. You going to be all right now?"

"I guess."

"Then I need to get back to work, ma'am."

"Gwen."

"Gwen. Yes, ma'am. Old habits, you see."

"You're not a jackal, Sean Keegan." She looked past him at the newspaperman who trembled at the shutter.

"Sure I am, Gwen."

She turned back to him. "What are you going to do, Sean? I mean, you're no longer in the Army. Have you thought about what you will do, where you'll wind up, how you'll make a living?"

He didn't answer.

"Nobody lives forever, but you ought to live while you can." She smiled. "What do you want to do? With the rest of your life?"

"Get out of Culpepper's Station," he told her.

Gwen Stanhope smiled. "Sean . . . I'm facing death. A hangman's waiting for me in El Paso. And —" She looked away, and found herself staring at the macabre sight of a dead man whose body had been nailed to the wooden shutters to offer some protection from marauding Apache warriors. When she looked back, she dabbed her eyes with a handkerchief. "You know what Griffin did, don't you?"

"I'm not sure, Gwen."

"He has taken some of that money from

the late Mr. Henderson's bags, put them in his own pockets."

He nodded. "That doesn't surprise me."

"I shouldn't have told you that. You might —

Keegan's head shook. "Pretty good chance he won't live to spend what he stole, Gwen. I'm a hard man. I've busted up saloons, gambling halls, brothels . . . begging your pardon, ma'am . . . and have more blood on my hand than all the kings in the Old Testament. But I won't deny even a heel like Alvin J. Griffin the Fourth the chance to die thinking he was rich."

"You're an odd man, Sean Keegan."

He nodded. "There's plenty that will agree with you, Gwen. And plenty more who'll think you could've chose a more appropriate name to call me."

"Like?"

"I've been raised not to use such language in front of a lady, especially a pretty lady."

She brought a hand to her face. "Do you think I'm pretty, Sean?"

"I've been taught not to lie, too. Don't always remember that. But I try."

"Thank you, Sean."

Their eyes locked.

"More?" she asked.

Keegan shook his head. "Best save what

we have, ma'am . . . Gwen."

"I understand."

"I do, too," he told her.

Her head tilted, and she studied him with hard intensity.

"Fifty thousand dollars," he told her. "That's a lot of money. It could get you out of the country, away from that hangman in El Paso. But I ain't the one to help you get it, ma'am — Gwen, I mean. I told that gent I just nailed to that window that I'd get all that money to his wife. And that's what I aim to do, God or the Devil willing."

He tipped his hat, and left her on the chair, but turned after only a few steps, and smiled. "But, Gwen, if you're still alive after all this is over, and the law hasn't locked you up, yet, you come see me. My share of the reward, even if McCulloch and Breen ain't dead and I only get my third, well, that's too much money for a man like me to keep. I'll see that you get some. Enough to get you across the Rio Grande. Maybe you ought to have one more cup of water, Gwen. You're looking a little off your feed right about now."

CHAPTER TWENTY-FIVE

The gallows were the finest Charles Van Patten had ever seen. El Paso had spared no expense in constructing the fine scaffolding behind the courthouse. Judge Martinez y Del Blanco had originally said the hanging of Gwen Stanhope would be by invitation only, but the editor of the Purgatory City newspaper, a man named Griffin, and some well-placed bribes had changed the judge's mind.

A hanging like this would bring in many people from miles around. It would be good for all the businesses in El Paso and the county. You didn't get a chance to see a woman dance from the end of a rope every day.

The murdered man was Kirk Van Patten. One of the finest men in that part of the country, he had done a great deal for the growth of industry and of the population, and knew important figures in Austin, New

York, San Francisco, Chicago, Kansas City, and Mexico City. The deceased's brother was the county sheriff, twice elected. The Democratic Party would help foot the bill for the gallows. The Democratic Party of Texas had helped Martinez y Del Blanco avoid scandal after that sordid little affair with that fifteen-year-old girl from Juárez. Sheriff Charles Van Patten had seen to that, too.

The sheriff wanted everybody in town, everybody in the county, everyone from Fort Stockton to the east and Lordsburg to the west, to see Gwen Stanhope's neck stretched. Nobody killed Kirk Van Patten and got away with it. Stanhope deserved to hang. Shooting that no-account brother of Charles Van Patten was going to make things difficult for Van Patten to keep his job as county sheriff. County peace officers didn't make much money, and now that his brother was dead, the sheriff wasn't going to get a percentage of the money Kirk somehow came up with. Texas Rangers, the U.S. Army, a federal prosecutor, and the state's attorney general were already investigating those little dealings going on in the salt fields and some alleged cotton thefts and how some revolutionaries down in Mexico were winding up with rifles stolen from the arsenal up in Jefferson City. And if Kirk Van Patten was around to see that some voting officials in the county got extra pay and bottles of fine Scotch whiskey, then chances were that Domingo Rodriguez would win the next election for sheriff.

That would likely mean Charles Van Patten would have to go back to rustling cattle and stealing horses. He had almost been hanged up around Tascosa for those very things.

Charles Van Patten was lean, his face darkened and chiseled by the wind and a life in the sun. His graying hair was close-cropped, unlike the drooping bushy mustache and pointed goatee. County sheriffs were supposed to be politicians, but that never was Van Patten's strong suit. He didn't act like a palm-greaser. He didn't dress like the governor. His boots were tall, scuffed, and worn, his spurs were plain, the tan britches were patched, his shirt was loose cotton with frayed sleeves, and his brown corduroy vest was missing two of its five buttons. About the only thing fancy about him was a bowler, and it hadn't cost more than two dollars at Strauss's General Store.

Well, his guns were fancy. He wore two, butts facing forward, and those were nickel-plated Colt .45s with mother-of-pearl grips. They were pretty, but Van Patten wore them because they served his purpose — they were accurate. And he was damned good with them.

Van Patten met Enrico Valdez underneath the trapdoor of the gallows.

The fat, one-eyed Mexican with the greasy hair and salt-and-pepper beard grinned when he saw the sheriff. "Amigo, *buenos tardes.*"

"Everything ready?" the sheriff asked.

"Sí, Señor Alguacil, sí. Todo lo que necesi-taré hacer —"

"English, you damned greaser," Van Patten said. "This town hasn't been part of Mexico for many years. Speak American."

"Very well." The hangman no longer smiled. "I shall just need to weigh *la patrona* . . . the lady . . . the killer of your brother . . . so I know what weights to use when we drop the door underneath her feet."

Van Patten grinned. "And when you don't get those weights calculated correctly?"

The hangman shrugged. "Well, it has been reported that a condemned person's head could come off." He shook his head in disgust. "It is not pleasant to see."

"But," Van Patten said, "of course it has

never happened to you."

"*Es verdad.* It is true. But even a hangman of my reputation can err."

Van Patten reached into his vest pocket and withdrew the pouch. He tossed it up, and when he caught it, the jingle of coins made Enrico Valdez smile. The sheriff tossed the pouch to the hangman, who caught it, jingled it some more, and shoved it into the deep pockets of his pants.

"Half now," Van Patten said, "the rest after the bitch's head comes off."

"And I still collect my five dollars from the county?"

"For the hanging. You get paid the five dollars if she's decapitated, if she just strangles, or if her neck pops in a clean execution. But you'll never live to spend it. That head comes off, Valdez. You savvy?"

"*Sí.* Yes. It will be as you wish, Mister Sheriff. I am good at these things."

"You better be." Van Patten turned and walked out of the courtyard behind the courthouse. He found his horse and was starting to swing into the saddle when Windy Bly, the telegrapher, called out his name.

Swearing underneath his breath, Van Patten held the reins and turned to meet the sweating, bald, fat man.

"It's from the marshal over in Sierra Vista, Sheriff." Windy Bly started to hand the yellow slip of paper to Van Patten.

"Sierra Vista's not my jurisdiction," Van Patten said. "That's two counties over."

"Yes, sir."

Van Patten looked at the telegraph with disdain and did not let go of the reins. "Read it," he ordered.

He had to wait for the old geezer to catch his breath. "He just says that the posse lost the trail of the bank robbers. He asked for you to keep a lookout." The fool's eyes widened. "Says they think it was the Hawkin boys."

"Yeah." He swung into the saddle.

"You want to answer him?" Windy Bly pulled the pencil off his ear.

"No."

The telegrapher frowned. "Well, are you gonna deputize a posse?"

"You volunteering, Windy?"

The man chuckled. "No, Sheriff, you don't want me. Last time I fired a gun —"

"You almost blew your foot off. Yeah. Don't worry. I'm not organizing a posse. If the Hawkin boys ride into El Paso and break the law, then I'll do my job. But I can't spare any deputies or any good men to go on some wild-goose chase. I've got a hanging to oversee." Van Patten swung into the saddle and spurred the black gelding toward the stagecoach station across from the Southern Pacific Railroad depot.

"It's still not here, Charles," the station agent said.

Sheriff Charles Van Patten fumed. "Ever been this late before, Vern?"

"Sure. More times than I can count."

"Even with Petey driving?"

"Petey can't fly a Concord coach over a road that's washed out. That's usually the case and —"

"When's the last time it rained, Vern?"

"It could have rained up in those hills, though, and —"

"Apaches?"

The station agent turned his head to spit tobacco juice onto some cactus. After wiping his mouth with his shirtsleeve, he sighed. "That's a possibility. I know Captain Trudeau sent out a couple of patrols yesterday. And you know about that bank robbery over in Sierra Vista. Jake Hawkin and his black-hearts could have waylaid the coach."

"With Rourke riding shotgun? Hawkin ain't that stupid."

"I can send out a rider, but Captain Trudeau come by before and said I shouldn't.

He's got Holy Shirt and some of those wild young bucks raising hell. Plus a bunch of others under some chief nobody's heard of yet cut down some patrol riding from Fort Spaulding over in Dead Man's Canyon."

"Don't send out any rider, Vern," the sheriff said. "No use getting some civilian killed. I'll go. The marshal from Sierra Vista telegraphed me and asked me to ride out, see if I could cut sign of Jake Hawkin."

"Are you going alone, Sheriff?"

"Not hardly. Where do you think Petey and Rourke would fort up? If it was Apaches, not bandits, not weather?"

"Well." Vern spit again. "We would have heard from them if they made it as far as Hueco Tanks. And we know they made it to Sierra Vista. Got a telegraph to that effect."

"Still leaves a lot of country."

"Yep. But that's one thing Texas has going for it. A lot of country. Even in this county."

"Culpepper's Station?" Van Patten asked.

"You know as well as I do, Sheriff, that if you're hit by a ton of Apaches or Jake Hawkin, the only place you'd want to have to deal with that would be Culpepper's."

"That's what I thought. Find Mr. Red, Mr. Black, and Mr. Blue for me, Vern."

The station agent almost swallowed his tobacco. Red, Black, and Blue weren't the real names of those gunmen — nobody knew their true names — but everybody knew their reputations. The reputations stank like a dead skunk.

Red was known for his red hair, and, if you believed all the stories from the saloons, sheriffs, and barbershops, for all the blood on his hands.

Black earned his moniker because of the slick black hair that fell to his shoulders . . . and that he could have been mistaken for an Apache if not for his pale skin and gray eyes. They also called him "Mr. Black" because his soul was blacker than Satan's heart.

Blue was perhaps the deadliest of the killers. His eyes were the color of the Texas sky, and everyone who saw him said those eyes chilled even the hardest man. They were eyes that ran cold, ever so cold.

They were hired killers from New Mexico, Arizona, up in Colorado and Wyoming, and over in Kansas and Missouri. The county typically frowned when Van Patten hired them for a posse, but the commissioner and the judge and the county solicitor had never said a word about it, publicly — at least back when Kirk Van Patten was alive.

They might say something now, but they wouldn't know about it till Van Patten was out of El Paso and raising dust for Culpepper's Station.

"Don't mention Apaches. Don't mention Jake Hawkin. Just tell them I'm deputizing them for a little scout. It'll pay them well. I'll meet them at my office. I need to pack some grub and get enough weapons to fight Gettysburg. Have them meet me there in a half hour. Tell them to be ready to fight a war. I sure don't want the county to get cheated out of a good hanging."

"Yes, sir."

The sheriff watched the station agent run to the red-light district. Charles Van Patten didn't know exactly how he felt. If the Apaches killed Gwen Stanhope, well, that would be sort of satisfying. Apaches had their ways of killing people, especially womenfolk. But he had really wanted to see Gwen Stanhope's head jerked off at the gallows behind the courthouse.

CHAPTER TWENTY-SIX

"You ought to stay behind the tables, ma'am," Matt McCulloch said without looking away from the cross in the corner shutter. He didn't have to turn his head to see who had walked up behind him. His wife might have been dead for years, but McCulloch knew what a woman smelled like — even a woman who had been trapped inside a jail, a crowded stagecoach, and a stuffy stagecoach station during one of the most savage sieges he had ever known.

"Are they out there?" Gwen Stanhope asked.

"Don't see them. But they're out there." A bird screeched from the barn, then was answered from behind the barn, and Mc-Culloch's head nodded. "Yeah. You don't have to see them."

He glanced at Breen's Sharps rifle leaning beside him, but did not touch it.

Sean Keegan stood at the left window, a

single-shot Enfield rifle — the Apaches had left it on the ground after their brief try at breaking Holy Shirt's edict about not using white man weapons to kill white men — nestled in his arms. The newspaper editor had been ordered to stand behind the shutter on the right, and although Keegan's Springfield trapdoor was leaning against the wall, Alvin Griffin did not touch it, did not even consider it. Keegan had warned him not to even look at the carbine. Jed Breen sat in the corner with Theodore Cannon, the former taking notes as the actor described all the contents inside the wagon, and how the wagon was held together.

There was no gunpowder left to load bullets, and the three frontiersmen in charge had nailed Harry Henderson's corpse up against the middle window's shutter, using more nails this time, thus there was no need to post a guard there.

Stanhope had been left alone, so she had decided to approach the Texas Ranger. "You would think they would have tried to bust open the shutters," she said, simply to make conversation.

"Can't." McCulloch pointed a finger at the cast-iron bolts. He held another weapon abandoned by the attacking Apaches, a cut-down Manhattan Colt that also used the percussion caps. It had only four caps, however, instead of six. "Locked from inside. They could pound all day outside and not knock one of these pieces loose. Try to shoot through it, and they'd find the plate of iron between the wood. Old man Culpepper knew what he was getting into when he built this place. That's why we're still alive."

"Do you think we'll stay alive?"

He lowered his neck and looked closer through the bar. Still studying the land outside, he said, "I'm not a betting man, ma'am. If you want to lay a wager, try Breen or Keegan."

"What was she like?" she blurted out.

Now, he did turn, and study her for a second, before he trained his attention on the terrain.

"I'm sorry. I didn't mean to bring up bad memories. It's just . . . just . . ." She stared at her feet.

He gave her a quick glance before he turned his attention to the Apaches outside, wherever they were.

"You were lucky," she said.

McCulloch did not look at her. "She wasn't."

"Yes, your wife was very lucky. She had you." Stanhope let out a little sigh.

Out of the corner of his eye, he saw her head shake and a handkerchief she held in her left hand come to dab her eyes.

"I never had any luck."

A mirthless laugh escaped his throat. "I don't believe that, ma'am. You were a gambler."

"You know what I mean. And don't call me ma'am. The name's Gwen."

He did not look away from the cross cut out of the wood and iron.

"I always wondered what it would have been like," she said. "My life. My older brother taught me how to shuffle cards when I was nine. By ten I could play blackjack and poker, and deal faro. My mother whipped the tar out of me when she found me playing poker — and winning — against about four other boys from our school. It was on the school porch. You never got such a beating."

McCulloch managed a weak grin. "You didn't know my old man." He turned and added, "Or my mother." His eyes trained again on the country.

"Well, by the time I was fourteen, I was playing poker with the schoolmaster, the man, Mr. Withersteen, who rented the building that served as our schoolhouse, and the president of the school board. I don't remember his name. I think he ran the sawmill."

"Did you win?"

That told Stanhope that he was paying attention.

"Depends on how you look at it, I guess." She signed again. "We were playing penny ante. Not a whole lot of money to win or lose. Mr. Withersteen, he always said it was for fun. That's what he said when he asked me to go with him to the barn."

McCulloch stared harder outside.

"I was sixteen then. And I . . . well . . . I guess I knew what he had in mind. Maybe I was curious." She wiped her eyes and her nose this time, and studied the piece of silk in her hand as though she could read the future in her dried tears and snot. When she looked at him again, she asked, "What was she like?"

"Spanish," he said stiffly. "You wouldn't dare call her Mexican. That would start a ruckus."

"Black hair?"

"Like tar."

Her other hand went to her hair, disheveled, dirty, in need of a currycomb and a new brush. "I never liked mine. Blond. And not like corn silk. Just plain, ordinary dirty blond. Dirty . . . like me."

"You look fine," he said.

She laughed. "Not now."

"Sure you do," he said.

"You're not a very good liar, Ranger Mc-Culloch."

"Because I don't lie, ma'am."

She cleared her throat and put her hands on her hips.

He smiled. "Missus Stanhope."

"Try Gwen."

He remained silent for a long time. "Well . . . Gwen . . . I don't lie. Breen, Keegan, they do. That newspaper editor, he most certainly does. But me?" His head shook.

"They taught you that as a Ranger?" she asked.

"No. I just never was good at it."

She stared again at her shoes, breathing in and out, lips flat, every now and then shaking her head at some distant memory. When she looked up, she said, "Mr. Withersteen. Kirk Van Patten. A lot of men between them. Never a decent man. Never a man like you. I'm a gambler, sure, but I've never known luck. Not like you have, Ranger Mc-Culloch." She grinned. "Black hair." Then touched her own.

"It was showing some gray," he told her without looking away from the window.

"We'd been together a few years. And it wasn't an easy life."

"I know all about hard living, Matt." She waited, and when he did not object, she said, "Your hair . . . it's nice, too."

"I still have some. And I'd like to keep it that way. You best go back to the tables, ma'am."

"Apaches don't scalp."

"Usually not, no. But after the hurt we've put on them, they might be inclined to act like Kiowas and Comanches . . . and Mexican scalp hunters."

"Well . . ."

He silenced her as he turned quickly, lowered the rifle, and pulled a cap-and-ball pistol from his waistband. "I've admired the companionship, Miss . . . Gwen . . . and the conversation. But it's time for you to get back inside the hole." He looked away. "Griffin!"

The newspaper editor jumped.

"Behind the table. Breen!"

Breen took the pepperbox pistol, which had been found in the tiny cellar, from his waistband, and helped the limping Sir Theodore Cannon make it to Fort Hopeless, where the bounty hunter left him and hurried to the window Alvin J. Griffin IV had abandoned.

"What you got?" Breen asked when he slid into his position.

"They're bunching around the cistern," McCulloch answered, then yelled, "Keegan?"

"Nothing over here," the Army veteran answered.

"Then you likely know what that means," McCulloch said.

"Yeah," Keegan said. "Breen!"

"Coming." The bounty hunter left the window, and, ducking so no Apache could catch his movement through the gunports in the front shutters, he ran to the corner window.

"How many shots does that thing hold?" Keegan asked.

"Four. Unless it blows up in my hand. Or shoots all four barrels by accident."

"No wonder Culpepper's boys threw that relic in the cellar." Keegan slid down the wall, crawled past the shutter, and rose. "Good luck, Breen."

"Yeah." The bounty hunter moved closer to the shutter. "You, too."

Once Keegan had crossed to the window Breen had abandoned, McCulloch looked at the tables. "Remember. We're emptying these guns. They're the worst of what we have left, and there's nothing else to load them with once we've shot them dry." He ducked and moved toward Breen.

Huddling behind the tables, Sir Theodore Cannon whispered, "I still do not know what they are planning."

"A fool's plan," Griffin said softly.

"A gamble." Gwen Stanhope smiled. "I know all about gambling. And it's a pretty good bet."

They heard the yips, followed by angry war whoops, and Sean Keegan rammed the Enfield barrel through the slots. "I hope we're right!" he yelled. "Here they come."

Thuds struck the shutters outside. Gwen Stanhope listened, but it was hard to hear anything inside the cellar. All she could make out were the whispered curses coming from Griffin and the prayer uttered by Sir Theodore Cannon.

Keegan waited, waited, waited. The shouts of the Apaches increased as they grew nearer. The staked body of Harry Henderson shuddered as arrows managed to slip through the cross and strike his dead body. Finally, Keegan touched the trigger. The Enfield roared, and Keegan left the barrel sticking through the cross at the base. He grabbed his Springfield and took off toward the far window. The .45-70's barrel poked through the center of the cross. Keegan fired, pulled out the rifle with his right hand while reaching with his left for Breen's Sharps. After he laid the empty single-shot Army carbine on the floor, he snapped a quick shot with the bounty hunter's long gun. That left the Sharps empty as well. Lowering that weapon — but not with the care he had shown with his own long gun — Keegan leaped up, took hold of a rafter, and pulled himself toward the low ceiling. He braced his boots against the rocky wall, body hanging above the openings in the shutters.

At the window Keegan had abandoned, the smoking Enfield rammed the hole in the wooden shutter. Apaches must have been trying to pull it through the hole, or maybe clear it so they could fill the inside of the station with more arrows. Arrows did come from the cross carving below Keegan.

Suddenly, Jed Breen was emptying the pepperbox pistol. Four quick shots, and he dropped to the floor. McCulloch stepped around him and pulled the trigger of the Manhattan. He took better aim. Once. Twice. Three times. Finally, the fourth, and last, round fired, and McCulloch moved to the side, trying to shove himself into the hard rocks.

They had guessed right. The Apaches had

tried a feint at the front of the station, then sent a charge toward the corner window. The pepperbox and Colt had turned them back.

It had been the shortest attack since the siege began. The arrows stopped coming through the crosses or slamming into a dead man's body, and the Enfield remained where Sean Keegan had left it.

Breen looked up and peered through the cross. He aimed his finger and said, "Bang."

"Let them carry off their dead," McCulloch said, and the bounty hunter studied the Ranger, wondering if McCulloch had been joking. Sergeant Keegan dropped from his perch between the ceiling and the wall, took the Springfield and the Sharps, and moved back down to the side table to reload both weapons.

The pepperbox and the Manhattan Colt were left on the floor.

"All right," Keegan said. "Sun's setting. So . . . who's volunteering to go find McCulloch's damned horses?"

CHAPTER TWENTY-SEVEN

"Me."

Every head stared at Gwen Stanhope.

"I don't think so, ma'am," Keegan said.

"Don't bet against me, Sergeant," the blonde fired back. "I'm the only one who can go."

Jed Breen laughed out loud.

"You think I'm joking? I'm not." She nodded at Matt McCulloch. "He has to go, of course. He's the only one who knows where he hid those mounts. You can't go, Mister Bounty Hunter, because you'll be busy all night fixing up your armor for those two horses that'll be pulling us out of this hell. Sir Theodore Cannon? He can hardly walk with one toe blown off. Our trusted member of the press? Do you think he'd ever come back with a horse? He'd be at a gallop for El Paso or Sierra Vista as soon as he could saddle up one horse. That leaves you, Sergeant Keegan. But if you go, well, who'd be here to protect us if the Apaches decided to attack at night? Or if McCulloch and whoever goes with him wind up being tortured by those red demons from Hell?"

She sat down and nodded. "I think I've made my point. Anyone think they can find any holes in that argument, I'm all ears."

"Miss Stanhope," the actor said, "do you know what those Apaches will do to you if they were to catch you?"

"Sir Theodore, do you know what waits for me in El Paso? I'm dead if we survive, and I'm dead if the Apaches keep up this assault. And that's another reason you have to send me with our brave, fine Ranger. My fate is the same. I have nothing to lose. And nothing to live for, except a hangman's noose, thirteen coils around my throat, and a short drop to eternity. Yes, gentlemen. Yes, yes, yes, I heard the gallant Mr. Rourke's screams. I know what's in store for me. But" — she grinned again — "nobody lives forever."

Breen looked at Keegan, and both men turned to McCulloch.

Alvin J. Griffin IV rose from his seat, cleared his throat, and said, "As much as I admire the lady's bravery, I'm sure I have no need to remind everyone that once she has gotten a horse, she will most likely ride for the border herself. We must think of that. She has nothing to live for? Horse apples. She has everything to live for. She'll be riding for her life. She'll be riding for Mexico to escape justice. Besides, are we yellow enough to send a woman to do a man's job?"

"I am," Jed Breen said, and he laughed.

"Galgenhumor," Sean Keegan said.

"What?" Breen and McCulloch said at the same time.

The old Army veteran shook his head and saw Gwen Stanhope smiling at him. "Nothing. A private joke."

"This is no time for jokes, Sergeant," Griffin said. "And that is why I am volunteering."

"Shut up," McCulloch said. "You're the last person I'd trust in this group. In fact, I wouldn't trust you if you were my only choice."

"Now see here —"

"Sit down," Keegan said. "You can write in your yellow rag that you bravely asked to do your duty and save our hides. No one in Purgatory City will believe it, but you can write it. And maybe a hundred years from now, some historian will come across the *Herald Leader* and write about Alvin Griffin, brave man, hero, a regular Davy Crockett,

Paul Bunyan, Kit Carson, and Natty Bumppo rolled into one."

For a few long minutes, no one spoke. The room darkened as the skies blackened.

"Breen?" Matt McCulloch broke the silence. "How long will it take you to rig up what we need?"

The bounty hunter shrugged. "I really won't know until we get all that gear out of the wagon and inside here."

"The Apaches will be watching."

Breen nodded. "Yeah. Maybe even attacking. They've got to be frustrated as hell after all the hurt we've put on those old boys."

Like a death shroud, another silence descended on the station.

The actor cleared his throat. "As much as I regret saying this, I'm afraid the point Mr. Breen just made is another reason why Sergeant Keegan must remain behind. To help us fight off the Apaches should they risk wandering in the spirit land forever after being killed in the dark of night."

"Thank you, Sir Theodore," Gwen Stanhope said.

Bowing, Sir Theodore straightened and sank into his chair. "That hurt my foot something god-awful," he said, and began massaging his leg.

"What were you thinking, Matt?" Keegan asked.

The Ranger shrugged. "Just wondering how long it would take Breen to fix up armor for the horses."

"And the driver," Sir Theodore pointed out.

"I know what you mean, McCulloch," Breen said. "But it's not good. By the time I could get that armor pieced together, and then go out with you to round up the horses, we'd never get out of here in time. The Indians would be upon us. We'd be dead."

Keegan nodded. "Yeah. The one chance we have is to get running out of this place before daybreak. Those bucks might be real hesitant to come after us in the dark."

"Yeah," McCulloch said. "There's a fair to middling chance they wouldn't even come after us." He shook his head. "And there's a fair to middling chance they will."

"Even money," Gwen Stanhope said. She rose and moved to the door. "And we're wasting time. Are you coming, Matt?" She looked at Keegan. "And, Sean, will you do us a big favor, darling, by getting that big stick out of those holders?"

McCulloch handed the blonde his hat.

"Take it," he whispered. "Your hair's light. This'll cover it. Apaches can see in the dark. Even in a new moon."

She pulled the hat tight over her hair. "I thought all the dirt and blood had already darkened my hair."

"And keep your mouth shut when we're outside. Follow me." He gave Breen and Keegan a grim nod, slipped through the crack, and moved quickly to Sir Theodore Cannon's wagon.

There he waited until Gwen Stanhope made it right beside him. Without speaking or acknowledging her, McCulloch hurried to the barn, and turned, watching the woman as she followed his every move. She pressed her back against the wall of the charred remnants of the barn. Her breasts heaved as she sucked in breath after breath, letting the air out of her lungs, but she was smart enough not to make any sound as she breathed. McCulloch had to give her that.

The noise came from the cactus and rocks, and he instinctively slipped in front of her, shielding her body with his own, while raising his knife and clamping his free hand over her mouth. Her eyes widened. He could see that much of her. He would cut her throat if the Apaches jumped him, kill her quickly, prevent her from . . . he tried to block out what had happened to his wife. The musky scent hit him, and he relaxed, releasing his hold, and pushing his body away from hers.

He almost laughed.

Javelinas grunted as they wandered out of the cactus and into the yard. Likely, they would find the remaining parts of the Apaches that Breen's bomb had blown to bits, and eat their fill.

As the javelinas moved past them, McCulloch took Stanhope's hand and pulled her behind him. They moved into the desert, maneuvering between rocks and cholla, creosote and yucca. Eventually, they reached a maze of rocks. McCulloch stopped and let Gwen Stanhope's hand fall free.

He could feel her, more than see her, as she rubbed the circulation in the hand he had clutched.

"You can turn back," he said, barely audible.

"No," she whispered, "but thanks for the offer."

"We'll wait here."

"Not on my account."

His head shook. His finger waved a few times toward the corral and the cistern.

She looked, saw nothing, but she dared not question Matt McCulloch, and when he moved that finger to his lips, she understood, and became mute.

For an hour, they waited, sweating in the coolness of the desert night. Eventually they heard the Apaches as they grunted and spoke in that guttural language.

Gwen Stanhope craned her neck. She could not see the Indians. She could hear them. And she cringed as she realized what must have excited those Indians so much.

The door squeaked like a rusty hatch opening in an ancient maritime vessel. Jed Breen figured the Apaches already knew where they were, so he helped Sir Theodore Cannon jerk the door open wider. As soon as the door was open, Breen hopped into the back and moved in the darkness until his boot slammed into something painful.

He swore, reached down, and felt the rough metal. He clutched the iron and lifted it off the floor. "Christ a'mighty, that's heavy."

"Ah, yes," Sir Theodore Cannon said. "That would be the mail habergeon."

"The what?"

"A shirt. Made of chain mail. Weighs thirteen and a half kilograms."

"Huh?"

"Thirty pounds, my friend." The actor

leaned forward and lifted a heavy helmet with a visor. "My bascinet, complete with a mail aventail. It weighs ten pounds."

"Let's get this stuff back inside," Breen said.

He and the actor staggered the few yards back to the porch and back inside the station. The visored helmet and the small shirt of chain mail were dropped onto the floor.

Breen stared at the shirt, then at the actor. "You wore this?"

"Not in thirty years, my good man." The actor rubbed his ample stomach. "But years ago, I could play Romeo more often that I could play Falstaff."

Keegan shouldered the Springfield carbine. "You got more of that stuff?"

"Yes."

"For playacting to Shakespeare?"

"No, Sergeant. Well, sometimes. The hayseeds in some towns thought armor was much manlier than robes. But usually, these were to bring publicity. Or to read Sir Malory and engage the patrons of some opera house with the tales of King Arthur. As you know, I even have armor for a horse. But that, my good man, will weigh ninety pounds."

"Griffin!" the sergeant snapped. "You

wanted to be a hero. Come on. Lend a hand."

They brought in a jousting harness and a plate harness, more habergeons, arm and leg armor. They found the broadsword.

"The tournament tin, as I like to call it, is much heavier than battle armor," Sir Theodore Cannon explained while hauling in more metal. "But do not believe these myths that a knight cannot move. You will be free, for you are an agile man, Mr. Breen. You can do somersaults, handstands, and cartwheels."

"None of which I've done since I was ten, Sir Theodore."

"One more load, my good men," Sir Theodore said. "Then we shall see what kind of medieval seamstress you are to rig this up to protect one driver and two horses."

Keegan pulled open the door, frowned, and peered into the blackness. Shrugging, he widened the crack, and Breen slipped out, followed by the limping actor. They had decided that Alvin Griffin was not needed to bring in the rest of the props and wardrobe. When Sir Theodore climbed into the wagon, the Apache who had sneaked close screamed and charged.

The muzzle flash from Jed Breen's Lightning blinded both the Indian and the actor.

The .38 slug tore through the Indian's shoulder, and down he went. Breen heard the shouts from the cistern and the corral and quickly jerked Cannon out of the wagon by his suspenders.

"Inside," he ordered.

"But . . ."

"Forget the rest," Breen barked. Ducking as an Apache slashed at him with a tomahawk, the bounty hunter fell to the ground, rolled over, came up, and sprinted for the charging warriors.

Breen snapped two shots, felt an arrow scratch his left arm, and the roar from Sean Keegan's Springfield deafened him. He backed up, started to shoot, but decided to save his ammunition and hurried into the station. Keegan slammed the door shut, and Cannon and even the newspaperman managed to get the bar over the holders as more arrows pounded into the heavy door.

"Let's get back to Fort Hopeless," Keegan said.

The men hurried to the makeshift shelter and settled in as more arrows fired through the crosses. Some of the arrows were flaming, but most hit the rock walls, and none of the sparks managed to ignite any of the hard wood in the building.

That still caused Breen to cringe. "If those

bucks fire up Cannon's wagon, we're cooked."

CHAPTER TWENTY-EIGHT

When the explosion of gunfire rocked the compound, Matt McCulloch did not say a word. He just grabbed Gwen Stanhope's arm and pulled her behind him, not letting go until they had climbed the path — or what might have been a path, for ants — to the ridgetop. He kept running, his moccasins making little noise, and did not stop until they reached some ancient mesquite. "You all right?"

She nodded.

The din of battle quieted.

"They're attacking," Gwen said, "at night."

He nodded. "Getting desperate. We get those horses, and get back to Fort Hopeless, we might have a chance after all."

Her heart pounded so rapidly, her chest hurt. She tried wetting her lips, but found no moisture in her mouth. She wiped the sweat off her brow and used that on her lips, instead.

"I thought you moved at a snail's crawl when you were around Apaches," she said.

He came to her, pulled her up, and started moving down the ridge. "I'm not one to tarry. Not when Apaches are trying to kill me."

They ran.

"What do you think?" Keegan asked before filling his mouth with the last of his chewing tobacco.

Breen stared at the horse's armor. "Well, if McCulloch brings back an elephant, this chunk of tin might work."

"Yeah. It was a silly idea to begin with. Here's what I'm thinking. When McCulloch and the woman come back with four horses, four of us ride away. Fast as we can."

"With the money, I presume!" the newspaperman shouted.

"Of course. That goes to that widow in El Paso," Keegan said.

"Who's the fourth?" Breen asked.

"They can draw lots."

Breen smiled. "That's a thought. But I've got a better one."

Keegan shifted the chaw to his other cheek. He saw Breen lifting the chain mail.

"We throw this over the horse," the bounty hunter said. "One of the horses, I mean."

"And an arrow or Apache lance guts the other horse. That puts a pretty quick and fatal stop to your getaway."

"I think, with a forge and some blacksmithing tools, I can get that horse's armor cut down to size. It won't be pretty. It might not even work." He found himself grinning at the possibility. "Then again, it might."

Keegan spit, wiped his mouth, and turned in the darkness to find the journalist. "Griffin, get your hands off Mr. Henderson's grips. And get a fire going in the fireplace. A big one."

"That'll light up the entire room," the editor protested.

"If you don't do what I said, I'll light you up, bubba."

Matt McCulloch released his hold on Gwen Stanhope. He needed both hands to guide his slide down the rough stones and into the slot canyon. The blonde came right behind him, landing harder on the old cactus and stones. She rubbed her buttocks as she somehow found a way to stand.

He stared down at her.

She asked as quietly as possible, "How much farther?"

His thumb hooked toward the south. Or was it west? She had lost all sense of direction. "Not quite a quarter mile."

They weaved along the winding path, moving at a desperate pace, but McCulloch did not pull the blonde behind him. They moved fast, not together but almost like one, as if she could read his mind, or at least anticipate his moves. When he stopped and braced his back against the limestone wall, she stopped, too.

A horse whinnied.

McCulloch smiled, but something answered the horse.

He brought the knife up as his face hardened. Turning toward Stanhope, he raised his free hand, motioned for her to stay still, and then moved quietly, like a mouse, but with a fierceness of a mountain lion. He came to the end of the canyon and slowly looked into the opening.

"Not that habergeon, my good man." Sir Theodore Cannon picked the larger of the chain mail shirts. "And certainly not this." He dragged the visored helmet down the hearth.

"Sir Teddy." Breen wiped his brow with his wadded-up shirt. "I'll be needing that for one of the horses." He had stripped down to the waist to work in the intense fire.

That was another thing old Culpepper had figured out. The fireplace inside the station had to serve several functions. To keep folks warm. To cook food. And to serve any blacksmith for any situation.

"You shall have to work on the horse's armor," the actor said, "and divide it so that it can fit over two horses, not just one big stud from the fifteenth century. You can use the other chain mail shirt."

"That's for me, Sir Teddy."

"Nonsense, my fine, brave, young friend. You shan't be driving."

Breen's head shook. "I suppose you think you'll be driving."

"Exactly."

Having removed the hobbles from the horses that had once belonged to three Mexican bandits, the Apache buck had slipped a hackamore over the pinto, and began leading the horse away from the others, whispering what must have passed as soothing phrases to an Apache. Then the Indian swung onto the horse's back, stopped the pinto, made it back up, turned the horse in a tight circle, and when he had it stopped, he let out a tremolo.

That's when Matt McCulloch stepped out of the canyon, leaped up, and drove the knife into the Indian's side. They fell down. The pinto bolted, but stopped only fifteen yards away.

Gurgling blood, the Indian rammed the palm of his right hand against McCulloch's chin. The former Ranger's neck popped backward, and he bit his lip. He figured the Indian would bleed out pretty quickly as deep as that knife had been pushed inside, and as much as he had twisted it, but the Indian brought the hand away from McCulloch's jaw, and next slammed it hard into his sternum.

He dropped onto his back, shook his head, cursed, and came up. The Apache tried to kick him, but McCulloch dropped the knife and caught the Apache's moccasin with both hands. He twisted the foot savagely, heard the ankle snap, and shoved the Indian away. He landed in cactus and tried to stand up, but McCulloch had found the knife and had recovered his senses. He drilled his foot between the brave's legs, then he slammed down quickly and rammed the knife into the Apache's heart. Again, he twisted the blade, hard, relentlessly. He drew it out, cut the Indian's throat, and then ran the blade across the dead warrior's head. His left hand took hold of the slick, greasy hair, and he jerked.

It sounded like a loud pop when he pulled the scalp free. He shoved the trophy into the dead Indian's mouth and turned around to see an older Apache, drawing back a spear over his right shoulder and preparing to let it sail.

The next thing McCulloch understood was that the spear was falling harmlessly maybe two feet in front of the Indian, who was collapsing onto his side.

Gwen Stanhope emerged from the shadows and dropped the stone she had been holding, letting it land on the man's groin. He did not flinch, or moan, or even move. Blood pooled beneath his crushed head. His eyes stared at the nothingness in the sky.

The Ranger came up, staring at the gambler.

She walked to him and held out both hands. "Let me help you up, Matt. Then we best get these horses saddled and ready."

"It's my wagon, Mr. Breen," the actor said. "I must drive the wagon. Besides, you are not a driver."

"Sir Theodore," Breen began.

"Our female friend, that charming little concubine named Miss Stanhope, she made her closing argument, which convinced me like it would any American jury. So here's mine. You have a Sharps Big Fifty. Am I correct?"

"Sir Theodore . . ."

"Am I correct, sir?"

"Yes, Teddy, you are."

"Do you think the woman, Miss Stanhope, or our illustrious newspaper editor from Purgatory City will be able to shoot that weapon with your accuracy?"

"No. And I see where you're trying to get to, Sir Teddy, but it's not going to work."

"It'll work well. Gwen Stanhope probably can't shoot a Big Fifty. And we will need all our top guns to be armed with guns. Mr. Breen, you are a fine man, sir, and I have enjoyed this meeting with you — although, naturally, a meeting in much less stressful, deadly, and damned terrifying situations would have made things better. Whether you are riding in this coach, or on some horse Matt McCulloch has managed to procure for you . . . we will need, we must have if we are to survive —" Sir Theodore stopped speaking a moment then went on. "It is imperative that we are outfitted with men who can shoot, and shoot with all accuracy, at the vermin Indians who are trying to wipe us off the face of the earth."

Breen started to make his argument, but bit off his curse and his statement, and looked at Sean Keegan.

"Don't look over here for no help, Breen," Keegan said. "I'm not a sergeant anymore. I don't give nobody any orders."

"You've been barking orders since I got to Culpepper's Station," Breen said.

"Yeah. But you know Sir Theodore's orders make a hell of a lot of sense."

Matt McCulloch saddled his buckskin and the Mexican's horses and slipped a lasso over the roan. He secured the lead rope to the black's halter and took the rope to the pinto, which Gwen Stanhope was saddling.

"We'll cut around to the north," McCulloch told her. "It'll take us too long to ride through that slot canyon, and once we come out, we'll have no idea where any of the Indians are. And this is a hard country to get around at night, anyway."

She climbed into the saddle and pulled down the hat — McCulloch's hat — low on her head.

When McCulloch moved toward his buckskin, he heard the clicking of a hammer behind him. He turned to see Gwen Stanhope holding a small pistol with a fairly large barrel.

393

He nodded. "Thirty-two is my guess. Teat-fire. Likely a Moore."

"I don't know what it is, Matt, except that it's got a brass frame and is loaded."

"Yeah."

"I'd appreciate it if you'd stop moving your hand toward that knife."

"I'd appreciate it if you'd stop aiming that relic at my middle."

"I appreciate you, Matt, but that's not happening."

"So Alvin J. Griffin Number Four was right all this time," McCulloch said, and let out a long sigh.

"No," she said, "he was wrong. But I'll be damned if I ride back to that station to get myself alive and well to El Paso, where I'll get hung up quicker than it usually took you to string up some Mexicans when you Rangers found them rustling cattle — and don't tell me that never happens. I've been around this part of the world for a damned long time."

"So you're taking one horse . . . ?"

"Two. In case I need to put some extra distance between me and the Indians."

McCulloch grinned. "So . . . which way will you be heading?"

She looked up, tried to find the moon and stars but quickly stopped. "Oh —" Her lips trembled, and she almost swayed in the saddle.

"Cloudy this night, and close to a new moon. Lot harder to find your bearings when it's this way. Besides, you don't want to leave us yet, do you, Gwen?"

"Why?" she asked, her shoulders sagging and her head dropping in defeat.

"That fifty thousand dollars of Mr. Henderson's," he reminded her. "It's back at Fort Hopeless. Unless the Apaches have overrun our fortress."

CHAPTER TWENTY-NINE

"Can you actually move with all that metal on?" Jed Breen asked.

The visor of the helmet was closed, and when Sir Theodore Cannon answered, neither Breen nor Sean Keegan could understand a blasted word he said.

Breen had to reach over and push up the metal. "You want to spit that out again?"

"Tally-ho, my good man," the actor said. "Yes. I can move. Even with my horribly maimed foot. The metal acts as a good cast, if I do say so myself. It's heavy, but, well, most people think that knights in those glorious but dark, lean, frightful times were immobile, but that is far from the case. As I told you earlier, I have seen actors do handstands and cartwheels while wearing suits even heavier than what I have on."

"The question is," Sean Keegan said, "can you work the reins to the horses?"

"But of course, my good man, but of

course."

Breen tapped a knife against the armor and shook his head.

"This particular getup," Sir Theodore said, and somewhere beneath the shadows and the metal, he must have smiled. "Did you enjoy my use of your Western parlance, gentlemen? *Getup.* What a fascinating word. Sir Walter Scott would have loved it. But I digress. The suit I don was made for jousting, thus it is thicker on this side." He tapped his left side.

"You can still work the reins," Keegan repeated. "And the brake."

"Yes, yes, yes. Come, gentlemen. If King Arthur's knights could not mount their horses without the help of their manservants, they would have all died." His right leg rose, and the heavy boot dropped with a clang. His left leg lifted and also banged on the floor. "Now, I do not think I shall be able to run very fast, crippled and weighted down, but . . ."

Keegan slapped the tin on the man's chest with the butt of his revolver. "I guess it will stop an arrow."

"Probably not a bullet, though." Jed Breen frowned.

"Then let's hope ol' Holy Shirt don't lose his charm."

"I'm excited," Sir Theodore said. "Nervous, but what actor does not feel sick before he first steps onto the stage? No matter how many times he has performed this play, he remains a total wreck, nerves tormenting him so, but then he finds himself treading the boards and all is well. Yes, all is well."

"Do you want to climb out of that airtight?" Keegan asked.

"Goodness, no! There's no telling how long it would take me to climb back into this bucket." He clanged away.

Breen chuckled. "That noise alone might scare off the Apaches."

Keegan was in no humor. "I don't like it."

"I don't, either," Breen said. "I don't think this will work at all."

"Then why are we doing it?"

"Because if we have to die, when they find us with a knight in medieval armor, they'll be writing about us for the next fifty years."

Keegan shook his head and spit on the floor.

"What time is it?" the newspaperman asked.

"No idea," Keegan answered absently.

Breen moved to the shutter and looked into the night. "We've got a while before sunrise, but McCulloch and that gambler, they damned well better hurry."

■ ■ ■

Getting past a number of Apaches in the dark while maneuvering through the rocks and cactus afoot had seemed almost impossible. Coming down the hill with four horses?

Maybe, McCulloch thought, *Stanhope had been thinking levelheaded back where they had found the horses.* Mount up. Ride hard and fast and as far away from Culpepper's Station. Leave all that money, a bounty hunter, a grizzled former Army sergeant, and a crazy actor to Holy Shirt and his boys.

They had made it maybe a quarter mile before they stopped. Stanhope kept her hand on the muzzle of one of the horses. Matt McCulloch left the two horses he was leading back with her and crept forward. His right hand held the knife. Anxious, he held his breath, sweating, hoping, and praying that the crackling of wood, probably the skeleton of a long-dead cactus, had been caused by a javelina, and not one of the Apache warriors. But he knew better.

"Apaches," an old scout had told him up in the Guadalupe Mountains a year or two back, "ain't human, son. It's the noses, you see. They's better than a coonhound for followin' a trail. They can smell anything. A white man. A white woman. Grease from a gun. Sweat from a trapped man. And the hair from a horse."

McCulloch knew they were downwind of whoever or whatever was coming this way.

The way the horses acted pleased him. So did the way the woman did not panic. He knew the horses would not stay quiet for long, but he did not expect the noise that broke the stillness.

Water sprayed on the rocks thirty feet behind him. If an Apache could smell the hair of a horse, then surely this one could smell the urine as one of the mounts relieved its bladder.

A rock skidded across the ground, and McCulloch felt the Apache step closer. He planned to bury the knife into the warrior's throat, hoping to sever the vocal cords before the brave could let out a scream, when another unexpected thing happened.

Gwen Stanhope shouted, "Look out!"

McCulloch was already moving toward the sneaking Indian when he stopped, and somehow sensed the presence of something dropping out of the sky.

He pushed himself away, landed on his back, somersaulted over, and sprang to his feet. The second Apache had leaped from the rocks above, and if not for Stanhope's warning and McCulloch's lucky move, the former Texas Ranger would be, if not dead, at least on the ground and about to be cut to ribbons.

The Indian who had jumped off the ledge came up, spitting venom and Apache curses, and swinging his tomahawk in defensive maneuvers, even though McCulloch was too far away to be any threat. The other Apache charged and yelled. Behind McCulloch, the horses stamped their hooves and whinnied.

McCulloch brought the blade of his knife up, deflecting the Apache's thrust. He threw a left punch that grazed off the Indian's bare shoulder, and as the Apache tumbled past him, McCulloch slashed with his knife. He must have missed, but that extra sense — what many Rangers said had kept him alive all these years — had him ducking.

The tomahawk sliced only empty air, and McCulloch dived to his right as the tomahawk came at him again. Then he heard the pistol shot. He turned his head to shield his eyes from the muzzle flash, and saw the first Indian coming at him. McCulloch buried his knife just beneath the brave's ribs. His free hand caught the warrior's wrist, and the Apache's knife slipped from his grip as

McCulloch twisted the blade.

"Aiiiiiyeeeeeeee," the dying brave wailed as McCulloch pushed him back.

One horse thundered past.

McCulloch whirled around and saw the shadow of the Apache with the tomahawk. He was on the ground, not moving, and McCulloch knew he owed Gwen Stanhope again. She had saved his life twice in as many minutes.

"Matt?" she called out in the darkness.

McCulloch ran. He found her holding reins to three of the horses, including McCulloch's buckskin. He took the reins from her, and the reins to the pinto. "Get on that one. I'll pull the pinto behind me."

"Where are we going?" she asked.

An arrow whistled over his head. Apaches yipped. A musket roared, and the bullet whined off a rock far beyond them. The pinto pulled hard, burning McCulloch's left hand with the leather reins.

"Where are we going?" She repeated the question, and her voice broke from total fear.

To Hell, McCulloch thought, but he said, "Ride for the station. Don't stop till we're there."

He waited till she managed to climb into the saddle despite the horse's dancing. Then a bullet hit the horse. It grunted and fell.

"Kick free!" McCulloch yelled.

Stanhope hit the ground, but away from the horse. McCulloch turned quickly, started to find his weapon and shoot, but knew better. Another bullet blew off the horn of his saddle.

"Get on the pinto!" he yelled.

He didn't have to. Stanhope was already leaping into the saddle as McCulloch tossed her the reins.

Another bullet whined off a rock. McCulloch almost lost the hold on the reins to his buckskin when the gelding reared. But he also heard an Apache yelling at his men. McCulloch understood just a few words, but nothing this one was saying. Even so, the former Ranger figured he must have been warning the Apaches not to shoot the horses. Or, maybe, he figured, not to shoot at all. Not rifles. Not revolvers. That would ruin Holy Shirt's medicine.

Whatever was being said, it gave McCulloch the chance he and Stanhope needed. He found the saddle and kicked the buckskin hard in the ribs. "Stay close!" he yelled.

"Don't worry about me!" she cried out.

He felt the wind as the buckskin exploded into a lope. He swung low in the saddle.

And he prayed he was riding in the right direction.

Sergeant Keegan had fallen asleep, but it wasn't his watch. He was supposed to be asleep. Sir Theodore Cannon was snoring something awful, but he was supposed to be catching a few winks, too. Jed Breen wanted desperately to sleep, but he wasn't about to leave Alvin J. Griffin IV to keep an eye out for Apaches — or the return of Gwen Stanhope and Matt McCulloch.

But his eyes were closed, and his breathing was steady.

He heard the footsteps, and he tried to tell himself that this was not happening. That Alvin J. Griffin was not that big of a fool.

The bolt started to slide, and Breen shook his head, opened his eyes, and brought up the double-action .38 that was in his right hand. He rolled over, quiet as a mouse.

Gunfire popped in the distance, causing Breen to frown. Apaches? McCulloch and the girl? He almost felt the urge to pray. For the Ranger. And the blonde. Silence returned. Breen wondered if the gunfire had unnerved the newspaperman. For several minutes, he heard nothing, so Breen started to fake his snores. The sergeant started snoring again, too.

A minute passed. Then five. No more gunshots sounded in the distance, and that could have meant good news or terrible news. After two more minutes, Breen was shaking his head. Alvin Griffin was trying to move the bolt off the door.

Sergeant Keegan's snores continued, but they sounded different. Breen turned his head to look at the blanket where the Army veteran was sleeping only to find Keegan on his belly, eyes open, Remington in his right hand, looking at the door — all the while snoring.

After a quick glance at Breen, Keegan nodded, and both men began crawling across the floor and around Fort Hopeless, Keegan to the left, Breen to the right. When they were ten feet from the door, they rose as Griffin tried to push up the cottonwood bar as silently as possible. The newspaperman realized something was afoot, and the bar slammed back into place as he spun around.

Two revolvers were aimed at his face.

"Going somewhere?" Keegan asked.

"To Hell," Breen answered. "That'd be my guess."

The newspaperman backed against the door and dropped the grip and the canteens.

"I . . . I . . . I . . . was . . . j-j-just . . . try-ing . . . getting . . . fresh air."

Breen laughed.

Keegan waved the revolver. "Go ahead. We won't stop you. But . . . you don't need the water."

"And I don't think those greenbacks need any fresh air." Breen waved the Lightning at the ugly bag the newspaperman had dropped.

"What do you think, Breen?" Keegan asked.

The bounty hunter shook his head. "Tak-ing money . . . that I understand. But water? That's low-down."

"I wasn't . . ." Griffin started, but stopped and gagged when Keegan shoved the barrel of the Remington into his gut.

"Shut up," Keegan said. "Did you think you could get away from all those Apaches?"

"I guess that much money drives people to gamble a lot," Breen said.

"You best say exactly what you were do-ing," Keegan said. "It'll go easier on you."

"Meaning you'll kill me quick!" the jour-nalist said.

Keegan shrugged.

"I was getting fresh air."

"Maybe he was opening the door so the Apaches could finish us off," Breen said.

Keegan straightened, realizing that was probably exactly what the newspaper editor had planned. "While those bucks are butchering us, torturing us, hell, he probably could have gotten away."

"No." Griffin's hands reached for the ceiling. "No, I swear. I wouldn't have done that."

"That much water would have gotten him to safety," Keegan said.

"And that much money could have bought him a new life," Breen added.

"No!" The man screamed. "No. I swear. I wouldn't . . . I wasn't . . ."

"Kill him," Keegan said.

"With pleasure," Breen said.

Then they heard the horses.

"Damn it all to hell," McCulloch said.

No Indians followed. He did not know why, and he did not care. Maybe Holy Shirt had ordered the braves not to risk the horses or not to risk the medicine man and war leader's medicine. It couldn't be that Apache superstition about fighting at night, because that was what had just caused McCulloch to swear.

The grayness had not seemed important. He hadn't even noticed it. He had not realized that he was seeing more than he should have been seeing at night. That's probably because all the pressure he had been under trying to get Stanhope and himself to the horses, and then trying to get the horses to the stagecoach station.

It was almost dawn. It had taken them that long.

On the other hand, he was alive. Stanhope was alive. They had two horses. One was dead. One was dying. But they had two, and that's all they needed to pull that wagon.

He shot a glance behind him, saw Stanhope leaning low, mouth set, eyes determined. They crested the hill, then raced down to the bottom, moved through the boulders and creosote, and saw the charred skeleton of the barn.

"Open the damned door!" McCulloch cried. "Open the damned door!"

Two Apaches sprang out of the bushes on the other side of the stagecoach road. They quickly brought their bows to the ready, while their left hands found arrows in their quivers. One shot first. The arrow just missed striking the buckskin in the throat. The other Indian was about to fire when he was blown about five yards back into the mesquite.

McCulloch looked back at the cabin to see Jed Breen kneeling beside Sir Theodore

Cannon's wagon and removing the empty .50-caliber shell from the breech of his Sharps. Sergeant Keegan appeared at the doorway and sent two rounds from his Remington revolver that chased the other brave away.

War whoops sounded behind McCulloch, and he pulled hard on the reins to the buckskin and leaped out of the saddle. Breen came to him, shifting the Sharps to his left hand.

McCulloch shoved the reins into the bounty hunter's right hand. "Get him inside!" he yelled, and rushed to Gwen Stanhope, who was leaning out of the saddle to the left as the pinto twisted and turned and kicked out with its hind legs. That sent the blonde to the dirt.

McCulloch leaped up and managed to grab one of the reins. He fell onto his knees, was pulled back about ten feet, but somehow managed to snag the other rein. The horse stopped just long enough for Mc-Culloch to scramble to his feet. He turned, saw Indians charging from the corral, and looked back as Sergeant Keegan managed to shove Stanhope through the open door.

"Come on!" McCulloch yelled, and headed for the stagecoach station. The horse followed obediently, or maybe fearful of the charging Indians behind him. McCulloch ducked and hoped the pinto would have the good sense to duck to get its sorry hide inside the station.

When he realized he was inside, and when he realized that Keegan and Breen were slamming and bolting the door before the Apaches made it in, he was jerked to the floor as the horse reared slightly.

McCulloch spun around, escaping the hooves as the pinto came down on all fours.

McCulloch blinked, trying to remember how to breathe. He couldn't blame the pinto for going a little wild inside the station. Seeing a man in a shining suit of armor would startle man or beast.

CHAPTER THIRTY

The desert, Alfredo Pagliotti thought as he crossed himself and removed his sugarloaf sombrero, did many strange and wonderful things. It was hot, yes, very hot, and that would have one believe that meat would rot and spoil, and sometimes, *sí,* it did just that. And yet there were other times . . .

Only the Lord in Heaven above could answer some things about that land. Perhaps, Pagliotti thought, on his next visit to see his family, kiss his mother, and confess his many sins to his kid brother — the priest in the Mexican village of Yelamos — he would ask him to explain why such things happened.

Billy Hawkin was dead. That much was evident. He had been shot at least once in the head, probably while he lay down where he was right that very moment. His eyes remained open, although the sun had baked them. Yet Billy Hawkin's body had not been butchered by Apaches, nor picked apart by vultures and coyotes. No flies or bugs even bothered the dead young brother of Alfredo Pagliotti's boss, Jake Hawkin. His face was becoming like a prune, not the prunes his mother preserved in gringo mason jars, but a dried prune. Like jerky.

That reminded Pagliotti that he had not eaten since yesterday around noon. He dug into his jacket, withdrew the pouch, opened it, dipped his fingers inside and withdrew a long piece. His teeth grabbed hold and he tugged, felt the meat tear, and he began chewing deliberately, feeling the saliva and tasty juices fill his mouth and coat his tongue. His kid brother was not only a fine priest in the village of Yelamos, he was one of the best makers of jerky in many, many kilometers north, south, east, and west. Perhaps Pagliotti would take his brother some cattle to butcher and dry. Young Padre Tomás would like that.

Jake Hawkin, on the other hand . . .

"What the hell was he doing out here?" asked the outlaw with the twin pistols, Colter Vaughn. He pulled off his black hat and slapped it against his thigh.

Alfredo Pagliotti shrugged. *"¿Quién sabe?"*

"Is he alone?" another of the gringo riders asked.

"*Sí.*" Pagliotti pointed at the tracks. "Well, there are the dead men over there, but those men I do not know."

"They's Mexicans, ain't they?" Vaughn said.

Alfredo Pagliotti looked up. "Mexico is a big country, amigo. And I know who I want to know." Pagliotti wished he did not know Colter Vaughn.

Another man began cursing in English and Spanish, and pointed to the smoke. "That's the second time we've seen that sign, Alfredo," he said in the true language. "I do not like riding in this country with Apaches running free."

"Nor do I," Pagliotti said in Spanish.

"Speak English, you turds," Vaughn said. "You're in Texas, not Mexico."

Pagliotti pointed at the smoke. "Eduardo merely points out that we are not alone."

"Hell's fire," another gringo said. "I don't like this."

"You like it for fifty thousand bucks," Vaughn said.

That silenced the gringo, but Pagliotti looked at some of the other riders, those from Mexico and those hot-tempered *norteamericanos,* and he realized that most of the men believed as Eduardo thought. Pagliotti could not blame them. They would rather be across the Rio Grande, and none of them, as far as he knew, had a brother who was a fine priest and knew how to make the best beef jerky between Denver and Mexico City.

Kneeling again by the corpse, Pagliotti plucked the piece of paper out of Billy Hawkin's pocket.

"What is that?" the gringo named Colfax asked.

"It is nothing you can spend on . . . whiskey or a *puta*," Pagliotti told him. "It is for Señor Hawkin. Señor Jake." He slipped it inside his jacket next to the pouch of his beloved beef jerky.

He walked to his horse, took the reins from Jacobo, who was holding them, and started to mount his horse.

"What about Billy?" Vaughn shouted. "Ain't you gonna plant his sorry hide?"

Alfredo Pagliotti turned and stared at the fool gringo. "You may stay and give him his last rites and see to his soul if you must. But I have a better idea." He nodded at the white smoke rising from the hills. "Let us leave Señor Billy as he is. But we shall tell Señor Jake that we buried him. *Vamanos.*"

Since the smoke seemed to be near Culpepper's Station, Alfredo Pagliotti led his men on a wide loop around those hills and canyons. They rode in a roundabout way toward Sierra Vista. It was about time to meet up with the boss and divide all that money that had been taken from the bank in Sierra Vista. Pagliotti planned to give at least fifty dollars to his kid brother Tomás when he arrived back in Yelamos.

To his surprise, he spotted dust about fifteen miles later. Apaches would not raise dust, and there was not enough dust to belong to a gringo posse or an Army patrol. He handed a spyglass to one of the younger Mexicans who rode for the gringo outlaw and sent him onto a mesa to see what fool or fools would be riding there at that time of day, especially with Apache smoke signals going up everywhere.

Forty minutes later, for it was a very hard climb to reach the top of the mesa and come back down, Rabaso emerged, returned the spyglass to Alfredo Pagliotti, and said, *"El Jefe."*

At first, thought that young Rabaso was calling him, Alfredo Pagliotti, the boss, and that made Alfredo Pagliotti beam with pleasure, but then he saw how nervous young Rabaso was, and that caused Alfredo Pagliotti to frown.

"Hawkin?" he asked.

The youngster's Adam's apple bobbed and he nodded quickly. *"Sí. El Jefe."*

After removing his sombrero and rubbing his long black hair with his gauntlet, Pagliotti let out a very long sigh, looked at young Rabaso, then at Colter Vaughn, and then at the smoke rising off in the distance.

"I'll be damned," he said in English, and nodded at young Rabaso and Colter Vaughn. "Ride out. Bring Señor Jake to us. He might like it here. We are at least in the shade."

Slowly, after hearing the words from the greaser named Alfredo Pagliotti, Jake Hawkin sat on a boulder and pushed back his hat.

"Was it them greaser banditos you found near him?" Hawkin asked. "Did they kill my brother?"

"No, Señor Jake." Carefully, the Mexican bandit reached inside his jacket and pulled out the page torn from a book. Hawkin looked at Galloway for help, found none, and reached up and snatched the page from Pagliotti's hand. He looked at the paper, realized that it came from one of those damned books the Texas Rangers carried, and wondered what the hell the fool Mexican meant by handing him a page about some burglar named Ed Haines who had busted into some homes and businesses in Round Rock, or a killer called Ham Harrelson whom Jake Hawkin knew had been hanged in Childress back in December. Then he turned the page over.

He saw the beginning of the entry for himself, and above that the shorter description and list of crimes attributed to his brother, young Billy. He saw the dried blood on the corner of the page and he read the scribbled note across the margin.

Billy Hawkin. Shot dead by Matt McCulloch while protecting himself.

"Matt McCulloch. That Ranger thimble-rigger. I'll see him in Hell for this. Nobody kills my brother and gets away with it." Jake wadded up the paper into a ball and tossed it to the dirt, but the wind caught it and carried it into a cactus.

"Where was he killed?" Hawkin asked.

"South of Culpepper's Station," the Mexican answered.

"And you buried him?"

"*Sí.* What kind of man would leave a poor young *norteamericano* to rot? Or not put up a cross, if only of cactus skeletons, over his grave?" He crossed himself.

"I appreciate that." Hawkin hitched up his gunbelt, drew his revolver, opened the loading gate, pulled the hammer to half cock, and rotated the cylinder on his forearm. Satisfied with the bullets, he brought the hammer back and softly down, snapped the gate shut, and shoved the hogleg into the holster.

"All right, boys, we're going to kill the man who shot my kid brother. Just know this. *I* kill him. You can shoot him all to pieces, but I want the SOB alive when I put a bullet through his manhood, his gut, his kneecaps, and finally right between his eyes. Make sure you remember that."

"The Apaches may have taken care of that for you," Pagliotti told him. "The tracks left by the Ranger headed toward Culpepper's Station. The smoke we saw came from Culpepper's Station. And there was much fire, much fire, in the night. I think the Apaches have burned the station to the ground."

"They can't burn that station," Hawkin said. "It's built like a damned fort."

"There was much fire in the night," Pagliotti said again.

"Barn maybe. It don't matter. We're riding to Culpepper's. We'll pick up McCulloch's trail. If the Apaches killed him, by thunder, I'll take some Apache scalps.

Nobody's killing that Ranger, boys, but me."

"He's not a Ranger no more, Jake," Colter Vaughn said.

"All the better. Rangers won't be so hard on our trail if we kill some murdering devil who's not a Texas Ranger no more." He nodded at Galloway and moved to his horse.

"Señor Jake?" the Mexican named Alfredo Pagliotti said pleasantly.

Hawkin turned around, frowned, and pointed at the Mexican's horse. "You ain't mounted."

"No. What about the money?"

"What money?" Jake Hawkin said bitterly.

"The money from the bank in Sierra Vista. The money we left with you, your brother Billy, Señor Galloway, and the strange little gringo from the bank. *¿Cuál era su nombre?*"

"Henderson," answered Jacobo.

"*Sí.*" Pagliotti's head nodded. "Yes. Henderson. You have the money, Señor Jake? We would like to split it up. I could be in Yelamos in three days."

"I don't have the damned money," Jake Hawkin barked. "That damned skinflint of a cashier, Henderson, he stole it."

Alfredo Pagliotti moved his right hand beside his revolver. Several of the other men put their hands on the butts of their revolvers or the stocks of their rifles.

"I'm telling you the damned truth," Hawkin said. "Tell them, Galloway."

"It's true," the gunman said. "We were at this little . . . well . . . in the whorehouse. Just the way we planned. The little cashier was in one of the rooms, too. He had the grips with the money. Nobody figured he'd have the sand to try to get away with it. But he did. Best we figured, he caught the westbound stage. Billy went after him. That's why you happened to find him shot full of lead. And that's why we're going. To get that fifty thousand dollars."

"The Apaches might have that, too, my friend," one of the Mexicans said from horseback.

"Then we'll steal it back from those red devils!" Hawkin roared.

"From Apaches?" Pagliotti asked.

"If they have it, yes," said Hawkin. "And if they don't, we'll get it off that stagecoach. We'll take it off Matt McCulloch." He found himself sweating. Saw the distrust and the doubt in the eyes of practically every man who was riding with Alfredo Pagliotti. "Boys, you don't take fifty thousand dollars sitting on your asses."

"And," Pagliotti said, "you don't lose it laying on your backs . . . in *el burdel*."

Some of the Mexicans in the bunch snickered.

"You boys are coming with me," Jake Hawkin said, and then tried to swallow as several guns were aimed at Galloway and him.

"Jake," Pagliotti said as he swung onto his horse. "We will leave you with your lives. Anyone here who wants to ride with you against Holy Shirt's Apaches has our blessing. We will take your saddle bags. And one canteen. And your money." He snapped his fingers, and four Mexicans moved quickly to the outlaw leader and Galloway, both of whom raised their hands, and let go their wallets, tobacco, watches, dice, and knives — along with saddlebags and Galloway's canteen, for everyone knew he filled his canteen with whiskey. The wallets were given to Pagliotti, who stuck them into his jacket pocket near his beef jerky.

"Who stays behind?" he asked.

Colter Vaughn nudged his horse out of the group. "Reckon I'll risk my hide for that much loot."

"*Bueno.*" The Mexican bowed and touched the brim of his hat.

Jake Hawkin looked around, hoping someone else would join him. His eyes landed on Mitchum, and he called out his name.

"You've ridden with me for two years, Buck."

"Closer to three," Mitchum said. "But before that, I rode with Cullen Baker. And before that, it was the Reno boys. And before that, it was with Arch Clements. And before that, William Quantrill. I know when it's time to pull out, boss, so I'm pulling out."

Pagliotti leaned his head back and laughed. *"Que tengas un buen día e ir al infierno,"* he called out, spurred his horse, and the men who had been part of the Hawkin Gang left Jake Hawkin, Galloway, and Colter Vaughn turning their heads from the thick, choking dust.

"What did that greaser say?" Jake Hawkin asked when the dust had settled.

"Something along the lines," Galloway replied, "of have a nice day and go to hell."

CHAPTER THIRTY-ONE

"It damned sure took y'all long enough," Jed Breen snapped.

"You think you could've done better?" Matt McCulloch was in no mood for argument.

"Hey!" Sergeant Keegan decided to play peacemaker. "He got here — so did the woman — with two horses. That's all that matters."

"We didn't have to come back," Mc-Culloch said.

"Yeah," Keegan said, "but if you'd deserted us, Breen and me would have tracked you both down — even if we were ghosts after the Apaches finished us off."

The pinto kicked over a bucket.

McCulloch, tired, irritated, hungry, and in general, just ticked off at everyone surrounding him, was about to fire back at the two men who had spent their evening in the relative safety of the stagecoach station. But then he saw Alvin J. Griffin IV. "What the hell is that about?"

Breen drew in a breath and exhaled. It was supposed to help one relax. It wasn't working. "He wanted to travel some. We wanted him to stay."

The editor was on a chair, his back to the window, making a pretty easy target for any Indians who wanted to shoot through the cross cutouts. He was gagged, tied to the chair — arms, hands, legs, ankles, and chest — and trussed up like a Christmas goose. His eyes remained wide open in terror.

"Surprised you didn't nail him up against the shutter like you did Henderson," McCulloch said.

The sergeant shrugged. "Out of nails."

"Oh, my God." Gwen Stanhope didn't say it desperately. She just stared, her mouth agape, at Sir Theodore Cannon in his medieval suit of armor. "Oh, my God," she repeated. She even managed to smile.

Keegan, on the other hand, wasn't smiling. "Heard gunshots. And not all of them was coming from your weapons."

"Yeah." McCulloch found the ladle, dipped it into a bucket, and took a couple of swallows. "I don't know if Holy Shirt's boys have turned their backs on him or what."

"If they're shooting bullets, we're not getting far at all," Keegan said.

"Even if they go back to arrows and lances," Breen said, "if they shoot our horses, we're not getting far."

"If they shoot my buckskin," McCulloch said, "I'll be right mad."

"I don't think they'll shoot our horses," Keegan said. "They didn't shoot the mules. Just stole them."

"Because they're hungry," Breen said.

"And they shot a horse last night," Gwen Stanhope said.

"But I think that was an accident," McCulloch said.

Keegan chuckled. "Well, we'll see. Apaches have peculiar notions, especially this Holy Shirt. He tells his braves they can't use anything from the whites — no guns, no clothes, nothing along those lines — but they're free to take horses and mules. They must've forgotten that they'd never seen a horse till the Spanish brought them over."

"We're wasting time," McCulloch said.

"Yes," came the muffled voice of Sir Theodore Cannon before he pulled up his visor. "It is time to play out the final act."

"Don't say *final,* Sir Theo," Gwen Stanhope whispered.

The newspaperman muttered behind his gag.

Everyone looked at the two horses, then at the harness. No one spoke for a while. No one looked excited at the prospects.

"We could wait till night," the woman said.

Keegan shook his head. "I've got cabin fever, ma'am. Time for me to get out of this dark, stinking hellhole."

"Besides," Breen said, waving at the actor in the suit of armor, "Sir Theodore Cannon might not want to spend twelve more hours in that tin can."

"Indeed!" the actor said. "This will be my greatest performance."

They knew the problem. Daylight meant the Apaches would be ready — with no superstitions about being killed in the night. They would have to hitch the two horses to the actor's wagon. That would leave them as open targets. It was one impossible job. But how much longer could they survive an assault on Fort Hopeless?

McCulloch nodded at the bound and gagged newspaperman. "Cut him loose. We'll need him."

Breen started to protest, but tightened his lips together, and Keegan grabbed a butcher's knife off the countertop and moved to Griffin.

"I'll have you all arrested for kidnapping!" the man said as soon as the gag was freed.

"I said we needed you, Griffin," McCulloch said. "I didn't say we need your mouth. I can put that gag back in, and I will, if you keep working your jaws, buster."

The man rubbed his wrists when the bindings were cut loose, trying to return the circulation, and began twisting his feet one way and the other. He sat there, frowning, working the stiffness and numbness out of his body. But at least he did not talk. Keegan threw the knife, which stuck in the floor between the newspaperman's shoes.

"The buckskin," McCulloch said, nodding at his horse, "isn't broke for pulling. But he'll do it. I still doubt if the pinto's much of a buggy horse, either, but that's what we have."

"We could draw lots," Breen said. "Two of us ride out. The rest stay."

"You'd ride for help, I'm sure," Keegan said.

"If I win," Breen says.

"I've heard how you play cards, Breen," McCulloch said. "You always win."

Breen grinned and moved toward the tack. "I guess that means we're riding out together . . . in Sir Theodore's wagon. Let's get the horses ready."

Keegan and the woman followed, but when the actor started clanking his way toward the animals, the buckskin whinnied and the pinto backed away, heads lowering and ears flattening.

"You stay put, Cannon," McCulloch said. "And you" — he pointed at the journalist — "keep your eye out. Let us know if the Apaches start something or even look like they're about to start something."

Frowning, Griffin pushed himself up, knocking the chair over. Apologizing, he stumbled toward the window.

The horses were stripped of saddles, blankets, and bridles, and the men began to strap on the rigging for the stagecoach, the regular harness, and Breen's concoction of medieval chain mail and armor. When that was completed, they stared at the door. None wanted to venture outside into the uncertainty beyond the walls — and the certainty of death.

"How many rounds in the Winchester?" Keegan asked.

"It's full," said McCulloch, who had reloaded the carbine upon his return.

"You'll have to cover us," Keegan said.

"No." Breen came over and took the .44-40 from McCulloch's hand. With a shrug and a sigh, the bounty hunter said,

"You've never seen me hitch a team. And you don't want to. I'll cover." He turned to the window. "Hey, jackass."

Alvin Griffin turned, frowning, but keeping his lips together.

"Come here."

When the editor stood in front of the bounty hunter, Breen pulled his Lightning, spun the revolver on his finger, and lifted it, butt forward, to the journalist. "Take it. You'll cover with me. It's got six beans in the wheel, and you don't have to cock it. Just squeeze the trigger."

Griffin decided to make a speech. "You know we'll all be killed."

"Nobody lives forever," the woman said.

"Let's go," Keegan said.

The horses protested, and that's what gave Jed Breen the idea.

"Mr. Cannon. Sir Theodore. How would you like to open this play with a scene that will steal the show?"

" 'But, soft! what light through yonder window breaks? It is the east, and Juliet is the sun.' " Sir Theodore Cannon, visor pushed up on his gleaming helmet, began Romeo's soliloquy as soon as Keegan pulled open the door. He clanged his way onto the porch, through the wreckage of the stagecoach, and about ten yards into the yard.

" 'Arise, fair sun, and kill the envious moon,
Who is already sick and pale with grief,
That thou her maid art far more fair than
    she:"

With the Winchester cocked, Jed Breen was out a moment later. He squatted beside a wooden column when the first arrow flew out of the desert and clanged against Sir Theodore's chest. The arrow bounced off. So did the second shot, which hit Sir Theodore's gleaming side. The actor never broke his stride or cadence.

"Be not her maid, since she is envious;
Her vestal livery is but sick and green
And none but fools do wear it; cast it off."

It worked. Breen wasn't sure how long it might go on, but for the moment, the Apaches were talking in excited, fearful voices as the man in the suit of armor walked this way and that, singing the praises of sweet Juliet, while McCulloch, Keegan, and Gwen Stanhope brought the horses out toward the tongue.

Breen felt Alvin Griffin standing behind him. He heard the revolver's hammer being pulled back.

"I told you that you don't have to cock that piece, Griffin," Breen said tightly. "And if you're thinking about putting a bullet in my back, you damn sure better kill me."

The editor said nothing.

"Just watch," Breen whispered. "This might work. At least till we get that team hitched."

The horses were being backed into position. McCulloch and Keegan started working furiously. "Get the guns out of the station," Keegan told Stanhope.

"And the canteens," McCulloch added.

"And the carpetbags!" Breen called out.

An Apache came out of the brush, nocked an arrow, and let it fly toward Sir Theodore. It slammed against the side of the helmet, and the shaft shattered.

" 'See, how she leans her cheek upon her hand!' " Sir Theodore called out and turned to face the Apache. " 'O, that I were a glove upon that hand, That I might touch that cheek!' "

The Indian fitted his bow with another arrow, but he aimed it at Breen.

"Mercy!" the editor said in a trembling voice.

"Don't shoot," Breen warned him. "That'll break the trance Sir Theo's got them in."

The arrow sliced through the air and lodged in the pole a few inches from Breen's head. The bounty hunter's nerve held. He kept his finger light on the trigger.

On the other hand, Alvin Griffin's nerves left him. He didn't fire. He just turned and ran.

Breen shot him a glance and saw him knock Gwen Stanhope down as she came out of the station. Having already managed to put the canteens in the coach, she was carrying the late Harry Henderson's grips. Griffin stopped, looked at her as she tried to stand. Reaching down, he grabbed one of the carpetbags with his free hand and clumsily raced toward the coach. He was climbing into the box when Keegan jerked him down.

The editor landed in the dust with a thud and a groan, but he pushed himself partly off the ground and lifted the cocked .38.

Keegan's boot kicked the newspaperman's arm, and the gun roared. The horses jumped, but McCulloch was already in the box pulling the lines tight. The coach, its brake set, dragged a few feet.

The Apaches started yelling furiously. Arrows thudded the wall. Breen shot twice from the Winchester, and yelled, "Curtain's closing, Theodore! Get in the coach!"

The actor bowed, another arrow bounced off his suit, and he ran noisily and unsteadily, favoring his mangled foot, toward the coach. Breen snapped another shot, jacked a fresh round into the rifle, and ran to Stanhope. Kneeling, he jerked her to her feet and shoved her after Sir Theodore Cannon. An arrow grazed Breen's side. Keegan shot twice from the Lightning he had picked up and helped shove Cannon into the back, helped Breen and Gwen inside, and then he climbed into the box beside McCulloch, who was releasing the brake. An arrow went through Keegan's left arm, between his elbow and wrist, and he groaned, but popped the revolver until it clicked empty. He settled into the seat, dropped the smoking, empty Colt by his feet, and hoisted the Springfield.

The wagon was moving. Alvin J. Griffin IV was up and leaping into the doorway, not inside yet, as the coach started turning around the building. The newspaperman screamed but held tight, his hands clutching the side, the door banging against him, flying back, then hitting him again.

The wagon turned sharply. The Apaches came out of the rocks and cactus in full force. Arrows flew. The newspaperman screamed even louder.

Jed Breen rolled over, looked up, and found Griffin starting to make his way into the back of the wagon. The bounty hunter rolled back, lifted his legs, and kicked forward. The boots caught the editor in his thighs. His hands slipped, and he toppled from the back of the wagon into the dust.

"Nooooo!" he yelled.

Breen came up, looked to the woman, and fired the Winchester through the dust. Two shots. Then he told himself not to waste lead.

Stanhope took Keegan's revolver, aimed, but did not fire as she sidled up beside the bounty hunter.

"Nothing to say?" Breen asked as he picked up the Lightning, reached into his pocket, and began filling the chamber with the last of his .38-caliber cartridges.

Her head shook. "I know why you did it. He was no good."

"That's not why I did it," Breen said. "I figured it would give the Apaches something to do. Give us a little time. Till they decided to finish us off."

CHAPTER THIRTY-TWO

"Move, horses, move, damn you!" Matt McCulloch desperately worked the reins. He glanced to one side, hoping to find a black-snake whip, but saw nothing.

Keegan's Springfield roared, and he dropped back, opened the breech, and shoved in another .45-70 cartridge.

"This isn't what we planned!" McCulloch yelled. "Cannon's supposed to be up here. The armor was supposed to protect him!"

"Yeah." Keegan came up, aimed, fired again, and dropped back down to reload again. "Well, what the hell do you want us to do? Stop. Let that demented old fool come up here to spell you!"

"Shut up. Just keep those Indians off my back."

"*Our* backs, pal." Leaning the Springfield between himself and the former Texas Ranger, Keegan broke off the bloodied point of the arrow, threw it away, and grabbed the shaft below the feathers.

"You want help?" McCulloch asked.

"Just drive," Keegan said. "I've had practice at this sort of thing!" He set his jaw and yanked the arrow out, fell back against the seat, spit, looked at the bloody wood, and tossed it into the dust, too. He untied his neckerchief, wrapped it around the bloody holes in his blouse and arm, and used his teeth to help tie off the makeshift bandage.

"You gonna be all right?" McCulloch bellowed.

"Till they kill me." Keegan rose again, braced his elbow on the top of the wagon, and aimed, but did not fire. "Griffin didn't make it!" he yelled.

"I can't say I'll miss the prairie rat!"

"But he's doing his part for us. Aw, hell." The Springfield roared, and Keegan dropped back. He pulled the cartridge from the carbine and flung it at the pinto's rear. "Move, hoss, move!"

"What was that 'Aw, hell' for?" McCulloch worked the reins harder. "Come on, hosses. You can run harder than that!" He looked at Keegan, who was drawing back the hammer.

"An Apache ended the fun the youngsters were having. Put a bullet into Griffin. Blew the top of his head off."

McCulloch's jaw tightened. He turned back and screamed harder at the two horses. The wagon hit a hole, bounced on two wheels, but dropped back onto all four. "Maybe Holy Shirt can talk his bucks out of using any more firearms!" he shouted over the squeaking of the wagon and the jarring noise from the hooves.

Keegan stayed seated for the moment. His head shook. "That ain't likely, Matt. That Indian with the rifle. He had silver hair."

"Damn," McCulloch said. "Old Holy Shirt?"

Keegan nodded. "I guess the old man's abandoned his religion."

"Then he can go to Hell."

Keegan stood. "He probably will. After he's sent us there."

"Lot of dust," Galloway said from the top of the mesa. "Lot of gunshots, too."

Jake Hawkin drank a swallow from the canteen and nodded. After wiping his mouth with the back of his hand, he said, "You still got that spyglass?"

"Yeah."

"Fetch it."

When the gunman handed the long brass telescope to his boss, Hawkin rose, extended the scope, and sighted on the road that ran out of the hills surrounding Culpepper's Station.

"You see anything?" Galloway asked.

"No. They're still in the hills. Wait. Wait." He leaned forward. "Wagon. Riding hell-bent-for-leather. About a half-dozen Apaches coming after them."

"Maybe Henderson's still on that stage-coach," Galloway said.

Hawkin shook his head and pushed the brass scope together.

"That's the hell of it, Galloway." He pointed the telescope at the dust. "That ain't no stagecoach them bucks are chasing."

They were out of the hills and the canyon, moving into open country, surrounded by mesas and buttes. The road stretched on, but riding across it felt like driving over a busted washboard. The wagon bounced this way and that. The Apaches spread out.

Stretched out on his belly, Breen aimed the Sharps. The door slammed shut, and he cursed, then the door bounced open. It closed again, but a bullet punched a hole through the wood. The door came open.

"Shoot!" Gwen Stanhope yelled.

"At what?" Breen barked back. "I can't

see a thing but dust, and I don't have more than six bullets left for this baby."

Lying on his back, Sir Theodore Cannon began reciting the entire play of Tom Taylor's *Our American Cousin,* adjusting his voice to fit all of the characters.

Breen shook his head, watched the door keep banging open and shut, and muttered under his breath. "The last play Lincoln saw, the last play Jed Breen ever heard. Who would have thought? What are the odds?"

"Gunfire," Mr. Red said. Riding point, he pulled his horse to a stop.

Mr. Black pulled up alongside him. "Dust, too."

"Excellent," Charles Van Patten said. "We can let them ride straight to us."

"The way they're moving," Mr. Blue said, "they'll ride right over us."

"You're being well paid," Charles Van Patten reminded him.

"And we know our business," Mr. Red said.

"You don't let a man come to you," Mr. Black said.

"You ride to the sound of the guns," Mr. Blue said.

The three killers spurred their horses into a lope. Charles Van Patten swore under his breath and kicked his mount to follow.

The Springfield boomed, and Keegan sank back to reload.

"How far behind are they?" McCulloch yelled.

"Not spitting distance." Keegan's left hand was stained with blood, which dripped off his fingers onto the cartridge as he shoved it into the breech. "But getting mighty close."

McCulloch couldn't figure out how the soldier could still stand and shoot. He cursed again and whipped the reins — and had to drop them or be pulled off the coach.

Releasing his hold on his carbine, Keegan leaned over and grabbed the waistband of McCulloch's trousers and pulled him back into the seat. Keegan fell into the box and pushed himself up. His left arm gave way, and he fell back, cursed, and let McCulloch help him up.

"Thanks," both men said at the same time.

Keegan shook his head and watched the team of horses ride away, sunlight bouncing off the metal armor that covered as much of them as possible. The lines and part of the tongue were dragging behind them.

"What the hell happened?" Keegan asked.

McCulloch shook his head. "With this old

relic of an ambulance, it's a miracle we got this far before it started to fall apart."

Keegan pointed. "Should we use the brake?"

"And let Holy Shirt's boys catch us?"

"They'll catch us sooner or later."

"I'd rather die in a wagon wreck than be tortured by Apaches." The Ranger helped Keegan onto the bench beside him. "Here." He untied the neckerchief, adjusted it, and retied it over the arrow wound in the sergeant's arm. "Before you bleed to death." He pulled it tight, and made the knot hard. "It didn't hit an artery," McCulloch said, shaking his head.

"Lucky me."

"Revolver?" McCulloch asked.

Keegan tilted his head toward the wagon. "Gave mine to the girl."

"I hope she knows what to do with the last bullet," McCulloch said as he drew his Colt revolver and eared back the hammer.

"Yeah. And puts it through Holy Shirt's brisket."

The horses, despite being handicapped by the tongue and rigging, began pulling away from the wagon.

Keegan turned his head to keep the dust out of his eyes. The wagon bounced hard, and McCulloch grabbed the soldier's left

441

shoulder, and pulled him back onto the bench.

They stared ahead, and then looked at one another.

"Aw, hell," both men whispered.

CHAPTER THIRTY-THREE

"What the hell is McCulloch doing?" Jed Breen said when the door opened.

Gwen Stanhope screamed as the wagon tilted on two wheels, bounced, and rolled her to one side.

Perhaps only the weight of Sir Theodore Cannon's suit of armor kept the wagon from overturning.

"We're off the damned road!" Breen shouted.

The door slammed again, and when it opened, ever so briefly, Breen saw the cactus and the Indians. They were close enough that he could hear them, and because the wagon was slowing, the dust had become minimal. He swore, brought up the Sharps, and was about to pull the trigger when the door slammed again.

"Hang on! McCulloch yelled toward the back of the wagon. He gripped the bottom of the seat as the runaway coach rocked left and right, bounced up, came down, and turned so that it was moving straight for a mound of rocks.

"Jump!" he yelled. "Get out! We're going to crash!" He leaped off one side, and Keegan hurtled himself off the other. They landed, bounced up as fast as they could manage, and checked their guns to make sure nothing had been fouled by sand. Keegan swung the Springfield up to his hip. He had no time to aim, so he just squeezed the trigger. The round caught a galloping horse in the middle, and the horse fell hard, throwing its rider in nothing but a breech-cloth into the dirt and taking out the two horses galloping behind it.

"Come on!" McCulloch yelled. He aimed the .44-40 in his hand, but held his fire.

Keegan rose, stumbled, and they ran after the wagon.

The door opened, and Breen saw two men racing after the wagon. He almost shot one with his Big Fifty before he recognized the figure as Matt McCulloch. "What the hell?" Then he understood.

"Hell." Breen came to his knees, grabbed Gwen Stanhope's arm and yelled, "Brace yourself, Sir Theo. We're about to crash." The door slammed shut and immediately bounced open. "Grab that repeater!" He shouted at Stanhope, and as soon as she had the barrel in her hands, Breen leaped out of the opening, his shoulder slamming against the door as it swung shut.

They hit the ground. Cactus spines raked his right arm and his cheek. He lifted his head, spitting out dirt and tasting blood, and heard the slamming of wood against immoveable rock.

Keegan went to him. Breen saw the blood-stained arm and let the sergeant pull him up. He blinked, heard the Winchester cracking, and saw the charging warriors wheel their horses. That told him that Gwen Stanhope was all right.

"To the rocks!" McCulloch yelled.

A bullet creased the right side of Breen's neck.

The wagon lay on its side, one wheel off on the top and the rear wheel spinning and squeaking. He could not see any sign of Sir Theodore Cannon, but the back door was closed. He could see the two carpetbags and one of the canteens lying on the ground just before the rocks.

Two mounds of rocks were about forty yards apart. The wagon had crashed into one, which was closer.

Gwen Stanhope started for that one, but Breen pulled her away and shoved her in the opposite direction. "That way."

"It's farther!" she yelled.

"But it'll steer those Apaches away from Sir Theodore." Breen started running.

"If he's still alive." Keegan shook his head, grabbed the woman's arm and led her after Breen. McCulloch followed.

Sean Keegan dived over the rocks as a bullet ricocheted just past his ear. Immediately, he rolled over, bounded to his feet, drew a bead on a screaming warrior, and knocked him off his galloping dun with a shot from the Springfield. Falling back behind the rocks, Keegan reloaded the .45-70 after he shoved Gwen Stanhope onto the ground. Stepping over her, McCulloch snatched the Winchester carbine from her hand and sent two quick shots.

While lying on his back and reloading the Sharps, Jed Breen nodded at the Texas Ranger. "I still think it was a fine idea."

McCulloch shrugged. "Maybe next time we'll have a newer wagon that won't fall apart."

An arrow smashed against the rocks over their heads. McCulloch ducked, and began fingering the holders in his shell belt. He swore, and turned to Keegan. "I've maybe five in the Winchester, maybe not that many, and only four in the pistol. How about you?"

They counted off. The number didn't make any of them overly hopeful.

"Those Indians are leaving the wagon alone," McCulloch said as another Apache round whined off the rocks.

"For now," Breen said.

"He hasn't come out yet," Keegan said. "I fear he's dead."

"Likely he'll have company soon." Gwen Stanhope screamed and pointed. "Here comes one of them!"

"I see him," Keegan said. "It's old Holy Shirt himself."

McCulloch braced his rifle on the rocks, and flipped up the rear tang sight. Breen moved to the side and aimed his Sharps.

Holy Shirt, naked except a breechcloth, rode a high-stepping brown horse. He carried a lance in his left hand and held the hackamore in his right.

"Sun just reflected off something in his right hand," Breen said.

"Knife?" McCulloch asked.

"I don't know."

"You get first crack, Breen," Keegan said. "When he's in range."

"He was in range a half-mile ago," Breen said.

"Can you hit him from here?" Gwen Stanhope asked plaintively.

"I . . ." He lowered the rifle, raised his head, and muttered, "What the hell?"

The door to the overturned wagon was being pushed open, and the sun reflected brightly, causing Breen to turn his head.

"It's that damned fool Cannon," Keegan said.

Breen turned back, brought up the Sharps again, and lowered it. He yelled, "Get out of the way, Sir Theo! Drop down. Get out of the way."

McCulloch's mouth hung open.

Gwen Stanhope stood. "What's he doing?"

The Apache reined in. The surviving warriors behind him stopped their chanting.

All that the four people hiding in the rocks could hear was Sir Theodore Cannon's voice.

" '. . . Handmart is preparing for a settlement of his heavy demand for the stables,' " Sir Theodore Cannon said in his Cockney accent. " 'Then there is Temper for pictures and other things for Miss Florence Trenchard's account with Madame Pompon, and —

" 'Confound it, why harass me with details, these infernal particulars?' " he continued, using a haughty English voice. " 'Have you made out the total?' "

The brown horse carrying Holy Shirt reared and turned in a circle as the medicine man got the horse in control. The Indian lowered his lance.

One of the Apaches let loose an arrow, but it clanged off the belly of the armor. The actor moved back to his Cockney dialect. "Four thousand, eight hundred and thirty pounds, nine shillings, and sixpence."

Holy Shirt reined in his horse.

"I don't have a shot!" Breen yelled. "Sir Theodore's right in my line of fire. Can you take him, Keegan?"

Two bullets whined off rocks above Keegan's head. "Not without getting my head shot off."

"Toss me your rifle," Breen said, and he moved toward the sergeant before bullets sent him diving for cover. "Sons of bitches. Now they decide to shoot guns."

"If they shoot Cannon, he's a goner!" McCulloch yelled.

But they weren't shooting at the knight, at least, not with powder and lead.

"Matt!" Keegan yelled.

"I'm empty," McCulloch said, and tossed his carbine into the dust.

Gwen gasped and shouted, "Holy Shirt's about to charge."

Carefully, the three men raised their heads

just enough to see.

Holy Shirt shrieked his war cry, kicked the stallion in the ribs, and galloped toward the actor, who had stopped *Our American Cousin* and had become Falstaff in *Henry IV: Part I.*

No longer able to take it, Breen came to his feet, and ran out from the rocks. Keegan jumped from his perch and joined the charge.

McCulloch shook his head, and hurried past Gwen Stanhope. "Nobody lives forever."

The woman stood, watching the three men charge at the charging Apache, and the other Indians whoop and cheer. Suddenly, she just smiled and took off, too.

McCulloch drew his pistol and fired twice from the hip, hoping to startle the horse. He cut loose with a Rebel cry.

But they knew they would never reach the actor in time.

Sir Theodore had drawn the heavy sword from its scabbard as he marched out to meet the charging Apache. The other Indians stood back, still cheering, still singing, and some of them, having overcome their fear of the man in the shiny metal, were laughing at him.

Those with repeating rifles opened up on

the charging white foursome. And all four dived to the ground for cover.

Holy Shirt let the lance sail. Sir Theodore Cannon blocked it with a shield.

Keegan, McCulloch and Breen lifted their heads.

The woman covered her eyes. "I can't watch."

The Indian reined in the frightened horse and leveled his right hand.

"He's got a gun!" McCulloch yelled.

Holy Shirt held a Remington derringer in his right hand, and he pointed it at the actor in shining armor.

In a proper accent and back to *Our American Cousin,* Sir Theodore said, " 'Well, of course we must find means of settling this extortion.' "

The .41-caliber hideaway gun popped. Once. Twice.

CHAPTER THIRTY-FOUR

Keegan cringed as the knight spun around.

"Nooo!" Jed Breen cried out, and he stood up.

The knight in all that armor twisted and staggered, and started to topple but managed to keep himself upright by stabbing the earth with his broadsword.

The Apaches in the distance cheered.

Breen came up and began running toward the actor and the Apache, whose horse bucked and reared. Suddenly, the knight straightened, turned, and walked toward old Holy Shirt.

The brown arched and reared again, and Holy Shirt fell to the ground as the horse galloped away from the staggering knight. The Apache came up, wiped his face, and lunged for the lance he had thrown earlier. He grabbed it and stood as Breen stopped and aimed the Sharps, then cursed.

"Shoot!" Keegan roared.

"I can't. I might hit Cannon, too!"

The Apache unleashed the lance and hit the knight dead center, knocking him backward, but not off his feet. The lance fell down. Holy Shirt drew his knife and charged.

Sir Theodore Cannon shook his rattling head and raised the sword just as Holy Shirt reached him.

Matt McCulloch had the best view. He saw the broadsword drive through the medicine man's body.

The Indian fell over dead.

Sir Theodore Cannon managed to stagger a few feet away then fell loudly on a bed of prickly pear. He did not move.

"Yiii-eeee!" One of the Apaches charged.

The other Apaches watched.

Keegan and Breen fired at the same time, and the brave was catapulted off his pony's back.

The three men turned their weapons toward the other Apaches, although Breen kept glancing at the pile of silver that did not move.

"How many bullets do we have now?" Keegan asked.

"Math and me never quite saw eye to eye," McCulloch said.

"Sir Theodore," Breen whispered. "Sir

Theodore . . ."

"Hey!" Gwen Stanhope laughed. "Look! They're leaving."

They watched as the Apaches disgraced themselves by leaving their dead, including the already disgraced medicine man, Holy Shirt, who had broken his own medicine by using a Remington over-and-under .41-caliber derringer and then had died at the hands of a warrior and weapon from the fifteenth century.

"I'll be the damnedest suck-egg mule I ever saw," Sean Keegan said, as he butted his Springfield on the ground. "We're still alive."

A bullet splintered the stock of Keegan's weapon and sent the carbine tumbling across the ground.

"Riders!" Breen shouted.

Three riders galloped their horses across the floor between the mound of rocks.

"More Apaches?" Gwen cried out.

McCulloch saw the puff of smoke from the charging riders and felt a bullet whine off a boulder somewhere. He turned back to see the last of the Indians dipping into an arroyo, out of view. "No, I don't think so."

The Sharps roared like a cannon, and one of the horses went down, sending its rider crashing hard in front of the animal, which rolled over the body. One rider glanced that way then leaned low in the saddle. Breen lowered the Sharps, opened the breech, and fished out another long cartridge. He studied the dust where horse and rider had fallen. Neither man nor beast moved.

"Spread out," McCulloch said. "Two men left. They can't take all three of us."

"Four," Gwen Stanhope said.

"You're right, ma'am," McCulloch said. "Four."

Keegan's gun roared, and another rider was booted from his saddle, landing with a thud, but that horse turned and galloped back toward El Paso.

"Odds," Stanhope said, "are getting better."

"Yeah, but I've got just one cartridge left," Keegan said.

About a hundred yards away, the third rider slowed his horse to a walk. When he reached fifty yards, he reined in.

"McCulloch!" he yelled. "Matt McCulloch."

The Ranger stepped forward. "Yeah."

"You killed my brother, McCulloch. I'm here to kill you."

"I've killed a lot of men's brothers," McCulloch said.

The rider swung down from his horse.

"I shot that damned fool off his horse!" Jed Breen yelled. "Not Matt McCulloch."

"That wasn't my brother. I'm Jake Hawkin!"

Breen whispered a curse, and then he grinned. "What's the reward on Hawkin's head now?" He started to ear back the hammer on the Sharps.

"This is personal, Breen," McCulloch said. "I'll take him."

Breen sighed. "All right. But if he kills you, I'm killing him. And the reward's all mine."

"He won't kill me," McCulloch said, and started walking toward the outlaw.

Breen butted the Sharps. Keegan cradled the Springfield in his arms. They watched as the Ranger strode across the ground, while Jake Hawkin wrapped the reins around a bush and walked toward the approaching Texan.

"Aren't you going to do something?" Gwen Stanhope asked.

"It's his fight," Breen said.

"He called it," Keegan echoed.

"But —"

Keegan shook his head. "If McCullough's a jackal like that yellow-livered Griffin claimed, then I'm a son of a soiled dove."

456

Breen nodded. "You are a son of a soiled dove, Keegan, but that man . . . McCulloch . . . well . . . he's a *man*. But don't ever let him know I said that."

"Don't worry," Keegan said. "I won't."

"I can't believe you two," the woman said. "You'll just let him face that killer, alone, without any help."

"Yes, ma'am," Breen said. "Because if Hawkin kills him, we get more money."

With forty feet between them, the outlaw and the former Ranger stopped.

"Jake," McCulloch nodded.

"Matt." Hawkin hooked his thumbs inside his gunbelt. McCulloch did the same.

"You didn't do Billy right, Matt," the outlaw said.

"I gave him a chance."

"You should have buried him."

"Then the Apaches might have buried me. Figuratively, you know."

Hawkin nodded. "Yeah. I guess you're right about that."

"I'm no longer a Ranger, Jake. Means I have no authority to bring you in. So you can ride out of here right now."

A gust of wind turned both men's heads, just slightly.

"I aim to do that, Matt. After I kill you."

"I ought to warn you, Jake." McCulloch

gestured behind him. "One of those men behind me is Jed Breen. I figure you've heard of him."

Hawkin nodded. "I have. He got that Big Fifty with him?"

McCulloch nodded.

"Well. I guess I'll have to kill him, too." Hawkin nodded and pointed with his left pinky. "What the hell is that big thing on the ground?"

"That's a knight, Jake. In full armor." Mc-Culloch didn't feel like explaining, so he changed the subject. "The bank robbery in Sierra Vista?"

"I thought you weren't a lawman anymore."

"I'm not. But I have to know. Was a man named Henderson involved? Harry Henderson?"

"I don't rat out friends or enemies, Matt."

"You're not. The Apaches got Henderson."

"Did they get the money?"

Matt McCulloch sighed. He did not answer the outlaw's query. Instead, he tried something else. "You wouldn't happen to know if Henderson has a wife in El Paso, would you?"

"You know me, Matt. I never pry into anybody's business. This'll be for Billy,

Matt. He was no good. But he was my brother."

"I know, Jake. But the thing is. You were no good, too." McCulloch palmed the .44-40, stepped to his right, and fired.

Surprised that a Texas Ranger would draw first, Hawkin had his gun halfway out of the holster when the bullet spun him around. He reflexively squeezed the trigger and blew apart the pear of a cactus plant as he dropped to his knees. Coughing, he turned a bit and felt another bullet punch his side. The revolver slipped from his hand, but he managed to stand, turn, and start walking toward McCulloch.

McCulloch let the outlaw come.

Hawkin had no weapon. He was a dead man, but he just kept walking. "You" — he managed to raise his right hand and point accusingly at the Texan — "you . . . drew . . . first."

McCulloch nodded.

Hawkin dropped to his knees, bent over, spit up blood, and lifted his head. "That . . . ain't . . . right."

"I told you, Jake. I'm not a Ranger anymore."

The outlaw coughed, blinked, and then a smile crept across his face. He was laughing as he fell to his side, then shuddered, and closed his eyes.

The wind stopped blowing. The sun no longer felt so hot, and the desert suddenly looked glorious. Texas could be that way, it seemed. Desolate, disturbing, and deadly in one moment, then glorious, almost like the Garden of Eden, the next.

When you suddenly felt alive, the place took on a new look, and gave you a new meaning.

Matt McCulloch felt that way.

So did Sean Keegan.

So did Jed Breen, even though he knew he could never collect the substantial reward on Jake Hawkin's head . . . unless Matt McCulloch met an untimely demise before reaching El Paso.

Keegan and Breen walked out to meet McCulloch, who carefully picked up the revolver Jake Hawkin had dropped and shoved it into his waistband.

The soldier and the bounty hunter waited by Hawkin's body.

"The wind carried part of your conversation in our direction," Keegan said. "I take it you two knew each other."

"In the war," McCulloch said. "We served in the same outfit."

"I see," Keegan said. "Wasn't prying."

McCulloch shrugged.

"You were pards?" Breen asked, and grinned when the Ranger looked at him. "Yeah. I am prying."

McCulloch gave another shrug. "It doesn't matter. He'd stop for remounts at my ranch from time to time."

"You didn't turn him in?" Breen asked.

"Wasn't a Ranger in those days."

"And you sold him fresh horses?" Keegan asked.

"Traded. Well, that's not exactly right. I'd wake up one morning to find some of my horses gone and tired horses in the corral."

"The Matt McCulloch I know wouldn't have allowed that without a few words," Breen said.

"The Matt McCulloch you know wasn't the same man back then. Besides, I usually got the better end of the trade. The horses he left were better than the horses he took."

"Knowing your reputation for horses, that's hard to believe," Keegan said.

McCulloch gave yet another shrug. "Believe what you want. That's the truth."

"Speaking of horses, we've got two horses now," Breen said. "The Apache's. And Hawkin's."

"If we can catch them up," McCulloch said.

Breen grinned. "We figure you can catch

461

them up. You're the wrangler of this bunch."

"Two horses," McCulloch said. "Four people. If that actor's still breathing, five."

"He can't be alive." Keegan shook his head. "He'd be moving around in that tin suit if he was alive."

"He was a good actor," Breen said. "A great actor. We should bury him."

"He was crazy as a loon," McCulloch said.

"The horses." Breen nodded at the Ranger. "You'll fetch them."

"I will."

"And you won't try to ride away? Without us?" Keegan said.

McCulloch shook his head. "You've got a long-range Sharps and a Springfield. I wouldn't get far on two horses, boys."

Breen nodded again.

"Two horses. We'll ride double," Keegan said. "It's not that far to Hueco Tanks. We can get extra horses there or wait till the next stage comes in.

Breen shook his head as he stared down at the dead killer. "That was one reward I would have liked to have collected." He raised his eyes and smiled at McCulloch. "From one profession, I salute you, Mc-Culloch."

"Speaking of rewards, there's one thing you boys should know," McCulloch said.

"Yeah?" Keegan asked. "What?"

McCulloch jutted his jaw toward the rocks, the wagon, the shining knight still not moving on the cactus, and Gwen Stanhope. "That woman's heading for the Apache's horse — with both carpetbags."

CHAPTER THIRTY-FIVE

Gwen Stanhope streaked across the desert floor. Breen shouted out a curse and bolted after her.

McCulloch yelled, "I'll see if I can catch up Hawkin's horse." He ran the opposite way.

Keegan started running after Breen, but soon gave up, and slowed to a leisurely walk. He was a horse soldier, he told himself, not a foot soldier. Retired or not. And he was not going to run anymore on that day. His feet hurt.

"Easy, boy," Matt McCulloch whispered as he approached Jake Hawkin's mount. "Easy." He smiled, began humming "The Yellow Rose of Texas," and raised his hand, letting the horse catch McCulloch's scent.

Behind him came Breen's shouts. "Stop! Stop! Stop, damn you, woman. Stop!"

The horse snorted, but McCulloch was

beside it and he put his left hand under the animal's nose, letting it take in the scent, while his right hand grabbed one loose rein, then reached under the animal's neck, and found the other. "You're a good —" He did not finish. He stepped back, studied the horse again, and moved past the saddle where he could read the brand.

It was a brand he knew well. After all, it was his old brand. He had to smile that an outlaw like Jake Hawkin would still be riding an M/M horse. It must have been swapped four years ago. The horse looked to be eight years old.

He put one moccasin in the stirrup and swung into the saddle, patted the scabbard to see it held a repeating rifle. He wet his lips and kicked the animal in the side.

He covered about a hundred yards before he reined up. "This nightmare just won't end," he said, and pulled Jake Hawkin's Winchester rifle, a big Centennial model, from the scabbard.

Gwen Stanhope stopped running, turned around, dropped the carpetbags and started to cock Keegan's big .44 in her right hand.

Jed Breen wasn't looking at her, however. He was focused on something behind her.

She was about to tell him that she was no

465

fool, that she would not fall for such an amateur's trick, when she heard the thundering hooves. Quickly she spun back and caught the hackamore to the dead chief's brown mare. Four riders galloped toward them.

"Oh, my God," Stanhope whispered. "It can't be. It just can't be."

Breen had moved up to her side. "You know them?" he asked. He counted four riders.

"I recognize the palomino. And the big white hat."

"The sheriff?" Breen guessed.

"Yeah. Charles Van Patten. Brother of the sidewinder I killed."

Breen took the horsehair-braided hackamore from her hand, climbed into the Apache saddle, and held out his free hand. "Grab hold. Swing up behind me."

"You're saving my hide?" she asked, but she accepted and let him pull her up.

"Not really, but if they shoot at me, they'll hit you first."

"But the money!" she said.

"You can't spend money if you're dead."

He turned the horse around, and the first shot kicked up dust about fifteen feet to his right. The Apache's horse needed no more encouragement. It struck out at a high lope back toward the wrecked wagon and the rocks.

A bullet shattered a stone about six feet from McCulloch's shoulder, and he helped Stanhope off the back of the Apache's horse. "Get the horse over there." He nodded to where he had tied Jake Hawkin's mount in the rocks.

"Four men," Breen said.

"I can count," McCulloch snapped.

"One of them's the county sheriff." Breen spurred the brown into the rocks.

McCulloch glanced at the woman. "Van Patten?"

"Yes."

He nodded. "That explains it."

"He'll kill me," she said.

"I expect that's his plan." McCulloch shoved her toward the wrecked wagon.

The riders were about two hundred yards from them when Keegan's Springfield boomed. The four men split into two pairs.

When they reached the crashed wagon, McCulloch held open the door. "Get inside," he told the woman.

"No," Stanhope said.

"Inside," McCulloch insisted.

"I'll be trapped."

"Where's the carpetbags?" McCulloch asked.

"Where we left them." Breen pointed. "Inside."

She crawled in and the door slammed shut, just as a bullet whined off the iron tire of the rear wheel.

In the rocks, Breen lined up one of the riders in his sights and squeezed the trigger, then felt the stock slam hard against his shoulder. One of these days, he thought, he might buy a rifle that didn't bruise his shoulder or come close to breaking the shoulder blade on the other side.

One of these days.

The rider was on the ground, and he wasn't moving. Few people moved an inch after having a .50-caliber Sharps slug tear through his body. The horse turned and galloped off toward the other set of hills where they had made their first stand after Sir Theodore's wagon had crashed.

Breen opened the breech, pitched the spent cartridge, and reached into his pocket. "Damn it all to hell." There were no cartridges left. If he hadn't shot them all, maybe one or more had fallen out of his pockets. He had been doing a lot of running lately.

A bullet smashed another rock just above,

blinding Breen, who dropped the Sharps, staggered a few feet, and fell onto the ground.

"I've got him, Mr. Blue!" someone shouted.

Breen tried to get to his feet, but another bullet punched off the heel of his right boot. He dived a bit farther and heard a bullet whine off a rock. Rolling onto his back, he heard the sound of hooves, a horse whinny, slide to a stop, and then the softer noise of a man's footsteps on the hard, rocky ground.

Breen reached for his Lightning, but it wasn't there. It must have fallen out when the wagon crashed.

He was unarmed, with no place to hide, when the man rounded the corner and squeezed off a shot. The bullet caught Breen in the left shoulder just as he threw the stone that caused Mr. Black to rush his shot and flinch.

The rock caught him in the lower lip and jaw, and he staggered back. Spitting out blood and teeth, he cocked the hammer and touched the trigger again. That bullet flew over Breen's back as he lowered his head and rammed his bleeding, burning, aching shoulder into Black's gut. Breen kept churning his feet and rammed Black's back against the rocks. The gun slipped from the killer's fingers and dropped into the dirt.

Breen straightened and felt punches tearing into the bloody bullet hole in his shoulder. He didn't care. Fury blocked all pain. He grabbed a fistful of Black's hair, jerked his head forward, and shoved it hard against the rock. Hearing Black groan, Breen pulled the head toward him again and rammed it even harder. When Black's head came forward, Breen saw the blood dripping from the rock. He smashed the head again. And again. And again. And . . . then he let the man fall, quivering and soiling himself, then twisting over and moaning.

Breen picked up the revolver the man had dropped. He started to put a bullet between the killer's eyes, but stopped, holding his fire. More bullets were ringing out beyond the rocky place, and Breen didn't know how many shots remained in the revolver. He simply stepped on Mr. Black's throat and pushed his boot down hard.

Hiding in the rocks, Keegan aimed the Springfield toward the clopping hooves and waited. The horse came into view, and Keegan swore, leaping back and looking up. Nobody was in the saddle. He had been duped by one of the oldest tricks in West

Texas. He blamed it on the wounded arm. A man didn't think that clearly when he was bleeding like a stuck pig.

He figured the rider was on his left.

But Mr. Blue leaped from Keegan's right.

The soldier dropped the rifle as he was slammed against the rock. Mr. Blue tried to club him with the barrel of his gun, but Keegan had spun around and blocked the hired killer's arm, hand, and big Schofield .45 with his right hand. His left knee came up and slammed into Mr. Blue's groin. The man staggered back, groaning, but recovering quickly. He fired.

But Keegan wasn't there anymore.

Keegan crawled through the narrow defile in the rock. He heard Blue's curse and his footsteps, but then those stopped. He had reached the narrow spot and had to crawl.

Light appeared, and Keegan crawled out. His left arm really hurt. It was bleeding hard again, and he had to fight off dizziness. He caught his breath, pushed himself up onto the rocks, and waited for the killer's head to pop out of the opening. When it didn't, Keegan spun around and bolted toward the other side.

He did not slow down. Reaching the side, he leaped, slamming into Blue's back as he was running toward his horse. The killer fell. The gun flew from his hand. He tried to get up, but Keegan planted his knee in the small of Blue's back.

Something stung Blue's nose. Something crawled across his face. Ants. Another bit him. Painfully. Keegan pushed the killer's head deeper into the mound, and more ants attacked. Blue screamed, twisted, tried to breathe. The knee dug deeper against his spinal cord as the ants attacked with fury.

When Blue no longer felt Keegan on top of him, he pushed himself to his feet and brushed the ants off his face. He snarled. His cloudy vision cleared, and he saw the cavalry trooper standing before him. Blue brushed off another ant then saw the gun — *his gun* — in the soldier's right hand. He saw the smoke and flame explode from the revolver's barrel. He felt the bullet slam into his chest and drive him back into the ant mound.

But he did not feel the bites of the attacking ants.

Charles Van Patten laughed as he levered a fresh cartridge into his rifle. He shot the door to the overturned wagon. Inside came the muffled scream of the woman.

"You like that, bitch?" he yelled gleefully. "How about this?" He sent two more rounds, splintering the wood.

Gwen Stanhope shrieked again. He fired once more. Then another. Around him, he heard his hired killers likely finishing off the fools who had tried to assist the killer of his brother. He aimed the rifle at the door, but realized he hadn't heard more screams. He started to lower the rifle, then thought better of it and shot twice more through the wood. Nothing. The woman inside never cried out.

"Hey, Gwen," the sheriff yelled. "What's the matter? You should be happy. The Apaches didn't rape you. And you won't live to hang in El Paso. I bet you're burning in Hell right now. But isn't this grand? You can be with Kirk for all of eternity. Burning in the fiery pit."

Laughing, Van Patten leaned the rifle against the wagon, found the handle to the wagon door, and lifted it up. He got it halfway, then shifted his hands, pushed it up, and looked inside. He saw Gwen Stanhope lying there.

Her eyes opened. She rolled over. And the Colt Lightning revolver she held punched two holes in his belly.

The door slammed shut.

CHAPTER THIRTY-SIX

Matt McCulloch, Sean Keegan, and Jed Breen stopped at the wrecked wagon. Sheriff Charles Van Patten lay on the ground, both hands gripping his bloody stomach, his mouth open as though he were laughing, his eyes staring at the sky, not blinking, not moving at all, and not seeing anything on this side of the hereafter.

Gwen Stanhope held the dead man's Winchester. It was pointed at the three of them. Breen's double-action .38 was shoved in her waistband.

"I take it," Jed Breen said, "that you're dissolving our partnership."

"You could say that."

"Taking the money for yourself?" Matt McCulloch asked.

"It seems the logical move." Stanhope waved the barrel. "Drop your hardware, boys."

"You plan on leaving us here afoot?" Keegan asked.

"No," she said. "I plan on leaving you here dead."

The three men just stared at her.

"It's not personal, boys, but Breen's a bounty hunter. He'd be coming after me at some point."

"Hell," Keegan said. "If that's all that's troubling you, go ahead and kill *him*. We won't stop you."

"I aim to," she said. "But he's a Ranger." She nodded toward McCulloch.

"*Was* a Ranger," he said.

"Once a lawman . . ." the woman argued.

"And what am I?" Keegan asked.

"What you would be, is a witness to two murders." She sighed. "Like I said, boys, it's nothing personal. I like all three of you. But I like fifty thousand dollars a hell of a lot better."

She stepped back, aimed at Keegan, and touched the trigger.

It snapped empty. She cursed, worked the lever, and fired again.

"No!" she screamed. Dropping the rifle, she jerked up Breen's Lightning she had discovered in the wrecked wagon. Slipping her finger into the trigger guard, she turned.

Three guns roared. Three bullets struck Gwen Stanhope in the middle, and she fell back, covering the dead sheriff's face. Her mouth moved once, and her eyes lost their focus.

"I know she was in custody, on her way to hang," Jed Breen said as he picked up his revolver that she had dropped, "but do you reckon there's still a reward posted on her?"

"How do you get this thing off?" Sean Keegan asked.

"Twist it," McCulloch said.

"Which way?"

"I don't know. Twist it and turn it and pray."

It took several tries, but the helmet was dragged off Sir Theodore Cannon, whose eyes shot open and were immediately blinded by the sweat that poured into his eyeballs.

"Get this damned stove off me before I'm cooked like the Christmas goose," he said, breathing heavily.

"You're alive, Sir Theodore?" Jed Breen said.

"Indeed. I was playing the greatest death scene of my career."

"It was almost the last death scene any of us played." Breen helped up the heavy man in the weighted armor but quickly dropped him back onto the ground, luckily missing the cactus, and began waving his hands in pain. "Hell, this tin is hot after lying in the sun."

"Just get me out of here, boys," the actor said.

Keegan fingered the side of the armor. "That derringer put two holes in you. Are you hit?"

"My good man," the actor said, "I informed you men earlier that this is a jousting suit of armor, meant for the fairs — like what Sir Walter Scott wrote about in *Ivanhoe* — not for battle. The lance would have struck this side, so this side is thicker. Yes, yes, yes, the two slugs penetrated this Scottish armor, but were spent after passing through such thick metal. I have two small bruises on my side. And if you can figure out how to get this tin bucket off me, I'll even let you see the sons of bitches." He stopped, panted, and let Sergeant Keegan give him a sip of water from the canteen.

Sir Theodore Cannon looked around. "I say, where is Miss Stanhope?"

Matt McCulloch shrugged. "Well, Sir Theodore, nobody lives forever."

"Let me get this straight." U.S. Marshal Devon Cody pushed back the bourbon he had poured for himself in his El Paso office.

477

"You're telling me that the county sheriff's dead. That old Holy Shirt's dead. That the woman that was to be hanged here is dead. That Jake and Billy Hawkin are dead. That a number of gunmen under certain aliases are dead. That the man who worked at the Sierra Vista bank is dead, the same man who is suspected of helping the Hawkin boys on that job. That at least two members of Hawkin's gang are dead. That many Apaches from Holy Shirt's reservation breakers and some of that crew that came up from south of the border are dead. That Petey and Rourke from the stagecoach line are dead, along with the paying passengers on that Concord. And that Alvin J. Griffin Number Four, editor and publisher of the *Purgatory City Herald Leader,* that he's dead, too. Hell, men, is there anyone left alive?"

"We are," Sean Keegan said, rubbing his arm in a sling.

"Kind of," Matt McCulloch rubbed his neck.

"There's an actor up in the hotel room," Jed Breen added as he massaged his shoulder. He also had an arm in a sling. "He's alive, too."

"He can confirm everything we've told you," McCulloch said.

"But you don't want to get him started,"

Keegan said, "Or he won't shut up."

Devon Cody twisted both ends of his mustache, frowned, grabbed the glass, and killed the bourbon. He found his hat and his gunbelt, and nodded at the front door. "All right, gents. Let's see what this actor has to say."

When no one answered the knock, Keegan took the key from McCulloch, turned the key in the lock, and pushed open the door to the hotel room. He saw the bed, unmade and empty of one Sir Theodore Cannon. Immediately, he looked at the dresser.

"Gone." He swore. He wasn't referring to the actor, specifically, but the two carpetbags.

"That swindling snake," Matt McCulloch said.

Breen spun around. "I'll check the train station."

"I'll see to the stagecoach," McCulloch said.

"I'll check the border crossing," Keegan said.

The U.S. marshal said, "I don't think any of you three are leaving my sight." He drew his revolver. "Let's go back to my office and talk this through once more."

Keegan, McCulloch, and Breen swore.

The lawman backed them out of the room, closed the door, and let Keegan lock it. The marshal brought up the rear as they went down the stairs. They were at the door when they heard the voice from the hotel's saloon.

"You believe that *The Seven Sisters* is great theater? My good man, it is nothing but trash. Low comedy. Not fit for a thespian like me. If you want burletta, go to a saloon. I, sir, am Sir Theodore Cannon, and have treaded the boards with Booth, and with Bartlett. I, my good man, am a thespian."

"Marshal" — Breen nodded at the saloon entrance — "that way, sir."

The marshal let the three men go first. They found Sir Theodore Cannon sitting in a booth, talking to a man in a long black coat, red cravat, and black silk hat.

"My friends!" Sir Theodore Cannon waved at them. "Welcome. Alice, be a dear sport and bring drinks, the best in the house, for these grand heroes, and for that strapping young man with them."

The man with the silk hat blinked, but seeing the badge on Devon Cody's coat, he quickly slid out of the booth and hurried out of the saloon. Breen, Keegan, and Mc-Culloch stood around the booth. Marshal Cody kept his gun out.

"Aren't you going to sit down, my friends?" the actor asked.

"We're just curious," McCulloch said. "So is the U.S. marshal. What about those two carpetbags of cash?"

"Oh." The actor's hands disappeared.

The marshal turned his pistol at the thespian, whose hands lifted two of the ugliest grips ever seen in that part of Texas.

He slammed them on the top of the table. "I did not think it wise to leave such important and valuable items lying around in the room, friends. This is not Paris. This is the raw frontier town of El Paso. Here. Here. Have a seat. Let's have a drink. Or two."

The men stared.

The actor laughed. "Oh, my. Oh, my. Oh, my. Now I understand. Bully! Bully, bully, bully!" He raised a hand and pointed at McCulloch, Keegan, and Breen. "You . . . you thought I had stolen the money and left you to pay for the crime. Oh, bully. What a comedy. I should write my own play. Here, here."

He paused as a woman carried a tray, set it on the table, and handed Sean Keegan, Jed Breen, Matt McCulloch, and U.S. Marshal Devon Cody tumblers of the finest rye whiskey to be found in El Paso, Texas. The marshal holstered his revolver before picking up his glass and killed his whiskey with one shot.

Sir Theodore Cannon's glass clinked against the tumblers held by the former soldier, the ex-Ranger, and the bounty hunter, who remained standing and looked completely exhausted.

"Boys, boys, boys. Won't you three ever learn?" the thespian said. "Not everyone in this lawless West of the United States happens to be a jackal."

ABOUT THE AUTHORS

William W. Johnstone has written nearly three hundred novels of western adventure, military action, chilling suspense, and survival. His bestselling books include *The Family Jensen; The Mountain Man; Flintlock; MacCallister; Savage Texas; Luke Jensen, Bounty Hunter;* and the thrillers *Black Friday, The Doomsday Bunker,* and *Trigger Warning.*

J. A. Johnstone learned to write from the master himself, Uncle William W. Johnstone, with whom J.A. has co-written numerous bestselling series including The Mountain Man; Those Jensen Boys; and Preacher, The First Mountain Man.